10/15

SCORPION SUNSET

CATRIN COLLIER

Published by Accent Press Ltd 2015

ISBN 9781783753772

Copyright © Catrin Collier 2015

For my cousin, Peter Johns, ex-Warrant Officer of the 1st Battalion The Black Watch (Royal Highland Regiment)

A wonderful man who taught me a soldier fights for many things, but once in battle, always for the man alongside him.

When a story is told

Three apples fall from heaven

One for the storyteller
One for he who listens
and
One for he who understands

Armenian proverb

Chapter One

The Road from Kut to Shumran
April 1916

Major Warren Crabbe saw the soldier marching in front of him waver, bend at the knees, and collapse. Crabbe dived forward but failed to break the man's fall.

A soldier who'd been marching alongside them crouched next to Crabbe. 'Sir, is Billy ... '

'Dead, Private Evans.' Crabbe closed the man's eyes and unfastened his identity discs from around his neck.

A Turkish private rushed up and hammered his rifle butt on Evans's shoulder. 'Yallah! Yallah!'

'Yallah to you, you bastard!' Forgoing caution, Crabbe grabbed the Turk's rifle and shoved it aside as he repeated the Turkish command to 'hurry'.

The Turk switched his attention to Crabbe, and brought his barrel down, full force, on the major's back. Fighting pain, Crabbe lifted the head of the dead soldier and held it up in front of the Turk. 'The waste of this brave man's life is down to you and your foul command. How dare you march sick, starving men who've suffered five months of bloody siege ... '

The Turk lashed out with his rifle stock a second time, slamming it into Crabbe's head. Crabbe reeled sideways and sprawled on the ground. Two naval lieutenants, Grace and Bowditch, fists clenched and faces grim, headed for the Turk. The Turk raised his rifle and pointed it at Grace.

'Back off!' Crabbe ordered the lieutenants. 'Go, notify the Brigadier. If anyone can stop the swine beating us, it's him.'

When the Turk saw the lieutenants heading for the knot of senior British officers he disappeared up the line.

Evans tried to lift Crabbe. 'Sir ... sir ... '

1

Major John Mason saw Crabbe on the ground and moved towards them.

'Major Mason, sir ...'

'I saw what happened, Evans.' John knelt beside the soldier who'd collapsed and checked his pulse. He knew it was useless, but even surrounded by death he instinctively adhered to medical procedure. He confirmed his suspicions before turning his attention to Crabbe and examining a cut that had opened below his eyebrow. 'Our prison escort is touchy. Best not to annoy them, Crabbe.'

'You know me. Never learned the gentlemanly art of tact and diplomacy.' Crabbe tried to rise and fell back on the ground.

John called to his orderly. 'Dira, bring the knapsack with the dressings.' He pressed down on Crabbe's cut. 'How many men have we lost from the Dorsets since we left Kut?'

Crabbe pushed his hand into his pocket and retrieved a handful of identity discs. 'I think seventeen. But I could have lost count. I'm not at my best.'

'Eight hours to march eight miles in this heat without food and water – none of us are. But looking at the state of the men, I'm surprised as many have made it this far.'

'Is it true we'll be travelling on from here by boat, sirs?' Private Evans asked.

Crabbe squinted up at the boy. 'Where did you hear that, Evans?'

'Rumour, sir.'

'Ah, rumour,' John repeated, 'if I ever track down rumour I intend to have a long conversation with that man.'

'Are we, sirs? Going on by boat to the prison camp, I mean,' Evans persisted.

'If I and the other medics have any say, we'll sail to our ultimate destination in a velvet lined barge complete with kitchen, chef, and all home comforts, but I doubt the Turks will pay much attention to our advice,' John replied. 'Have you been issued with biscuits by the Turks, Evans?'

'All the men have, sir. Two and half each.' Evans reached into his tunic and pulled out three filthy lumps of black biscuit about five inches in diameter and three-quarters of an inch thick. 'I tried breaking one with the heel of my boot, but I couldn't make a dent, sir. They're as hard as the cobblestones in Ponty market square.'

'Where?' John was bemused by Evans's turn of phrase.

'Never ask Evans to explain any of his mysterious communications, Major Mason,' Crabbe warned. 'He's Welsh.'

'And that means ... sir?' Evans bristled in indignation at the perceived slight.

'It means you never stop talking gibberish, Evans.' Crabbe allowed John to help him up to a sitting position.

Evans stared downwards as he cradled his dead mate's face so the officers wouldn't see the expression on his face.

'I told the men to pass the order down the line. No one, officer or rank, is to attempt to eat that hard tack biscuit until they've soaked it in water,' John warned Evans. 'Nine out of every ten men have dysentery and the remaining one, diarrhoea. After the starvation diet the Kut garrison's been on since December, something as hard as that could prove fatal to a weakened stomach. That's without accounting for the bacteria and dirt baked into them.'

'What water, sir?' Evans looked around as if he was expecting a water cart to materialise.

John pointed to the river. 'Boil it before you use it. If you pour it on the biscuit while it's hot, the heat might even kill some of nastier additions in those black bricks.'

'What about ...' Evans finally looked up from his mate.

'As we seem to have reached our destination for the night. I'll look for Reverend Spooner after I've seen to Major Crabbe. He'll know what arrangements have been made,' John offered.

'It will be burial at sunset, won't it, sir?'

'If it can be organised that quickly, Private Evans,' John qualified.

'Thank you, sir. I'll pass the word on about soaking the biscuits, sirs.' Evans rose and managed to stand in an approximation of attention. He saluted and left.

Dira arrived with the knapsack. John opened it and rummaged through the meagre contents. 'Hardly anything left.'

'Those are the last of our medical dressings, sir. Captain Vincent told me to warn you there are no drugs. When he asked the Turkish officers for medical supplies they said they didn't have any for their own troops. They insist they have nothing to give us, not even antiseptic.'

'Given the state of the Turkish troops, I believe them, but someone has to petition for the medical care of our ranks. We're the Turks' responsibility now.'

'You volunteering?' Crabbe rose gingerly but didn't remain upright for long. He sank down on the muddy riverbank.

'If senior staff isn't prepared to do the job, yes.'

Dira signalled to two Indian sepoys who brought a stretcher. They loaded the dead soldier on to it and carried the corpse away.

John took a needle from a tin in Dira's knapsack, struck a match, and held it in the flame for a minute. He wiped the soot from it with a corner of gauze, threaded the needle with fine silk, and stitched Crabbe's wound. The major didn't flinch. When John finished, he lit another match and sterilised the needle before returning it to the knapsack. 'Dira, do me a favour. Find Reverend Spooner and ask if there's a burial service scheduled for sunset?'

'It won't be sunset, sahib. The men are too weak from marching to dig. I heard the brigadier say dawn might be a more appropriate time.'

John nodded.

'If you need me, sir, I'll be with Captain Vincent. He's treating the worst dysentery cases with what's left of the chalk.

'Tell him to send for me if he needs help.'

Crabbe saw John looking at the mud stains on his uniform. 'My clothes are so filthy a little extra dirt makes no difference. Besides, mud's cooling. Damn the hot season.'

'The temperature is higher than it was in the desert when we marched overland to Amara last year.' John sat next to Crabbe with the same disregard for his uniform, which was no cleaner and even more threadbare than Crabbe's.

'It's probably no higher, just our memory playing tricks.'

'I wish I hadn't smoked my share of the cigarettes the Turks handed out when we marched from Kut.'

'My last one.' Crabbe took a battered specimen from his pocket and contemplated it. 'If I don't light it soon, it'll turn to dust. If you have a Lucifer we can share it.'

John felt in his pockets and produced a box of matches. He struck one, shielded the flame with his hand, and lit Crabbe's cigarette. Crabbe inhaled and passed it over. 'As defender at your court martial, I need to make enquiries into your status as a double

4

prisoner of the British and Turks.'

'Presumably as a British court martial passed down a death sentence to be carried out as soon as my medical skills are no longer needed, the British brass can execute me any time they like.' John inhaled and savoured the sensation of smoke in his lungs.

'They'll need to borrow a Turkish firing squad to do so. If I remember the Hague Convention rules on the treatment of POWs, which Turkey pledged to follow, we aren't allowed to shoot one another.'

'Even if said prisoner is under sentence of death?'

'I have the brigadier's signed document stating, "Major Mason is no longer to be treated as a prisoner but as an officer and doctor of the Indian Expeditionary Force D, his sentence to be reviewed after the relief of Kut", safe in my pocket. And from where I'm sitting it looks like the senior officers are more concerned with survival than reviews. The only ones who wanted you shot were the ones who trumped up the charges against you, Perry and Cleck-Heaton. As they both developed "funk fever" that fooled the Turkish medics and gained them a coward's place on an evacuation boat downstream, you're safe until the end of the war. You're a doctor and from the state of the men, I'm talking Turk as well as Expeditionary Force, neither side will want to kill a medic. Not while men are dropping like flies.'

John studied the soldiers around them. Most of the British had long passed weariness and were on the point of collapse. Officers as well as ranks were slumped on the ground. A few senior men were trying to remonstrate with the Turkish officers in an effort to get food and better treatment for their men, but from the expression on the Turks' faces, they weren't in a mood to listen.

'Speaking of the Hague rules, it also states that prisoners of war have to be fed and sheltered. I see no evidence of food, tents, or the Red Cross.' John took another drag on the cigarette before returning it to Crabbe.

'This far behind the Turkish lines it'll be the Red Crescent.'

'I doubt any one of us will be fussed which turns up as long as it's one or the other. Halil Bey promised Townshend we'd be fed when we reached here, didn't he?' John checked.

'He also promised we'd be treated well and with respect on the journey. It would appear Townshend's surrendered to a liar.'

A crowd of men rose en masse from the ground and rushed, as much as it was possible for anyone in their condition to move quickly, towards the Turkish lines. Evans limped back through the throng on bare feet. He was hugging two loaves of black bread to his bare chest.

'Where the hell are your boots and shirt, man?' Crabbe reverted to his sergeant major parade ground voice, reminding everyone within earshot that unlike most officers he'd risen through the ranks.

'Swapped them for bread, sir. I'm starving. The Turks have set up a market in front of their lines. Boys are exchanging all sorts for food. Anything has to be better than the bricks the Turks gave us. I know you told us to soak them in water, sir,' Evans said to John, 'but the water just sits on top of them and laughs at us. I tried putting mine in my tin mug and covering them, but they're no softer now than they were when they went in ten minutes ago.'

'You did boil the water?' John took the mug Evans unhooked from his belt.

'The Indians did, sir. They're always the first to start a cook fire. But begging your pardon for my French, sir, they, like the rest of us, have bugger all to cook.'

John eyed his finger and decided it couldn't be any grubbier than the biscuits in the bottom of Evans's mug. He poked them. As Evans said, they were as hard as cobblestones for all the grimy layer of water on top of them.

Evans held up one of his loaves. 'This isn't as soft as our bread, sirs. At least I don't think it is, but it's been so long since I tasted decent bread, I won't know the difference. It seemed to make sense to swap my boots. We won't need half the kit we're carrying, and in this heat every ounce weighs as heavy as a ton.'

'And when you have to march tomorrow?' Crabbe demanded. 'How far do you think you'll get without boots?'

'The Turk who gave me the bread ...'

'Gave you, Evans!' Crabbe thundered.

'Swapped me, sir,' Evans corrected. 'He said we're all going up river to Baghdad on steamers. Ranks as well as officers. There's one berthed behind us. I saw it.'

'Even if the Ottoman Army does give us river passage to

Baghdad and by some miracle transport on to whatever Godforsaken corner of Turkey they decide to send us, do you think the prison camp will be next to the quayside?' Crabbe raged. 'The enemy knows every man jack of us will try to escape. Ranks as well as officers. They'll lock us up well away from the river and any towns or villages where people may be inclined to help us, and that, you idiot, means we'll be trekking miles. Your feet will be cut to ribbons, and when you can't walk one more step you'll be left behind to the mercies of the Bedouin and the vultures. I'm not sure which will be worse.'

John frowned. 'What other kit are the boys exchanging for food?'

'Overcoats ...'

'Overcoats!' Crabbe thundered.

'We'll be well shot of them in this heat, sir,' Evans declared defiantly.

'Have you seen the Turks queuing up to give you blankets?'

'No, sir, but they have to give us bedding ...' Evans faltered. 'Don't they?'

'Has it escaped your notice that we're at the mercy of the Ottoman Army? They don't "have to" give us anything, boy. Not even water. I haven't seen a Turk shed a tear for the boys who've died on this bloody forced march from Kut. Have you morons forgotten how cold it gets at night in the desert even in the hot season? And when this stifling weather ends the rains and winter set in. How long do you think you'll last without boots in your tropical kit?'

'Winter ... sir ... we'll be home before winter. Won't we?' Evans blanched beneath the layer of grime on his face.

Crabbe shook his head in despair. 'Do you have a telegraph to the India Office, the War Office? Or the Kaiser or Halil Bey? You're just one bloody fool in an army of bloody fools, boy. We're going to be imprisoned for the duration. That means until the end of the war. My prediction is it's likely to be years, not months.'

'Go, find your friends and eat your bread, Evans,' John advised. He felt sorry for the boy and all the others who hadn't thought further than their next meal. Given the blows, kicks, foul water, and inedible food the Turks were distributing among the British

7

POWs, who was to say that the men who'd settled for a full stomach weren't right, when it looked highly likely they'd all be dead soon.

'Bloody fool,' Crabbe muttered as Evans left.

'He is,' John agreed. 'But only a fool would be here. The wise men sorted themselves cushy berths in Whitehall before Force D was dreamed up by the Indian Office.'

Crabbe gave a crooked smile. 'You have to laugh.'

'Why?'

'They called us Force D and sent us to Sinne. You know what the Arabs say about Mesopotamia. 'When God created hell it was not bad enough so he made Mesopotamia ...'

'And added flies.'

Crabbe and John turned to the man who'd spoken. An immaculately tailored German captain, who looked cleaner than any man had a right to given the country they were in, bowed and clicked his heels.

'Gentlemen, you are British officers?'

'We were,' Crabbe replied dryly.

'Hauptmann Meyer at your service.'

'Major Mason.' John indicated Crabbe, 'Major Crabbe. Excuse us for not rising. We're tired after taking our daily stroll, Captain Meyer.'

'You British and your sense of humour. Major Mason, Major Crabbe. Cigarettes?' Meyer took two packets from his tunic pocket and handed them one each.

Crabbe eyed the captain suspiciously. 'What's this for?'

'A gift to enemies I admire. The odds were stacked against you but you fought bravely, and held out through many more months more of siege than your king or country could reasonably expect of you. Skeletons would be fatter than your officers and men.'

John asked. 'Do you know where we're being taken?'

'The Turks don't confide in we Germans and contrary to what you might have heard, German Command doesn't wield any authority over our Ottoman allies, but I suspect you'll be taken to Turkey and housed well away from the front lines.'

'So we've heard,' John opened his packet of cigarettes.

'Our rank and file?' Crabbe pressed.

'They need labourers to build the final sections of the Berlin-

8

Baghdad railway.'

'Surely they won't expect the men to work until they've recovered their health?' Crabbe questioned.

'The Turks can and will, Major Crabbe.'

'Then they'll kill even more of our men than they already have.' Crabbe had difficulty containing his anger.

'I have a cousin who was captured on the Western Front. He wrote to his mother from a prison camp in England to assure her that he is being treated well, as are all his fellow German POWs. Germany is caring for the British POWs just as conscientiously. I know, because my father is in charge of one of the prison camps and he takes his responsibilities for the welfare of the soldiers who have surrendered to the Germans very seriously. But the Turks,' Meyer shrugged, 'are different. They do not place the same value on life as we Europeans. I doubt ten out of every hundred British soldiers here will live to see your country again. Good evening, Major Mason, Major Crabbe.'

Armenian Christian Apostolic Church, Kharpert Plain, Ottoman Empire
April 1916

An icy cold permeated upwards from the flag-stoned floor and filtered through the stone walls of the church. It froze the air and Rebeka's blood. It didn't help that she, like all the Armenian women and children packed into the building at rifle point by Turkish gendarmes, was too paralysed by fear to move. Terrified of what lay ahead, surrounded by the dispossessed, deafened by the wails of hysterical women and the cries of children upset by the sight of their mothers' tears, she remained crouched on the floor, aware that whatever fate had in store, it was out of her hands.

Like their menfolk who had been ordered to report to the town square three days ago, the women and children had been told to make their way to the church at two o'clock that afternoon with sufficient food for three days travel and a change of warm clothing. After waiting patiently in a slow-moving line for over an hour a Turkish gendarme had ticked her, her mother's, grandmother's, and sisters' names off a list so thick it resembled a

9

book.

Her mother had settled their family as close as she could to the altar rail on the premise that proximity to hallowed ground would ensure God and the Blessed Virgin would look after them, especially her grandmother, who was confused as to what was happening. Their neighbour Mrs Gulbenkian, the dairyman's wife, laid claim to a patch of floor next to them.

'You know all our men are all dead?' she whispered.

'How dare you suggest such a thing?' Rebeka's mother demanded indignantly. 'The men have been marched south to work on farms where we will join them.'

'You choose to believe the gendarmes' lies?'

'They wouldn't have asked the men to bring warm winter clothes as well as food for three days if they had meant to kill them. The gendarmes would have shot them in the town square when they assembled. They collected them to work in the fields to produce food for the Ottoman Army. Everyone knows that the Turks make poor farmers.'

'They want to get rid of all of us Armenians because we are Christians. The Turks want a Muslim country, which is why they killed our men. The gendarmes shot the old men who couldn't walk and the cripples first,' Mrs Gulbenkian asserted.

'They loaded them into carts. I saw them pass at the end of our road.'

'As soon as the carts were out of sight of the town, the gendarmes pulled the weakest from the carts and shot them. Don't tell me you didn't hear the sound of the rifles.'

'They were warning shots.'

'The American missionary Mr Brackett and Mr Bilgi followed the men when they were marched out. Mr Brackett told me himself that he had seen the bodies of all our men, including the old and the crippled. He recognised your husband's corpse and my husband's, and Anusha's Ruben. Every last one of them, all of them had been shot and their bodies heaped up in Green Horse Canyon.'

'I don't believe you.' Rebeka had never seen her mother react so fiercely. 'And I'd appreciate you keeping your lies and stories to yourself, Mrs Gulbenkian. Do not repeat them in front of my mother and daughters.'

'First they killed the men, now it's our turn,' Mrs Gulbenkian persisted. 'Soon there'll be no Christian Armenians in Turkey or the whole of the Ottoman Empire. They only waited three days to collect us so they could be sure there'd be no men left in hiding to fight for us or our honour.'

'Enough! Stay away from my family!' Rebeka's mother ordered.

Mrs Gulbenkian shrugged and turned her back to them.

'Do you think Mrs Gulbenkian could be right?' Rebeka whispered into her mother's ear.

'I think she is talking a lot of nonsense. Look after Mariam and your grandmother while I see to Veronika and Anusha. Too many of the gendarmes are looking at them for my liking.'

Rebeka, the second of four daughters, had long accepted that she was the 'plain one'. She had been relegated to working in the jewellery business founded by her maternal grandfather, because there was little hope of her attracting a financially secure husband. She didn't resent her status, though; rather she revelled in the independence it gave her, like her mother's spinster sister.

Her mother retied the scarves around Anusha and Veronika's heads so the cloth hid as much of their faces as possible, as well as their hair. Mrs Gulbenkian occasionally looked in their direction but when Rebeka's mother glared back at her she didn't attempt to speak to them again.

Time crept on. The shadows within the church lengthened and more and more of the gendarmes entered the church. Apparently oblivious to its holy purpose they shouldered their rifles as they stood in front of the door, laughing and joking amongst themselves. Occasionally one of them would point to an exceptionally pretty girl and the others would snigger and make lewd comments.

Her sister Veronika was the first to be singled out. The gendarme who grabbed her arm, Mehmet, had always had an eye for her, and a reputation every girl in the town feared. When he tried to drag Veronika forcibly from them, her mother screamed and clung to her, locking her hands around Veronika's waist.

Horrified, Rebeka grabbed Veronika's leg, Anusha her arm.

'You will not dishonour my daughter.'

Those were the last words her mother spoke.

Mehmet released his hold on Veronika, and her mother clasped her in her arms. He turned, lifted his rifle, aimed, and fired.

The bullet lodged in Veronika's temple.

Her mother screamed. A second gendarme fired. Her mother's body fell across Veronika's.

Mehmet reloaded his rifle, pointed it at her and Mariam, and stretched out his hand to Anusha. Her eldest sister didn't protest, she rose and allowed herself to be led outside, as so many other girls were.

The church door remained open. The screams of the 'chosen' women and girls wafted in, high pitched, harsh, disturbing and discordant.

'They are being dishonoured.'

Rebeka looked into Mrs Gulbenkian's eyes.

'Come, child, I'll help you cover your mother and sister.'

She took two sheets from one of the bags her mother had packed and handed one to Mrs Gulbenkian. The whole time she helped the older woman lay out her mother and younger sister, she listened to the screams and wondered when it would be her turn to be 'dishonoured'.

Chapter Two

Basra
May 1916

Dr Georgiana Downe left the Lansing Memorial Mission House, where she lived with the staff when she wasn't on duty in the Lansing Mission Hospital, and closed the front door behind her.

'Good. That's what I like, a punctual woman.' Major David Knight stepped down from the carriage he'd hired and held the door open for her.

'What else do you like in a woman, Major Knight?' Georgiana flirted mildly as she stepped inside.

'Wit.'

'Beauty?' Georgiana sat with her back to the driver.

'Can't have everything, Dr Downe, and your spectacles are slipping down your nose.'

'My eye-glasses invariably slide down when I use face cream.' She pushed them back up.

'Perhaps they're telling you that you don't need to use face cream.'

'Is that an attempt to flatter me?'

'Not at all, you wouldn't be with me if you were too ravishing. I'm allergic to women who are more handsome than me.' He sat opposite her and ordered the driver to move on.

Georgiana laughed. 'Harry used to warn me about good-looking men who were too besotted with themselves to love anyone or anything else.'

'I miss Harry. Life was always fun when he was around. Everyone who knew him adored him. You were fortunate to have him for a brother.'

'Harry wasn't just my brother, he was my twin.'

'Even better, for you that is. So, to return to my favourite topic

13

of conversation, me, do you consider me exceptionally good-looking?'

'Not enough to outweigh your faults.'

'For a woman who's only met me in the company of others until this moment, you have very decided and fixed opinions on my personality.'

'You drank too much at the lunch Charles organised when you, Peter Smythe, and my brother Michael came downstream after the surrender of Kut.'

'You kept a tally of what I was drinking? Knowing I'd been besieged, under fire, and starved in Kut for months and months.'

'Harry's warnings about unsuitable men also extended to drunkards.'

'That's rich coming from Harry. I've watched him open a fresh bottle of brandy when every other man in the room was under a table.'

'Including you?'

'Including me,' he conceded. 'Every man with sense drinks too much in war. It's the only escape.'

'I'm tired of discussing you.'

'Surely not – but never mind, we can always return to the riveting subject later.'

'Where are we going?'

'You need to ask? How long have you lived in Basra?'

'This is only my second free evening since I arrived and I slept through the first. I don't know how hard you work in the Basra Military Hospital but we doctors in the Lansing Memorial are drowning in patients. Not just the Turkish POWs you send us but the locals who can't get treatment anywhere else. Our shifts last round the clock.'

'So you know nothing of Basra's wonderful nightlife?'

'From what Michael tells me, it's centred on the Basra Club, the Basra Club, and the Basra Club.'

'Your younger brother is right. Although he seems to have found an interesting place to live. Abdul's has quite the reputation among British officers.'

'Michael lives there from a sense of duty.' She had trouble keeping a straight face as she said it and he knew it.

'Don't tell me you believe what you've just said.'

14

'A war correspondent needs to keep up-to-date with events and from what I gather most events in Basra start in the back rooms of Abdul's. Or so Michael tells me.'

'Or upstairs in the brothel,' David added. 'Or so Harry told me. He had a room there too.'

'I know, I used to write to him there when I worked in London.'

'About this dinner ...'

'You're wondering if I'd prefer to eat in the respectable security of the dining room or risk scandal by accompanying you to one of the private rooms?' she questioned.

'Some of the private rooms are very comfortable.'

'With bedroom and bathroom attached, or so I've heard.'

'I've been told that too. So, public dining room it is.'

She smiled. 'The privacy afforded by a private room may help me to understand you better.'

'You want to understand me?'

'I'm curious as to whether or not you deserve your reputation.'

'I have a reputation?' He gave her the full benefit of his smile.

'You didn't know?' She had to concede, if only to herself, that he was *very* good-looking. Possibly the most handsome man she'd ever met. His hair was white-blond, his eyes a deep cerulean blue. Piercing and full of mischief.

'You amaze me.' He laughed a deep throaty chuckle that had the effect of broadening her own smile.

'You most certainly do among the nurses who've worked with you,' Georgiana elucidated. 'I would like to discover if you're really as dangerous and wild as they've suggested.'

'I take it that you have talked to these nurses who've been privileged to work with me?'

'Angela Smythe organises tea parties for them. She invited me along.'

'I thought you were too busy working for a social life.'

'I manage to spare the odd hour occasionally to drink tea.'

'What happens if you find out that I'm not "dangerous and wild"?'

'I'd be disappointed.'

'Really?'

'It would mean that I'd have to look elsewhere for excitement on my rare leisure evenings.'

The ground was even colder than the air, the only warmth emanating from Mariam's small body as she lay on Rebeka's lap. Rebeka pulled her sister even closer, covering her ears with her skirt as the women who'd been picked to 'entertain' the guards that night were dragged from the group. A few – those who had not yet learned that fighting back wasted energy better put to use in trying to survive – screamed and attempted to lash out at their assailants. The only rewards they received for their efforts were beatings.

Rebeka saw her sister Anusha rise when Mehmet beckoned and her heart went out to her.

'Even as a baby everyone could see Anusha was going to be a beauty, not just in your family but in the town. Men's heads would turn when she passed them in the street when she was small. It pains me to sit here and watch while that filthy beast puts his hands on her. He's not fit to wipe her boots ...'

'What was that you said, Grandma?' A guard thumped Mrs Gulbenkian's ankle with the barrel of his rifle.

She stared up at him defiantly. 'I said we need food, water, and milk for the children.'

The man laughed. 'And where do you think we're going to get them? There are no shops here.' He lifted his head and stared up at the sky, 'Only the heavens. You're a Christian, pray to your God. He might send something down.' The man grabbed Rebeka's chin, and wrenched it towards him. Rebeka closed her eyes but she still sensed the man staring at her.

'You're ugly.' The man released Rebeka and grabbed the girl next to her. 'You'll do.'

Rebeka exhaled slowly lest he detect her relief. She felt sorry for the milkman's daughter who'd been sitting beside her but not sorry enough to volunteer to take her place. She opened her eyes again and winced as fingers clamped painfully on her shoulder, digging into her flesh.

'I'll take care of Mariam.' Mrs Gulbenkian reached out and lifted Mariam from Rebeka's lap.

Rebeka didn't protest. She'd tried to fight the first time she'd been 'chosen' and still bore the swellings and bruises.

The gendarme dragged her to the fringe of the group of women. He grabbed the neck of her dress.

'Strip!'

It was her last and only garment. If he tore it from her she'd be left naked, as some of the other women already were. She did as he ordered and stood before him, shivering. He poked and prodded her breasts and thighs, laughing as he did before pushing her to the ground and kicking her legs apart. All around, women and girls were suffering the same indignities she was being subjected to.

The man unbuckled his trousers and dropped them before landing on her, bruising her flesh. His breath stank of rotting food, his body of filth and stale sweat. His eyes, wide dark pools in egg-shaped whites, stared crazily into hers.

She left him and what he was doing to her and retreated to her 'memory table'. One of the best gifts her grandmother had given her and her sisters. She could still hear her grandmother's voice the first time she told them about it.

'Everyone has a memory table, but not everyone knows how to use it. The women in our family lay them with Great-Grandmother's lily-embroidered linen cloths, the white ones we keep for Easter and birthdays, but they are not set out with plates, silverware, almond cakes, and wine. They are furnished with your own very special memories. Some gleam silver with reflected moonlight, some with the tarnished light of the dying sun on a summer's evening, and some dance, bright and cheerful: red, pink, white, cream, and blue, like newly opened flowers at sunrise. But be careful to select only the best. The ones when you were happiest.

'When your days are difficult, and you are unhappy, go to your table and pick and take a memory. Hold it close, relive it, and remember the good times and believe with all your heart that there are more to come. Keep your chosen memory with you throughout the entire day and relive every precious second, because you will have to wait a whole sunset and sunrise before you can take another.'

She picked one. It wasn't one of her special memories or even one she would have chosen to remember. But it was one she couldn't blot from her mind because it marked the division between her old life and the new.

Rebeka's family home, Kharpert Plain
April 1916

Anusha thrust open the door, charged into the house, and dropped her basket of shopping. 'Mehmet's back in town,' she announced breathlessly.

'Surely not. You must be mistaken.' Their mother calmly carried on chopping red and white cabbage for winter salad.

'He's wearing a gendarme's uniform.'

'Mehmet's father is such a nice man.' Her grandmother, who insisted on believing the best of everyone, dropped her sewing and tucked her needle into the linen. 'The way he runs his stables, he can't do enough for people. When the farmers don't have enough money to rent a plough horse, he gives them one and waits until harvest before asking for payment.'

'Mehmet is not his father, Mother,' her mother replied. 'Have you forgotten what he did to the spice seller? Beating him and stealing his takings from the shop.'

'I thought Mehmet was sentenced to ten years in jail. Not just for beating up the spice seller but ...'

'That's enough, Anusha.' Her mother spoke sharply after looking to Veronika and Mariam who were sitting on the window seat plaiting rags to make rugs.

Her mother wanted to protect her youngest daughters but she, like Anusha, knew it was too late. Mariam, Veronika, and every girl in town had heard the tales of the girls Mehmet had done despicable 'dishonouring' things too. Girls who didn't dare make a complaint to the police because they knew they'd be expected to stand up in court and speak against Mehmet. And that would forever taint them as 'used goods'.

Her father walked in from the school where he taught. 'Anusha,' he'd kissed her cheek. 'You must go home to your husband at once.'

'Why, Father?'

'Just go, quickly, girl.'

Her mother set down the knife and sat down. 'The stories are true?'

'I've just watched the gendarmes post the notice on the church door. All Armenian men and boys over the age of fourteen are to report to the church before nine o'clock tomorrow morning. We are to take enough food for a three-day march, stout shoes, and warm clothing.'

'You must go to the Americans at the mission … you must …'

Her father went to her mother and gently, tenderly helped her from the chair. 'We older men have to go, my love, so we can care for the boys and the younger men.'

'But …'

He silenced her mother's protest with a kiss. 'Go, pack food and my warm clothes and while you do put your trust in God, my love.'

Northern Mesopotamian Desert
May 1916

The man who'd raped Rebeka spat in her face as he climbed unceremoniously off her. 'You're ugly.'

She wiped his spittle from her eyes with her fingers, grabbed her dress, and pulled it over her head.

'If a man chooses to favour you again, try moving. Making love to you is like making love to a potato sack.'

Rebeka knew she was taking a risk but she could not remain silent. 'You call what you just did to me "making love"?'

'It's more love than someone as ugly as you deserves. Don't look at me like that. Bitch!' He lashed out. She ducked to avoid the blow and fell to the ground. Bruised, battered, and bleeding, she stumbled back to Mrs Gulbenkian.

'Mariam … did she …?'

'She saw nothing,' Mrs Gulbenkian assured her. 'She's so tired she hasn't opened her eyes, the angel. Come, it's cold. Sit next to us, Rebeka. Have you heard the story of the Golden Bird?'

Rebeka had, many times, but she shook her head, curled close to her sister, and prepared to listen.

Basra Club, Basra
May 1916

'Any complaints about the dinner?' David asked Georgiana.

'None, but as all you did was order the food I hardly think you can give yourself an accolade.' Georgiana sat back in her chair and sipped her glass of wine.

'Can I order us brandies without running the risk of you calling me a drunkard again?'

'Brandy can affect the body in so many ways. I'd rather visit that bedroom first.'

'You're very direct, Dr Downe.'

'I've discovered honesty saves time, especially in war when there are so few leisure hours to enjoy the limited pleasures that are available.'

David stared at her.

'Lost for words, Major Knight?'

'Out of my depth. I'm used to …'

'Please continue.'

'I don't want to risk offending you, Dr Downe.'

'In that case let me guess. You were about to say, honest whores and dishonest husband-seekers.'

'You don't appear to fall into either category.'

'How discerning of you.'

'You're not looking for a husband?'

'Absolutely not. I lost a wonderful one to the war. Gwilym was perfect in every way and irreplaceable. Besides, the demands of my present post as a doctor in the Lansing allow me so little free time a husband would prove an encumbrance at the moment. However, I do like sex.' She left the table, went into the bedroom, and pressed down on the mattress. 'Seems comfortable. What do you say we give it a try?' She removed her wire-rimmed spectacles and placed them on a side table.

He tugged at the buckle on his belt. Before he'd succeeded in unfastening it, she'd unbuttoned the pearls that decorated the shoulders of her cream lace dress and allowed it to fall to the floor. She stepped out of it, picked it up, and folded it on to a chair. Her chemise and drawers followed.

'Stockings on or off?' she rested her right foot on the chair and pulled at her garter.

He stared at her.

'You have no preference? About the stockings,' she added when he failed to reply.

He found his voice and murmured. 'You don't wear a corset.'

'You prefer your women in corsets?'

'Yes … no …' he stammered

'Stockings are at such a premium in wartime I think I'll take them off rather than risk tearing them.'

'Georgiana …'

'I find formality to be out of place in the bedroom, David. Please, call me Georgie.' She knelt on the bed and unbuttoned his trousers.

Afterwards David propped himself up on his elbow and looked down at Georgiana. 'I dread the reply but I have to ask. Did I rise to your expectations?'

'You'll do.'

'Until you find something better?'

'That goes without saying, but I have so little time to look for something better, a more apt maxim might be, "until one of us moves on".'

'You're thinking of going somewhere?' He rearranged the pillows, lay back, and lifted her head on to his chest.

'Not immediately. But I have some control over my life and where I work. You, however, are army property – I believe the term Harry used was "one hundred per cent military for the use of".'

'Unfortunately Harry was right. No soldier is in control of his own fate. I go where I'm sent. But while I remain in Basra I would like to repeat this evening as often as feasible.'

'That would be fun. You can order that brandy now.'

'If it's all the same to you I'd prefer to stay here a while longer. You?' He ran his fingertips lightly down her arm and over her naked breasts.

'Only if you continue to dispel boredom by amusing me.'

'Georgie …'

She pulled his head down to hers and kissed him long and thoroughly before slipping her hand between his thighs. Then, for a while, there was no time or need for words.

When they finally lay entwined, pleasantly exhausted, and too close to sleep for Georgiana's peace of mind, she turned back the sheet.

'Do you have to move?' he mumbled without opening his eyes.

'If I don't, I won't wake until morning and I don't relish the thought of explaining why I stayed out all night to Mrs Butler.'

'Tell her you were kidnapped by a doctor who wanted to discuss treatments for heart failure.'

'She thinks I'm having dinner with Clary and the nurses who share her bungalow.'

'Why would Mrs Butler think that?'

'Because that's what I told her.'

'You're ashamed of me?'

She smiled. 'Should I be?'

'I think I'm a charming fellow …'

'I already know what you think of yourself. I doubt Mrs Butler would agree. She's suspicious of the motives of all British officers, especially where ladies are concerned. I'm amazed she allowed an American like Angela to marry Peter Smythe.'

'It was Angela, not Peter, who persuaded Mrs Butler to give them her blessing.' He opened his pocket watch. 'We have time for that brandy, if you want one.'

'Please.' She went into the bathroom and filled the basin from the jug on the washstand.

He padded naked into the dining room and rang the bell for service. By the time she'd finished washing and dressing the brandy had arrived.

'What are you doing tomorrow night?' he asked when she returned to the bedroom and retrieved her spectacles.

'Working.'

'Really?'

'There are only three doctors in the Lansing. I have, however, been promised Saturday off, if you're free.'

'I'll make sure I'm free. Georgie …'

She laid a finger over his mouth.

'Now I'm not allowed to talk to you?'

'Ground rules. Tonight was lovely and fun.'

'Thank you …'

'But that's all it will ever be between us, David, lovely and fun. I don't care if you have a wife in India or England …'

'I don't.'

'I don't want to make plans with you. I just want the here and now. Understand.'

'No I don't, Georgie. I've never met anyone like you and …'

'No ands, no past, no future. Beyond Saturday that is.' She picked up her brandy. 'Dress, please. I don't fancy riding through the streets in a hire cab alone at this time of night.'

Chapter Three

Shumran
May 1916

Captain Johnny Leigh tottered unsteadily towards Majors Mason and Crabbe.

'Brigadier's compliments, gentlemen. He's invited all officers to join him at the wharf for a briefing.'

John studied Leigh with a professional eye. 'You have a temperature?'

'Difficult to know in this blasted heat,' Leigh slurred.

'Fighting stomach cramps and diarrhoea?'

'Me and everyone else in this man's army.'

'Find a place where you can lie down, preferably in the shade.'

'There is none.'

'There might be under a cart.' John couldn't see Dira but he spotted the guard he'd been given after his court martial, Sergeant Greening, overseeing a platoon of sepoys who were digging a latrine trench. He waved to him and Greening made his way over. 'Find Captain Leigh a place where he can lie down and rest, sergeant. If Captain Vincent's around, ask him to administer chalk.'

'We ran out of chalk half an hour ago, sir.'

'Damn! Does Captain Vincent know about the briefing?'

'Already left, sir.'

John checked Leigh's pulse. 'I'll take another look at you after I've seen the brigadier, Leigh.' John rose. His muscles felt as though they'd turned to stone since he'd sat down.

'I'm all right, Mason ...' Leigh's eyelids fluttered. He crumpled to his knees.

'I'll get Captain Leigh into one of the tents, Major Mason. You go along to the briefing, sir.' Greening slung Leigh over his shoulder and walked away.

'I wish I had one-tenth of Greening's strength left to me.' Crabbe accompanied John as he negotiated his way around the groups of men who'd lit fires along the river bank to boil water in their billy cans. A few attempted to struggle to their feet when they saw John and Crabbe approach. Crabbe called out in advance.

'At ease, men.'

The brigadier was slumped on a camp chair in front of one of the carts they used to haul their equipment. Give the debilitated state of the available donkeys and mules, only the most essential items of kit had been loaded. A fire burned next to the cart and an Indian orderly was making tea. John noticed the bleached state of the leaves he was spooning into the tin pot, and wondered how many times they'd been used.

The brigadier saw him staring at them. 'There's enough life left to colour the water, Mason.'

'I'll take your word for it, sir.'

'Rumour has it the Relief Force has dispatched a supply ship under a white flag that should reach us tomorrow.'

'I thought that was more definite than just a rumour, sir.'

'Relief Force asked the Turks' permission, I received the news via our wireless in Kut before we smashed it. The senior man here informed me it was on its way when I arrived.' The brigadier watched the officers limping and straggling in then spoke to his orderly. 'Lieutenant Grace will take over brewing the tea, Patel. Pass down an order to the non-commissioned officers asking them to ensure we receive privacy during the briefing.'

'Yes, sir.' Patel saluted and disappeared. Just one more grey figure blending with the others in the twilight.

'Cigarettes, gentlemen?' The brigadier handed out packs. 'These are the last from the Dorsets' mess. Don't hoard them. In this dry heat they're already turning to dust.'

John opened the pack Bowditch handed him, extracted one, and lit it immediately.

'Thank you all for answering the summons. I realise you're dispirited as well as exhausted but I thought it as well we exchange views on the situation. As senior ranking officer I approached the Turkish Officers on arrival, hoping to negotiate more suitable and humane treatment for the ranks. I regret without success. I have, however, officially registered my disgust at the conditions we find ourselves in, particularly the lack of shelter, clean drinking water, sanitation, food, and transport that has resulted in a high death toll among both officers and men on the march out of Kut. I also registered my revulsion as to the amount of violence meted out by both Turkish ranks and officers towards our men. I asked the Turks to make note that in the opinion of our senior officers and medics, our casualties would have been considerably less if the Ottomans had organised and furnished basic amenities.'

'And was your protest noted by the Turks, sir?' John asked.

'Noted, and documented by them and me, Mason.'

'Are we being shipped to Baghdad, sir?' Alf Grace poured the 'tea' into tin mugs and passed them down the line.

'That is the Turks' intention. I've received assurance that the worst of our casualties, ranks as well as officers, will be conveyed there by steamship but I've been warned the majority will have to march. Please!' The brigadier held up his hand to silence the hubbub of protest. 'All decisions about evaluating and transporting the sick will be made by our medics as well as the Turks.'

'That doesn't bode well for our sick given the way the Turkish doctors dismissed the advice of our medics in Kut,' Crabbe observed.

'All we can do is to try and make them listen.' John finished one cigarette and lit another.

'Will we be held in Baghdad, sir?' Lieutenant Bowditch asked.

'No, we're being sent on into prison camps in Turkey.'

'Ranks and officers?' Crabbe pressed

'Ranks and officers, Major Crabbe. Officers will be separated from the men at the earliest opportunity and our Indian troops will be separated from our British troops. From what the sepoys have told me, the Turks are doing all they can to try to bribe our Muslim soldiers to change sides and fight for them.'

'Our Hindu and Sikh troops, sir?' Vincent asked.

'Are not being treated as well as our Muslim troops, or our ranks. And despite my protests the Turks absolutely refuse to allow more than one officer to remain with each regiment.

Crabbe rose to his feet. 'Permission to remain with the Dorsets, sir?'

Other officers jumped to their feet and the brigadier held up his hand again. 'I've been assured we'll remain with the men until we reach Baghdad. All decisions as to deployment of officers will be made there. I'd appreciate a report on the medical situation, Major Mason.'

'Grim, sir.' John looked to Captain Vincent. 'Would you like to elaborate on the supply situation, captain?'

'We're out of medical supplies, sir.'

'You've applied to the Turks, Captain Vincent?'

'I talked to their medical officers, sir. They don't have medical supplies to meet the needs of their own troops, let alone ours,' Vincent confirmed.

'Let's hope the supply ship the Relief Force has promised us exists on more than paper and turns up soon. Anyone else want to say anything?' The brigadier looked around the silent group of demoralised men. 'Good night, gentlemen. Although I doubt any of us will get much sleep. I have a premonition that even worse times lie ahead, so I advise you to get as much rest as you can, while you can.'

John lingered after the other officers dispersed. 'Permission to discuss medical matters, sir?'

The brigadier nodded and offered John his flask.

'I'd like to volunteer to act as rear guard and follow the men who will be marched to Baghdad, sir. Dysentery, scurvy, beriberi, and diarrhoea are endemic. If the way the Turks drove us to this point is any indication of their future behaviour towards us, they won't be expending their resources caring for our men. Not while they treat their own ranks so abominably. I suspect that when, not if, our ranks fall out they'll be left where they lie to die.'

'I believe your suspicions to be correct, Mason. What are you proposing?'

'That if the supply ship exists and appears, Captain Vincent set up a floating hospital on board to ferry the worse cases of sickness amongst our men to Baghdad. As we haven't enough medical officers to delegate one to each regiment, I'd like to travel with volunteer orderlies behind the Dorsets, Norfolks, and Hampshires with whatever tents and equipment I can scrounge and set up respite centres to care for our men who can no longer walk.'

'I'd be happy to give you permission, but even should the Turks agree, they'll insist on giving you a Turkish guard.'

'I'm aware of that, sir.'

The brigadier lowered his voice. 'You've no thoughts of escaping?'

'Not while any of our men requiring medical help remain in Turkish custody, sir.'

'You do realise that you can expect to be held in Turkey for the duration?'

'Can't be helped, sir. As a doctor I took an oath.'

'You won't be able to do much without medical supplies.'

'I'm confident that when the Red Cross or Red Crescent hear of our predicament, they'll send us at least some of what we need. But even if they don't, after almost two years of improvised doctoring in the desert I may be able to alleviate some of the men's suffering.'

'Even if it's only to help them on their way? No – don't comment on that remark, Mason. It was fatuous of me to make it. Some things are best left unsaid. As for marching over the desert, you're as skeletal, sick, and exhausted as the rest of us.'

'I'm fine, sir,' John lied.

'David Knight wanted you to go downstream with the worst of the casualties we exchanged for Turkish POWs, didn't he?'

'We tossed, sir. He won.'

'That's not the version I heard. You have a two-headed sovereign and a wife in Basra?'

'My wife and I are estranged, sir.' John avoided mentioning the sovereign that had been a birthday gift from Harry Downe.

'You volunteered to stay with the main force to avoid your wife?'

John smiled. 'I doubt any man would choose to be here simply to avoid his wife even if she was a demon, sir. Maud and I agreed to divorce before I left Basra last July. I'm certain she no more wants to see me than I do her.'

'She does know you weren't shot at dawn after that ridiculous court martial when Perry and Cleck-Heaton levied trumped-up charges against you?'

'If she didn't know it before we surrendered at Kut, I don't doubt Smythe told her when he and Mitkhal smuggled dispatches to the Relief Force last January, sir.'

The brigadier lowered his voice. 'Can you honestly tell me that your decision to remain with the Force has nothing to do with your personal circumstances?'

'I volunteered to stay with the Force because I've been in Mesopotamia longer than Knight and have more experience of treating tropical diseases, sir.'

Realising John had said as much as he was going to about his private affairs, the brigadier changed the subject. 'When you say "travel behind with orderlies", presumably you mean your Indian orderly?'

'Dira, yes, sir, but only if he volunteers.'

'Sergeant Greening?'

'He's my guard, sir.'

'Since you've proved yourself a model prisoner, I've heard that under your tutelage Greening's become proficient in administering various medical procedures?'

'He has, sir.'

'Do you think Greening would happy to stay behind with you and your Indian orderly and assist you?'

'As with Dira, the choice would have to be his, sir.'

'You'll probably need more help.'

'I'll take any that is offered from experienced orderlies, sir, but the choice has to be theirs.'

'Ask for volunteers. I'll talk to the Turks and do what I can to help you implement your plan. Can I leave it to you to delegate responsibilities to the other medics?'

'I'll call a medics' conference for first thing tomorrow, sir.'

'I'll send someone to notify you if that supply ship is spotted. This is not a corner I'd have chosen to be pushed into, Mason, but it's good to have men like you and Crabbe with me.'

'Thank you, sir.'

When John walked away he saw Patel returning to the brigadier's cook fire. He made a detour to the shelters that had been erected next to the river. Leigh had been packed into a two-man tent with half a dozen other officers. Dira was using a sponge attached to a stick to moisten his lips.

'Good work, Dira, but there's little we can without supplies, so try and get some rest yourself.'

'Yes, sir. Thank you, sir.'

'If you need me I'll be with Major Crabbe.'

'His bearer has set up his tent next to the Dorsets' cook fire, sir.'

'Thank you, Dira. Good night.'

John found Crabbe sitting outside his tent, staring down into the flames. He saw John and handed him a flask. John opened it and sniffed the contents.

'French brandy from our mess. I told my bearer to hide the flasks in the contaminated laundry sacks in case the Turks searched us. That one is yours.'

'Thank you.'

John buttoned it into his shirt pocket.

'Not drinking tonight?'

'I swallowed enough brandy to last me a lifetime a year ago. Given my absence of sense in those days I don't recall thanking you properly for taking care of me.'

'Wasn't just me. It was Charles, Smythe, even Leigh, Bowditch, Grace and ...' Crabbe hesitated before saying the names of the dead, 'Harry, Amey ...'

'I miss him.' John didn't have to say who 'him' was.

Crabbe knew John had been closer to his cousin Harry than most men were to their brothers. 'Harry would find something to get up to even here.'

'Probably annoying the Turks to the point where they'd start shooting us,' John suggested, not entirely humorously.

'There are worse ways to go. Like dying inch by inch on a long dry march over the desert.' Crabbe rose from the stool his bearer had foraged from one of the carts. 'I'm for bed. My bearer made a cot up for you in my tent as your man was busy helping Dira.'

'Thank you.' John reached for his cigarettes.

'Don't stay out too late. Damned mosquitos are out for blood and they've brought their forks and carving knives. I doubt we'll get any rest tomorrow.'

'I'll turn in shortly.' John struck a match, lit his cigarette, and looked around the camp. Most of the officers had managed to bring their tents but the men were sprawled on the ground around their camp fires. He considered what the brigadier had said about Maud. Had he stayed with the Expeditionary Force simply to avoid her?

31

If Maud had remained faithful when he'd left India – if she hadn't been pregnant with another man's child when he'd been shipped downstream with fever last year – if she'd told him she still loved him …

He suppressed the thoughts almost as soon as they arose. There were simply too many 'ifs'. A vision of Maud as she'd looked the first time he'd seen her in the officers' mess in India came to mind.

Maud's gown had been gold silk decorated with amber beads. He'd described her afterwards in a letter to his mother as looking like 'a Botticelli angel who'd stepped off of an Italian altarpiece.' There was no denying Maud's beauty, but for the first time he wondered if that was all he'd ever seen in Maud? Had he simply fallen for a pretty face?

He tried to recall conversations they'd shared but the only ones he could remember were about trivialities, furnishings, food, balls, parties, Maud's gowns … Maud had been so young when they'd married. He'd been ready to resign his commission and settle down to the life of a rural doctor in his native West Country, but would Maud have settled for life as a country doctor's wife?

He finished his cigarette and tossed the stub into the fire. The question had become academic after war broke out. Who knows what they would have done if Britain hadn't declared hostilities and called up the reservists? In all probability Maud would have chafed at the boring routine of life in an English village after growing up in India and Mesopotamia. She might have sought out excitement in affairs just as she'd done when he'd left her in in India.

And him? Would he – could he – have turned a blind eye to an unfaithful wife?

He left his stool and turned towards the medical tents. Thoughts – especially those of the future or 'might have beens' were pointless when he was surrounded by the sick and dying.

After presiding at the burial of so many of his fellow officers and men he was certain that an unmarked grave in a desert he'd never wanted to visit, and had learned to loathe, was all the future he could expect or hope for.

What was worse, he couldn't see how his presence, along with that of his fellow sufferers, was in the slightest use to King or Empire.

The Wharf, Baghdad
May 1916

Bowditch tiptoed, balancing precariously as he wove a path around the bodies of men who'd stretched out wherever they'd found space on the deck of the steamer. He continued to head for the ship's prow where he'd spotted the shadowy figure of Major Crabbe leaning on the rail, smoking.

'You're up early, Major Crabbe.'

'Couldn't sleep, Bowditch. You?'

'I've been waiting for the order to disembark.'

'All night?' Crabbe asked in amusement.

'Bastards seem to enjoy tormenting us. When they didn't move us when we dropped anchor, I thought they'd wait until we were all asleep then blow a whistle.'

'They won't move us in the dark, Bowditch.'

'Because they're afraid we might run off?'

'That's the least of their worries. They know we have nowhere to run to. Not here.'

'Then when will they move us, sir?' Bowditch persisted.

Crabbe stared down at the undulating mat of flotsam and faeces that lapped sluggishly around the hull. 'They'll move us after the town wakes and there's enough of a crowd to abuse us as we're marched down the gangplank and through the streets.'

'We're British, sir. They wouldn't dare expose us to humiliation and ridicule ...' Bowditch began.

'Oh yes they would,' Crabbe cut in sharply. 'Halil Bey has scored a major victory in forcing Townshend to surrender to him and he's going to exploit it to the full. The whole town will be out to throw brickbats at us. So I suggest you brace yourself and warn the other junior officers, non-coms, and ranks to do the same.'

'Most of us are sick, sir.'

'So much the better for Johnny Turk and the natives. We're not in a condition to fight back.'

'Do you think they'll keep us here, sir?'

'In Baghdad?' Crabbe shook his head. 'Not a chance. But hopefully we'll be given reasonable quarters in the city until transport has been arranged to take us to the POW camps in Turkey. If they try marching us there I doubt any of us will survive the trek.'

Bowditch stared at Crabbe and whether it was the subdued light that emanated from the oil lamp affixed to the mast, or the darkness that swirled like fog around the deck, the senior officer appeared wraithlike. He reminded Bowditch of the illustrations of ghosts from the Netherworld that had adorned the pages of the *Illustrated Police News* that he and the other boys in his prep school had devoured from cover to cover by torchlight under cover of the blankets on their beds. Bowditch shuddered.

'You look like someone just walked over your grave, Bowditch.' Crabbe tossed the stub of his cigarette over the side.

'I feel as though someone has just walked over my grave, sir.' Bowditch took a pack of Turkish cigarettes from his pocket and offered them to Crabbe

Crabbe shook his head. 'Keep them. We may have plenty at the moment but I've a feeling they'll soon be in short supply.'

'You think so, sir?'

'Like food they'll become a memory.'

Bowditch leaned on the rail next to Crabbe. 'Have you any idea what kind of accommodation we can expect? I've never been a prisoner of war before.'

'None of us have. The brigadier said there was talk of housing the officers in a hotel, but I'm guessing that even if there is a hotel, the rooms won't be up to Ritz standard, or even that of a doss house. But whatever they are they'll be better than the accommodation the ranks will be given and that's where I'm headed. I cleared it with the brigadier last night. The Turks are allowing one officer to remain with every regiment. I'm staying with the Dorsets.'

'The men will be put to work?'

'They will.'

Bowditch was feeling too demoralised to ask what work Crabbe thought the men would be forced to carry out. He studied the horizon. 'Dawn is breaking.' He stared at the wharf as the square outlines of warehouses on the bank emerged from the night shadows. 'Baghdad doesn't look much of a place, does it, sir?'

'If there is anywhere that looks like much of a place in this bloody country, I haven't seen it.' Sensing Bowditch's despair Crabbe gripped his shoulder. 'All we can do is make the best of it, boy, and remember we're not as badly off as some. It's the poor beggars marching behind us I feel sorry for.'

'You're thinking of Major Mason, sir.'

'He won't sleep, eat, or rest while there's a man who needs care, and when a man is past saving he won't leave him unburied. If he hasn't the strength to pick up a shovel, he'll scrape out a grave with his bare hands.'

'He has Sergeant Greening and his orderlies to help him, sir,' Bowditch reminded.

'And hundreds of sick and dying men who are being force-marched. Much as I don't want to spend any time here, I'd like to see him before we move off if only to reassure myself that he's made it this far.'

'Odd isn't it, sir?'

'What?' Crabbe asked.

'How close we've become since we've surrendered. While we were under siege I saw men fight over a tin of bully beef, now ...'

'We have no tins of bully beef to fight over and the Turks' black biscuits don't warrant expending any energy.' Ignoring his own warning about rationing cigarettes Crabbe reached into his pocket.

'That mention of bully beef has made me hungry. I'll go and forage. You never know, the Turks might have come up with something for breakfast.'

'I'll say this much for you, Bowditch, you're an incorrigible optimist.'

Crabbe watched the lieutenant pick his way back over the sleeping men carpeting the deck and resumed the calculations he'd been making as to how much longer the war was going to last.

Chapter Four

The desert south of Baghdad
May 1916

John was on a ship. The sky was blue, the breeze fresh. He was surrounded by light. It danced and shimmered, clear, beautiful, and blinding above and around him. Below the sea glistened with reflected sunbeams that tipped the surface of the waves with winking gold and silver flashes. The wind carried the taste of fresh salt air. The vessel moved out from the land, gliding slow and stately past the anchored boats in the harbour.

A woman stood next to him, a child in her arms. She looked ahead towards the horizon. A shawl covered her hair. He felt an overwhelming love for her and the child. He lifted his arm intending to embrace her ...

He woke with a jerk. Momentarily disorientated, it was a few seconds before he realised he'd been sunk deep in a recurring, disturbingly realistic dream that had first surfaced in Kut.

He opened his eyes, rubbed the desert grit from them, and blinked. He was encased in darkness. There was no salt breeze. The air was as cold as only desert air can be in the hour before dawn. A few sticks smouldered weakly at his feet, barely glowing in the embers of what would have been a cook fire if they'd had anything to cook.

He stretched, rose, and walked over to the tent Greening and Dira had erected. Behind it under the watchful eye of Baker and Roberts, lay the bodies of four men who'd died during the night.

'Have you been on duty long?' John asked Baker.

'Relieved Sergeant Greening ten minutes ago, sir. The natives have been creeping out and about under cover of night. The sergeant was concerned they might try to steal the clothes and boots from the dead.'

'We need to dig a grave.'

'Already done, sir. Jones and Williams finished it before they turned in. Sergeant Greening told us to hold off putting the bodies in it until this morning.'

John nodded. He'd expected six, not four deaths in the night. He ducked into the tent. Greening was sitting bolt upright, his back against a tent pole, but his eyes were closed and judging by the noise he was making, he was sound asleep. Dira was watching over the four men lying on ground mats.

John examined them. All four had dysentery and two were so dehydrated he hadn't expected them to last the night but they still clung to life. The other two were burning with fever. He opened a water bottle and moistened their lips.

'Private Jones caught a couple of fish last night, sir,' Dira volunteered,

'Edible ones?'

'We'll find out at breakfast, sir. About the burial party …'

'We'll leave it until the sun is up, Dira.'

John left the tent and looked out over the desert. Touched by the first rays of sun the gravel was turning gold. Soon the sun would blister the air until it wavered in mirages. The air temperature would rise from cool, to warm and before the hour was out reach unbearably hot where it would remain until sunset.

He wished he'd slept longer, remaining in that other wonderful world that had begun to haunt him. A world where he was sailing … to where?

Home? With a woman who loved him. He thought of Maud, the way she'd looked at him whenever they'd been alone together. A secret look he'd believed she'd kept just for him … then he remembered her baby.

Baghdad
May 1916

The house was no different from any of the others that lined the street opposite the bazaar, except in size. It was treble the width of its neighbours. The outside was plain, with nothing to indicate the inner life lived behind the four-storey walls. The front was studded with massive heavily carved double doors that looked as they would withstand a battering ram. High above them a roof terrace capped the building. Thatched by swathes of palm matting, it afforded some shade from the glare of the sun.

A tall slim Arab dressed in a gumbaz and abba, his head covered by a kafieh and plain black agal, stood behind the balustrade. Coffee cup in hand, he watched a procession of ragged, sick British troops being whipped and bullied by Turkish soldiers and Arab irregulars as they were driven along the street and through the entrance to the bazaar. A few had tabs on the collars of the remnants of their tunics. Tabs that identified them as British officers, but officer or ranker, all were clothed in rags and most were doubled over by the pain of dysentery or cholera.

The natives lining the streets shouted, screamed, and jeered at the men, spitting in their faces and throwing slops at them whenever they passed within range. But most of the Jews and Christians in the crowd stood back in sombre silence, to the annoyance of the guards who frequently lashed out at them as well as their prisoners.

A shorter, slighter man wearing an eye patch joined the Arab on the terrace. He stood next to him watching the scene being played out far below for a few minutes before speaking in Arabic.

'They could have marched the British along the river where there wouldn't have been so many people to throw filth at them. It's not enough that the bastards forced them to surrender, they have to expose them to insult.'

He took the coffee a servant handed him. 'Have you seen anyone you know?'

'Major Crabbe, Lieutenants Grace and Bowditch, and the brigadier.' Mitkhal continued to watch the stream of men being herded at gun and whip point into the bazaar.

'John Mason?' Hasan's pronunciation of the English name sounded odd, as if his command of the language had grown rusty from disuse.

'No.'

'Peter Smythe?'

'No, nor David Knight nor any of the other doctors. I've heard the Turks abandoned all the sick who weren't exchanged for Turkish prisoners. The doctors probably stayed with them.'

'Do you know where they're taking these prisoners?'

'They've fenced off an area on the river bank five miles upstream for the ranks.'

'Some of those men look as though they can't walk five steps.' Hasan watched a man collapse. A guard kicked him. An officer behind the fallen man pushed the guard aside and tried to pick up his comrade, only to receive a blow from the guard's rifle.

'I'm going down there ...'

'No, Hasan.'

An unveiled woman walked out of the door behind them. 'You and Mitkhal can do nothing against so many. My father has returned. He says the Turks are sending the British into Turkey.'

'You mean the ones that live to see the sun set,' Hasan muttered.

'My father was told most will have to walk there.'

'They'll die on the journey.'

'The officers are being billeted in the old transport offices on the other side of town, close to the American Embassy. You and Mitkhal might be able to talk to some of them if you go there.'

'There would be to no point in us speaking to them, Furja.' Mitkhal moved away from the wall. 'We can't help so many and they need more than talk.'

'You can give them money for the journey to buy food from the tribes. You know the Turks ...'

'They won't feed them.' Hasan shook his head. 'I can't stand here and do nothing while ...'

Furja looked anxiously at him. 'You are Bedawi.'

'A Bedawi who won't stand back and watch British soldiers being murdered, Furja.'

'Not even to save your own life?'

'Not even that, Furja.'

Bank of the Tigris
May 1916

John officiated at the funeral of his eight patients an hour after sunrise. The two men he'd expected to die of dehydration during the night had died shortly after dawn, the two who'd succumbed to fever, minutes later. It was almost as though the light had drawn what little strength remained from their bodies, taking with it their will to live.

The sun burned mercilessly overhead when he read the burial service. Afterwards, when he stared down at the blanket-wrapped corpses and sprinkled the parched sandy earth over the bodies, he found himself actually envying the dead. Their agony was over; his, never-ending. He wondered how many more mass graves like this lay ahead, waiting for him to preside over them.

Dira, Sergeant Greening, Corporal Baker, and the three privates joined him in reciting the Lord's Prayer. Their Turkish guards remained at a distance, smoking cigarettes, talking and laughing amongst themselves. If they had intended insult they'd succeeded, but John couldn't help thinking their behaviour was simply down to indifference as to whether their captives lived or died.

The orderlies filled in the grave. John was careful to note the exact position and coordinates against a future when it might be possible to retrieve the bodies and give them the burial they deserved, before ordering the carts brought up. He commanded Corporal Baker to drive them over the spot until the surface was indistinguishable from the rest of the desert, lest the Bedouin dig up the bodies in search of clothes or blankets.

Leaving the corporal to his task he joined Dira and Sergeant Greening and helped them dismantle and pack up the tent. It was hot, heavy work and John was exhausted by the time Baker brought the carts back for loading.

Their Turkish guards mounted their donkeys. Baker climbed on to the seat of one cart, Greening the other, and the rest, John and Dira included, walked behind. They'd been travelling for what seemed like days to John when Greening shouted.

'Men ahead, sir!'

John quickened his pace. Greening jumped down from his cart and handed the reins to Dira. He walked alongside John.

'They looked close, sir.'

'It's the mirage.' Breathless, John struggled to keep pace with the sergeant.

'They are men?' Greening asked doubtfully.

'We'll soon see.'

John walked until he was within a few feet of a row of a dozen naked men stretched on the ground. 'They were men, Greening. But not any longer.'

'Their throats have been slit and they've been stripped,' Greening said angrily. 'Abandoned by the Turks for the Bedouin to finish.'

John knew he should be shocked, or at the very least feel anger at the sight of so much carnage, but he was too numb to feel anything.

'Shall I order the men to start digging, sir?' Greening asked.

John straightened his back. Greening's prompt had reminded him that he was the senior officer.

'Please, Greening, and unharness the carts to rest the mules, but hold off from erecting the tents. There's no point when we have no patients.'

Canal running from the Shatt al-Arab into Basra
June 1916

Sister Kitty Jones sat back on the cushions the boatman had arranged to cover the planking in the stern of the boat and leaned close to Charles Reid.

'This has been a lovely afternoon, thank you for inviting me to spend it with you.'

Charles wrapped his arm around Kitty's shoulders. 'And we have the entire evening ahead of us. You haven't forgotten Tom and Clary's wedding breakfast in the Basra Club with Georgie, David, Michael, Peter, and Angela?'

'How could I?'

'You have an elegant gown to wear?'

'As elegant as Angela Smythe's Jewish dressmaker could patch together. Haven't you heard, Major Reid, there's a war on, and as Matron keeps telling all us poor nurses, we have to sacrifice fripperies.'

'Surely women's gowns can't be classed as "fripperies".'

'Exactly that.'

'Seems to me that that some people are expected to sacrifice more than others in this war. Women's gowns should never be counted among the casualties.' He lifted her hand to his lips and kissed her fingertips. 'When is your next afternoon off?'

'Monday.'

'Can you ride?'

'Ride what?' she asked in her Welsh lilt.

'A horse.'

'Don't be silly, where would I learn to ride a horse? The only ones I saw when I was growing up in the Rhondda were pulling milk, brewery, or coal carts.'

'I'm sorry, I didn't think. That was crass of me.'

'There's no need to apologise, Charles. We're from very different worlds, you and I. As my mother would say, "there's more of a difference between a lump of coal and a diamond than a layer of dirt".'

'I take it you're describing yourself as the diamond.'

'Hardly,' she laughed, a soft low chuckle he had come to love, 'I'm coal, and definitely from the wrong side of town, even in the Rhondda. You're …'

'A common soldier.'

'An officer, a gentleman, and, I'm guessing, one who will inherit a house with more rooms than the entire street I grew up in.'

'Officer, I agree, gentleman would be disputed, and not just by me.' He frowned as a memory he desperately wanted to forget surfaced. 'House? There is a house, but it's the sort of solid square house a retired general buys because he lacks the imagination to look for anything different. It also happens to be on the edge of Clyneswood, the estate owned by Michael Downe's family. His father is a close friend of my father's.'

'Which explains your friendship with Michael.'

'I was closer to his older brother, Harry, just as I was with Tom Mason's older brother John. The Masons own Stouthall, the estate next to Clyneswood.'

'Two landowners among your close friends! We would certainly never have met if it wasn't for the war.'

'Of course we would have,' he countered.

'I suppose it's possible I could have entered the servants' entrance of one of your friends' houses as a nurse, but if that were the case I would never have been allowed to speak to you.'

'You have a peculiar idea of life on estates. Of course everyone speaks to everyone else, servants, family … we live together, why would we not speak to one another?'

'Your father employs a parlour maid?'

'Yes.'

'And a cook and a butler?'

'And a footman, and a valet who used to be my father's orderly before he retired from the army.'

'Their names?'

'The maid's Florrie, the cook, Alice, the butler is Stevens, the valet Esher, and the footman is, or rather was, so young when I left home he was known as Billy. Does that make me Fabian enough for you?'

'Fabian is too posh for the Valleys. My father is a Marxist.'

'I don't blame him. If I had to hew coal underground for a living, I'd be campaigning for equal shares for all. But I don't know why we're having this discussion.'

'We're having it because you and I are ridiculous together.'

'Now you're being silly.'

'Am I?' she questioned. 'Be honest, Charles. How would your fine friends react if you took me to dinner?'

'We're going to dinner tonight. In the Basra Club.'

'I mean in one of their houses back in England.'

'They'd be delighted to see you.'

'They'd say they were delighted, because I'd be with you and they're polite. But they'd have trouble understanding my accent and I'd have problems sorting what cutlery to use with each course.'

'Like a lot of other things, class, cutlery, and dinner parties with endless courses won't be a problem after this war. We'll have more than we can cope with just trying to survive.'

'Things won't change that much.'

'They already have. Kitty ...' He hesitated. They had only known one another a few weeks but he knew he was in love with her. He knew because he'd been in love two years before, with a married woman who'd sent him away and told him to forget her. Emily Perry, Maud's mother, had died the day he'd left her. Apparently from a scorpion bite, but he'd been haunted by her death until something even more traumatic had happened to disturb the equanimity of his life.

'If you're trying to tell me that you have another girl in England, that's fine, Charles. I have no right to expect ...'

He laid a finger across her lips. 'You have every right to expect me to behave honourably towards you, Kitty.'

She laughed. 'You sound like a character in a melodramatic romance novel, Charles. What on earth does,' she mimicked his accent with uncanny accuracy, '"behave honourably" mean?'

'There is no other woman, at least not one I love, but I have a past.'

'I would be very concerned if a man of your age didn't.'

'I'm sorry, I'm probably not making much sense …'

'You're not.'

'I need a little time to sort out my responsibilities. And when I have …' There was so much he wanted to say but it wasn't the right time. 'We'll talk again.'

'We're coming into the wharf.' She picked up her shawl.

Charles glanced at the boatman as he reached for the stick that had become indispensable since he suffered a leg wound. The man was too concerned with avoiding the other boats in the dock to watch what his passengers were doing. Taking advantage of his preoccupation, Charles bent his head to Kitty's and kissed her.

To his amazement, even after the conversation they'd had, she kissed him back.

Open prison for British Ranks, Baghdad
June 1916

Mitkhal rode his horse slowly out of the city towards the fenced off area the Turks had set aside to house the British ranks. The air grew putrid with the stench of raw sewage, men's sweat, and rotting flesh long before he reached the high metal wire that enclosed the camp. He dismounted at the gate, turned his horse's reins over to Ibn Shalan's servant, Farik, who'd accompanied him, and lifted a bundle from his saddle.

He approached the guard and handed him a fistful of silver. The guard counted it before unlocking the high wooden doors that had been reinforced with barbed wire. Mitkhal held the bundle close as he walked into the compound. As on all his visits, the ground around the single pump, the sole source of water for over four thousand men, was crowded with men patiently queuing to fill the motley collection of containers they'd scavenged to hold drinking water.

He looked for Warren Crabbe. He'd told him he would return at midday, but apart from the sun, the major had no way of knowing when midday was. Pocket and wrist watches, like everything of value – right down to the men's boots and underclothes – had been stripped and stolen from the British POWs by their Turkish and Arab guards.

He spotted Crabbe in the north-east corner of the fenced off area, shifted the bundle he was holding under his arm to protect it, and, stepping carefully, headed towards him. A few platoons were sitting in closed circles from force of habit. There were no camp fires because anything that could be used as fuel had long been burned, and the only food in evidence was the dreaded, thick black Turkish 'biscuit'.

The handful of senior officers who'd been allowed to stay with the men and their sergeants had ordered latrine trenches to be dug, siting them at the furthest possible point from the entrance, but they had proved pitifully inadequate to cater for the needs of so many, especially as dysentery and cholera were endemic. As a result the ground around the northern half of the camp was damp, and slimed with human waste and excrement.

'I meant to meet you at the gate so you wouldn't have to smell the aroma.' Crabbe pointed to the 'facilities' behind him. 'Am I late or are you early?'

'Does it matter when both of us have time to spare?' Mitkhal handed the bundle he carried to the major. 'Bread, cigarettes, dates, a couple of flasks of brandy.'

'Thank you. I and some of the other men here wouldn't have survived this hellhole if it wasn't for you.'

Mitkhal lowered his voice to a whisper. 'You won't have to survive it much longer.'

'We're leaving?'

'I spoke to an officer in Turkish HQ. They're clearing the camp in stages. The Dorsets will be marched out first thing in the morning.'

'Marched – no transport?' Crabbe paled.

'The American consul, Mr Brissel, is negotiating with the Turks. He's offered to supply carts to accommodate the sick and haul supplies. He's doing all he can as are some of the locals.'

'Will Mr Brissel succeed in getting the Turks to accept the

carts?'

'He's hopeful.'

'We need more than hope.'

Mitkhal slipped his hand inside his abba and unclipped his belt. He glanced around to make sure they weren't being watched, but most of the men around them were lying on the ground, their eyes closed.

Mitkhal rolled up the belt and handed it over. 'Keep this hidden. There's a hundred gold sovereigns stitched into the lining.'

'That's too much.'

'Not for the number of men who'll be marching with you. You'll come across tribes along the way, Kurds, Bedouin, Yazidi … Armenian, if there are any of them left alive. The Turks are killing them faster than they're wiping out the British. Some of the tribes will hate the British, all will hate the Turks, but all love money and most will be prepared to sell you food if you offer them gold.'

'Thank you. I'll take care to see you're repaid when the war is over.'

'No need. As Harry would say, it's only money.'

'As Harry would have said,' Crabbe corrected. 'I pay my debts, Mitkhal.'

Mitkhal looked across to the gate where sappers' bodies were being piled on a cart. 'The best way you can repay me is by surviving until the end of the war. How many have died here?'

'Around twenty a day for the last week and the Turks don't give a damn. We've two medics with us but they have nothing. No drugs, no dressings, nothing.' Crabbe buckled the belt Mitkhal had given him around his waist. 'Only this morning I sent six men down to the gate to wait for a cart to take them to hospital. Two died before it arrived.' Crabbe finished fastening the belt and closed his hands into fists. 'Damn the bloody Turks. Doesn't anyone in the Indian Office or War Office know what's happening to us? Or don't they care?'

'They know,' Mitkhal assured him. 'Mr Brissel has sent telegrams to Washington with instructions to pass the information on to London and the War Office and the Indian Office.'

'Too damned late for some men,' Crabbe cursed.

'Mr Brissel is also filling the carts I told you about with

blankets, disinfectant, food, and clothing to be sent into Turkey with you, but,' Mitkhal glanced around. 'Even if he persuades the Turks to allow you to take them, the supplies won't be enough once they're divided among so many.'

'But they'll help.' Crabbe's anger had been short lived. Weariness and resignation had again taken control.

Mitkhal didn't blame Crabbe. The more he gazed at the surroundings the more he found it difficult to believe that men could live in such foul conditions and remain sane.

The cart arrived to take away the dead and the guard was looking back into the camp, probably for him. A fistful of silver didn't buy more than a few minutes.

'I have to go.'

Crabbe nodded.

'I'll follow you after you march out and bring you more food and money if I can. Don't look for me. I'll turn up when you least expect me, and always with the natives so as not to arouse your guards' suspicions.'

Crabbe clasped Mitkhal's arm. 'Don't risk your life on our account. We're all dead men, Mitkhal.'

'Not if I have a say in the matter. Besides, I'm an Arab, I risk nothing.'

'Harry could pass as an Arab, and the Turks killed him,' Crabbe reminded him.

'I could still get you and perhaps one or two others out of here and back to Basra.'

Crabbe gave Mitkhal the same reply he'd given him the first time Mitkhal had made the offer. 'I can't leave the men. Coming up through the ranks I understand them better than any other officer.' He lifted the bundle and beckoned to his sergeants. 'Thank you again, Mitkhal. If any of us live to see the end of this war it will be because of your bravery and kindness. We won't forget it.'

Chapter Five

Military HQ, Basra
June 1916

Charles limped into his office, propped his stick in the corner behind his chair, and sat behind his desk. Ignoring the pile of files in his in tray he took a clean sheet of paper, opened his ink bottle and picked up a pen.

Dear Maud,
*   Please believe me, I'm not writing this note to you to begin yet another argument. I need to talk to you urgently about your son – and other matters. Please meet me. The Basra Club would probably be best. I can book a private room where we can have coffee or lunch and talk in privacy without risk of disturbance.*
*   I can't leave things the way they are between us, so please can we meet within the next day or two? With the push upstream likely to start at any moment, I could be transferred out of Basra at short notice.*
*   I appreciate friendship between us is out of the question, but I hope we can manage civility, for Robin's sake.*

Yours sincerely,
Charles Reid

Charles blotted what he'd written, folded the paper, and placed it in an envelope. He sealed it and wrote Maud's name on the outside, then realised he didn't know which bungalow Colonel Perry had been allocated. There were only two orderlies on duty at that time of day and he could hardly send one round knocking on doors in search of Maud.

He left the envelope on top of his out tray and headed back to his quarters to bathe and change before picking up Kitty.

Bungalow, British Military Quarters, Basra
June 1916

Maud Mason straightened the chairs in the dining room and checked the dining table. She'd moved into the officer's bungalow her father had been allocated that morning, and had spent the day directing the servants to make the quarters as comfortable as possible given the limitations of the solid, inelegant military furniture. She'd taken her parents' personal possessions from storage, polished the family silver, cleaned the Royal Doulton china, and arranged the framed photographs of family and friends on the sideboard. The new cook had concocted the colonel's favourite curry to Maud's stringent specifications, but if her father didn't turn up soon, the meal and evening she'd planned would be spoiled.

She paced through the French doors out on to the veranda. The sound of ribald songs resounded from the officers' mess and the evening air was warm, too warm to linger outside. She returned to the dining room, slammed the French doors, and waved the servants back into the kitchen with a curt, 'Keep the meal hot.'

The air was oppressive, adding to her sense of foreboding. Maud poured herself a brandy and added ice from the bucket before carrying her glass into the drawing room. She placed it on a table next to a chair she'd earmarked as 'hers'. Needing to do something, she walked down the corridor that led to the bedrooms and looked in on the nursery. Her six-month-old son, Robin, was asleep in his cot. The native nursemaid, who she'd brought from the mission to look after him, sat beside him in a chair angled in front of the window so she could watch the sunset.

Maud closed the door. She checked her father's room. His Indian orderly was unpacking the kit left in Basra when the Colonel had joined Townshend's campaign.

She went into her own bedroom and saw that the girl she'd engaged as her lady's maid had hung her clothes away as ordered. Finding no fault with the maid's work she opened the bureau and removed her account book. Whichever way she calculated the figures, she was hopelessly in debt with no prospect of receiving any income to repay what she owed for months.

She had been granted an officer's widow's pension and an allowance for her child when she'd received notification of John's death last Christmas. She'd also been paid the first instalments of an annuity John had purchased to give her additional security. Unfortunately she'd spent more of the money she'd received than she could repay from her wife's allowance, which was all she'd been left with since John had been reported alive by the sick troops sent downstream after Townshend's surrender.

Both the army and insurance company had pressed for repayment. By emptying her bank account she'd managed to reimburse the insurance company, but not the army. The clerks had retaliated by freezing her wife's allowance, until such time as they reclaimed the over payment. She'd appealed, but the officer who'd interviewed her had tersely dismissed her suggestion that small amounts be taken from her allowance over a longer period. She'd walked away wondering if John had notified the military that he intended to divorce her, in which case she'd soon be entitled to no money whatsoever from the army.

She picked up the silver framed photograph of John that her maid had set next to her jewellery case. She looked at it – really looked at it for the first time since he'd left her to join the Expeditionary Force.

They'd met in India before the war. Her father had sent her and her mother from Basra, where he was ranking officer, to visit friends at his regiment's HQ. Ostensibly they went to escape the heat of a Mesopotamian summer, but she knew her father expected her to find a husband among the senior officers. He'd been concerned about her friendship with a young subaltern, Harry Downe, who'd been sent to Basra as punishment for bedding a senior officer's wife in India. To her disappointment, despite her father's concerns she'd been far more infatuated with Harry than he with her.

After John had asked her to marry him she'd told him she'd fallen in love with him at first sight. Had she? Or had she merely been attracted to his good looks? Tall, well-built, with dark auburn hair and deep brown eyes, women turned their heads whenever he entered a room – but unlike most of the other handsome officers she'd met, John had been unaware of his good looks.

Her father hadn't been enamoured of her choice when he'd discovered John Mason was an army medic, not a career officer. John had intended to return to England after their marriage, a plan that had been set aside like so many others when war broke out. Her father had been even more disappointed when he'd discovered John and Harry were not only close friends but cousins.

Harry! She smiled as an image of him came to mind. His fair hair tousled, his grey eyes glittering with mischief. How he'd loved shocking people, particularly the pompous. When her father sent Harry to negotiate a treaty with a Bedouin tribe, Harry had sealed the bargain by marrying a sheikh's daughter. She'd been as appalled as the rest of military society by Harry's native 'marriage', but that didn't stop her from admiring Harry's complete disregard of anyone's opinion other than his own.

The last time she'd found herself in financial difficulties was shortly before Robin's birth. Everyone knew John couldn't possibly be the father of her child as he'd been on active service for over a year. To make matters even worse, the Gulf was awash with well-founded rumours of her infidelity and scandalous behaviour in India. Instead of judging or ostracising her, as all John's other friends had, Harry had visited her in the American mission she'd taken refuge in and given her money.

If only she could talk to him now – he would understand her plight and lend her money. But Harry was dead, killed by the Turks, and she was left with a father she'd never really known. An officer and a gentleman who'd made no secret of preferring the masculine confines of the officers' mess to domesticity and family.

She glanced at the clock, then headed for the kitchen to check if the curry was still edible.

Officers' Mess, Basra
June 1916

The moment Colonel George Perry stepped through the door, an orderly materialised before him.

'Good to see you back in Basra, Colonel Perry, sir.'

Perry knew he'd seen the man before but if he ever knew his name, he'd forgotten it. 'Good to be back.'

'Can I get you a drink, Colonel Perry, sir? Your usual?'

Perry looked at him blankly.

'Large whisky with ice, Colonel Perry, sir?'

'Just the ticket.' Perry headed for the table where his immediate subordinate and fellow Kut survivor, Major Cleck-Heaton, was holding court with a group of younger officers. From the immaculate state of the junior officers' uniforms he assumed they were stationed in HQ.

Cleck-Heaton and the officers rose from their chairs as he approached.

'Colonel Perry,' Cleck-Heaton effected the introductions. 'May I introduce my godson, Major Reginald Brooke.'

'Good to meet you, sir.' Reggie Brooke saluted.

'Informal, captain. We're in the mess.'

'Saluting a survivor of Kut, sir. A hero.'

Cleck-Heaton continued. 'Lieutenant William Bowditch, Royal Navy ...'

Perry peered at the young man. 'We had a Bowditch in Kut.'

'My brother, sir. I was hoping he'd be sent downstream when Townshend surrendered.'

'As I explained, Bowditch, only the most severe cases of wounds and sickness were repatriated. Unlike Colonel Perry and I, your brother was fit to march,' Cleck-Heaton countered. 'He's better off than us. Able to sit on his rear end and take his ease in a prison camp for the duration, while we continue to campaign.' He continued. 'Colonel Perry, I present Captain Grace.'

'Related to the naval officer who was also with us in Kut?' Perry enquired.

'Yes, sir. The Grace and Bowditch families tend to do everything together, sir,' Grace replied. 'We live in the same town and when our elder brothers joined the navy we decided to follow suit.'

'All four of you opted for the navy?' Perry stated the obvious.

'As did our fathers, Colonel Perry. How was my brother when you last saw him, sir?'

'As Major Cleck-Heaton said, well enough to march. Your brothers will be sitting out the rest of the war in comfort in a Turkish camp, Bowditch, Grace.' Perry turned to the orderly and took his drink.

'Shall we sit, sir?' Cleck-Heaton pulled out a chair for Perry.

'I've been telling Reggie and the others of the hell that was Kut.'

'I'm grateful to be out of the hospital and eating something other than mule and horseflesh. In any other circumstances, ninety per cent of our strength in Kut would have been regarded medically unfit for active service,' Perry added thoughtlessly.

'Yet the Turks sent so few downstream,' Grace couldn't resist the comment after the 'well enough to march' remark.

'As I said, only the most severe cases,' Cleck-Heaton glanced at Perry. 'Colonel Perry and I weren't discharged from Basra hospital until this morning. Fourteen died after admission and that was just on our ward.'

'They were in addition to those who died on the journey,' Perry added. 'More than fifty per cent of the medically unfit who were exchanged for our Turkish prisoners didn't live long enough to see Basra.'

'Can we trust the Turks to provide medical care for our sick and wounded, Colonel Perry?' Bowditch enquired.

'Absolutely!' the colonel was emphatic. 'I'm certain the care they'll provide will be comparable to our own once the POWs reach Baghdad. Until then they'll be no worse off than Major Cleck-Heaton and I were, along with the rest of our sick on the journey downstream.'

'I'm billeted with a medic. He said most of the men who were sent downstream from Kut, the survivors that is, will be discharged back to Blighty as unfit to return to active service,' Reggie Brooke observed.

'Says something for our stamina, Colonel Perry,' Cleck-Heaton enthused. 'Can't keep a good man down, or from doing his duty. Someone has to go upstream to teach the Turks our surrender at Kut was down to chance, not superior soldiering.'

'It was down to the abysmal leadership of the Force sent to extricate us, Cleck-Heaton,' Perry was vehement. 'If the Relief Force had a general worthy of the name, the Expeditionary Force would have been spirited out of Kut in January and we would never have been forced to surrender to the infidel.'

'Things will be different when we go upstream. Next objective Baghdad, and once we take that the bloody Turk will have to leave Mesopotamia and the Anglo-Persian Oil Company in peace and keep their noses out of British business,' Cleck-Heaton added.

'You think the Turks will surrender when we take Baghdad, Colonel Perry?' Grace asked hopefully.

'The Turks will surrender all right – in Mesopotamia, but even when we overcome them here, they'll carry on fighting this sideshow elsewhere in the Middle East. Bloody as it is, it is a sideshow. I attended a debriefing in HQ this afternoon, and we all agreed that whatever we accomplish here will be minor in the scheme of a world war. The Turks won't surrender until the Germans capitulate. When the Germans surrender it will have a skittle effect and the Ottoman Empire and all its Johnny Turk soldiers will follow suit but until then the infidel will fight on, even after we drive them back into Turkey.'

'And our POWs, sir?' Bowditch asked. 'Can we trust the Turks to treat them well, even when we're pushing them back into Turkey?'

'No doubt about it,' Cleck-Heaton signalled to the waiter to refill his glass. 'The Turks have agreed to abide by the Hague Convention. Our men will remain prisoners but in the best of oriental tradition they will be treated as honoured guests. The enemy make poor soldiers but they are gentlemen. They not only gave every one of our officers but also our ranks cigarettes when we surrendered. There's no need to concern ourselves about the men who were marched into captivity. They'll be feather bedded.'

Perry wondered if Cleck-Heaton hadn't seen, or had simply chosen not to see, the Turkish rank and file inflicting blows on the men who'd been forced to surrender, looting their pitifully few possessions and stealing their shirts, underclothes, and boots.

Grace and Bowditch exchanged glances. 'If you'll excuse us, sir, sir, we're dining with ladies in the Basra club.'

'A gentleman never keeps a lady waiting,' Cleck-Heaton agreed. 'Nurses?'

'Yes, sir,' Grace smiled. 'An influx of new blood came in on the boat last week. Some of them are quite presentable.'

'No lady for you, Brooke?' Cleck-Heaton asked as Brooke raised a finger to the waiter.

'No, sir. I've drawn night duty in the wireless office tonight.' He turned to the orderly. 'Another round of drinks, for the colonel, the major, and myself, on my tab.'

The orderly looked to Perry and Cleck-Heaton. 'Whisky, sir,

sir?'

Perry and Cleck-Heaton nodded.

'During your debriefing did you receive any inkling as to when we'll begin the advance on Baghdad, sir?' Cleck-Heaton asked Perry.

'Only "soon". Do you have better information, Brooke?'

'Everyone's waiting on Gorringe. They're expecting better things of him than they did Aylmer …'

'You mean General *Faylmer*, don't you?' Cleck-Heaton laughed loudly at his own well-worn joke. The General had been rechristened by the troops of both Relief and Expeditionary forces after his disastrous failure to relieve Kut.

'There's talk of a new commander being appointed, but no one is certain who it will be. Although my money's on Maude.' Brooke placed his empty glass on the orderly's tray.

'Good man,' Perry agreed, 'but all urgency appears to have left the Relief Force now Kut has fallen. From what I've heard the directive is still the same. Take Baghdad and consolidate our position in Mesopotamia.'

'To quote my CO, "Time is all that's needed to bring success to our endeavours".' Reggie changed the subject. 'I trust you have been allocated suitable quarters, Colonel Perry, Major Cleck-Heaton?'

'I've been given a bungalow. Not as good as the one I had before I went upstream, but it will do. My daughter's there now. Fussing round as only a woman can.' Perry checked the time on the mess clock. 'Another round before dinner?'

'Or two. You're fortunate to have a daughter here, sir. Mrs Cleck-Heaton is in India, which is why I'm staying here, in the mess.'

'Your daughter's been waiting for you in Basra throughout the siege of Kut?' Reggie enquired archly. He knew Maud Mason was Colonel Perry's daughter and was eager to pay her back for rejecting his offer to become his mistress after they'd made love in a 'private' room he'd hired for the purpose. Believing herself a widow, Maud had been happy to bed him when she'd assumed he was about to propose. When he realised Maud expected marriage, he was shocked that a woman with her reputation could even consider herself suitable wife material for a Brooke.

'My daughter is married,' Perry barked, raising his voice as he always did when he was forced to talk about something he found disagreeable. 'She has a husband with the Expeditionary Force, now a prisoner of war. Not a regular – a, a medic. John Mason.'

'Major John Mason?' Reggie feigned surprise.

'You know him?' Perry asked.

'I was in school with John Mason, Charles Reid, and Harry Downe.'

'Harry Downe! Now that's a name to conjure with,' Cleck-Heaton sniggered.

A major raised a glass at the table behind them. 'To Lieutenant-Colonel Harry Downe. A great soldier, diplomat, and one of the rare breed who understood the Arab. We could have done with his assistance when we were trying to negotiate with the Bani Lam today.'

'Smythe, didn't see you sitting there,' Perry blustered loudly in an attempt to conceal his irritation with Cleck-Heaton's tactlessness.

Peter Smythe rose to his feet and indicated a fair-haired young man in civilian clothes sitting next to him. 'Michael Downe, war correspondent.' He deliberately reversed protocol and introduced the younger, less important man to the higher rank. 'Downe, this is Colonel Perry. Your brother Harry's commanding officer before the war. Colonel Perry, Harry Downe's brother, Michael Downe, war reporter.'

Perry snorted. 'I see the family resemblance.'

Half a dozen political officers who were sitting close to the door rose to their feet and raised their glasses. 'To Lieutenant-Colonel Downe. May he rest in peace wherever he lies.'

'He's where he deserves to be. In an unmarked grave in the desert.' Cleck-Heaton had loathed Harry Downe for frequently making him the butt of his jokes.

'You didn't like my brother, sir?'

Cleck-Heaton realised Michael was watching him. 'No, I didn't,' he retorted defiantly. 'Any more than I like civilians who sit on their arses behind the lines while real men engage in combat.'

'You insult Mr Downe, Major Cleck-Heaton.' Peter rebuked. 'He's just returned from the front, where he distinguished himself.'

Cleck-Heaton had headed for the mess as soon as he left the hospital. He'd spent the entire day drinking. Although not as sick as he would have liked his fellow officers to believe him to be, the brandies he'd downed had affected him more than they would have if hadn't spent months subsisting on starvation rations in beleaguered Kut. 'There's no insult strong enough for a man who chooses to remain a civilian when his King and country are at war.'

The silence that fell over the mess was intense, asphyxiating. The political officers remained on their feet.

Perry intervened. 'Major Cleck-Heaton is about to tender his apologies to Mr Downe, gentlemen. He was with me at Kut. We were only discharged from the hospital this morning.'

A ripple of sympathy dispelled the silence.

'Major?' Perry prompted.

Cleck-Heaton stared belligerently at Perry. Perry returned his hard look.

'Apologies, Downe,' Cleck-Heaton muttered after a silence that seemed interminable.

'Accepted, major.' Michael nodded to Peter and they left the mess.

Colonel Perry watched them walk out. 'Smythe a major! Astonishing! I never saw him as a candidate for promotion when he was under my command. No military tradition among his people. His father – a nobody – was the first to take a commission in his family. The vicar in his Smythe's parish had to get up a subscription to buy his uniform when his status as an officer's orphan managed to get him a commission. And, to top it all Smythe married an American. A missionary type who lives in the Lansing Memorial.'

'Casualties were so high during the Relief Force's attempts to reach Kut, brass have been forced to promote all sorts beyond their capabilities. I've heard Smythe tipped for a colonelcy. Something to do with the dispatches he brought out of Kut when he escaped, and his insistence on remaining with the Relief Force against the advice of medics.' Reggie failed to keep the envy from his voice.

'I've heard it all now. Smythe! That pathetic little subaltern is on his way to a colonelcy.'

'They gave Harry Downe one,' Cleck-Heaton reminded them

bitterly.

Perry glanced at the political officers before lowering his voice. 'Not in a regiment. Everyone knows political officers are unprincipled scoundrels ...'

Reggie risked a second interruption and turned the conversation back to the topic he wanted to pursue. 'Have you seen your daughter since your return to Basra, Colonel Perry?'

'Maud?' He looked blankly at Reggie. 'Of course. She visited me in hospital as soon as she heard I was there. Told you, she's in my bungalow.'

'She's happy to keep house for you?'

'Couldn't wait to move out of the American mission she's lived in since Mason went upstream. Never realised until now, but it must be the same place Smythe's wife lives. Silly girl, mixing with Americans. Maud wasn't brought up that way. Should have known better than to go near them. Smythe's wife must have persuaded her. Can't understand why Maud allowed it. Mason's a major, his rank would have secured her a bungalow or at least rooms in one shared with a fellow officer's wife.'

Reggie smiled. 'I know exactly why she moved into the American mission, sir.'

Colour flooded Perry's cheeks at the perceived insult to his daughter. 'Explain yourself, sir.'

'I've said more than I should have. My apologies, sir. It's been a long day. I'm tired and have had more brandy than is good for me.'

'You maligned my daughter. I repeat my demand. Explain yourself.'

Reggie took a deep breath and plunged headlong into the revelation he'd been framing since he'd spotted the opportunity to take revenge on Maud. 'It was rumoured Mason intended to divorce your daughter, sir. As soon as Mason was listed dead, she arranged to marry an American doctor ...'

'First I've heard about a divorce. Sounds like malicious tittle-tattle to me. And so what if she was going to marry again? She received official notification of Mason's death last Christmas. The army doesn't often make mistakes.'

'It doesn't, sir,' Reggie agreed. When she'd refused to become his mistress Maud Mason had dealt a blow to his pride. He suddenly saw an opportunity to exact revenge. 'And the proposed marriage to an American was understandable. Mason didn't see your daughter for a year before she had a child. The whole of Basra knows her son isn't Mason's. She wanted to marry the doctor because no man or woman in decent society would associate with her. I'm sorry she didn't tell you this herself. Forgive me if I've spoken out of turn, sir, but I refuse to stand back and remain silent while a man of your courage and integrity be made to look a fool. Even if the one sullying his reputation is his own daughter.'

The colour drained from Perry's face.

Conveniently forgetting the earlier plea that he'd had too much brandy, Cleck-Heaton lifted his finger to the orderly. 'Brandy all round, here, boy. Now.'

Chapter Six

Colonel Perry's bungalow, British Military Quarters, Basra
June 1916

Maud entered the kitchen and told the cook to take the curry from the heat. He wasn't pleased. Anxious to avoid a shouting match she retreated to the drawing room where she found her father ensconced in the most comfortable chair, with a brandy at his elbow.

'Father.' She ignored the hostile expression on his face and forced a smile. 'I didn't hear you come in.'

'Evidently.'

'Shall I ask the servants to serve dinner?'

'You can ask but I won't be eating with you.'

'You've eaten?' she proceeded warily.

Her father had always had an unpredictable temper, especially after visits to the mess. Her mother had been adept at shielding her from the worst of his outbursts. As a result her father had been a remote figure during her childhood. Her marriage to John had exacerbated the situation, driving them even further apart, if that was possible in a relationship that barely existed.

Perry finally looked up at her. 'I've eaten in the mess, and that's where I'll be taking all my meals from now on.'

Shocked by his unpleasantness Maud went to the kitchen, informed the cook they wouldn't be eating and ordered him to clear the table. When she returned, her father had finished the brandy in his glass and was pouring another.

She sat down and picked up her own glass.

'Did I invite you to sit with me?' Perry snarled.

'You invited me to move into this bungalow with you when you returned from Kut. I assumed you wanted to live with me and Robin as a family.'

61

'Family,' he sneered before setting down the brandy bottle.

She saw the red light of anger in his eyes and attempted to defuse his temper. 'I'm your daughter. Robin is your grandson.'

'From what I heard in the mess today, Robin is your bastard. A daughter whose child is disowned by her husband is no daughter of mine.'

'Who told you Robin is a bastard?'

'Every man in the mess knows.' He evaded her question. 'You're the talk of the regiment. The colonel's daughter who'll open her legs for any man who crooks his finger. Not that I have any time for Mason, but I won't blame a man for refusing to acknowledge a child conceived when he's away on active service. What the hell were you thinking of. Moving in with me ...'

'You asked me to run your house,' she interrupted.

'When I assumed you were a respectable woman.'

'I'm not?' she challenged.

'You're a whore and I want you out of this bungalow. Tonight!'

'Where do you expect me to go?'

'When Bedouin women disgrace themselves, they and their bastards are sent out into the desert.'

'To die?'

He refused to meet her eye.

'You know I've nowhere else to go, and no money after repaying John's death insurance.'

'Return to your bloody American missionaries. They take in charity cases and fallen women, don't they?'

'There's no room for me at the mission.'

'There was room for you and your bastard before I arrived.'

'The Reverend and Mrs Butler only invited me to stay until Robin's birth.'

'And after his birth they wanted you out because they discovered you were a whoring slut?'

Her father's words stung more than the gossip that had led to her ostracism. 'I couldn't stay there. Not with Dr Wallace living in the Mission. Not after we'd planned to marry.'

'Hard luck on you having your damned husband alive. Surprised you baulked at bigamy but I suppose that would have broken criminal as opposed to moral law.' Perry downed his brandy.

She hated begging but she had no option. Not when she had Robin to care for. 'I have nowhere to go, Father. I have no money. The army is demanding I repay my widow's pension ...'

'Pay them out of your wife's allowance.' He left his chair, paced to the window and turned his back on her.

'They've stopped paying it. The last time I saw John he said he wanted to divorce me. He's probably written to the paymaster.'

'As is his right. No officer wants a whore for a wife, not even a soft bugger like Mason.'

'Please, Father. I can't stay in Basra without your protection. I can't return to India. I know no one in England ...'

'You should have thought of before you opened your legs to every Tom, Dick, and Harry.'

She left her chair. 'You're drunk.'

'If I'm drunk, I drink to forget you're my daughter. Out by first light tomorrow, Maud. That's an order,' he barked as if he were admonishing a junior officer.

'You'd put me and your grandson out on the street?'

'I'd see a whore and her bastard on the street. And take your damned maids with you.'

'If I don't?' she challenged with a fragile defiance.

He raised his hand and slapped her across the face, hard. She reeled into the wall. Something warm and wet trickled down her cheek. She lifted her fingers. When she withdrew them they were covered in blood.

'Whoring bitch!' He raised his hand a second time.

She ran into her bedroom, slammed the door, and locked it. Terrified, she leaned against the wall, waited and watched the minutes tick off her bedside clock. When ten had passed in silence she picked up her cape, threw it over her shoulders, and unlocked her door.

The passageway was quiet and empty. Forgetting her child, she ran through the kitchen and out of the house. She had no idea where she was going. She only knew she had to get as far away from her father and the bungalow as possible.

When Maud saw the sentries at the gate to the compound, she slowed to walking pace. Once past the military boundary she kept her head down, looking neither left nor right. She sidestepped whenever she glimpsed anyone walking towards her because she knew they'd assume, not without cause, that any woman out alone in the evening was a streetwalker hoping for trade.

Angry with her father, more terrified of the future than she'd ever been, she found herself on the thoroughfare that led to the Lansing.

Then she remembered Theo Wallace ... he'd wanted to marry her until the news that John was alive had reached Basra. Given the number of casualties that had flowed into the town since the fall of Kut, he'd have to be at the hospital. It was the only place that treated Turks ... Theo would help her ... he had to.

Lansing Memorial Hospital, Basra
June 1916

'Dr Wallace is examining a patient.' Sister Margaret crossed her arms and glared at Maud, reminding her that the nurse had never liked her, even when she'd done her utmost to try and please the woman during her short stint as a nursing assistant in the Lansing.

'May I wait in his office, please?'

'You can wait in the general waiting room.' Sister Margaret pushed open a door. The room was packed with women, children, and babies. Maud stepped inside, stood behind the door, and prepared for a long wait. Less than five minutes later Theo pushed his way into the room.

'Maud? What on earth are you doing here?'

'I wanted to see you.'

'Come into the office. There's a cut on your face that should be seen to and I need to change my coat.'

She followed him into the office. Sister Margaret sniffed loudly as she passed and she noted that Theo made a point of leaving his office door wide open. He stripped off his soiled coat, tossed into an open linen bin, opened the cupboard, and took a clean one from a neatly laundered pile.

'Sit down.'

She sat in the visitor's chair in front of the desk.

He took a bottle of sterile water and a gauze pad from a tray on his desk and cleaned the cut on her face.

'Leave it, Theo. I didn't come here for medical treatment,' she said impatiently.

He threw the bloodied gauze into the bin. 'You shouldn't be here. Aside from carrying the risk of infection to your child, you shouldn't be out alone in the evening.' He sat behind his desk. 'You are alone?'

'I am, and I wouldn't have come here if I had anywhere else to go. My father's thrown me out of his bungalow.'

'Your child?'

'Is in the bungalow with his nurse, but I have to find somewhere else for us to live from tomorrow.' She braced herself. 'I don't have any money, Theo, but I have jewellery that can be sold. It will bring a better price in Europe or America than here. We can still go to America as we planned. With John alive we can't marry but if I call myself Mrs Wallace ...'

'Maud, please, not another word. We might have succeeded in silencing the gossips if you'd been widowed but you weren't. Have you heard what people are saying about you? You're the talk of Basra. The major's wife and colonel's daughter who's slept with half the men garrisoned in the Gulf while your husband and father starved in Kut.'

'I only slept with Reggie Brooke, he's ...'

'The one spreading the gossip, Maud.' He turned impatiently to Sister Margaret who was standing in the doorway. 'Yes?'

'Dr Picard needs your assistance.'

'Tell him I'll be there in a few minutes,' he said tersely. When the nurse didn't leave, he added. 'You can assist him until then, Sister Margaret.'

Maud waited until the nurse left before appealing to Theo again. 'You won't help me?'

'It's more than my reputation as a doctor is worth. My colleagues at the Lansing Mission warned me against marrying you when they thought I was marrying a widow with a slightly dubious reputation. If I booked passage home with a married woman who's considered no better than a streetwalker by everyone in Basra, including the Americans, word would reach the United States before the ship we were travelling on dropped anchor.'

'But I have jewellery that could be sold to buy you a share in a doctor's practice in America.'

'A doctor needs more than a practice, Maud. He needs patients and in order to attract them he needs a family life above reproach.

That includes a respectable wife.' He put on the clean white coat.

'If John hadn't been alive we would have been married by now ...'

'You're wishing your husband dead, Maud? After presenting him with a bastard?' He looked at her for a few moments. 'I've a feeling we're both going to regret this conversation. Maud, please, don't make a bad situation worse by asking more of me than I've already given you.'

'I slept with you ...'

'When I thought you were free to marry me. That cut isn't deep but you need to put ice on that bruise.'

'I have nowhere to go ...'

'Dr Wallace!' Sister Margaret's voice resounded from the corridor.

He left his chair and went to the door. 'Frankly, there are only two places a women like you can go, Maud. A whorehouse or a convent. You know your way out.'

Basra
June 1916

Maud ran from the Lansing with Theo's words ringing in her ears. She stumbled on in the direction of town until the heel of her evening slipper caught in a hole and she stopped to free it.

'I regret, madam, no unaccompanied ladies are allowed inside.'

She glanced up at a liveried steward of the Basra Club and realised she was outside the front door.

'I have no intention of entering the club,' she retorted, gathering the few shreds of dignity that remained to her.

'Neither can you linger here, Madam.'

'I'm not lingering. My shoe ...'

'The lady's waiting for me, steward.'

'If you're sure, Mr Downe.'

'Quite sure, steward.' Michael Downe offered Maud his arm. 'Please accept my apologies for keeping you waiting, Mrs Mason.'

'No apology is necessary, Mr Downe.' It was easier to take his arm than refuse. Besides, she knew Michael Downe by reputation although they'd never been introduced.

'Captain Mason has booked a table for nine in a private room.

As Mrs Mason is joining us, we'll now need a table for ten.'

'We have everything ready for your party, Mr Downe. You're the first to arrive. I'll order a waiter to set an extra place.'

'Thank you. We'll go up. You'll inform Captain Mason and the other guests we're waiting for them.'

'Of course, Mr Downe.' The steward ushered them up the stairs and into a first floor room. He pulled out a chair for Maud, shook a napkin over her lap, and handed her the menu.

'Would you like to see the wine list, sir?' the steward asked Michael.

'As the only wine that travels here without spoiling is Chianti, we'll settle for that.'

'Yes, sir. I'll send in an extra chair and cover.' The steward closed the door as he left.

Maud stared blankly at the menu. A waiter appeared with a bottle of wine. He poured two glasses. A junior waiter brought in a chair, cutlery, and crockery.

'Can I get you and the lady anything before the other guests arrive, sir?' the senior waiter asked.

'No, thank you.'

The waiters left.

'Everyone said you look like Harry, but it's more than a resemblance. You have his gestures, his voice ... you could be him,' Maud said.

'Hardly surprising when we had the same parents.' Michael picked up his wine glass and touched it to Maud's. 'Shall we drink to peace?'

'How did you recognise me?' She lifted her glass and drank.

'Tom Mason pointed you out when we were walking along the wharf last week. You were in a carriage with Mrs Smythe and Mrs Butler so he couldn't introduce us.'

'He wouldn't have acknowledged me even if I'd been walking.'

'It's a difficult situation. Tom has always been close to his brother, so close it bordered on hero-worship.'

'And it's upset him to discover that his brother's wife has the reputation of a whore.'

'He was disturbed to discover that your child isn't John's,' Michael commented diplomatically.

'Yes, well, there's no denying that.' She drank her wine.

He refilled her glass. 'Mrs Smythe told me you'd been raped.'

'What's done is over and finished with. There's no point in talking about it.'

'You're obviously upset about more than what Tom thinks of you,' Michael ventured. When she didn't answer, he said. 'Tell me to go to hell if you think I'm prying.'

Maud looked at him. He was so like Harry, it would be easy to fool herself that she was talking to Harry. Wasn't that just what she'd wished for earlier that day?

'What happened tonight to send you out on to the street without a hat, shawl, or gloves?' he pressed.

'Nothing,' she said quickly. Too quickly.

'You have a cut and the beginnings of a spectacular bruise on your face.'

Maud instinctively lifted her fingers to her left cheek.

'Mrs Smythe told me that you were moving in with your father.'

'I did. He went to the mess straight from his office this evening …' She fell silent.

'And?'

'He returned drunk and ordered me out of the bungalow.'

'After hitting you?'

Michael was shocked at the silence which confirmed his suspicions. 'You left your baby with him?'

'The child will be fine. His nurse is with him.'

The door opened. John's brother Tom Mason walked in with his bride Clarissa, David Knight, and Georgiana Downe.

Tom stared at Maud. The silence was absolute, claustrophobic, and embarrassing until Tom broke it. 'This is Clary's and my wedding breakfast.' He pointed at Maud. 'I didn't invite her, so what in hell is she doing here?'

Maud left her chair. 'I'm leaving.'

'Not until I've seen to that bruise. Michael, send down to the kitchen for ice.' Always the doctor, Georgiana examined Maud's face. 'How did this happen?'

'I hit myself on a cupboard door. Please, excuse me. I really do have to go.'

'Can't bear to be in the same room as your brother-in-law,' Tom taunted.

Maud slipped past him and fled down the stairs.

'I'll make sure she's all right.' Michael went to the door.

'I'll go with you.'

'No, Georgie.' Michael stopped his sister from following him. 'I was the one who managed to get Maud in here, which in retrospect was not the wisest move I could have made. And as Basra's been flooded with sick and wounded since Kut fell, you and David have scarcely had a free moment in weeks. Stay with Tom, and wait for the others. Order me a pilaff. That can be easily heated up if I'm delayed. I'll be back as soon as I've seen Maud somewhere safe.'

'I heard she'd moved in with her father.' Tom realised Clary was looking at him. 'I haven't been watching her but until John divorces her she's still my sister-in-law.'

'If she doesn't want to return to her father's bungalow, Mrs Butler might find her a bed in the mission, at least for tonight.' Georgie advised. 'If there's no room in the Lansing, Angela and Peter might take her in. I'll ask them when they get here.'

'Thanks, Georgie, I'll try the mission first. That's if Maud will go there.'

'You sure ...'

'Stay here, toast the bride and groom, and enjoy your meal, Georgie. You work such long hours you get hardly any free time.' Michael ran down the stairs and out on to the street. He spotted Maud walking in the direction of the British compound. Hailing a carriage he ordered the driver to follow her. He told the driver to stop when they drew alongside her.

'May I offer you a lift?'

Maud turned around. 'A lift to where?'

'Georgie said the Butlers would find you a bed at the mission.'

'The Butlers have been very kind but I've overstayed my welcome there.'

'Angela Smythe ...'

'Peter and Angela have only just moved out of the mission and into their own bungalow. They may have been married for over a year but they've spent hardly any time together. I'd feel like a gooseberry.'

'So where are you going?'

'Back to my father's bungalow to pack my things and Robin's.'

'Get in. You'll be safer in a carriage than you would be on the street.' He stepped out and helped her inside. Sitting beside her he closed the door and asked the driver to take them to the British military compound. 'I need the number of your father's bungalow.'

Maud looked at him quizzically.

'For the sentry at the gate.'

She gave it to him.

'Where will you go after you pack?'

'I don't know.' The enormity of her situation overwhelmed her. Her lower lip trembled and the tears she'd managed to keep in check since she'd run out of the bungalow finally fell. 'I've nothing. No reputation, no money ...'

Michael reached for her hand. 'Don't you get a wife's allowance?'

As the tears fell so did her last remnants of pride. Words tumbled out between the sobs. She didn't stop until Michael knew exactly how destitute she and Robin were.

Aware of the attention they were attracting, wishing he'd selected a closed rather than open carriage, Michael handed her his handkerchief.

'I would invite you stay with me, but aside from the fact that it would attract gossip I live in Abdul's and it's well known that he runs a brothel behind the coffee shop.'

'You're very kind.' Mortified at spilling all her troubles out on Michael – a stranger until that evening – Maud dried her eyes and straightened her shoulders.

'I have to take you somewhere.'

'I told you, back to my father's bungalow.'

'After he hit you and threw you out?'

'He can hardly object to me returning to pack my things.'

'Where will you go from there?'

'He'll have passed out from the brandy he drank in the mess by now. I'll stay at the bungalow tonight and find somewhere tomorrow morning.'

Michael felt in his pockets and pulled out a leather purse. He pressed it into Maud's hands.

'What's this?'

'Money.'

'I can't take your money.'

'Call it a loan if you must. Pay me back when you can afford it.'

'That might be never.'

He shrugged. 'I won't miss it.'

She opened the purse. 'There has to be ...'

'Two hundred sovereigns,' he whispered, conscious of their driver sitting in front of them.

'What are you doing with that in your pocket?'

'A war correspondent occasionally has to pay for information.'

Maud remembered Harry and how free he'd been with money. 'You're not working for the Political Office, are you?'

'What makes you say that?'

'Harry always had money in his pocket to bribe ...'

'I'm a civilian. A war correspondent, and I bribe no one.' Michael said quickly and too emphatically.

The driver turned into the British compound. Michael spoke to the sentries guarding the gate. They lifted the barrier and Michael gave the driver directions to Perry's bungalow.

'I won't leave until I see you safely inside and you assure me your father is sleeping,' he warned Maud. 'Go in. If he's asleep come out and wave to me. I'll wait until I see you. I'll be back at five o'clock in the morning with a cart and carriage to take you wherever you want to go.'

'There's no need.'

'Yes, there is,' he contradicted. 'As Tom said, until John divorces you, you're his sister-in-law. That makes you the responsibility of John's family and friends.'

'I don't want anyone to take responsibility for me.'

'Then tell me, where you intend to go tomorrow?'

'I'll think of somewhere. I'm responsible for the mess I've made of my life and I'm the one who has to pick up the pieces.'

'Most of the ship's captains come into Abdul's. I could ask around, find out if any of them are carrying passengers down to the Gulf where the ocean liners that carry civilians berth. They may know if one is heading back to Europe soon.'

'You think I should leave Basra?' she asked.

'I think you have no reason to stay,' he replied diplomatically.

'If I'd married Theo, I would have gone to America.'

'If you want to go there you can, although you may have to

travel via Alexandria or one of the Mediterranean ports. Legally you're still married to John. You could ask if there's a free berth on one of the military vessels that are repatriating the sick.'

'I'd rather not ask for anything from the army.'

'I understand your reluctance.'

'I have no idea what I'll do if there's no ship carrying civilian passengers leaving Basra soon.'

'Would you like me to look for rooms for you?' Michael offered.

'I doubt anyone respectable would take me in.'

'Perhaps not in British military quarters,' he conceded, 'but I have friends in the French consulate. One them asked me today if I was interested in renting his house as he's been recalled to France. I'll call in to see him on my way back to Abdul's tonight.'

'Please don't go to any trouble on my account.'

'No trouble.'

'Thank you. We're here.' She leaned forward and spoke to the driver. 'Stop, please.'

'Five o'clock tomorrow morning. Will you have much luggage?'

'Not much.'

'A trunk?'

'And baby things.'

'I'll bring a couple of men to move everything. You'll be packed.'

She nodded.

'Think of where you'd like to go?'

'I will. Thank you, Mr Downe.'

'If you called my brother Harry, you must call me Michael. I'll wait until you wave.'

She ran up the path and entered the house through the veranda door. She reappeared a few moments later waved and returned inside, closing the door behind her.

Michael continued to wait. When he saw the drapes close in a room at the end of the building he spoke to the driver.

'Back to the Basra Club, please.'

'Yes, sir.'

Michael reached into the inside pocket of his coat for his cigar case. He lit one and drew on it. He had no doubt that Maud had

72

treated John abysmally, but she was being punished for her actions and a small part of him couldn't help feeling sorry for her. In fact, when he considered the situation he felt more sympathy for Maud than he did for his own estranged wife. Perhaps picking the wrong woman to marry ran in the family. He only hoped his cousin Tom would fare better with Clary.

Chapter Seven

Basra Club
June 1916

'And a pilaff for Mr Downe.' Tom Mason closed the menu and returned it to the waiter. 'Everyone ordered?'

'More food than the Kut garrison consumed in four months,' Peter Smythe answered.

'More wine, sir?' the waiter asked Tom.

Tom looked around the table. 'At least three more bottles, please. We've a wedding and the promotion of a good man to celebrate.'

'A well-deserved promotion.' David raised his glass to Peter who was sitting across the table from him with his wife Angela. 'To Major Peter Smythe, who will soon be a colonel.'

'Put a sock in it, David,' Peter retorted. 'My promotion to this dizzy height highlights how desperate the force is for officers – any officers.'

'To the very good health of Mrs Angela Smythe,' Georgiana lifted her glass to Angela. 'Where would officers be without their ladies?'

'Miserable.' David locked his fingers into Georgiana's and lifted her hand to his lips.

Oblivious to David's romantic gesture, Georgiana stared at the door. 'Michael's taking his time.'

'Not if he escorted Maud back to the British compound.' Charles pointed out. He and Kitty had arrived at the club after Maud had left, but Tom hadn't wasted any time in updating them on Maud's unwelcome appearance at his wedding breakfast.

'I didn't like the look of that bruise on Maud's face,' Georgiana frowned.

'Some women deserve to suffer. When I think of the way Maud

75

behaved and treated my brother ...'

'No one, woman, child, or man, deserves physical punishment. John would never hit anyone weaker than him no matter what they did,' Georgie admonished Tom.

'More the pity. If he had hit his wife, maybe she wouldn't have had another man's bastard.' Tom glanced at Angela. 'And don't try telling me Maud was raped. I refuse to believe it after hearing the rumours flying around Basra.'

Charles's colour heightened. He dropped his napkin to the floor and bent down to retrieve it.

'Rumours aren't necessarily true, Tom,' Angela reminded gently.

'Most have a germ of truth in them. Especially the one that suggests you're far too nice and forgiving, Angela.'

'She is,' Peter was tired of talking about Maud. 'Thank you for this invitation, Tom. You've no idea how marvellous it feels to be sitting here celebrating your wedding. Especially after the rough time you've been having. Three bouts of fever in two months are no joke.'

'I hate being invalided out. When I think of John ...'

'John would be the first to tell you to get on that boat at midnight with Clary,' Charles insisted. 'It's bad enough the rest of us are stuck here. Believe you me, I'll be headed home first chance I get.'

'What about you two?' Tom looked to Georgie and Michael who'd just walked through the door. 'Civilians can go home any time they want.'

'I'd hate to have to face my editor if I returned to London before the cessation of hostilities, after hearing his insistence that correspondents are always the last to leave a theatre of war. I believe I even promised to pull the curtains after me,' Michael reclaimed his chair.

'I'm doing work at the Lansing I could only dream of in London. There, they mock female surgeons here, they hand me the theatre and experienced surgical nurses.'

'Food,' Peter beamed as the waiters carried in trays of appetizers.

'I've never seen anyone eat as much as Peter has since he came downstream from Kut,' Angela teased.

'I'm looking forward to a good dinner after all those months cooped up with only a slice of mule to look forward to for supper.'

'I'll second that,' David, who'd been sent downstream from Kut with the sick and wounded after Townshend's surrender, added. 'I never want to eat mule ...'

'Or horse,' Peter added.

'Or strange-looking weeds ...'

'Weeds?' Angela interrupted David.

'The Turks surrounded the entire town. We had no access to fields so we couldn't grow anything and the farmers in the area couldn't break the siege to bring their vegetables to market,' Peter explained.

'Even if we'd been able to get into the fields they were all full of mud and Turks,' David explained. 'So on medical advice ...'

'Yours?' Georgiana checked.

'I believe your cousin John's. He ordered the cooks to forage and cook anything that was remotely green.'

'With the proviso that the green wasn't down to mildew or mould,' Peter qualified. 'I've never been so hungry.'

David fell serious. 'I hope the Turks are feeding our men. You know what John's like, he'd give a man his last mouthful if he thought he needed it more than him.'

'That's my brother.' Tom emptied an open bottle of Chianti between their glasses. 'To John and all the British taken at Kut. May they live and eat well in Turkish captivity until the end of the war.'

'To John and all the POWs,' Michael echoed.

'What have you done with Maud?' Tom asked.

'Left her at her father's bungalow, but she'll be moving out tomorrow.'

'Where will she go?' Angela asked.

'As long as neither I nor John will see her again I couldn't give a damn.' Even as Tom spoke, he had a feeling he and his brother hadn't seen the last of Maud. He preferred not to think about her but knew his brother. Wherever John was, he'd be feeling unaccountably guilty over the end of his marriage. Even though he was entirely blameless.

'Another toast, to the bride and groom and a safe and pleasant journey back to England.' Michael refilled their glasses.

Their food arrived and while everyone was passing plates and condiments Georgiana laid her hand on Tom's. 'Don't forget to give everyone at home our love.'

'Even your parents after what they said about Gwilym?' Tom questioned.

'Water under the bridge.'

'I wish I could be as forgiving as you.'

'If you're thinking about Maud, it's for John to forgive her, not you.'

'I suppose it is.'

'You'll be home by August, in time for a summer that will feel freezing cold after the heat here, and then you'll have a beautiful cool, mosquito-free autumn to look forward to.'

'My father would love to have you work with him in his clinic, Georgie, you do know that.'

'Perhaps I will when the war is over.'

'That could be years, and in the meantime ...'

'Michael is here.'

Tom glanced at David. 'And so is David.'

'He amuses me, and at the moment I amuse him,' she smiled. 'It's not serious on either side.'

'You haven't given up on looking for Harry, have you?'

'Let's just say I feel closer to him here than I did when I was in London.' She kissed his cheek. 'Be happy with Clary, Tom. For all our family. Me and Gwilym, John and Maud, Harry and Furja, Michael and your sister Lucy ...'

'That was a marriage made in hell. I tried telling both of them that they weren't suited to one another.'

'As did we all.'

Tom slipped his arm around Clarissa's shoulders. 'We'll be happy, Georgie. I promise you.'

Smythes' Bungalow, British Compound, Basra
June 1916

'That was a lovely evening. One to remember.' Angela sat at her dressing table, removed the clips from her hair and dropped them on to a pin tray.

'It was.' Peter sat on the bed behind her and unbuttoned his

78

tunic.

'As Tom said, "a good way to celebrate a wedding and the promotion of a good man".'

'I hope you haven't believed a word David, Tom, or Michael said. I'm no better than any other man in this man's army.'

'Yes, you are,' she smiled at him in the mirror. 'You escaped from Kut for a start.'

'I did not escape. I was sent out of Kut by command because they needed a messenger boy to carry dispatches, and I wouldn't have made it more than a foot through the Turkish lines if I hadn't been with Harry's orderly, Mitkhal. He's the hero, not me.'

She took the last pin from her hair, ran her fingers over her scalp to make sure she hadn't missed any, and picked up her hairbrush. She didn't stop looking at him in the mirror, while she counted out the strokes.

'You like watching men undress.' He hung his tunic on the back of a chair.

'Not men, just you. It's wonderful to have you home, and even more wonderful to have a home to call our own.'

'You were tired of living in the mission?'

'Reverend and Mrs Butler were very kind, and it was good to be in the same house as Theo, not that anyone saw much of him, Dr Picard, or Georgie Downe. All of them practically live in the hospital. But I much prefer living with you.'

He wrapped his arms around her, looked at her in the mirror, and kissed her neck. 'Unbutton my dress, please.' She rose from the stool and turned her back to him.

As he slipped the line of pearls from their loops, he considered how far they'd come since his first fumbling attempts to make love to her on their wedding night.

'Do you think you'll be sent upstream soon?' She tried to sound casual but she knew he'd picked up on the tremor in her voice.

'There are whispers in HQ that we'll be making a move next month, but no one really knows when it will happen. My guess is after our failure to relieve Kut command will be cautious and won't advance until we've consolidated and strengthened both our supply lines and the Relief Force with all the men we'll need to take us to Baghdad.'

'Including you?'

'According to Charles Reid, who's more in the know than me, I'll be sent because I'm one of the few who has enough first-hand knowledge of conditions upstream to brief command on what's needed.'

'Will I have you for the rest of this month?'

'And possibly a week or two of next.' He unfastened the last button and she stepped out of her dress. 'Disappointed I'll be here for a few more weeks?'

'I wish you could stay here with me forever.' She wrapped her arms around his neck and stood on tiptoe, but he still had to bend his head to kiss her.

'You'd soon be bored with me if I was under your feet all day.'

'No, I wouldn't.' She slipped out of her underclothes, turned the sheets back and climbed, naked, into bed.

He lay beside her, pressed the length of his body against hers, and breathed in her scent, lemon from her hair and rosewater tinged with cinnamon from her skin. Imprinting the scents and sensations, together with the exact feel of the texture of her beneath his fingertips, storing the impressions against a future when he sensed he'd need memories.

They made love slowly, tenderly, without haste. Afterwards he lay on his back and pulled her towards him, wrapping his arm around her and cupping her breast. 'Have I told you how much I love you today?'

'Not today.'

'I love you.'

She spread her fingers through the hairs on his chest. 'Is it true you're on your way to colonelcy?'

Peter laughed. 'I know it's a wife's duty to boost her husband's morale but I've only just made major and I didn't deserve that promotion. David and Charles were just making jokes at my expense.'

'David said you'll be one before the end of the year.'

'David knows nothing about how regiments and promotion work. The Indian medical service is full of doctors like him and Tom who are naïve to the point of believing that the world is fair and the army efficiently run.'

She frowned. 'I wish Tom wasn't so angry with Maud.'

'When you consider what Maud did to John, Tom has every

right to be angry with her. No man likes the thought of his brother's wife being unfaithful. Especially when the result is an illegitimate child.'

'But Maud was …'

'Raped,' Peter interrupted. 'I know she told you that, but do you really believe her, sweetheart?'

'I do.'

He dropped a kiss on to her forehead. 'I love you all the more for wanting to think the best of everyone.'

'You don't believe Maud?'

'I don't know her well enough to know what to believe. But even if she was, what do you think John should do? Accept another man's child as his? That's hardly fair, is it?'

'How would you react if it was me who had another man's child?'

'I'd rather not think about it.'

'I mean if I was raped.'

'That is a question I hope I never have to face.' Peter sat up and left the bed.

Angela gripped his hand. 'Please don't go.'

'You know I have to.' He pulled his hand free.

'Please, Peter. Just this once. I'd give anything to wake up next to you in the morning.'

He shook his head and reached for his robe. 'I'll never forget what I did to you in Amara.'

'That was my fault. I shouldn't have visited you so soon after you fought a battle.'

'I damn near killed you. The sight of those bruises on your face will haunt me until the day I die. Knowing that I put them there …'

'It wasn't your fault. You were asleep. You'd been fighting the Turks. You had a nightmare, you lashed out.'

'I lashed out and if it wasn't for John and Crabbe I would have killed you. I'll never risk anything like that happening again. I'm going into the dressing room. I'll bolt the door on the inside, but please turn the key in the lock on this side in case I open the bolts in my sleep.'

'I don't want to.'

'Please, Angela. The only way I can sleep is if I know there's a solid door between us.'

'Am I never going to sleep next to you again?' Tears fell from her eyes as she sat up on the pillows.

He wiped her tears away with his thumbs. 'I'm sorry, darling, but after Amara, it has to be this way.' He walked into the dressing room and closed the door. She heard the bolts being pulled across the inside.

'Angela?'

'I'm doing it.' She left the bed and turned the key in the lock.

Colonel Perry's Bungalow, British Compound, Basra
June 1916

Maud carried the last of her gowns from the wardrobe and dumped them in her trunk, on top of the clothes she'd already piled into it. She squashed the contents down. There was an inch or two of space free.

She sat on the bed and looked around the room for something else to pack. All the drawers in the chest and dresser were open and empty. The wardrobe, tallboy, and cupboard doors yawned, revealing bare shelves and hanging spaces. She'd packed everything she owned except the clothes she was wearing. The only things remaining were a travelling desk, two jewellery boxes, and a flat black case on the dressing table.

She unpinned her watch and opened the smallest jewellery box with a key threaded on the chain. She'd given her wedding ring to Harry to return to John last November, and she had no way of knowing if Harry had even seen John before he'd been killed. Her engagement ring, a four-carat solitaire diamond set in a platinum band, winked up at her in the lamplight. She touched one of the matching earrings John had bought to complement it as a wedding gift. Next to them was a pearl necklace Mrs Hale, the widow of John's commanding officer, had given her before she'd sailed back to England.

In a drawer below the diamonds she kept the jewellery her parents had given her. A gold ring and locket which she'd worn as a child and set aside in the hope that one day she'd have a daughter to pass them on to. A larger, more ornate locket that held a photograph of her mother and a heavy gold link bracelet her parents had given her on her eighteenth birthday.

She removed the diamond earrings and engagement ring, stowed them in their original boxes, and placed them in an envelope. Then she locked the box. Other than the pearls there was nothing left inside that would bring much money even if she was inclined to sell any of the pieces her mother had given her. It had been her mother. She doubted her father had ever chosen a Christmas or birthday present for her in his life.

She opened her mother's jewellery case which she'd found packed away with the furniture from the house. She was familiar with every piece. She'd been allowed to play with them as a child. She knew exactly which rings, bracelets, and necklaces had been inherited by her mother from her grandmothers and great-grandmothers, and which pieces her father had bought her mother.

There were strings of pearls, pearl rings, and pearl bracelets, the staple of every officer's wife's jewellery collection. Below them on a separate tray were the ornate gold bracelets, necklaces, and earrings, some studded with sapphires and rubies, that her father had bought for her mother when he'd been stationed in India. She closed the box and left it on the dresser. It had been her mother's and she felt she had no claim to anything her mother had owned, not after the way she'd behaved.

The last box was different. If it was possible for a woman to earn a gift of jewellery, she'd certainly earned that one. When John had left her in India she'd missed him to the point of insanity. Not just him, but his male presence in her life and especially her bed. Within weeks she'd found solace in the arms of a young lieutenant, and after he'd been posted to Basra other lovers had followed. The jewellery had been given to her by a Portuguese, Miguel D'Arbez, and it had been their liaison that had given rise to the gossip that had destroyed her reputation in India.

She opened the box. It contained magnificent pieces more suited to Indian royalty than an Englishwoman. A massive ruby and heavy diamond-studded tiara, a multi-strand necklace with a thick chain, and four bracelets to be worn above and below the elbow. There were also long pendant earrings and a nose ring, like the tiara all encrusted with enormous rubies and diamonds. The set was far too ostentatious for European taste. When John told her he intended to divorce her, she'd given it to Harry to sell. He'd paid her for it but the set had been returned to her on Harry's death, which suggested either he hadn't found a buyer, or hadn't looked for one.

Like the ancient mariner who'd shot an albatross and had been forced to carry its corpse around his neck as punishment, the set had become a permanent and humiliating reminder of her bitterly regretted infidelity. If only she could turn the clock back to the day of John's departure from India. If only she'd concentrated on immersing herself in the charity garden parties and afternoon teas that the other officers' wives spent their days organising. If only she hadn't succumbed to temptation …

She glanced at her watch. Two o'clock. Not much time and she still had a great deal to do.

She opened her travelling desk and removed a sheet of notepaper and an envelope. After spending a few moments trying to compose what she wanted to say she picked up her pen and wrote quickly, instinctively, without putting too much thought into her words.

Dear Mrs Butler,

Thank you for everything that you have done for me. I regret having to impose on you further, but circumstances dictate that I have to leave Basra. Lack of funds and friends has made my current situation precarious and you and the trustees of the Lansing Memorial are the only people I can think of to entrust with the upbringing of my son.

You are aware of his antecedents. My father has disowned me and my child. Both of us are now reliant on the charity and goodwill of strangers.

It would be too much to ask or expect you to bring Robin up personally but I hope you will find a sympathetically run orphanage, here or in America, willing to take my son and if possible his nursemaid as he is accustomed to her.

I have paid her one year's salary and I have sent a box of jewellery with her that I hope the trustees will be able to sell to recover some of the cost of rearing Robin.

I am so sorry to have to appeal to your goodwill again, Mrs Butler. Thank you for your many kindnesses towards me, and please accept my apologies for this, my largest imposition, which I assure you will be my last.

Yours very sincerely,
Maud Perry

Maud folded the notepaper and placed it in a large box together with the jewellery case that contained the ruby and diamond set. She closed the box, tied it with string, and wrote Mrs Butler's name and address on the outside.

She addressed a second envelope to Charles Reid, and again wrote quickly without putting too much thought into her words.

Dear Charles,

My father, quite understandably, has ordered me to leave his bungalow. As the army has rescinded my widow and dependent's allowance on the perfectly reasonable grounds that John is alive, your son and I have been left destitute.

By the time you get this I will have already left my father's house. I will send my son and his nursemaid to the American mission and ask Mrs Butler to place him one of the orphanages run by the Lansing Memorial. I have also sent Mrs Butler the ruby and diamond jewellery I asked Harry to sell, that you retrieved from Harry's strongbox and insisted on returning to me. I hope the jewellery can be sold, and the money used to defray the cost of Robin's keep.

I regret I cannot love my son the way a mother should, but as I have no idea what the future holds, or even where I'm going, Robin will be better cared for by the Lansing Memorial than me.

I am more sorry than you can ever know for what happened between us, Charles. I regret even more the way I betrayed John. He loved me. I didn't realise how valuable that love was until I'd thrown it away. I'm not expecting you to do anything other than tell John, if you see him again, that I don't expect him to forgive me but I hope in time that he can forget me and find a woman more worthy of his love.

I enclose the engagement ring and earrings John gave me and hope that you can return them to him. I gave Harry my wedding ring but I have no way of knowing whether Harry had time to give it to John before he was killed.

I hope I never see you again, but I wish you and yours, and especially John, a long and happy life. I hope and pray he will survive the war and find a wife worthy of the name of Mason.

If you are ever in position to help Robin and see fit to do so, I would be very grateful for his sake, not mine. He didn't ask to be brought into this world.

Maud

She folded the sheet of notepaper into the envelope that held her engagement ring and the earrings and sealed it.

She'd made a start, but she still had a great deal more to do before dawn broke and she and Robin had to be on their way.

Chapter Eight

Mesopotamian Desert
June 1916

'We are being driven further into the desert every day to the point where there will be no one to see the gendarmes murder us. There are many places in this wasteland where they can hide our bones. We'll lie there forever, never to be found by a living being, and no prayers will be said for our souls,' Mrs Gulbenkian whispered close to Rebeka's ear.

Terrified of being overheard by one of the gendarmes who surrounded them, Rebeka remained silent. Her former neighbour constantly voiced suspicions about their fate, but Rebeka shuddered all the same. She realised Mariam had heard Mrs Gulbenkian when her sister tightened her grip on her hand. The rumours had begun days ago, echoing from one woman to another when realisation dawned that they were being taken east.

A scream resounded from somewhere in the centre of the huddle of women. Rebeka kneeled upright. The moon and stars were bright and she made out Mrs Saroyan, the baker's wife, foaming at the mouth. Her four daughters were trying to quieten her, without success. The women around them watched the girls tend to their mother, but none dared offer help. Not after seeing the way the gendarmes beat women for extending the slightest kindness to one another.

She wondered if she would have been braver if she hadn't had Mariam to look after. Then one of the gendarmes unslung his rifle from his shoulder and she knew she wouldn't have dared. As unbearable as her existence had become, she could still breathe, feel, and think. She wasn't ready to relinquish life. Not yet. Not while Mariam crouched next to her and she could still see Anusha, although Mehmet wouldn't allow her or Mariam to approach their eldest sister.

A gendarme scooped up the youngest Saroyan girl by the neck. He held her high in front of Mrs Saroyan.

'Don't look,' Rebeka muttered to Mariam. She covered her sister's eyes with her fingers as the gendarme dashed the four-year-old to the ground. The toddler cried out just once then fell silent. The gendarme kicked the child's body as it lay limp on the ground, before reaching for his rifle. He shot Mrs Saroyan in the back. Two more shots rang out as his colleagues targeted two of the other girls. The fourth, Hasmik, ran to Mrs Gulbenkian, who was holding out her arms ready to embrace her in a show of defiance only a childless woman would risk.

The gendarmes looked at Hasmik and Mrs Gulbenkian and laughed.

'Enjoy your new foster daughter, old woman, while you can. You'll soon all be ...' One of the gendarme drew his finger across his throat.

Rebeka tightened her grip on Mariam's hand and huddled back close to the ground, focusing determinedly on the desert floor lest she catch a gendarme's eye and draw attention to her or Mariam.

The sound of the river flowing on their right escalated her burning thirst. Needing distraction, she concentrated on conjuring the 'memory' she'd taken from the table earlier that night.

Rebeka's Family Home
December 1915

Anusha's wedding. Not the celebratory mass held in the town church, nor even the wedding feast prepared by her mother and aunts for the entire extended families, her sister's bridegroom Ruben's as well as their own. But late evening, long after her eldest sister Anusha and her new husband had driven off in Ruben's father's carriage to the house his family had built for them, and she, Mariam, and Veronika had retired to the bedroom they shared.

Mariam had fallen asleep on their mother's lap after Anusha and Ruben had left. Veronika had carried their youngest sister upstairs. Mariam hadn't opened her eyes, not even when she and Veronika had washed her and changed her bridesmaid's dress for her nightgown and tucked her into the bed they shared.

While Veronika prepared for bed, she'd folded away their bridesmaids' dresses. All three had been lovingly hand-stitched and decorated with white embroidery and cream crocheted lace by their grandmother. She wrapped each one in layers of fine cotton cambric then canvas before placing them in the chest where they kept their best gowns, petticoats, and shawls.

Mesopotamian Desert
June 1916

She wondered where those dresses were now. Had their Muslim neighbours broken into their house and looted their belongings? Had the Turkish police burned all the Armenian Christian houses in their town as they'd threatened?

Rebeka's Family Home
December 1915

'I'm going to treasure that gown forever and pass it on to my daughter when she's old enough, so she can pass it on to her daughter.' Veronika brushed out and plaited her black curls.

'And if you have sons? Will you make them wear it?' she teased.

Veronika wrinkled her nose. 'I won't have boys, only girls. Four of them.'

'What if Gevorg wants boys?'

'Gevorg will get what he is given.' Veronika waited until she'd closed the lid on the chest before passing her the pin tray for her hair clips. 'Besides, I may not marry Gevorg.'

'Does Gevorg know you may not marry him?'

'I have no idea what Gevorg thinks,' Veronika plumped up the pillows. 'It's strange to be without Anusha.'

'Even stranger to think she'll never sleep here again, but as Mother said, every woman has to give up her home to make another with her husband.' She eyed Veronika. 'Aram Saroyan is very good-looking?'

'Who said anything about Aram Saroyan?'

'Me. I saw the way you were looking at him in church today

when you thought no one was watching. More importantly I saw the way he was eyeing you.'

'Did anyone else ...'

'See you two lovebirds making sheep's eyes at one another? I don't think so. Father won't be pleased if you throw Gevorg over for Aram. Aram will become a baker like his father whereas Gevorg ...'

'Will become a professor like his father and ours.' Veronika made a wry face.

'What's wrong with being a professor?'

Their father taught French, English, and Arabic Literature at the school and college in the town where Gevorg's father was the senior instructor in mathematics.

'Nothing, teaching is an honourable profession. I'm making a face at mathematics. All Gevorg talks about these days is how clever he is and how he can solve this equation or that, or how many numbers he can put into letters. I don't understand a thing he says and what's more I don't want to.'

'Sounds like you two have been quarrelling about more than mathematics.'

'Perhaps. Perhaps it's just seeing how happy Anusha and Ruben were today and how excited Anusha was the first time she visited Ruben's family's farm. She's so looking forward to working beside Ruben every day and helping him with his livestock and crops. As she said to Papa when she pleaded with him to allow her to marry Ruben, there's more to life than books.' Veronika slid beneath the bedcovers.

'I can see that a baker who makes delicious bread and cakes would be a more agreeable and entertaining husband that one who talks in logarithms. And Aram is very good-looking,' she continued when Veronika didn't answer her. 'Much more so than Gevorg.'

'I suppose he is.'

'The thought hadn't occurred to you?'

'Do you think Aram is better looking than Razmik?' Veronika bit back.

'Razmik is the best-looking boy in the town, but Aram comes a close second.' She refused to rise to Veronika's bait.

'You'd marry Razmik tomorrow, wouldn't you?'

90

'No,' she assured Veronika, 'First because I have my career to think about, and secondly because I don't expect to marry at all and if I did, it certainly wouldn't be to a handsome boy. I have no illusions about my looks.'

'But if Razmik asked you ...'

'He won't because there's nothing between Razmik and me.' There wasn't but that hadn't prevented her from dreaming. She knew Razmik only talked to her because he was being polite and felt sorry for her. She also knew she put too much store by what he said to her.

'You know Father's views as well as me,' Veronika said mournfully. 'None of us to marry before our seventeenth birthday. I have another eight months to go. Whereas you could marry Razmik tomorrow.'

'I couldn't because he hasn't asked, and I wouldn't if he did. Has it occurred to you that even if you agreed to marry Gevorg you couldn't marry him on your seventeenth birthday?'

'Why not?' Veronika demanded.

'Because you'd have to wait until he finished his studies and found a paid position that could support you both.'

'Have you thought what it would be like to be married?' Veronika asked seriously.

'To sleep with a husband who didn't kick me the way you, Mariam, and Anusha have done in this bed for years? It would be bliss – that's if I wanted to marry, which I don't.'

'You know what I mean and I'm not talking about kicking.' Veronika moved Mariam who'd rolled sideways so she could get into the bed.

'You heard what Grandmother told Anusha before she left. That love between a man and a woman can be very beautiful ... beautiful ... beautiful ...'

Mesopotamian Desert
June 1916

Only it wasn't beautiful. It was ugly, brutal, demeaning, and humiliating beyond measure. Rebeka hoped she'd die before she had to endure it again, and that Mariam would never discover how much pain a man could inflict upon a woman.

Abdul's Coffee Shop, Quayside, Basra
June 1916

'Can't you sleep? It's the middle of the night,' Michael complained when Kalla left the bed and lit the oil lamp.

'I'm thirsty; besides, we haven't slept yet.'

'Only because you won't let me.' He watched her cross the room and admired the smooth lines of her naked body and the golden glow of her skin. 'You look like a classical bronze of a goddess. A Venus or Juno. Or give you a bow and arrow and you could be Diana.'

She glanced back at him as she went to the table 'The goddess I understand – what is a classical bronze?'

'The Greeks and Romans liked to decorate their towns with metal statues of beautiful women. Diana was the goddess of hunters, Venus of love …'

'I'd like to be the goddess of love if you are the god.'

'I'm too short to be a god. The statues are always tall.' He rearranged the pillows and sat up in the bed.

She poured two glasses of water and handed him one. 'But if I was made of metal and you weren't I wouldn't be able to make love with you.'

'That would be a disaster for me.' He fondled and kissed her breast when she climbed back onto the bed.

She cupped his face in her hands and caressed him, holding him close to her. 'Take me with you when you go upstream, Michael.'

He stopped kissing her and looked into her eyes. Huge liquid pools that suddenly appeared more reproachful than loving. 'Who says I'm going upstream?'

'Daoud, Abdul – everyone in Basra knows that soon the British will march on Baghdad to avenge the defeat at Kut, and where your forces go reporters like you must follow.'

'There'll be fighting. I can't take you into battle.'

'Then leave me behind in the camp with your horses, syce, and bearer.'

'Daoud follows the fighting with me.'

'Then I'll stay with your bearer. I don't need looking after, Michael. Please, don't leave me here on my own again,' she begged.

'I'll give you money like last time. Abdul will take care of you.'

'I don't belong to Abdul, but Zabba. If she sends for me I will have to go, and because she owns me she can make me do whatever she wants.'

He'd been half asleep but he suddenly woke. 'Sleep with other men?'

'If that's what she wants.'

Michael sat up. 'Did she send for you when I was away?'

'Yes.'

'You went?' His voice was sharp.

'No, but only because Abdul reminded her that you could return at any moment, and as you paid for my company you would be angry if I wasn't here to greet you. He also reminded her he was paying her for me to spy on you, so she was already getting double money for my services.'

'I've been meaning to ask. What do you report to Abdul and Zabba about me?'

'Only what you tell me you've written for your newspaper.'

'In which case Abdul isn't getting much for his money.' He pulled her down beside him. 'After all the chaos and death upstream, I was so glad to return to you, I forgot you're a slave.'

'I never forget it.' she lay quietly and made no attempt to cover herself.

When Michael didn't say anything, she added, 'You knew I was a whore and I told you I was a spy shortly after you took me into your bed.'

'Don't call yourself a whore, Kalla.' He glanced at the clock, 'I have to leave shortly, but later this morning I'll visit Zabba and ask her to sell you to me.'

'If she refuses?'

'I'll keep offering her more money until she does,' he said recklessly, thinking of the strongbox in the bank which the army had filled with gold sovereigns for him to bribe any native tribes he might 'persuade' to join the British cause. He, like his brother Harry before him, was finding his status as political officer – albeit an undercover one – extremely useful.

'You'll really buy my freedom?'

'I will,' he promised solemnly, 'and when I do ...'

'I'll be yours.'

'No, you'll be your own person. Free to make your own decisions about your future.'

She smiled triumphantly. 'Then you won't be able to stop me from travelling upriver with you.'

'The army would stop you. They don't allow women into war zones. Besides, if you were with me I'd only worry about you.'

'Then you will have to worry.'

'I won't,' he said decisively, 'because you won't be accompanying me. I'm serious, Kalla. I will buy and free you. I'll also ask Abdul to take care of you, even if it means locking you up in this room and paying a man to sit outside the door.'

She'd never seen Michael so forceful, or so close to anger. Forgetting her determination to accompany him – for the moment – she said, 'Please don't visit Zabba. Daoud and I will go. If she sees you, she'll set my price too high.'

'You're being very careful with my money.'

'Not that careful. I'll ask Daoud to walk me back through the bazaar. I need new clothes so any money I save I'll spend on myself.'

'Profligate.' He smiled in attempt to take the edge from his earlier outburst.

She kissed him again. One kiss led to another – and another – and as they began to make slow, satisfying love again, Michael's only thoughts were of Kalla, and how fortunate he was to have found a woman like her to share his life after his brief and embarrassingly disastrous sexless marriage to his cousin Lucy.

Kalla's thoughts were on journeys and how to accompany Michael without him knowing – at least for a while.

Colonel Perry's Bungalow, British Compound, Basra
June 1916

At five minutes to four Maud picked up the last item she wanted to take: her jewellery case. She stuffed it on top of the few essentials she'd packed into a Gladstone bag. There was a tap at her door. She opened it to see her new maid.

'The cart is here, ma'am.'

'Wake the nursemaid and Master Robin. Tell the nursemaid to

give Master Robin's boxes, crib, and bedding to the gardener to pack on to the cart.'

'And this trunk, ma'am?'

Maud considered its contents, but there was no way she could take it. 'If my father asks about it, tell him I will send for it when I'm settled.'

'Yes, ma'am.'

Maud wrapped her cape around her shoulders, picked up her handbag and carpet bag, and walked out to the cart. She watched the servants load Robin's crib and box. The nursemaid left the house with the child wrapped in a shawl. Maud kissed his forehead and pressed the parcel for Mrs Butler and twenty sovereigns into the woman's hand. 'Your pay for the year.'

The driver climbed on the cart and she watched him drive away. She followed as far as the manned barrier, nodded a 'Good morning' to the soldier on duty, and left the British compound.

She had one hundred and eighty pounds, two changes of clothes, and a string of pearls that might bring a decent price, but she'd been close to and fond of Mrs Hale and resolved not to sell them unless she was desperate.

Other than the wharf to find a ship she had no plans. No idea where she wanted to sail. She only knew she couldn't bear the thought of imposing on Michael Downe or any friend of John's who'd give her another of the pitying looks Michael had last night.

She continued to walk, and as she walked she recalled all the people she'd met in her life. For the first time she realised how superficial most of her acquaintanceships – she could hardly call them friendships – had been. They'd either been based on mutual sexual obsession, like Miguel D'Arbez and the junior officers she'd bedded after she'd married John, or empty, meaningless social contacts among fellow officers' wives. She couldn't think of a single person she could turn to other than those who'd been more John's friends than hers – and Angela Smythe. Angela would certainly offer her help and accommodation but she could hardly impose on her just after she and Peter had moved into their first home, especially as Peter still hadn't recovered from his experiences at Kut.

Theo's words resounded in her ears. 'Frankly there are only two places a women like you can go, a whorehouse or a convent.'

Then she thought of someone who would help her no matter what she'd done. Not because they loved her but from motives of pure charity.

She would leave Basra after all, and go to the one place people would least expect to find her. She quickened her step and looked along the wharf. A white woman would attract attention but not a woman in a bourka.

She saw a native opening his shop.

A moment later she was inside it.

Chapter Nine

Mesopotamian Desert
June 1916

Rebeka sat up as the order to wake was shouted from gendarme to gendarme. The moon and stars were fading, the sky slowly lightening from dark to pale grey but the air was still uncomfortably chill. She looked around and realised they'd been corralled like sheep on to a tiny peninsula of rough ground that jutted out into the river. She studied the white pinched faces that surrounded her and knew the same thought was in all their minds. They were in for yet another hungry, thirsty, burning hot day, long, painful, and full of humiliation.

'Drink!'

The moment the gendarmes gave permission, there was a stampede to the bank. Rebeka kept a tight hold on Mariam's hand as they trailed behind the others. Even in the early morning gloom she could see the water at the river's edge was thick with mud and rubbish.

'Wait, Mariam.' She untied the scarf from her head and strained water through it into the tin mug she'd threaded on to her belt. Trying not to think of the filth she hadn't managed to filter out, she gave the water to her sister. Only when Mariam had finished did she fill the mug and drink herself, and by then the gendarmes were yelling at the women to move back from the water.

Anusha pushed close to her. She looked up. Saw Mehmet watching them.

'Anusha, Mehmet ...'

Anusha leaned forward, embraced and kissed her. 'I love you, Rebeka. Take care of Mariam for both of us.'

'I love you, Anusha, but ...'

'I'm sorry.' Anusha wrenched her hand from Rebeka's and

waded into the river. Within seconds she lost her footing and was swept out into the mid-stream.

Mrs Gulbenkian, Rebeka, and Mariam screamed as the current carried Anusha swiftly away from them.

'You don't want to drown, do you, Grandma?' A gendarme kicked Mrs Gulbenkian and Hasmik, who hadn't left the older woman's side since the night her family had been killed, back into the throng.

A shot rang out. Anusha's body jerked then sank.

'Shut up, bitch.' A gendarme knocked Rebeka, who was crying, on to the muddy bank. She reached out for Mariam, struggled to her feet, and moved close to Mrs Gulbenkian simply because it was reassuring to be in the company of someone familiar from better days. She closed her eyes and tried to retreat from what was happening.

She pictured the bedroom she'd shared with her sisters. The patchwork eiderdown her mother had stitched from their outgrown dresses and stuffed with feathers from their poultry yard that she'd washed and dried and scented with herbs and lavender. The photographs of their grandparents in silver frames that hung on the walls. The rag rugs she and her sisters had inexpertly plaited. Their 'best' white Sunday shoes ranged in a row below the curtains in front of the window ...

'You! Ugly sister!'

Mehmet knotted his fingers into her hair and hauled her close to him. Mariam's cries escalated. Mrs Gulbenkian covered Mariam's eyes so she wouldn't see what was about to happen. As if her sister hadn't seen it already so many times she'd lost count.

Mehmet dragged Rebeka by her hair to the edge of the crowd. The pain of her hair being torn out by the roots was excruciating, the sound even more so. Her dress was ripped from her. Then, amidst savage, mocking laughter, Mehmet wielded a whip, bringing it down on her back, shoulders, legs and buttocks.

'I forbade you to talk to your sister ... you knew she was mine ... you made me shoot her ... You! ... No one else. You ... killed her ...'

She tried to think of home – safety – her grandmother – her father – her mother – but it was no use. She wanted it to be over. She wanted to die. To join Anusha and Veronika, but she couldn't.

Not while Mariam still lived and needed what little protection she could give her.

Military HQ, Basra
June 1916

Charles stared at Maud's letter for a few seconds before reading it a second time.

If you are ever in position to help Robin and see fit to do so, I would be very grateful for his sake, not mine. He didn't ask to be brought into this world.

He folded it, returned it to its envelope, and glanced up at his aide.

'When was this delivered?'

'Early this morning, sir. A guard brought it up from the front gate because it was marked urgent. He said it was delivered by a native woman.'

'Order a carriage to meet me outside the main entrance in ten minutes.'

'Yes, sir.' The private saluted and left.

Charles reached for the letter he'd written to Maud, which was still in his in tray. He folded it into the pocket of his tunic, picked up his stick, rested his weight on it, and rose awkwardly from his chair. He walked slowly, testing the strength of his damaged leg as he limped down the corridor. He tapped a door at the end.

Peter Smythe shouted. 'Come in.' He looked up from the maps spread out on his desk. 'Charles, you've news about the advance?'

'Nothing. I received a letter from Maud. Did she write to you or Angela?'

Peter ran his fingers through his bright red hair, brushing it back from his face. 'Not me. She might have written to Angela but nothing came before I left the bungalow this morning.'

'Maud's father has thrown her out.'

'That would explain why she was so upset last night.' Peter perched on the windowsill, leaving the single chair in his cupboard-sized office for Charles.

'I didn't like to ask last night in the club as Tom was so angry with Maud, but did you and Angela actually see her?'

'No, like you and Kitty, Angela and I arrived at the Basra Club after Maud had left. Michael was the first to arrive for the dinner, then Tom, Clary, David, and Georgie. From what David told me we missed an ugly scene. Tom completely lost his temper when he saw Maud. Michael had found her standing outside the club. She was upset, so he took her in to try to calm her down. Then Tom arrived and gave her a hard time.'

'Understandable after what Maud did to his brother,' Charles sat and propped his stick against the wall.

'I'll not argue with you on that score. Michael offered to take Maud home. You were there when he returned and said he'd sorted her problems but with Tom breathing fire every time Maud's name was mentioned I didn't have a chance to ask Michael what he'd done.' Peter looked up as the orderly knocked on his open door. 'Yes?'

'Mr Michael Downe's here, asking if you can spare him a few minutes, sir.'

'Show him in.'

'You've had a letter from Maud?' Charles asked as soon as Michael walked in.

'No.' Michael frowned. 'You've heard from her?'

'I had a letter a few minutes ago.'

'What did it say?'

'Among other things, that she's leaving Basra.'

'Why did she write to you?'

Charles suddenly realised just how incriminating Maud's letter was, not only to her but him. 'Possibly because I'm John's oldest remaining friend in Basra and I was a friend to her mother as well as her.' He hoped that neither Michael nor Peter would suspect just how close a friend he'd been to Emily Perry.

'I was supposed to meet Maud outside her father's bungalow at five o'clock this morning,' Michael revealed. 'I'd arranged to move her ...'

'To where?' Charles interrupted.

'When we talked, she didn't know. Maud's father told her to leave his bungalow yesterday evening. I promised to find her somewhere. Last night I arranged for her to rent a house from one of the people who works at the French consulate. His wife has returned to France ...' Michael realised he was digressing.

100

'Anyway, when I arrived at Colonel Perry's bungalow this morning with a cart and carriage ready to move Maud, her baby, and belongings, she'd already left. Colonel Perry refused to allow me inside. I'd told Maud I was living in Abdul's so I returned there in case she'd gone looking for me. She hadn't. The only other place I could think of that she would have gone to was your bungalow, Peter, but the maid said you and Angela were out.'

'Angela's teaching at the Lansing,' Peter explained. 'What did Maud say in her letter?' he asked.

'That she was going to leave her baby at the Lansing in the hope that Mrs Butler would place him in an orphanage.'

'Good God!' Peter exclaimed. 'Why on earth did she write to you, Charles, and not Angela? Angela's her friend ...'

'Maud mentioned the effect military gossip was having on her,' Charles divulged. 'It was the reason her father ordered her to leave his bungalow. She probably didn't want Angela to become tainted by association.'

'That still doesn't explain why she wrote to you and not me after we talked last night,' Michael protested.

'As I said, I'm the last of John's close friends in Basra,' Charles persisted. 'She doesn't know either of you as well as me. Tom said some devastating things to her last night. She was probably concerned that you both despise her for being unfaithful to John.'

'You don't?'

Charles avoided Peter's question. 'Perhaps she felt she couldn't abandon her child in an orphanage without telling someone where she'd left him.'

'Did she hint where she might be going?'

'No.' Charles left the chair. 'I asked my orderly to arrange a carriage. I thought someone should go to the Lansing and talk to Mrs Butler. I doubt she's happy at having the child dumped on her, even if it turns out to be on a temporary basis.'

'I'll come with you,' Peter volunteered.

You don't have to,' Charles demurred.

'I'll grab any excuse to leave the office and see Angela, especially in the middle of the day. What about you, Michael?'

'As I have nothing planned for this morning, I'll tag on. Just as well Tom's already left Basra.'

'I agree, he's best out of this,' Charles observed.

'I'm not sure what any of us can do,' Peter followed Michael out of the door.

'First we establish how Mrs Butler feels at having the child sent to her,' Charles suggested.

'And if she refuses to take responsibility for the baby?' Peter ventured.

'Someone else will have to.' Charles picked up his hat and closed the door behind him.

Lansing Memorial Mission, Basra
June 1916

'More tea, Major Reid, Major Smythe, Mr Downe, Angela?' Mrs Butler beckoned to the maid who was manning the tea trolley.

'No, thank you, Mrs Butler.' Charles declined. The other guests followed suit.

'Leave us,' Mrs Butler ordered the maid. 'Close the door behind you and ask the cook to find you something to do in the kitchen until it's time to serve lunch.'

'Yes, ma'am.'

'To return to your question, Major Reid,' Mrs Butler continued after the girl left the drawing room. 'Yes, I was shocked when Mrs Mason's nursemaid arrived here with the baby before five o'clock this morning. Shocked and angry that Mrs Mason should think of imposing on us here at the Lansing. She's lived among us. She knows how busy we are, but I could hardly turn the woman and child out on the street, which is why I've accommodated them, temporarily, in the room Mrs Mason used when she stayed with us as our guest. However, I have stressed to the maid their residence here can be only an interim measure.'

'The maid has accepted responsibility for the child?' Charles asked.

'Hardly,' Mrs Butler set her cup on a side table. 'Before I found her the position of nursemaid to Mrs Mason she worked as a maid in our orphanage for native children. She has no home and no resources of her own beyond the money Mrs Mason gave her before she came here.'

'Maud gave her money?' Michael made an effort to sound casual lest anyone suspect his generosity.

'A year's wages, twenty pounds, but nothing whatsoever towards the woman's or the child's living expenses. Maud did, however, send this.' Mrs Butler handed Charles the jewellery case Maud had given the maid. 'I have no idea how valuable those pieces are or if indeed they have any value at all.'

Charles opened the case. 'This is a set Harry left to Maud. It's valuable and its worth will probably increase after the war. Particularly if the gold is melted down, and the stones sold through a reputable jeweller.'

Angela left her chair and looked at the pieces over Charles's shoulder. 'If those rubies and diamonds are real, few officers could afford them, and fewer wives would have the courage to wear the jewellery for fear of losing or breaking one of the items.'

'I wouldn't know where to begin to look for a buyer for them,' Mrs Butler said. 'As to taking the child, the Reverend and I are run off our feet between making improvements here, and opening the new orphanage and training facility for destitute girls. Our sister centre in Amara will be operational next month. It is taking up every minute of the Reverend's time which makes my presence here more vital than ever. We're simply not in a position to care for a child. It really was most irresponsible of Maud Mason to send the baby to us.'

'Is the maid is capable of looking after the boy?' Michael checked.

'At the moment, when the child only needs feeding, changing, and nursing, but babies have a habit of growing and when they do, they need more attention than a nursemaid can give them.'

'As it's difficult for you and the Reverend to look after Robin, Peter and I could take him until Maud returns,' Angela volunteered.

'Steady on, Angela,' Peter remonstrated. 'We're not in a position to adopt a child. You teach here and I'll be going upstream as soon as the Relief Force regroups.'

'No one said anything about adoption. It will only be until Maud returns. She will, and soon,' Angela declared. 'She dotes on that baby.'

Mrs Butler snorted in derision. 'I saw little evidence of Mrs Mason doting on that child when she was here.'

'Maud doesn't find it easy to show her feelings,' Angela

defended her loyally. 'And the child won't present a problem, not immediately. The nursemaid and the baby can live in our bungalow. I'll bring them here with me here on the days I teach, and if you agree, Mrs Butler, they can stay in Maud's old room. They'll be out of the way there and I can check on them during my lunch break. When I've finished teaching I'll take them back to our quarters.'

'And when I go upstream? Peter asked.

'The baby and the nursemaid will be company for me.'

'You're taking on a huge responsibility, not to mention expense,' Peter warned.

'A baby won't cost much and Maud's paid the nursemaid a year's wages, so it will only be their food. Our cook always makes far too much. I doubt we'll notice any difference in the housekeeping.'

'In my opinion Maud won't be back any time soon to reclaim the boy,' Mrs Butler prophesised. 'Frankly, given that Robin isn't her husband's child I doubt she'll ever return.'

'I'd like to contribute towards the upkeep of the child,' Charles offered.

'Why would you do that?' Mrs Butler enquired suspiciously.

'Because John Mason is my closest surviving friend and no matter what happened between him and Maud, he wouldn't want to see her or the child in need. He has enough problems being held captive by the Turks without worrying about Maud and her baby being left destitute.'

'I heard that Major Mason intends to divorce Mrs Mason.' Mrs Butler blatantly fished for information.

'The last time I saw John we were at Nasiriyeh and too busy fighting the Turks to discuss our personal circumstances.' Charles deliberately moved the conversation on from John's marital problems. 'There's an innocent baby adrift in Basra, which in my opinion is not a suitable town for army wives, let alone children. If Peter and Angela are prepared to take the child on a temporary basis until something more permanent can be arranged, the least I can do is contribute to his upkeep. I'll open an account in his name, make a monthly deposit, and arrange for Angela and Peter to draw on it so they can purchase whatever he needs.'

'Then that's settled, thank you, Charles.' Angela smiled at

Peter.

Peter didn't return her smile. 'What about clothes and furniture? We don't even have a child's cot.'

'Maud sent everything the child needs. I'll ask the gardener to cart it to your bungalow,' Mrs Butler offered.

'Thank you, Mrs Butler,' Angela said gratefully. 'We have two empty rooms in the bungalow so accommodating Robin and the maid won't inconvenience us.'

'Shouldn't someone look for Maud?' Michael suggested. 'When I left her last night she was in quite a state. I doubt she was thinking straight.'

'She most certainly couldn't have been thinking straight. If she had been, she wouldn't have sent her child here,' Mrs Butler declared.

'Are you volunteering to look for her?' Charles asked Michael.

'I'll make enquiries, but I had a cable from my editor this morning. A source in the War Office has tipped him that the push to Baghdad is imminent. He asked me to head upstream and write a series of articles on the Relief Force's plans to wreak revenge for the surrender at Kut al Amara.'

'Plans,' Charles smiled. 'I can tell you what they are now. Two words will cover it. "Under discussion".'

'I was thinking of writing "Not yet formulated".'

'That will do just as well. When will you be going?' Charles asked.

'Early next week, so I'll have a few days to look for Maud.'

Charles glanced at Peter. He knew the same thought was in both their minds. 'How long before they'd be ordered back into battle – and would they survive a 'next time'.

Chapter Ten

Mesopotamian Desert, Ottoman Empire
July 1916

When the gendarmes shouted the order to halt at dusk, Rebeka sank to the ground without relinquishing her hold on Mariam. They were on the outer edge of the group, close to the police, but she lacked the energy to crawl deeper into the mass of bedraggled humanity.

Mrs Gulbenkian and Hasmik were next to them. Rebeka looked to her old neighbour, but Mrs Gulbenkian was too sunk in her own misery to respond. Plagued by thoughts of Anusha's horrific murder, none of them had spoken for days.

They had left the river behind them over a week ago. Since then, the gendarmes had permitted the occasional stop at wells, but never frequently enough to assuage their thirst. The water bottles they shared were heavy to carry when full and never held enough to satisfy everyone's needs.

She was beginning to think her previous life had been no more than a beautiful dream. Every muscle in her body ached; her feet were cut and bleeding, and each footfall brought fresh agony. Her skin was on fire from a combination of sunburn, mosquito bites, and bruises, inflicted during the nights when – in Mrs Gulbenkian's terms – 'her honour was violated'.

Her nerves were as shredded as her feet, and she only had to hear one of the guards raise his voice for tears to start in her eyes. Her dress was torn and hung so loose it was in danger of falling from her. Crippled by agonising stomach cramps she could no longer walk upright, but her craving was for water, not food. Her mouth and throat longed for one of the buckets of cool sweet water she'd drawn from the well at home. She'd stand in the garden, and after making certain neither her mother nor grandmother was watching, drink from the bucket. At the height of summer, she'd tip the rest of the water over her head, allowing it to trickle down her neck and on to her dress. Cool, wet, soothing …

She raised her head, hoping to catch sight of a well or failing that a pool. But the desert yawned back at her, flat, dry, and gritty. The only visible plant life was an occasional clump of camel thorn that she suspected even the animals they were named for might reject.

The gendarmes swaggered, an intimidating armed line of masculinity. She watched them nod to one another as they pointed to the women and children who'd stretched out on the ground. Holding Mariam close she was careful to sit upright. At a snapped command from Mehmet, four of the younger gendarmes moved among the women and children and picked up those who'd collapsed. They carried them away from the group and dropped them next to a shallow trench carved out by the rains during the wet season.

Suspecting what was coming after the events of previous nights, Rebeka dug in her pocket for a crust of bread she'd hoarded from the loaves that had been distributed days ago by the last group of American missionaries who'd dared come near them. The bread was rock-hard but she gave it to Mariam.

Mariam took it and whispered, 'Water.'

Rebeka shook the tin bottle she carried. 'It's empty.' Like the bread, she gave it to Mariam anyway.

'You, Beka …'

'Not hungry or thirsty,' she lied. 'Put your head on my lap, it will be cold soon. I'll wrap my skirt around you to keep you warm.'

Mariam did as she suggested and Rebeka covered Mariam's eyes as well as her back and shoulders. The gendarmes pulled out their knives. The women and children they'd taken from the group didn't even cry out as the gendarmes slit their throats.

Rebeka lifted her head and stared up at the blue-black sky studded with silver stars and a low hanging, enormous brilliant moon. The heavens were vast, infinite, beautiful – and indifferent. She found it difficult to imagine it was the same night sky that had watched over her home and family.

She heard the gendarmes moving, but refused to look when she heard them flinging the bodies of those they'd slaughtered into the gulley. The corpses landed in a series of ominous thuds. When silence reigned again it was only to be shattered by a chilling scream.

The gendarmes retreated into the black desert. Huge, terrifying, shadowy figures crept out of the gloom and swooped down on the captives. Rebeka watched, mesmerized as the giants moved among the women. They were massive – and strong. She saw one lift a woman from her feet and hold her high as another stripped the clothes from her.

Mrs Gulbenkian wrapped her arms tightly around Hasmik. 'Lie beneath me. Don't look. Don't make a sound.'

Before Rebeka could follow suit with Mariam, she was grabbed by her neck. As she was swung from her feet, a man, his head half-hidden by a turban, materialised in front of her. He inserted the point of his dagger in the neck of her ragged dress and sliced it from her. She fought with all the strength she could muster but it wasn't enough. After the man had stripped her of her clothes he threw her aside, picked up her dress and Mariam and tossed both to a shorter, slighter figure wrapped in a cloak and kafieh.

The man caught Mariam, who was catatonic with terror. Rebeka saw her sister's mouth open but if Mariam screamed, it was silent. Devastated at the prospect of losing the last member of her family, Rebeka charged towards the man. She was only vaguely away of the cries, bloodshed, and chaos around her. Young girls and children were being wrenched from the arms of their mothers and sisters. Women and children tried to fight as the clothes were ripped from their backs. Most ended up knocked to the ground. Rebecca tripped over them, falling more than once on to mounds of bare flesh.

She didn't even realise she was stark naked until she found herself running alone in the moonlit desert. Somewhere ahead was a resounding drumbeat of pounding hooves. That was the moment she realised the bandit tribesmen who had robbed her and the other women of their clothes and children were riding off.

Even as she summoned the last of her strength to run after them she knew it was futile. That she could never hope to catch them. But she kept running and crying Mariam's name.

A blow rained on her back. She plunged headlong to the earth.

A second blow sent coloured stars shooting across the horizon. One by one they burst into shards of light and when the last sliver fell to earth there was only darkness.

Abdul's Coffee Shop, Basra
July 1916

Georgiana knocked Michael's door.

'Enter.'

Her brother was sitting, writing, his travelling desk on the table beside him.

'Georgie,' he left his chair and kissed her cheek, 'this is an unexpected pleasure.'

'No boat of Turkish casualties came in this morning. Dr Picard and Theo Wallace insisted they could manage without me, so I thought I'd come and torment you before you go upstream.'

'How do you know I'm going upstream?'

'Angela Smythe told me when she visited her brother in the Lansing this morning.'

'Can't keep any secrets in this town. I'm pleased to see you, but Abdul's is no place for a woman.'

'Some people would argue that point. From what I've heard it's exactly the place for enterprising women. I've been curious about the opportunities it offers to both sexes for a while. Besides, your girlfriend seems to manage living here. Now what did Charles say her name was?' she mused unconvincingly as if she didn't already know. 'Kalla, isn't it?'

'I supposed you're shocked.'

'If you're happy with her, I'm very pleased for you, little brother. You should never have married Lucy.'

'You did all you could to stop me.'

'I'm only sorry I didn't succeed.' She looked around the room. 'Where is Kalla? As I called in unexpectedly I was hoping to meet her.'

'Visiting …' He hedged. 'An acquaintance.'

'An acquaintance, not friend?'

'Kalla belonged to a woman …'

'Belonged? She was a slave?'

'There are many in this country.'

110

'Nothing about this place should surprise me, but that does,' Georgiana answered.

'I'm in the process of buying her, which is proving complicated possibly because Kalla insists on doing the negotiating with my orderly Daoud's help. They didn't trust me. Said I'd end up paying too much. Frankly I would have rather given double the money to have the business over with by now. I find the whole idea repugnant.'

'Hasn't it occurred to you that most civilised people would?' she asked in amusement.

'Sorry, Georgie, I've been too long in this country and talked to too many people like Abdul who think it's normal for one human being to own another.'

'A word of caution: have you considered what you're going to do with Kalla when you buy her?'

'Free her, of course.'

'That's it? Just say, off you go, Kalla, you're free?'

'No, of course not. Kalla wants to go upstream with me. We've been arguing about it.'

'She realises there's going to be serious fighting up there?'

'Yes.'

'But she still wants to go?'

'When the bullets start flying I could leave her behind the lines with the orderlies. She'd be safe – or relatively safe – there.' He gave her a disarming lopsided smile that reminded her of Harry. 'I'm still thinking about it, but,' he shrugged.

'From what you've just said I think she's already persuaded you to take her.'

'I think I love her, Georgie.'

'Think?'

'I do.'

'If you love her, and she's prepared to risk her life just to be with you, take her.'

'I didn't expect that advice from you.'

She laughed.

'What's funny?'

'Us. Me marrying a Welsh miner, Harry a Bedouin girl, and now you falling in love with an Arab slave girl. Our poor parents. They put such store by what the county thinks. Can you imagine

111

the sensation you'd create if you turned up at mother's next garden party with Kalla.'

'They'd approve of David Knight,' Michael commented.

'They probably would.'

'Is he serious?'

'About what?'

Irritated by her evasion, he snapped, 'You, Georgie.'

'Good Lord, no. David and I have fun together. Nothing more. Besides, David's far too good-looking for any woman, especially me with my plain face, to take seriously. He's like the flashy impractical gown you long to buy even though you know it's going to disintegrate the first time you wash it.' She went to the window and looked down at the wharf.

'Do you love him?' Michael asked.

She turned to face him. 'No, but I do love my post at the Lansing because it means I can stay close to you. I can't bear the thought of losing you. Not after Harry ...'

'It's not as though you're in the same situation Clary was,' he broke in. 'I could understand her refusing to marry Tom until he was sent home sick, because it would have meant her having to give up nursing, and she was doing important work in the Basra Hospital. But the Lansing's a charity. They're not even paying you. They're so desperate for doctors they would keep you on, Georgie, whether you were married or not.'

'I know.'

'Then why not marry David?' he asked.

'One, David hasn't asked. Two, Gwilym may be dead but his death hasn't stopped me from loving him and you can't simply replace one husband with another. Then there's the future – when I dare think about it. I married one man who went off to war and never returned. Gwilym promised me he'd be safe behind the lines as a stretcher-bearer. David's a doctor with field experience. If he went upstream and was killed I ...' She turned back to the window.

'Would it be easier if David was killed and you weren't married, sis?'

'Probably not,' she admitted. 'I can't bear the thought of losing anyone else I know and love as a friend.'

'What did you just say to me? "If you love her you should take her with you." That applies to you too. If you love David you should marry him.'

'I told you, he hasn't and won't ask me to. Are you expecting Charles?'

'Is that your way of changing the subject?'

'No, Charles just walked in downstairs.'

'That's his stick hitting the stairs.' Michael went to the door and opened it.

Charles hobbled into the room. 'Georgie, I didn't expect to see you here.'

'If you want to talk men's rubbish, I'll clear off.'

'No, please. Not on my account.' Charles removed his hat and dropped it and his swagger stick on a side table before lowering himself on the divan. 'I heard you're going upstream soon.'

'I am,' Michael confirmed.

'Any news of Maud?'

'None. Abdul and Daoud have had men out scouring the wharf and Basra. It's as if she's stepped off the earth.'

'Not into the Shatt al-Arab, I hope.' Charles fell serious.

'Daoud checks the bodies with the civil authorities every morning. A female of Maud's age and colouring would attract instant attention and there haven't been any answering her description.'

'I ran into Angela in the stores yesterday morning, She seems to be coping with looking after Maud's child,' Charles took the glass of whisky Michael poured for him.

'I think she secretly loves having a baby to care for.' Georgie nodded when Michael offered her a glass as well. 'But Peter isn't too keen. Like all men he wants his own children and he's probably wondering how Angela will cope with two babies.'

'Angela's going to have a baby?' Michael asked.

'Not that she's confided in me,' Georgie glanced at Charles. 'When are you going upstream?'

'When HQ decides I should go.'

'Peter?'

'I shouldn't be telling you this but he was given two days leave this morning. He went back to his bungalow so I assume he's giving Angela the news now.'

'So the push is coming and Peter will be going in three days?' Georgiana sipped her whisky.

'Peter will be leaving in three days,' Charles confirmed, 'the push to Baghdad will only happen when the new command believes we're ready.'

'New command?' Michael picked up a pen.

'General Maude's been put in overall command.'

Michael scribbled the name.

'Before you go rooting around the Basra Club and the bars, I can tell you now, the men like him. He's aggressive, a brilliant tactician, and controls every detail of his command. He never takes unwarranted risks, and performed miracles with the 13th Division after the Dardanelles fiasco. It was shot to pieces but within six months he'd transformed it into a fighting force second to none.'

'You think he'll take Baghdad?' Michael asked.

'In his own good time, and only when he's ready,' Charles qualified. 'He won't advance until he's confident of success.'

'Will David be going upstream?' Georgiana asked.

'To quote the senior MO, "Knight will be invaluable to the medical service because he has experience of conducting surgery on trestles."'

'Then he'll be leaving on the same boat as Peter?'

'Ask David that question,' Charles evaded.

'I don't have to now, Charles.' She set down her glass and went to the door. 'Time to say a goodbye.'

'I'll walk you back to the Lansing.' Charles reached for his stick.

'I walked down here perfectly well on my own. I'm equally capable of walking back among the natives, who are nowhere near as dangerous as British Military would like to have their womenfolk believe.'

'I'm not offering protection, Georgie, just asking for your company and given the state of my leg the assistance of a doctor should I need it. I have to get back to the office so I'm going in your direction. Dinner tonight in the Basra Club for as many as can make it, my shout? I'll pass the message on to Kitty, Peter, and Angela and book a table.'

'I'll be there,' Michael agreed.

'Neither David nor I are on duty so we'll join you.' Georgiana opened the door and strode ahead of Charles.

'Are you going to tell me why you really called on Michael, Charles?' Georgiana asked after Charles had given in to her demand they hire a carriage for her sake, although he knew she wouldn't have considered doing so if she'd been alone.

'You heard me talk about the push upstream.'

'Something Michael would have found out for himself as soon as he went down to the coffee shop.'

'Dinner tonight …'

'Was an afterthought and don't try saying it wasn't. Your first question was about Maud.'

'I'm concerned for her. I recalled what Michael said, about her being upset. Mothers don't abandon their children …'

'Unless they have nowhere to turn to. Maud's father had thrown her out. From what Michael told me about your visit to the Lansing, Mrs Butler wasn't exactly enthralled at the prospect of having Maud's child dumped on her, which makes me suspect she wouldn't have given Maud house room – or in her case, mission room – if Maud had taken the child to the Lansing herself.'

They were approaching the Basra Club and the turning to the broad avenue that swept up to the European quarter and the Lansing Hospital. The palm-lined boulevard was wide and almost devoid of people at that time of day as the military were working and the locals sleeping away the heat of the afternoon.

'This is me you're talking to, Charles,' Georgiana added impatiently. 'We were raised in the same nursery. You may be a major now but I remember you wearing baby dresses and romper suits …'

'Remind me not to allow you anywhere near my subordinates.'

'What makes you think I haven't already spoken to them?'

He winked at her. 'It's good to have people I grew up with to talk to – sometimes – and in moderation.'

'So out with it,' she pressed. 'What's the problem, Charlie?'

'It's years since anyone called me that.'

'It's years since anyone dared. I'm waiting,' she prompted.

'It's bad enough that I know what I've done, I couldn't bear to have you think any the less of me.'

'Does it have something to do with Maud's baby?'

'How did … what makes you think …'

'I fed him a bottle of milk when I visited Angela. That child is a miniature replica of you. He has your exact shade of blond hair and the same blue eyes.'

Shocked, he stared at her. 'Does anyone else suspect?'

'No one has said anything to me and I haven't said anything to anyone until now,' she reassured. 'You've turned white. The Basra Club is only five minutes away. We could ask the driver to turn around and have coffee in a private suite so you could lie down.'

'I could do with a drink. John is my closest friend …'

'John isn't here. He was divorcing Maud,' she reminded, 'and I'm guessing whatever went on between you and Maud happened when John wasn't around. After he'd left her?'

'What happened between Maud and me should never have occurred. I was drunk.'

'Was she?'

He shook his head. 'It would be all too easy to say she was, but she wasn't, and to be truthful and at the risk of losing what little good opinion you have of me, neither was she totally willing.'

'You raped her?'

He remembered all too clearly Maud straddling him after he'd aroused what could only be described as her lust. 'At first she wasn't willing, then …'

'Her husband wasn't there and wouldn't be for months, possibly years, and you were.'

'You understand?'

'I understand the power of the sexual urge, for all that women aren't supposed to have one. After Gwilym left me in London and went to France I was actually grateful for eighteen-hour shifts because they left me fit for nothing except sleep. Did Maud blame you afterwards?'

'She explained the pregnancy by telling a medic she'd been raped.'

'So bloody unfair.'

'I wish I could …'

'I didn't mean for Maud and you in particular, I meant for women in general. We're badly designed. Women should be born with switches that have to be operated by a man willing to take moral and financial responsibility for a child before we can get pregnant. There are times in every woman's life when lovemaking is just too damned seductive to turn down.'

'This whole situation is a mess.'

'On that I agree. That drink you wanted? I think we'll make it two.'

Chapter Eleven

The desert east of Baghdad
July 1916

The gendarmes hauled a handcart loaded with rags towards the group of naked women and children hunched on the ground. They stopped a few yards away from them and flung out the contents.

'You wanted clothes,' Mehmet growled. 'We found a tribe prepared to give you some. Put them on. In five minutes we start walking.'

Mrs Gulbenkian whispered in Hasmik's ear. The child ran to the garments the naked women were already fighting over. She pulled out two long black robes and carried them back to Mrs Gulbenkian. Mrs Gulbenkian handed one to Rebeka.

'It stinks of goat but beggars can't afford choice.' Mrs Gulbenkian pulled her robe over her head and clambered to her feet. She turned to Rebeka who remained crouched, eyes downcast. 'Put that robe on and exert yourself, child. If you don't, you'll never find Mariam.'

Rebeka looked up at the older women through dark tormented eyes. 'You really think I'll see Mariam in this life again?'

'Those tribesmen took her with them. They wouldn't have bothered if they had no use for her. They would have killed her right away as they did the babies and the older women.'

'You think they took her to be a servant or ...'

'Don't trouble yourself wondering why they took her,' Mrs Gulbenkian interrupted. 'It's enough they burdened themselves by carrying Mariam away. The chances are, whatever their reason, they'll feed her. She'll be given more water to drink than we will today, that's for sure.'

'I hope you're right,' Rebeka said feelingly.

'Think about it and you'll know I am. Come on, Rebeka,

Hasmik,' she softened her voice. 'Time to toughen the soles of our feet and walk.'

Rebeka looked around. Over a thousand women had left her home town at the beginning of the trek. She counted nineteen women and ten children. 'There's hardly anyone left.'

'While one of us still remains upright we have to fight to stay alive.' Mrs Gulbenkian glanced at Hasmik. 'For the sake of the children and those who are no longer with us. It will be our duty to tell everyone who'll listen, how the Turks forced us from our homes, stole our land and all we had, killed our men and children, raped our women, and drove us like animals into the desert to die of thirst and starvation.'

Rebeka stared ahead into the wasteland. 'You were right when you said if we die in the desert no one will be there to see it.'

'God has answered my prayers. Help will come.' Mrs Gulbenkian spoke with conviction.

Rebeka wanted to believe her. 'You're not just saying that to comfort me?'

'We wouldn't have lived this long if God wanted us dead. It will come,' Mrs Gulbenkian repeated firmly. 'And when we least expect it.'

'How can you be so sure?'

'Because God has not turned his back on us. We have to trust in him and have faith.' Mrs Gulbenkian held out her hand to Rebeka. The girl slipped on the robe that did indeed stink of goat before taking it.

'Now we walk as upright and as tall as we can, like princesses at a court to show these evil men that they haven't broken our spirit.'

Rebeka took her place beside Mrs Gulbenkian but her thoughts were of home and the past, not mythical help that may, or what she thought was more likely for all of Mrs Gulbenkian's confidence, may not, lie ahead.

Turkish Hospital, Baghdad
July 1916

The Turkish guards escorted John's party to the gates of the Baghdad hospital that had been requisitioned by the Ottoman army. They spoke to the sentry, who opened the gates and ushered John, Sergeant Greening, Corporal Baker, and the three privates with their two carts inside the compound. Their guards didn't follow.

John turned when the gates closed behind them. One of the guards, the youngest, waved to him before walking down the street behind the others.

'I hope we never see any of those beggars again,' Greening said feelingly. 'They never lifted a finger to help us.'

'They didn't beat us either,' John pointed out mildly. 'And they were the ones with the guns.' He saw an entrance to the building and leaned on the cart as Baker drove towards it. A man in a white coat came out to meet them.

'You are British soldiers?'

John stood to attention and saluted. 'Major John Mason, medical officer with the Indian Army. We have six sick men in the carts.'

'Colonel Muller. I am also a medical officer, Major Mason.' The German officer saluted John before walking around to the back of the carts. He looked inside. 'Dysentery?'

'Cholera,' John corrected. 'They need …'

'Hydration, care, ice, and chalk. My officers and nurses will look after them, Major Mason. Where have you come from?'

'Shumran.'

'I thought the last of the British POWs had been sent up from there weeks ago.'

'We followed the men who were marched up, taking care of the sick and the dying on the way.'

'Yet you only have six patients.'

'Six we found in a Bedouin tent yesterday. We sent ten up river by steamboat. All the others died en route.'

'I am so sorry,' the colonel sounded sincere. 'The Turkish command made poor provision for your troops.'

'They made no provision,' John countered.

Colonel Muller shouted an order through the open door. Half a dozen orderlies ran out and went to the carts.

'I need to see what treatment you will be giving the men,' John insisted.

'Of course, but if I may, might I suggest that first you and your men see to yourselves. We have spare rooms and a bathroom in the staff quarters. I can arrange clean clothes and meals.'

'The sick ...'

'I promise you, Major Mason, they will be well looked after. I will take you to see them as soon as you are clean, fed, and rested. Afterwards perhaps we can discuss the future. You and your men are prisoners of war. Your men will be expected to work. We could certainly use another doctor and orderlies here. I assure you the conditions at this hospital are far more pleasant than those of a Turkish prison camp.'

'I have to follow my regiment, Colonel Muller.'

'At least think about it. We'll talk later.' The colonel led them down a path that ran in front of the hospital.

'Are the British prisoners still in Baghdad?' John asked when Muller opened the door to the staff quarters.

'I can't tell you anything about the British regiments other than they have been sent on at intervals out of Baghdad for the last few weeks.'

'To Turkey?'

'That's what the authorities are telling us, Major Mason. Quite a walk, wouldn't you agree?'

John pushed an image of dead men littering the desert from his mind, only to have it supplanted by one of flattened, obliterated graves.

'Quite a walk,' he echoed grimly.

Turkish Hospital, Baghdad
July 1916

John woke in complete darkness. He opened his eyes and stretched his limbs. He was warm; lying on something so smooth and soft it felt peculiar. It took him a few moments to realise he was no longer in the desert but in a Turkish hospital in Baghdad.

He revelled in the sensation of a comfortable mattress beneath him and clean sheets against his bare skin while he waited for his eyes to adjust to the darkness. Then he recalled seeing a candle on the locker next to his bed. He reached out, found a box of matches, opened it, struck one, and lit the candle. He left the bed and washed in a travelling washstand that stood in the corner of the cubicle-sized room.

Every muscle ached and the skin on his face and arms was raw, sore, and sensitive from sunburn. The water was cool, sparkling, and, after the muddied Tigris, unbelievably clear even in the subdued light of a single flame. The lather from the soap was soft, the towels sheer luxury. Someone had cleared away his filthy uniform while he'd slept and left a clean shirt, trousers, and socks in their place.

He dressed and ran his hand ruefully over his unshaven chin. His razor – if he still possessed it – was in his depleted kit bag somewhere in the back of one of the carts.

He opened the door of the cubicle and looked up and down the corridor. Oil lamps flickered in sconces on the wall. Hearing voices in the distance, he headed towards them and found himself in a room furnished with basic wooden chairs and tables. Sergeant Greening was sitting with Corporal Baker, Dira, and the three privates. Bowls of yoghurt, chopped melon, mint, jam, butter, cheese, and a wooden trencher that held great hunks of Turkish bread were set out in front of them.

'Sir.' Sergeant Greening leapt to his feet and the others followed suit.

'As you were, sergeant. That looks good.' John pulled out a chair and joined them.

'It is, sir.' Greening handed John a bowl and spoon.

'Anyone any idea of the time?' John looked around as his question was met with silence.

'The four o'clock morning prayer call was about half an hour ago,' Baker volunteered.

'I slept all afternoon and night?' John helped himself to yoghurt.

'You slept two afternoons and two nights, sir.'

John froze, holding the ladle over his bowl.

'But you don't have to worry about the men we brought in, sir,' Greening assured him. 'They're all alive and on the mend. I saw them myself before I went to bed last night. The German colonel's done us proud, sir. The men are being looked after and we've all been given proper beds and as you see, as much food as we can eat.'

'Have you talked to any British officers?'

'Not outside this hospital, sir. The brigadier's here, along with about a hundred others. In fact there are two entire wards full of our men. They all seem to getting good care as far as I can see, although of course I'm no medical man.'

'Which is more than ...'

'Baker, let the major eat in peace.'

'Whatever it is, I'll find out so you may as well tell me now, sergeant,' John prompted.

'My mate Alfred's in here, sir, with dysentery and fever,' Baker divulged. 'He told me that most of our men have been sent on into the desert, sir. The blasted Turks are walking them to Turkey.'

'The Dorsets?'

'Left Baghdad two weeks ago, sir. Major Crabbe went with them.'

'If our sick are being well cared for here, we should go after the men who are heading into Turkey as soon as possible.' John lifted the spoon to his mouth. The yoghurt was thick with the consistency of clotted cream, the melon ripe and sweet, but his stomach cramped at the smell of the food. He dropped his spoon and the food untasted back into the bowl.

'Are you all right, sir?' Greening looked at him in concern.

'Not used to food, Greening. Good food, that is.' John poured himself a cup of water from a jug on the table.

'Right, you lot, to work on the wards,' the sergeant ordered. 'I'll be along presently to check you're making yourselves useful.'

The corporal and privates left.

'They've been put to work?' John asked.

'Taking care of our men. They're happy to do it, sir.'

John left the table. 'If the brigadier's here, I should talk to him.'

'You haven't eaten, sir.'

'I'll eat later.'

'There won't be anything laid out here again for four hours or more.' Greening picked up a piece of bread and handed it to him. 'You have to eat something, sir.'

'It's been a long time since I needed a nanny, Greening.'

'Someone has to look after you, sir. We wouldn't have made it to this place if it wasn't for you and we need you to lead us into whatever lies ahead.'

'If anyone brought us through, it was you, sergeant. You're

even capable of taking command when your CO decides to fall asleep for two days and nights.' John went to the door. 'Which way is the ward?'

British POW Ward, Turkish Hospital, Baghdad
July 1916

The brigadier's voice was so faint John had to lean forward to hear what he was saying.

'The Turks split the officers into four groups. The first two comprised all the high-ranking officers and generals, about a hundred in each. They left three weeks ago. They were given transport of sorts, principally mules and a few carts.'

'They were sent into Turkey?' John checked.

The brigadier nodded.

'They were allowed to take orderlies?'

'Two apiece. If you don't have two with you, take one from the convalescents here. The ranks stand a better chance of surviving if they're detailed to serve us.'

'The third group?' John asked.

'Junior officers and orderlies. They left Baghdad last week on foot. The fourth were mainly sick and wounded. Some ended up here some were sent elsewhere. I don't –'

It was so painful to hear the brigadier speak in his weakened voice, John interrupted him. 'I'll find out where they are and try to see them, sir.'

'I visited the men's camp every day before I ended up here with this blasted fever. The ranks were kept in the most appalling conditions. Open field, no water, no latrines, except what they could dig themselves, and they had no strength left for fatigues. I've since heard they've all been marched out to Turkey …'

'I'll check, sir,' John promised.

'Turks said the men were going to construct railways …'

'I've heard that too, sir.'

The brigadier managed a small smile. 'Your sergeant told me you've been sleeping for two days.'

'I have, sir.'

'From the look of you could do with another two months.'

'I'll sleep on the boat home when the peace treaties have been signed, sir.'

'Did you manage to save any of the men the Turks forced us to abandon on the march here?'

'Some, sir, not many. I found a few of them berths on steamboats. I hope they were cared for afterwards. Most of our time on the journey here was spent comforting the dying and burying the dead.'

The brigadier's eyes closed and his voice dropped even lower. 'Look after yourself, Mason. You'll be no good to our men if you succumb. We need all our doctors. Too many were sent downstream from Kut with our sick and wounded. No Englishman would treat a dog the way the way the Turks have treated ...'

John saw the German doctor enter the ward. He grasped the brigadier's hand.

'I'll talk to you again before I leave here, sir.' He rose and pushed the stool he'd been sitting on back beneath the brigadier's bed.

'Good to see you up, Major Mason, even if you are tiring my patient,' Dr Muller said.

'The brigadier's very weak,' John diagnosed.

'He was close to death when he was brought in here.'

'I didn't mean that as a criticism.' John looked around the ward. It was clean, as were the patients and the bedlinen. 'You run a fine hospital.'

'We do our best. It was easier before the war when we only had patients from the European civilian and local communities.'

'This is not a military hospital?'

'It wasn't until the war broke out. Although you wouldn't think it now from the number of soldiers we're treating. As for the brigadier, I would like to keep him here for at least another two weeks, three would be better. The American consul is attempting to get some of the British sick exchanged for the Turkish POWs your forces are holding in Basra, but the Turks are loath to release any of the British higher ranks because they make good bargaining chips.' Colonel Muller glanced at the clock on the wall. 'I usually have coffee and a roll in my office at this hour. I would be pleased if you would join me.'

John followed Muller. A coffee pot, cups, plates, knives, and a basket of cheese rolls stood on the desk.

'Please, help yourself,' Muller offered.

'Thank you.' John took a roll and set it on a plate.

'I meant what I said about offering you a post in this hospital. We are short of doctors. You wouldn't have to treat Turkish military personnel, only your own soldiers and local civilians. The men who arrived with you have proved themselves excellent orderlies. You could all stay here and sit out the rest of the war in safety with sufficient food and reasonable accommodation.'

'As opposed to the starvation rations and appalling accommodation our comrades will have to endure in Turkey.'

'You and I both know the Turk won't care for his prisoners, Major Mason. Your rank and file have been treated very badly in Baghdad and your officers not much better.' Muller picked up the up the coffee pot and poured two cups of coffee. 'What do you say to my offer? Will you accept my invitation to work alongside me and my colleagues?'

'If I thought our men who are being marched into Turkey would be cared for, I would be delighted to work alongside you, Colonel Muller. I'm grateful for your offer. I hope you understand why I cannot accept. I couldn't remain here well fed and in comfort for the remainder of the war while our troops suffer and die for want of medical attention in Turkey.'

'Spoken like an English officer and gentleman, Major Mason. Is there anything I can do for you before you leave?'

'I would be grateful for any drugs, food, equipment, blankets, or clothes you can spare.'

'I will see what I can find, Major. When are you thinking of leaving?'

John's hand shook as he picked up his coffee cup. 'As soon as possible, Colonel Muller. If not today, then first thing tomorrow morning.'

David Knight's Bungalow, British Military Compound, Basra July 1916

David Knight walked through the door of the bungalow he shared with Charles and shouted for his bearer.

'He's running your bath and I've told him we're dining out.' Georgiana leaned against the living room doorway and handed

David a glass of brandy.

'You look ravishing and beautifully clean after all the filthy bloody, broken, and battered bodies I've seen today.'

'Another steamboat came in from upstream?'

'Baghdad.'

'I'm surprised Dr Picard and Theo didn't send for me.'

'There were only British on board. Casualties from the Baghdad hospitals the American consul arranged to exchange for our Turkish prisoners. One of them told me he'd been treated by John in a makeshift medical tent on the march from Kut to Baghdad. John managed to get him a berth on a steamboat bound for Baghdad. Poor blighter has abscesses on his liver as well as dysentery which is why he was put on the list for exchange as soon as he reached the city.'

'Did he say how John was?' Georgiana was as close to her cousin John as she was to her brothers.

'Overworked, skeletally thin, putting the welfare of others before his own. All the things you'd expect of John.'

'He's had to play the eldest brother, and look after others his entire life, including my two incorrigible brothers. He's not likely to change now.'

David took the brandy she offered him. 'I feel guilty being here while he's God knows where, trying to look after thousands of starved, sick men.'

'Take your guilt to the bath and wash it away with the dirt.'

'You said we're dining out?'

'Charles has booked a table for the usual crowd in the Basra Club.'

'What time?'

'Nine o'clock.'

'We have three hours.' He winked. 'Want to go to bed first?'

'When you're clean, but not if you're going to fall asleep.'

He laughed, a deep chuckle that had first attracted her to him. 'You'll never allow me to forget that, will you?'

'No.'

'I'll have that bath and be with you in five minutes.'

Georgiana took her brandy, sat at the table, and looked around the room. There were no photographs, no books, only a box of cigarettes on the table. She presumed that Charles, like David, kept his personal possessions in his room. Military life! She'd never thought about it until she'd reached Basra and been invited into soldiers' quarters. It made little difference if the men were single or married. Some wives, like Angela, made an effort to create a home, but it wasn't easy when the choice of furniture and furnishings was taken from them.

'You look pensive. Penny for your thoughts.'

She glanced up David was watching her from the hall. 'They're worth more than that.'

'I did say five minutes.' David walked in, dressed only in a towel he'd slung around his waist.

'Your hair is wet and dripping down your back.'

He removed the towel and rubbed it over his head.

'If your or Charles's bearer walks in, they'd make assumptions about our relationship.'

'I rather think they're already doing that – and about Charles and Kitty come to that. Charles seems to like her.'

'That's an understatement.' She went into the bedroom.

He followed and closed the door. 'What were you thinking about?' He finished drying his hair and dropped the towel to the floor.

'The bungalow.'

'This bungalow?'

'As it happens, yes.' She unbuttoned her dress.

'I was hoping you were thinking about me and what a wonderful lover I am.'

She stuck her tongue out of him.

'You don't think I'm a wonderful lover?'

'You have your moments. You're also on your way upstream.'

'How do you know?'

'I know.'

'Charles?' he guessed.

'Georgie ...'

'If you're about to say something serious, don't.'

'Why not?' He climbed into bed.

'Because it will spoil the mood.' She slipped out of her dress and draped it over a chair.

'It's not serious – really serious. Just a thought about the future.'

129

'The future isn't something to consider when we're in the middle of a war.' She unclipped her garters and dropped them on top of her dress.

'You're a doctor –'

'You've noticed.' She sat on the edge of the bed and unrolled her stockings.

'You thinking of staying on in the Lansing after peace is declared?' He reached out and stroked her arm with the back of his finger.

'I'll let you know after the treaties have been signed.'

'Before John and Maud left India to marry here and go on to England – or at least that was their intention until the war messed up their plans – I went to his bachelor party in the mess. When John talked about the life he wanted for himself and Maud, it was the English village, the old Georgian house in a huge garden with an orchard, outbuildings, with plenty of room for his children, dogs, cats, ducks, pigs, and geese, a garden to sit and dream in after work was finished for the day …'

'Sounds like he was describing his parents' house, Southall.' Georgiana's eyes misted when she recalled the upbringing she'd shared with her cousins.

'Whether he was or wasn't, I envied him that dream, until I realised I didn't even have a girl to call my own and for a dream like that – house, domesticity, ducks, dogs, and so on – you need a woman you love who's equally in love with you.'

'Sounds like John's bachelor party turned maudlin.'

'Not the party, just me. Then when things became quite jolly in the mess and we moved on …'

'To the rags?'

'Women aren't supposed to know about rags.'

'Women who don't dine with their garrulous retired officer fathers and uncles might not. I'm not one of them.' She left the bed and dropped her stockings on the chair. 'Harry and Tom were expert at tapping into their elders' more risqué reminiscences.' She slipped off her chemise.

'No corset again, Dr Downe?'

'It's too damned hot to wear one.' She slid into the bed beside him.

'Marry me,' he whispered turning towards her and cupping her face in his hands.

'Not today.'

'I'm serious.'

'So am I.' She moved on top of him.

'Georgie …'

'Not now, David. As I said earlier, you're spoiling the mood.'

Chapter Twelve

The Smythes' bungalow, Basra
July 1916

'It's good of Charles to invite us to dinner, but frankly after the day I've had I'd rather have a quiet evening in with you.' Peter locked his arms around Angela's waist.

'We only have to stay for the meal. Charles will want to spend time with Kitty, Michael will want to get back to his Arab girl, and David will try to commandeer as much of Georgie's time as she will allow.'

'What is going on there?'

'Between Georgie and David? I've no idea.'

'Just wondered if it's serious between them.'

'It's none of our business.'

Peter smiled down at her. 'I'm just so happy with you I want the whole world to feel the same way.'

'You old romantic.' She tried to fall in with his mood, but all she could think of was that in another day he'd be gone again.

He sensed her thoughts and held her close, dropping a kiss on top of her head. 'We're almost there, Angela. With Maude in charge we'll take Baghdad in no time.

'And then?'

'With luck I'll be posted out of this damned country.'

'To where?'

'Wherever the army sees fit to send me.'

Even as she returned his kiss she supressed the disloyal thought that Peter's allegiance was more to the army than her. She'd known what she was getting herself into when she married a soldier. But now ... now there was Robin, and if she wasn't wrong, there would soon another small being for her to care for ...

Mesopotamia, west of Baghdad
July 1916

John stood as close to the fire Dira and Corporal Baker had built as he dared without risking singeing himself. The night seemed colder than usual and he was unsure whether it was because he had become accustomed to the scorching days or because the temperature had dropped as the hot season was drawing to a close. In which case the rains would soon start, bringing in their wake, winter. He shivered at the prospect.

'Here you are, sir, one of Dira's strong teas to set you up.' Sergeant Greening handed him a scalding tin mug. 'There are two sugars in there, sir, just the way you like it.'

'I'm surprised you remember, Greening. It's so long since we had sugar I've forgotten how many I take.'

'That German colonel was generous when it came to giving us rations for the journey, sir. Reckon we'll be better fed for the next few weeks than any other men in the British army in Mesopotamia.'

'Unless we stumble across an abandoned division, in which case our supplies will be gone in an hour.'

'It's not done to meet trouble halfway, sir, as my mother used to say. Dira's making dried beef stew with potatoes and vegetables. The bread's still soft and there's fig jam and olive oil for afters.'

'A veritable feast, Greening.' John wasn't joking. He'd eaten a greater variety of food since they'd reached Baghdad than he had done during the entire siege in Kut. Although he was so accustomed to starvation rations he was having difficulty keeping food down.

'A banquet we deserve, sir. We covered a lot of miles today.'

'I thought we'd see more evidence of our men passing this way than two Bedouin in British tunics.' John drank his tea. It tasted good. He only hoped it wouldn't leave him with a craving for sugar when the German colonel's stock ran out.

'If the brigadier was right about the Dorsets leaving Baghdad a month ago, the regiment will have long gone from here by now, sir,' Greening commented. 'If any of the men fell sick or died on the march they'd be in their graves.'

'If there wasn't anyone to dig one, they'd be left for the vultures, Greening. In which case we would have seen their bones.'

'Not a pleasant thought, sir. I wouldn't say it in front of the men, but I can't help feeling that we – I mean all of Townshend's men – are being deliberately punished by command for losing Kut.'

'You could be right; Townshend's surrender couldn't have pleased the Indian or the War Office.'

'Do you think they've forgotten about us, sir?'

'I hope not, Greening, for all our sakes.' He handed the sergeant his empty mug. 'Thank Dira for me. That was the best cup of tea I've had on the march. It's given me the energy to take a stroll before dinner.'

'Not too far, sir,' Greening warned.

'Have you seen anyone out there?'

'Private Jones thought he did.'

John laughed. 'That man jumps a mile every time he catches sight of his own shadow.'

'Whatever it was, Corporal Baker saw it too.'

'In that case I'll be careful.' John glanced at their Turkish guards. The six men appeared to be even more indifferent to the fate of their British charges than the soldiers who'd escorted them from Kut to Baghdad. They were circled around their fire which they'd lit some distance from Dira's. Judging by the noise they were making they were also well oiled by raki or Turkish brandy.

'Don't walk out of sight, sir,' Greening warned as John turned.

'I won't, but reassure the men that if there are any tribesmen snooping around our escort should see them off. That's what they're there for.'

'If the tribesmen only wanted to kill us I don't think Johnny Turk would be too bothered, sir. If we were wiped out they could pack up and return to Baghdad.'

John instinctively reached for his empty holster. 'I'd feel happier if I'd managed to hold on to my gun.'

Greening lifted his eyebrows.

'You haven't …'

'What you don't know can't hurt you, sir, and Johnny Turk's too handy with his fists for my liking. Especially when he thinks we're hiding something from him.'

'Where've you hidden …'

'Any problems, sir, shout for me, Dira, or Corporal Baker,' Greening answered loud enough for the Turks to hear. He lowered his voice to a whisper, 'our backs are broad enough to take a few Turkish lashes.'

'You've been ill-informed, sergeant. They beat their prisoners on the soles of their feet these days, or so I've been told.'

'That sounds nasty, sir.'

'You need a stronger word than nasty to describe it, Greening. Be back in a few minutes.' John walked away. When darkness closed around him he turned and studied the circle of light emanating from their campfire. Baker, Jones, Williams and Roberts were thrown in sharp relief as they sat huddled around Dira's cook fire, smoking Turkish cigarettes. Dira was stirring a pot suspended over the flames and Sergeant Greening was standing over them.

Their figures silhouetted against the flickering embers of thorn reminded him of the woodcut illustrations in his nursery edition of *Grimm's Fairy Tales*. It was a scene that had been played out in army camps throughout the centuries. One he could imagine the Greeks and Romans who'd invaded this same desert enacting it. He turned his back and faced the profound blackness. The air was so dense, so thick he felt as though he could almost rub it between his fingers.

The silence that punctuated the intermittent conversation of his companions and the guards was total and absolute. Not for the first time he reflected it was no accident that the three greatest world religions had been born in the desert. After more than two years soldiering in the wastelands, he suspected that even the sanest of men walking alone in the barren country would fall prey to hallucinations after a few hours, let alone the biblical forty days and forty nights.

When he judged himself far enough from the camp, he relieved himself. He was buttoning his trousers when he heard Sergeant Greening calling out to him. As he turned he glimpsed something large moving in the shadows to the left of their camp. Reality or hallucination?

He retraced his steps and shouted, 'Is anyone there?' When

there was no response, he repeated the question.

Sergeant Greening and Private Jones ran towards him.

'You see something, sir?' Greening asked.

'Not sure.' John pointed in the direction of the movement he thought he'd glimpsed.

'Yallah!' A Turkish guard joined them and pushed John and Greening back towards the tents with his rifle butt. He yelled to his comrades. Two of his fellow guards thrust branches of brush into their fire. Brandishing the flaming sticks they and the Turkish lieutenant in charge of the platoon rose and walked to the perimeter of the camp.

John continued to peer into the darkness but the more he looked the more he felt his eyes were playing tricks on him. He could no longer distinguish between ground and air and had the oddest sensation that he was perched on the edge of a precipice. One step and he'd hurtle into an abyss …

Then he heard it. A loud inhuman groan, resounding eerily from the black void. Seconds later there was a harsh crack.

'A whip?' Greening asked.

The lieutenant barked another command. The guards inched forward, reluctantly continuing their inspection. The lieutenant shouted again. A herd of camels charged out of the darkness and bore directly down on the Turks. The crack of a rifle shot was swiftly followed by another and another.

Greening yelled, 'Hit the ground, sir!'

John flung himself on to the desert floor. Greening landed next to him with a thud. Gunshots continued to be fired overhead. John turned his head and found himself staring into Greening's eyes.

'Bedouin by the sound of them,' Greening whispered as the assailants shouted to one another in Arabic. He raised his voice. 'Williams, Roberts, Baker, Dira, Jones?'

'Lying low, sir,' Baker's voice echoed over the ground.

'Any lower and we'd be under the worms, sir,' Jones added.

'If there are any bloody worms in this gravel.' Roberts added.

'Enough, Roberts. Stay put the lot of you,' Greening ordered.

'We weren't planning on going anywhere, sarge,' Baker called back as more bullets whistled overhead.

John heard camels snorting, and boots hitting the ground as the tribesmen dismounted. He raised his head again and saw a brown

Bedouin hand extended towards him.

'You can get up now, Major Mason. Your Turkish guards have all been killed.'

The desert between Baghdad and Turkey
July 1916

Mitkhal and John sat beside the fire Dira had lit in front of John's tent. The Bedouin who'd ridden in with Mitkhal were crouched around Dira's cook fire, sharing their food and the Turkish brandy and raki they'd found in the Turks' saddlebags with Sergeant Greening and John's orderlies.

'There's no need for you to continue on to Turkey, John,' Mitkhal advised. 'We can get you and your men back through the Turkish lines to the Tigris and Basra.'

'If my men want to go with you, I won't stop them, but I won't abandon our men who've been marched into Turkey. The way the Turks are treating them they'll be in dire need of medical care.'

'You're the only doctor who can give it to them?' Mitkhal questioned.

'There's a shortage of doctors. Townshend sent too many downstream with the sick.'

'They say Townshend didn't care what happened to his men. He was too busy being feted by the Turks at welcoming dinners. Apparently the Ottoman government has set aside a fine villa for him overlooking Constantinople.'

'Who's "they"?'

'Officers and men of the Relief Force.'

John nodded. He envied Mitkhal's freedom which enabled him to roam from British, through Bedouin, to Turkish encampments at will. 'Townshend might not have given a damn but I do. Have you seen many of our men in the desert?'

'Yes.'

'In bad condition?'

'The worst were bones, the ones who still breathed not much better. Your Indian troops, the ones that aren't Muslim, are being treated very badly. We buried twenty yesterday, not ten miles from here. Your rank and file aren't being cared for any better.'

'Who was looking after them?'

'No one and they had nothing. Everything they possessed had been stolen from them by their Turkish and Arab auxiliary guards. The sick die where they lie from starvation and dysentery.'

'If I'd been there …'

'You have food and medicines?' Mitkhal interrupted.

'Some.'

Mitkhal glanced at the two mule carts. 'Not enough for thousands of men.'

'But enough for a few, and every life is precious,' John countered.

'Harry always said your greatest fault was putting every other man before yourself.'

'You haven't mentioned our officers.'

'They are faring better. They have been given horses and mules to ride into Turkey to the prison camps.'

John leaped to his feet at the sound of camels' hooves.

'The other half of our party.' Mitkhal carried on smoking his cigarette.

'How many men do you have with you?'

'About a hundred, all Shalan's men.'

'Scavenging from the Turks?'

'Doing what we can to protect our allies – the British,' Mitkhal smiled. 'But a hundred men spread between Baghdad and Turkey can't accomplish a great deal against the Turks.' He tossed his cigarette butt aside and went to meet the men who'd joined them. A thickset heavily built man ordered his camel to kneel, slid to the ground, and lifted a child from his saddle.

'More Armenians?' Mitkhal called.

'We found three alive. But all are close to death.'

'Get them into my tent.' John looked at the young man holding the girl. 'Farik, isn't it?'

'I am surprised you recognise me, sir.'

'The time I spent in your master's house in Basra just before the war was memorable and happy. How are you, Farik?'

'As well as an Arab can be when his land is invaded by so many infidels, sir.'

'With luck we'll leave you in peace soon.'

'I hope so, sir.' He ducked under the tent flap and carried the child inside.

John shouted for Dira who came running with water bottles.

John followed Farik and examined the girl. 'She's just a baby, no more than three or four years old. Poor thing is skin and bone.'

'The Turks don't feed Armenians. Not even the babies.' Mitkhal took a water bottle from Dira, opened it, and handed it to John.

Farik left and returned carrying a middle-aged woman. She was unconscious and in the same deplorable starved and dehydrated state as the girl. Farik settled her on a blanket next to the child, before lifting a young woman from a man just outside the tent.

'All three, even the child, have been raped, and brutally, sir,' Farik informed John.

'Then I'll need to examine and stitch them. Dira, I'll need catgut, needle, more water and gruel, and that cream the colonel gave us to put on sunburn. And bring more lamps,' John added.

Mitkhal entered the tent after John had examined the women. 'Will they survive?'

'Difficult to say.' John moistened the woman's lips. 'They're dehydrated like everyone and everything else in this damned country, even the camel thorn. They're malnourished and exhausted, their skin is burned, and their feet like their genitals are cut to ribbons. The damage done to the child is significant, but there's no sign of venereal disease, which frankly is a miracle after being raped by the Turks. I'm sick of seeing the signs in soldiers who've been used by the guards.'

'We gave them sour camel milk. It was all we had,' Farik said apologetically.

'When did you find them?'

'First light this morning. They were with around twenty others in a dried-up wadi about six miles from here.'

'The others?'

'All dead,' Farik said shortly.

John continued to spoon feed the child water. Her eyes were closed but she was conscious enough to open her mouth and swallow. The two women were both comatose. Neither reacted when he wet their lips.

'Where did they come from?' John asked Mitkhal.

The Arab shrugged. 'Somewhere in Turkey.'

'The Turks are sending their own women and children on death marches as well as British soldiers?'

'They're not Turks, they're Armenians.' Mitkhal said as if that were explanation enough.

'I don't understand. Armenian, Turk – both peoples live in Turkey, don't they?'

'Armenians are Christians. The Turks want a Muslim-only country. They've been killing them so they can steal their lands, farms, and houses.'

'Openly?' John was appalled at the idea of the slaughter of an entire race.

'Everyone who lives in Turkey can't fail to see what's happening,' Mitkhal continued.

'So they just march them into the desert ...'

'I've heard that first they order all the Armenian men and boys over the age of fourteen to report to the authorities in a hall, church, or the market square of their town or village. Then they take them somewhere away from the houses and roads and shoot them.'

'What if the men and boys refuse to report?'

'They kill the family of the men who object.'

'How do you know?' John was having difficulty believing what Mitkhal was telling him.

'Furja's father heard it from the American consul in Baghdad. Mr Brissel and the American missionaries in Turkey have been trying to help the Armenians as well as the British prisoners of war. Once the Armenian men and boys are out of the way and can't protect their women and children, the Turks order the Armenian women and children to report. Then they march them into the desert. Some of the women have tried to give their children away, but the Turks shoot anyone who takes them – or in the case of American missionaries, deport them.'

'The Turks shoot the women and children as well?'

'No. Bullets cost money and there are so many of them it would prove expensive, so they just march them until they drop dead from hunger and thirst.'

'All the Armenians?' John sat back on his heels and stared at Mitkhal. He was still having difficulty comprehending the enormity of what Mitkhal was telling him. It didn't help that the Arab was speaking in the same deadpan, heavily accented unemotional way, he used in normal conversation.

'Not all, some of the pretty girls are kept by the Turkish officers, either for their own use or to sell as slaves. Furja bought two at the market last month because she felt sorry for them.'

'How many people are we talking about?' John asked.

'The American Consul thinks that a million have already been killed. He also said the Americans, who run missions in the towns where the Armenians lived, believe it's not the Turks who organised the killings but the Germans. It's possible. They are allies.'

John looked down at the small girl and the women.

'The desert is covered with bones,' Mitkhal said. 'British troops, your Indian sepoys, Armenian men, women, and children, and Turks too, when your army gets the chance to kill them. It's war.'

'War should not be waged against women and children,' John said feelingly.

Mitkhal heard whispering outside and lifted the tent flap. He nodded to the person he'd spoken to and dropped the flap. 'Can you do any more for the women?'

'Not until they wake and they can describe their symptoms.'

'Tomorrow you will move on?'

John shook his head. 'The women won't be ready to move on for a few more days. That's if they survive.'

'Then we'll stay with you, look around, see if we can find any more British soldiers for you to doctor. Can your orderly take over here for a while?'

'I'd rather stay.'

'I fetch you, sir, if one of the patients wakes,' Dira offered.

'I have a friend with me who would like to talk to you,' Mitkhal said.

'You are offering to translate?' John asked.

'If I need to.'

John left the tent. A short, slight man was sitting beside the small tent Dira had erected for his use. The man turned towards him. John saw that he had an eye patch covering one eye. The man rose to his feet.

'Harry ...'

John embraced his cousin.

142

Chapter Thirteen

The desert between Baghdad and Turkey
July 1916

John couldn't look anywhere but at Harry. It was as though he were afraid if he glanced away from his cousin for a second Harry would disappear.

'I'm real, John.'

'Why didn't you let me know you were alive?'

'Because ...' Harry hesitated and when he spoke again his speech was slow, halting, heavily accented, and John realised his cousin's lack of fluency was down to more than simply disuse. Harry was groping for words because English no longer came easily to his mind or his tongue. He was translating every word he said from Arabic. 'Because I haven't seen you.'

'I was in Kut. We had radio contact ...'

'With Basra HQ, not with the Arabs. Harry Downe is dead, John. When the Turks tortured me they killed him. The survivor is the creation of the Political Office, Hasan Mahmoud. He was born in a paper file in an office,' he held out his arms, 'but now he lives.'

John saw the bandaged stump at the end of Harry's right arm. 'How did you lose your hand?'

'The Turks removed it for me. Quarter inch by quarter inch.'

'Dear God, Ha –'

'Hasan,' Harry finished for him. 'It was painful, but not as painful as losing my eye. They burned that out with a hot iron. There are other scars on my body, but the worst are branded on my mind.'

'I can imagine.'

'I hope you can't. I wouldn't wish anyone to live through that pain, not even in imagination. There is no need to look at me like

143

that, John. The hurt is over. Now it seems like a bad dream. Unfortunately one I still occasionally relive in my nightmares.'

'How did you escape?'

'I didn't. When the Turks believed they'd killed me they handed me to one of their Arab auxiliaries to bury. The auxiliary was Mitkhal. He'd followed me into the camp and waited his chance to get me out. It was Harry Downe's bad luck that he was too far gone to be rescued.'

'But now you know who you are ...'

Harry shook his head and laughed. A sound that was all the more poignant because John thought he'd never hear it again. 'Harry Downe is dead and will remain dead, John.'

'The army wouldn't expect you to serve again. With your injuries you'd be invalided out and returned to England. At the moment your parents, Michael, and Georgie all believe you to be dead.'

'Michael and Georgie have seen me.'

'You talked to them?'

Harry shook his head. 'I was boarding a boat with Mitkhal, Shalan, and Furja in Basra just after Kut fell. Michael and Georgie were watching from a window in Abdul's. I know they recognised me.'

'They didn't try to stop you.'

'There was no time. They saw me as our boat was casting off.'

'You'll look for them when the war is over?'

'I'll write to them and my parents and ask them to try to understand why I've chosen to live the way I have.'

'Understand? I don't understand why you're walking away from everything and everyone you've ever known, and you're here in person to explain it to me. Is it Furja and the children, because you could ...' John faltered.

'Take them to Clyneswood? Can you imagine the expression on my parents' faces if the parlour maid ushered me and my family into the drawing room? Especially if we were all wearing Arab robes.'

'I remember you telling me when you married Furja that you promised Ibn Shalan you'd never take her to live among Europeans.'

'It's not just Furja and the children, although they mean more to me than anything in this world. I'm not sacrificing anything to be Bedouin, John. Sometimes think I was born Arab. That's why I was always in trouble when I was growing up. I find it easier to live with the tribe, than to live with English people – particularly those in the school we attended. The tribe forgive me my faults.'

He laughed softly again. 'Most of the time I even manage to keep the tribe's rules, something I never did when I was living with my father, or after I took a commission in the army. And, yes, I promised Furja and her father that I would remain with the tribe and bring up my children respecting their ways, but being Bedouin and being accepted by the tribe – it feels as though I've come home.'

'But you can't turn your back on your family,' John protested.

'My old family. I already have, John. Even if they don't understand why I've chosen to live as Arab when they find out what I've done, I hope they will in time.'

'I'm trying to understand. But …' John fought a tide of emotion welling inside him. 'I can't bear the thought of losing you.'

'You'll never lose me, John. You, me, and Charles. What we shared – the brutality of English public school – all those nights of drinking and fun – the complete insanity of desert warfare – they'll stay with us forever.'

'It is a stupid, meaningless war,' John agreed.

'First it was "secure the oilfields". That at least I could understand, pure greed on Churchill's part: he didn't want to pay for oil to fuel our ships. Then it was "let's order Force D to go upstream and take Baghdad because the news from the Western Front isn't good and civilians need something morale boosting to read in the morning newspapers while they consume their kippers and boiled eggs." And now?' he stared at John through his remaining eye. 'A lot of good men have starved to death trying to hold on to Kut, a town that had little strategic value other than as a buffer to Baghdad. As if that isn't enough, those men are now being ground into bones to carpet the floor of a desert they should never have been sent to in the first place.'

'I'll not argue with you. Not while I spend most of my time easing men out of pain and life. When you write to your parents and Michael and Georgie, will you write to Charles?'

'I'd rather you told him I was alive. When the war's over you might enjoy passing on some good news. That's if Charles considers the existence of Hasan Mahmoud good news.' Harry laughed. 'I loved him dearly but he can be a stuffed shirt.'

The 'loved' wasn't lost on John. Harry's pronouncement had brought the realisation that the Harry he knew had gone forever and the man sitting beside him really was someone else.

'What are you doing for money? You must be owed a fortune in back pay, and if you're determined to keep Harry Downe dead, his widow is entitled to a pension.'

Hasan grinned in amusement. 'Can you imagine Furja calling into the paymaster to claim a pension? "Marriage certificate?"

"We never had one, but Harry Downe did lift me onto his horse and ride me around my father's camp three times".'

'You've never been serious about anything in your life.'

'I have some sovereigns in a box in the bank in Basra, but my father-in-law has more money than I or my family are likely to need for several lifetimes. Just one thing, if you do tell Charles that I live on as Hasan Mahmoud, swear him to secrecy so this happy Bedouin can carry on living his undistinguished life.'

'Are you really happy, Harry – Hasan?' John asked seriously.

'I'm as happy as a man can be with these.' Harry indicated his eye patch and the stump on his arm. 'My twin girls, Aza and Hari, are a delight. My son, Shalan, is four months old and grows stronger every day. And,' he raised his eyebrows, 'as I enjoy making babies with my wife I hope for many more children.'

'You're living in the Karun Valley?'

'At the moment Furja is with Shalan in his house in Baghdad. When I leave here I will return there; after that, who knows where we'll go. The desert, Basra, Baghdad, Amara, Qurna, my father-in-law has properties in most of the towns in Iraq.'

'Iraq?'

'It's what the Arabs call Mesopotamia. They've outgrown the Biblical name.'

'Is Shalan's house in Baghdad as comfortable as his house in Basra?'

'Of course, you honeymooned there with Maud. Shalan's house in Baghdad is larger and even more comfortable.'

'Yet you live there under Ottoman rule.'

'It may surprise you to know that for the ordinary people who

146

haven't annoyed any officials, there isn't a great deal of difference. The British courts may be fairer in the areas under British rule but only if no bribe-taking locals are employed in them. As for food and money – both are always in short supply among the poor, whoever rules the land.'

John was afraid of what the answer might be but he had to ask the question. 'So whose side are you on now?'

'The side of Furja, my children, Shalan, and the tribe, and at present they fight for the British.' Hasan took the cigarette John offered him, lifted a stick from the fire, and lit it. 'Shalan accepted more guns from the British just before Kut fell. In exchange he promised to keep the Karun Valley clear of Turks and to look out for, as far as possible, the British POWs in Turkish hands. Securing the Karun Valley against the Turks is easy, just a question of leaving enough men in the area. The POWs are another matter.'

'The Turks have treated all of us: ranks, sepoys, and officers abominably.'

'I watched British officers and men being marched through the bazaar in Baghdad. I doubt many will survive to see the end of the war. But Shalan has ordered all the men in the tribe to do whatever they can to help the British and give the officers in charge of the men, money, and food.'

'The Turks allow you to help the POWs?'

'The Turks employ Arab auxiliaries to do their work for them. They assume all Arabs are as brutal as them. Most are. Shalan's men are not – to the British anyway.'

'In the bazaar – did you see anyone we knew?'

'Crabbe, Grace, Bowditch. Did Mitkhal tell you that we can get you and your men back through the Turkish lines to Basra?'

'He told me.'

Hasan stared balefully at John through his good eye. 'You won't go, will you?'

'I won't stop my men from going back with you if they want to risk passage through the lines …'

'With Mitkhal as a guide there'd be very little risk.'

'It's out of the question for me. You said it yourself. Our men are in dire straits. They need medical care. I'm a doctor. It's my duty …'

'Duty!' Hasan repeated. 'Do you never think of yourself?'

'All the time when I'm not needed by anyone, at the moment it happens I am. And you're a fine one to talk, giving up your country, your family your people ...'

'My people are my wife and children. I love them and want to spend as much time as possible with them. That's hardly the act of an unselfish person.'

John frowned. The mention of a wife had reminded him of Maud. 'You said you left Basra after the fall of Kut.'

'I did.'

'Did you hear anything of Maud?' John tried to make his question sound casual. It didn't.

'I wasn't moving in British military circles.'

'You don't know if she'd had her child?'

'No, but as she was heavily pregnant when I last saw her before the battle of Nasiriyeh I presume she did. You told me when I left Kut that you were divorcing her.'

'Not easy to arrange in wartime. I'm wondering if she's all right.'

'You know Maud. She'll be fine. Next time you see her she'll probably be waltzing on a general's arm, if not as his wife, then his mistress.'

'I hope so, pregnancy's rarely easy on a women and it can take its toll in this climate. Which reminds me, Sergeant Greening's wife was pregnant and by now he should have has a son or daughter in Basra. If anyone should go back it's him.'

'Didn't he marry Mrs Perry's maid Harriet?'

'He did.'

'You'll talk to your men and tell them of our offer to get them to Basra?'

John glanced at the other fire, where the laughter was growing louder and the jokes more ribald, at least the ones he could understand among the British. 'I will, tomorrow morning when they're sober.'

'It's late, old friend. Time I fetched my blanket roll. We'll speak tomorrow.'

'I'll ask Greening to put up a tent for you.'

'I like sleeping under the stars, as do the men with me.'

'Really?' John was sceptical. 'With no mosquito net and the

sand flies and bugs biting every inch of skin they can prise their jaws into?'

'I've learned to ignore them.'

Dira left the tent. 'Major Mason, sir?'

'Coming, Dira.' John rose to his feet. 'See you in the morning, Ha ... Hasan.'

Harry embraced John, kissing him on both cheeks, in the fashion of the Arabs. It was a spontaneous, natural gesture, and more evidence to suggest that Harry Downe was dead and Hasan Mahmoud lived.

John watched Harry walk away, his robes billowing around his feet, his kafieh pulled low, covering most of his face. He watched him greet the men he'd travelled with. Someone handed him a bottle of Turkish brandy, Greening a pack of cigarettes. Hasan sat on the ground alongside the men. The conversation and the laughter escalated.

John felt as though he'd just lost his cousin all over again. Harry was only a few feet away yet he was already missing him.

Sick tent, the desert between Baghdad and Turkey
July 1916

John crouched beside the child and laid his hand on her head. It was cool. He spooned more water into her mouth and she swallowed without opening her eyes.

'The two ladies are burning with fever, sir.'

John laid his head first on one forehead then the other. 'You're right, Dira, but the Arabs said that they found them in the desert. Chances are they've been forced to walk in the heat of the day for days if not weeks. The high temperature could be the result of sunburn.'

'And if it's not, sir?'

'The treatment is the same. Fetch my medical bag and the morphine, please.'

'And if our own men need it, sir? We haven't a large stock.'

'We give the drugs to anyone who needs them, on a first come first served basis, Dira.'

'Even Turks, sir?'

'Even Turks. And I need to examine these patients; as they've been raped they may need stitching.'

'I'll get the phials and syringe, sir.'

Dira returned with the equipment. John opened his bag and prepared to examine the child.

'Permission to speak, sir.'

'When have I ever refused you permission, Dira?' John asked.

'Lieutenant-Colonel Downe's orderly, sir, Mitkhal ...'

'Best to think of Lieutenant-Colonel Downe as dead, Dira. The man here is Hasan Mahmoud.'

'Yes, sir. Mitkhal told me he was an Arab. Sorry, sir.'

'No need to apologise, his sudden appearance has been a shock to us all.'

'What I wanted to say, sir, is that now that our Turkish guards are all dead, Mitkhal offered to take us through the Turkish lines and back to Basra. He said that you told him you'd have no objection to any of us going with him.'

'I wouldn't, Dira.'

'You'd come with us?'

'No, Dira.'

'Even without the guards you're going to follow our men into Turkey, sir?'

'They need medics, Dira.'

'They need medical assistants and orderlies too, sir.'

'I won't ask you or the rest of the men to stay with me, Dira. This is your chance to return to base and from there possibly home. You must be due leave.'

'I won't go without you, sir, and neither will the others. We all talked about Mitkhal's offer. You say the men need medics – they need good orderlies too.'

'You're the best, but I can train others in Turkey.'

'You can try and persuade the others to go with the Arabs if you want to, sir, but I'm staying with you, so you can stop trying to talk me out of it.'

'I will, and thank you, Dira.' John offered his orderly his hand and Dira shook it. 'I'm overwhelmed by your sacrifice.'

'It's no sacrifice to stay where you're needed, sir.' Dira unscrewed the cap on the water bottle, filled it, and moistened the young girl's lips.

Two hours later John left the tent that housed the sick women. The Arabs who'd ridden in with Mitkhal had rolled themselves into their blankets and were lying around Dira's cook fire. Sergeant Greening was standing outside the men's tent, smoking. John joined him.

'Can I get you anything, sir?' Greening asked as John approached.

'No, thank you, sergeant.'

'The Turks had plenty of brandy and raki, the Arabs too, and theirs was better quality.'

'You didn't save me some?' John asked in amusement.

Greening held up a flask. 'I did, sir.'

'Thank you, but you can drink it for me. The women the Arabs brought in might need medical attention in the night.'

'They're still alive, sir?'

'Against the odds. I spoke to Dira earlier about Mitkhal's offer to smuggle any of you who wanted to go, back through the Turkish and British lines to Basra.'

'He's staying, sir. We all are.'

'You have a wife and by now a child in Basra, Greening.'

'And I'm looking forward to hearing from them once the Turks put us in a prison camp and I have an address to send her.'

'That's insanity, Greening. If Mitkhal says he can get you through the lines he will. You've a chance to see your family ...'

'I won't leave you and the others, sir. Not while I'm needed, and I dread to think what state the survivors of Kut's garrison will be in when they reach Turkey. They'll need medical care and fit men to look after them and begging your pardon, sir, but I'm fitter than you and the rest of the orderlies. If there's heavy lifting to be done, including live or dead bodies, I'm your man.'

'Is there nothing I can say to you, Greening, that will persuade you to go with Mitkhal?'

'Nothing, sir. I'm staying with you and the rest of the boys and that's that. Mitkhal said the Arabs will move out tomorrow to scout around. Will they take the women with them?'

'They're not fit to be moved, and won't be for another few days, that's if they survive.'

'So what do we do, sir? Sit here and wait for the women to get better and the Turks to turn up.'

'As we can't be sure where the Turks were taking us, I can't think of a better plan. Can you?'

Chapter Fourteen

David and Charles' bungalow, Basra
July 1916

Georgiana slipped the key David had given her into the lock of the bungalow he shared with Charles. She muffled the sound of the door click with her glove and crept inside. Charles's bearer, Chatta Ram, was slumped snoring in a chair in the hall. She stepped out of her shoes, stole past him, and tiptoed down the corridor to David's room. She entered, closed the door quickly, and leaned against it.

David's bearer hadn't drawn the curtains and moonlight streamed in through the windows, silvering the mosquito net and bedsheets. David was lying on his side, his right arm under his head, his breath soft and even. His blond hair was the same hue as the moon, his features as regular and fine as a Greek god's. Not for the first time his beauty took her breath away.

She walked over to the chair, slipped off her cloak, and undressed. Naked she went to the bed, turned back the sheet, and slipped in beside him.

David opened his eyes and stared disorientated at her. 'Georgie?' he mumbled groggily.

'You were expecting someone else?'

He closed his eyes and stretched out. 'I live in hope of beautiful women climbing into my bed, but you'll do.' He moved close wrapped his arm around her and pulled her back against his chest. 'Ow! What was that for?' he demanded when she kicked his shin with her heel.

'For suggesting "I'll do".'

'I take it back. You're the most stupendous, gorgeous beautiful woman in the world ... ow!' he exclaimed when she kicked him again.

'And that's for lying.' She turned to face him.

'How did you get past Chatta Ram? He's supposed to sound the alarm if someone breaks in, especially bossy female doctors. You could have walked in on a private moment between me and ...'

'And?' she raised her eyebrows.

'A passing siren?'

'Even if there was one, Charles's bearer was too tired to care.' He kissed her. 'What's the time?'

'I left the hospital at three. Must be about half past by now.'

'The boat's leaving the wharf for upstream at nine.'

'Which allowing for travelling and packing time leaves us about four hours.'

'For what?'

'I was hoping you'd think of something.' She returned his kiss.

'As you're lying naked in my bed, I can think of one way to dispel boredom.'

'The problem with you is you're all words and no action, and this is not a time for talking.'

She moved on top of him and soon all that could be heard in the room was their mingled breathing.

The Smythes' bungalow, Basra
July 1916

Angela was already awake when she heard Peter knock the dressing room door. She left the bed and unlocked it. Peter stood before her, holding a pillow over his ears.

'Do babies ever do anything except cry?' he demanded.

'Lots of things,' Angela whispered, keeping her voice low lest she disturb Robin even more. 'Sorry he woke you, darling. The nursemaid will soon have him back to sleep.' Even as Angela spoke the baby fell silent.

'Every time that happens I wonder if the nurse has smothered him.'

'She knows that if she kills Robin she'll be out of a job.'

Peter laughed. 'I'll remember that the next time the baby suddenly goes quiet. I'm getting a glass of water. Do you want one?'

'Please.' Angela snuggled back under the sheet.

Peter soon returned and handed her a glass. 'There were a

couple of pieces of ice left in the bucket, so it's cold.'

'Thank you. It's been marvellous having you all to myself the last couple of weeks.'

'Because I bring you iced water in the middle of the night?'

'Among other things. I'm going to miss you.'

'I'm going to miss you too. The crazy thing is going back to the front seems like returning to normality which says a lot for the way I've been living since this war started.'

'I was only thinking the other day that we've never talked about the future, Peter,' she said seriously.

He sat on the bed next to her. 'I don't mean this in a morbid way but you married a soldier against your brother's advice, sweetheart, and just like every other soldier fighting this war I can't guarantee I even have a future beyond this hour, and possibly not even that long. When the guns start blazing I have to go wherever my superiors order me.'

'You have to survive this war. You simply have to,' she reiterated fiercely as though she could keep him alive by sheer force of will.

'I promise you I'll do my best.' He sat on the bed next to her.

'And when the war finishes, what then? For us I mean, Peter.'

'As I'm neither trained nor fit for anything else, I suppose I'll carry on soldiering.'

'Here?'

'Wherever the Indian Office posts me, which in all probability will be India. Why the questions?'

'I love you, I always want to be with you, and I thought that ...'

'What?' he persisted when she didn't finish her sentence.

'I think I must have spent too much time talking to Clary. As soon as Tom discovered that he was being invalided out of the Force because of his recurring spells of fever they started making plans. Tom's father owns an estate in the English countryside. Apparently there are several cottages on it and Tom and Clary intend to settle down in one and start a family ...'

'And live on fresh air?' Peter interrupted. 'Bills for food and fuel arrive even in a cottage you're not paying rent on.'

'Tom's father offered Tom a doctor's post in a clinic he owns not far from the estate, at least until he's recovered his health.'

'Tom is a doctor. He has a profession to fall back on. I was talking about this with Charles Reid only this morning. For regular soldiers like Charles and me there is no choice. No one wants to employ a retired soldier simply because there's no call for warfare in the civilian world.' He took her glass from her, set it on the bedside table, and reached for her hand. 'Would it be so terrible to spend the rest of your life in married quarters as the wife of a serving soldier?'

'No, of course not.' She squeezed his hand.

'What brought on this "cottage and family" dream?' he asked. 'Was it really Clary or is it having a baby to care for?'

'Partly the baby,' she admitted. 'I know Robin cries at night, but he really is a very good baby and ...'

'He's not ours, Angela, he's Maud's,' Peter reminded. 'And knowing Maud and how fickle she can be I wouldn't put it past her to dance back into Basra someday soon and reclaim him. So please, as much for Robin's sake as yours, don't get too attached to the child.'

'That's easy to say, but difficult to do when he looks up with those enormous trusting blue eyes and wraps his tiny fingers around yours.'

'You already regard him as yours, don't you?'

'I'm fond of him,' Angela admitted. She was good deal more than fond of him but aware of Peter's feelings about the child, and his determination to keep his affection for their own children – when they had them – she was wary of saying more.

Peter left the bed, dropped a kiss on her cheek and went to the dressing room. 'There's time for another couple of hours' sleep. You'll lock me in?'

'If I must.'

He looked back at her. 'I love you, Mrs Smythe.'

'Love you too.'

'I'm sorry I have no father with a landed estate like John and Tom's ...'

'I don't want a landed estate, just a ...'

'Cottage with roses round the door?' He ran his fingers through his thick red curls, brushing his hair away from his face. Then he grinned at her. The same boyish grin that had won her heart the first time she'd seen him at a ladies' evening in the Basra mess. 'Roses wither in winter, sweetheart, and in my experience, most

156

English cottages are damp, draughty, and have chimneys that smoke terribly.'

'None of which would matter as long as you were inside.'

'We'll talk again when the war is over and the Indian Office has decided what to do with me.' He kissed her lips and held her close for a moment before going into the dressing room. As she locked the door behind him she heard Robin cry again. Leaving her slippers at the side of the bed, she left the room quietly, lest Peter heard her and guess where she was headed.

The desert between Baghdad and Turkey
July 1916

A thin grey light on the horizon heralded the advent of dawn as John left the hospital tent. He stood in front of the flap, shivered in the cool wind, and looked around. The Arabs were already awake. They'd gathered around Dira's cook fire to drink the tea Corporals Jones and Williams had brewed and were dispensing in tin mugs. He studied the men's shadowy silhouettes, black against the breaking light, but failed to pick out Mitkhal's massive figure.

'I told Williams and Jones they could give the Arabs sugar, sir,' Baker handed John a mug. 'After what they did for us yesterday … I thought they'd earned it.'

'They did, Baker.' John agreed. 'As for the sugar, better it's used than left for the flies. They always get into the sacks no matter how tightly we fasten them.'

'They do, sir. I fished out a fair number of bodies last night. It was too dark to see them this morning.'

'So I'm probably drinking a few sand flies.' John squinted into his mug but the light wasn't good enough to see if anything was floating on the top.

'And mosquitoes, I should think, sir, the way they were biting last night. If there's a lump in your mouth chances are it's more likely to be a fly than a tea leaf.'

The sun suddenly inched high enough over the horizon to flood the desert with soft golden light. A line of four camels moved towards them from the horizon. John squinted, but because they were directly in front of the sun it was impossible to make out more than the wavering outline of beasts and riders.

'Probably Mitkhal, sir, he went out to scout a couple of hours ago and said he'd be back at dawn.'

'Mitkhal left the camp?'

'He said he wanted to make sure no Turks were about to disturb us at breakfast sir. Roberts is making bully beef stew and we've the last of the bread to go with it.'

'Sounds a good solid meal to set us up for whatever the day brings.' John walked ahead to meet Mitkhal. Harry – Hasan, as he was forcing himself to think of him, was riding alongside him. Mitkhal joined the other Arabs but Harry rode his camel to meet him. When he reached him, he pulled up the beast and slid down.

'Good morning, Hasan.'

'Good morning, John.' Hasan smiled.

'I wish I could ride a camel the way you do.'

'You'd manage it if you had Mitkhal whipping you every time you made a mistake.'

'Whipping?' John smiled back.

'With words, which can hurt a sensitive being as much as leather thongs.'

'Tea, sir.' Greening handed Hasan a mug.

'Thank you.' Hasan took it and beckoned John aside. 'Turks will be here in about two or three hours.'

'How many?'

'We counted about fifteen Turks, and twenty Arab auxiliaries. Bakhtairi Khans, and they can be bastards.'

'Then we'll have to be careful not to give them any reason to lose their temper with us.'

'They're escorting about a hundred British ranks. All look as though they're hospital cases. They abandoned four men in the first ten minutes we watched them. We took them to a local tribe who promised to care for them. They'd better, we paid them enough, but I'll be checking on them again when I pass back that way.' Hasan squatted on the ground in the position peculiar to Arabs. John perched on his heels next to him and offered him a cigarette.

'They're definitely headed this way? They're not likely to take a detour?'

'While you remain camped here, there's no way they'll miss you. Mitkhal and I talked. He suggested that he stay here with a

158

couple of our men and tell the Turks you were attacked by tribesmen who left the women after they were driven out, but,' Hasan chuckled and John again caught a glimpse of Harry. 'Not before the tribesmen had killed all your Turkish guards, although they didn't manage to kill all the Arab auxiliaries. That story shouldn't arouse suspicions as several of my father-in-law's men are working for the Turks. That way Mitkhal and the men who stay with him can remain with you until you reach Turkey. They'll do their best to curb the excesses of the Turks and the Bakhtairi Khans but it would be better if you didn't annoy either group.'

'We'll try not to, but what about the Armenian women? Will the Turks try to kill them?'

'They'll want to but they won't dare if you tell them they're under British protection.'

'And you?'

'I doubt any Turk would recognise me, but they might recognise the signs of torture. A missing eye could be a murderer's punishment. A missing hand the mark of a thief that the average Turk sincerely believes gives him the right to remove the other hand. So I prefer to avoid the company of the Ottomans; besides, I've been away from Furja and our children quite long enough.'

'The happy family man?' John questioned.

'Very happy.' Hasan took the stick he used to spur on his camel and started drawing in the sand. 'When this is over, one way or another ...'

'You think the Turks will win?' John broke in.

'I don't know and I don't much care. I think the Ottoman Empire is crumbling, but like an old lion with one rotten tooth it might have a bite or even two left.'

'So many men are dead.'

'At the beginning of this war I thought the Indian Office wanted to colonise Mesopotamia with sepoys who'd retired from the Indian Army. I even remember a civil servant saying that as the locals were nomads they'd welcome industrious Indians moving into the country as they'd be prepared to work the land and grow crops for the locals. There was talk of resettling "surplus" Punjabi population here. Now I wonder if the British have any plans for this country beyond taking it. Look around you. How in hell can anyone govern this wasteland? No one really knows how many people live here or, which tribe owns what in the way of land and buildings. The climates so foul it's as much as anyone can do to survive one more day. The only thing of any value here, besides whatever treasure might have been buried in the remains of ancient cities and civilizations is the oil, and the Anglo-Persian oil company has laid claim to that. Even if the British take the place – at God only knows what cost in lives and blood – they'll have no more luck governing it and extracting taxes from the Arabs than the Turks did.'

'That won't stop the India Office and the British Government from trying to take the place to rule it.'

'Probably not.' He looked at John. 'I'll be riding out with most of the men. I have no idea when I'll see you again.'

'Or even if we will meet again, but let's not get maudlin.'

'I'll try not to. When you see Georgie and Michael ...'

'If ...'

'No, when,' Hasan corrected. 'Tell them how much they both mean to me, and if you're all in Basra take them to my father-in-law's house. If I am anywhere close by I will come and see you.'

'I doubt I could find the house again. I only went to and from the place by boat.'

'So you did. If you can't find it, go to Abdul's. He'll tell you where it is and I'm sure he'll remember you. After all, you did perform the medical checks on his girls.'

'I'll ask him.'

'And give Charles my regards and tell him not to be such a stuffed shirt.'

'You think he'll listen to me?'

'No. And last of all, tell my parents I regret being such a disappointment to them, but try to explain I'm living my life the way I want.'

'You'll never be a disappointment to anyone who knows you – Hasan.' John hugged his cousin. Behind them the Arabs were already mounting their camels. Hasan climbed on to his, hit it with a stick. The beast rose and Hasan followed the rest of the men out of the camp.

John watched until the camel train was no more than a series of specks on the horizon. Only then did he turn and retrieve the tin mugs they'd used to drink tea.

He saw the rough sketch Harry had drawn in the sand. A cartoon of three schoolboys holding up glasses of foaming beer and smoking cigars.

He looked back to the horizon. School seemed so long ago, as if it had been experienced by another person a world away, but it was good to know that a little of that schoolboy still existed, not only in him, but Hasan, even if Harry was to all intents and purposes dead.

Chapter Fifteen

Shatt al-Arab
August 1916

Peter and Charles stood side by side on the deck of the steamer and watched the flat roofed mud brick buildings of Qurna loom slowly into view. Practically every building they could see had a roof terrace complete with awnings, tables, and chairs set out among potted palms and bushes. Black-robed women sat sewing in the shade, while men drank tea and gossiped and children played at their feet.

'I wish I was up there in one of those shady spots with Angela and a bottle of iced wine,' Peter said wistfully.

'I have a bad case of deja vu,' Charles grumbled, 'Maybe it's the optimist in me but I'd hoped I'd seen the last of this place when I was shipped downstream after the Battle of Nasiriyeh. Granted, I have no memory of the place then because I was too far gone from wounds and fever to even know I was here but I swear I sensed it.'

'This town is all some men are going to see of the Basra Wilayat.' David joined them. 'I've just ordered fifteen sappers and two doctors to the hospital. The sickness rate is alarming. At the rate we're going there'll be no one left to march into Baghdad, provided of course we ever get near the place.'

Charles eyed the men on the lower deck. 'What does the Indian Office expect when they send us so many raw recruits? When are they going to realise six weeks in India to "thin the blood" isn't enough to prepare untrained boys for war.'

'You've been delegated responsibility for supplies, not manpower. So don't borrow another officer's worry.' Peter slapped Charles on the back, 'If my memory serves me right, there wasn't a bad officers' mess in Qurna. They may even have palatable whisky on offer to cheer you up.'

'And fresh river ducks,' David murmured. 'Roasted, with pomegranate sauce and sautéed potatoes. I'll meet you there after I've delivered the sick to the hospital.

'There's no necessity for you to leave the wharf, Knight.' Perry strode along the deck. 'You can hand over the sick on the dock. I've sent a message to the hospital requesting ambulances and doctors to receive our patients. We'll be here long enough to offload them and refuel the boat and not a moment longer.'

'Yes, sir.'

Perry continued walking along the deck, Cleck-Heaton hovering in his wake, an undersized tug lapping behind an oversized liner.

'Is he wearing a brigadier's uniform?' stared at Perry.

'Apologies, I should have warned you. The Force has been so decimated by sickness, it's resulted in mass promotion of the unworthy. Perry was posted brigadier yesterday evening.' Charles couldn't stand Perry and was wary of mentioning him in conversation lest someone pick up on just how deep his dislike of the man actually ran.

'May as well surrender to the Turks now,' Peter muttered.

'We may be able to use him as a buffer between us and Turkish bullets.' David suggested.

'He was my CO in Basra before the war. The one thing I can tell you about Perry is that he never – and I mean never – stands in any location where bullets are likely to fly. When battle starts, he'll be dug into a nice comfortable hidey-hole at the furthest possible point from the front line.' Peter reached for his cigarettes.

'First man to track down Perry's lair gives me the location so I can use it for fever cases,' David chuckled. 'If we can't get the useless being one way we'll get him another.'

Charles smiled. 'Glad to have you with us, Major Knight.'

'Glad to be here, Major Reid.'

'The musketeers. One for all and all for one,' Peter chanted.

Charles looked over the side at the sun-baked wharf and the thick clouds of flies hovering over clumps of rotting vegetation. He'd spoken earlier about sailing downstream. He hadn't lied, he didn't remember that journey, but he did remember the last time he'd been on a steamboat heading upstream. He'd been with John and Harry. The original three musketeers – and that memory was almost too painful to bear.

Desert outside Baghdad
August 1916

'This is bloody disgraceful.' John stood in the doorway of the reed hut and looked down at the four naked skeletal men, who lay inches deep in their own filth on the dirt floor. The eyes of the one lying closest to him flickered open.

'Get water, Dira,' he ordered.

Dira was out of the doorway before John finished speaking. The Turkish captain who'd assumed command over John's unit and Mitkhal's auxiliaries took his place.

'We have no time to waste here, Major Mason. We have to move on.'

'I and my orderlies are not going anywhere,' John contradicted. 'Not until we've ministered to these men.'

The captain pulled out his gun.

'Shoot them and I'll make sure the world knows about it.'

'You are a prisoner ...'

'A prisoner of the Turks and your Arab auxiliaries, some of whom can speak English. We are on the edge of a village. Kill me and there'll be witnesses. Or do you intend to kill them too?'

'These men are as good as dead.'

'These men fought bravely and deserve to be treated with dignity. Allow me to treat them, and look after the female patients in my care, and I will make sure you are known to the British authorities as a good and admirable man.' When the captain hesitated, John added, 'There are many Turkish prisoners, officers included, in British hands.'

'You have,' the captain held up all the fingers on one hand, which John knew from experience meant five minutes.

John shook his head. 'We have to stop here and make camp, now.'

'There is an hour of daylight left. We can travel a good distance in that time.'

'I won't risk moving these sick men.'

'I didn't think I would have to remind you again, Major Mason.

I'm in charge of this party.'

'And I didn't think I'd have to remind you, captain, the garrison of Kut surrendered to your countrymen on the understanding that your forces would accept full responsibility for the care and welfare of our men.'

'Your men ... not women and children.'

'The women and child travelling with us have been displaced by the war. They have nowhere to go.'

'They could have stayed in any village we passed through.'

John met the captain's glare. 'As slaves?'

'They would be fed and have a roof over their head.'

'And no status. And what if they fell ill again as a result of being starved and mistreated by the police that drove them from their homes?'

The captain held up his hand to silence John. 'Tomorrow, Major Mason, we cross the border into Turkey. Within one week we will be at our destination. I suggest you begin preparing yourself for separation from the women. A prisoner of war camp is no place for a female – even "a slave". It is not for you to determine the future or treatment of the women who travel with you.' The captain walked away and Dira, who'd been standing behind him, handed John a water bottle.

'I'll clean these men up, sir.'

'We'll do it together, Dira.' John crouched down and wet the lips of the man closest to him. He studied the others. The only one that showed any sign of life was the one he was leaning over.

Treading carefully to avoid the worst of the waste that carpeted the floor Dira walked around to the far side of the hut. He held his hand in front of the faces of the other three men.

'They are all breathing and alive, sir, but close to death.'

The man closest to Dira spoke without opening his eyes. 'Please, I beg you, let me die.'

'We'll soon have you clean and feeling better,' Dira consoled him clumsily.

'Please, I can't stand this pain any more.'

John looked at Dira. 'Get the morphine, and bring Jones and Williams here. We need to get these men clean and comfortable.'

To John's surprised Dira returned with the men, and with the two Armenian women: Mrs Gulbenkian, and a younger woman,

Rebeka.

'You haven't recovered from your ordeal or regained your strength,' John warned the women. 'These men are filthy, they could be carrying disease.

'Like we were before you healed us and took care of us?' Mrs Gulbenkian challenged.

'Like you were,' John agreed.

They set to work washing and cleaning the men, and wrapped them in blankets before carrying them outside the hut.

Evans and Greening had erected all the tents they hauled with them and they carried the sick men into the one John rather grandly referred to 'as the hospital tent'. Once the men had been settled on clean sheets and blankets, John sat on a stool just inside the flap and waited for the inevitable.

He'd done what little he could, given the men morphine to dull the pain and cramps that came with dysentery, moistened their dried, cracked lips, and applied cream and dressings to the worst of their sores. It wasn't enough to save them but he doubted any of them would have survived even if he'd been able to take them into the military hospital in Basra, which was equipped with all the latest medical aids.

'Am I dying, sir?'

John looked down at the boy. Notwithstanding the stubble that covered his chin and cheeks, he looked about twelve years old.

'I'm doing my best to care for you ...' he read the boy's name tags, 'Wilkinson.'

'I don't mind, sir. Anything has to be better than that hole they put us in. No food ... no water ...' The boy turned his head and, without another word, sighed and died.

John was ashamed when the first thought that crossed his mind was whether he'd wasted a dose of morphine that could have eased someone in an even worse state out of life.

He looked at the other men. Their breath was shallow, barely perceptible. He stretched his legs, climbed to his feet, and went outside. The sun had set and darkness loomed dense and threatening outside the circle of light surrounding the cook fires. He lit a Turkish cigarette. Their tobacco was much stronger than the one used by British manufacturers and tasted foul, but he couldn't break the habit of reaching for a pack every time things didn't go as he wanted them to.

Greening joined him. 'Burial party, sir?'

'The only man I thought had a chance of living until morning has just died. Please ask Jones and Williams to dig a grave for four and leave it open and ask Baker and Roberts to remove the body to the grave site.'

'I'll do that, sir.'

Greening left and John saw a group of men from the village staring at him. There was no sign of any local women and he assumed they were in their huts making the evening meal.

'Tea, sir.' Rebeka walked towards him carrying a tin mug.

'Thank you, and thank you for your help, and Mrs Gulbenkian's, earlier.'

'We are glad to do something for you, sir, after you have done so much for us.'

John stepped away from the tent when he saw Baker and Roberts approach.

'You want us to put the body in the grave when it's dug, sir?'

'Please.' John saw a villager still watching him. 'Put a guard on the grave as well, change every two hours so no one misses too much sleep.'

'Will do, sir.'

Greening joined him with Mitkhal and two Arabs. 'I've been given permission by the captain to go out with the auxiliaries and look for any more of our men who've been left behind, sir.'

'I offered Sergeant Greening a camel but he prefers to drive your cart,' Mitkhal didn't meet John's eye. They'd been careful to avoid all but the most essential contact lest they arouse the Turkish captain's suspicions.

'You'll need it if you find anyone.'

'That's what I thought, sir.'

'You have plenty of water bottles in case you come across any men.'

'I do, sir. Jones and Williams are digging the grave.'

'You told them to make it large enough for four?'

'I did, sir. See you when we get back.'

Baker and Roberts removed the body of the man who'd died and John returned to his stool. A deathly hush hung over the village and the surrounding desert. It was so quiet he could hear the rattle of spoons as the men ate around Dira's cook fire.

Rebeka pushed back the tent flap. 'I brought you food, sir.'

'Thank you.'

She handed him the bowl and sat cross-legged on the floor beside him.

'Shouldn't you be eating?'

'I've finished my meal, sir. Mrs Gulbenkian says it's not ladylike to eat quickly, but I can't help it. After being starved for so long, I'm afraid I can't eat slowly.'

'Your English is very good.'

'My father taught me. He was the English and French professor in the school in our town.'

'Do you know where he is now?'

'Dead. The Turks ordered all the Armenian men in the town to report to the church at nine o'clock in the morning. They had a list and any man who didn't report was hunted down. When they had gathered all of them, they marched them outside town and shot them. An American missionary visited the valley where they'd killed them. He was a friend of Mrs Gulbenkian. He recognised my father's body and that of my sister's husband.'

'I'm so sorry. That must have been devastating for you and your family.'

'It was, sir, but we had no time to mourn him. A few days later all the women and children were ordered to report. Just like with the men, those who didn't, were hunted down. Then we were marched into the desert and made to keep on marching until we started dying. The rest you know.'

He wanted to ask if she'd been with anyone else from her family but he recalled Mitkhal saying that she and her two companions were the only ones found alive. No matter how tragic Rebeka's story, he was no position to help her or any of his fellow prisoners.

'Your town?' He hoped to prompt pleasanter memories. 'Was it here or in Turkey?'

'In Turkey, sir, on the Kharpert Plain. Have you been there?'

John shook his head. 'I've travelled very little. Here, India, Britain, a few holidays in France before the war, and that's it.'

'The Kharpert Plain is very beautiful, endless fields of wheat, barley, and crops, surrounded by mountains, some softly rolling

169

covered by woods. Others rocky and craggy. Even the buildings are beautiful. All the houses and churches in the towns and villages are painted white. And inside the churches are colourful paintings of the saints and Jesus and the Magdalene.' She looked up at John and her dark eyes glowed, bright with tears in her thin pale face. 'Tell me to be quiet if I'm talking too much, sir. My family at home were always telling me not to talk so much.'

'I like to hear you talk. It gives me something other than my patients to think about.' John left the stool and checked the pulses of the three remaining men. Like their breathing, all were low, barely perceptible. He moistened their lips, wiped their faces, and returned to his stool. Rebeka was still sitting cross legged on the floor.

'Was your family large?'

'I was the second of four girls, sir. Our father's parents lived with us until they died. My mother said she was glad that my grandfather didn't live to see what the Turks were doing to us. My grandmother was old and confused, the gendarmes made us leave her behind in the church with the other old women. We heard the shots as we were marched away.'

'You said you father was an English professor. What about you and your sisters?'

'I worked with my aunt in the family's goldsmith's business. We designed and made jewellery.'

'That sounds like hard work.'

'I loved it. After my eldest sister Anusha married everyone looked to me to marry, but being the plain one in the family ...'

'You're not plain,' he interrupted.

'I am, sir, and I really don't mind. My sister Anusha had many boys who wanted to marry her, as did my younger sister Veronika. They could take their pick. The only men who asked to marry me were widowers with large families who needed looking after. After I turned down the third proposal, there was a family argument. My aunt, who'd never married, suggested I join her in the business my family owned and she ran. I loved the work. Within two months I was designing and making my own pieces.'

'So you were an independent woman. What else did you do beside work?'

'Help my mother to keep house. She taught me to cook and

clean and my grandmother taught me to sew, but most of all I liked to read my father's books. He had a fine library of English and French classics.'

'What authors did you like?'

He sat back and listened while she told him of her admiration for the Brontës, Jane Austen, Dickens and Dumas and Flaubert, and while she talked he watched her slowly come to life again.

He couldn't help but think of the incongruity of the situation. Here he was, on the borders of Turkey, discussing European literature with a young woman, almost as if they'd met in a civilized drawing room. Yet she was destitute and had lost her entire family. It made the suffering he'd endured seem inconsequential.

'Sir.'

John jerked upright. He looked around. The oil lamp he'd lit when the sun was setting was flickering low. Rebeka was still curled at his feet and Greening was shaking his shoulder.

'Greening?' he mumbled finding it difficult to focus on the sergeant.

'We found more men, sir.'

'Alive?'

'Only one survived the trip here, sir. Private Evans.'

'Private Evans from the Dorsets?'

'That's the one, sir. The Welshman with the peculiar sense of humour. Jones and Williams are cleaning him up now, sir. They'll bring him in when they've finished.'

'Thank you, Greening.' John kneeled and examined the men on the floor. He checked their pulses and laid his hand in front of their mouths.

Greening read the expression on his face. 'They've gone, sir.'

'While I was sleeping,' John shook his head in dismay. 'So much for the care I gave them.'

'If any of them had made a noise you would have woken, sir. No man can expect more than a clean place to lie down and something to take the pain away. Dira was making tea when I came in. Go and have a brew, sir, while the boys take these men out.'

'Thank you, Greening.' John reached down and shook Rebeka

awake. Like him she woke with a start.

'Mrs Gulbenkian will be wondering where you are. I'll walk to your tent.'

She rose to her feet and yawned. He saw her to the small tent Greening had allocated for the use of the women and went to the cart. Corporal Baker was washing Evans, but like all the men they'd found who'd been abandoned, he was comatose.

John checked Evans's pulse and pinched his skin.

'Dehydration, dysentery, and sunstroke, sir,' Baker announced.

'You'll be a doctor by the time this war finishes, Baker.'

'I wouldn't mind, sir. I'd like to put some of the things I've learned from you to use.'

'You regular army, Baker?'

'Me, sir? Not ruddy likely, begging your pardon for the language, sir. I was dull enough to volunteer when the call went out for conscripts. Thought I be a hero in France killing Fritzes, sir. Never crossed my mind I'd be a prisoner of these heathen beggars.' He glared at the Turks who were clustered around their own fire.

'I don't think any of us thought we'd end up here, Baker.'

'Why did you ask if I was regular, sir?'

'If you were I could recommend you for medical training. The RAMC are looking for good men like you.'

'Kind of you to say so and kind of you to offer, sir. Although if I'm lucky enough to survive this war and get back home in one piece I'm hoping my old man will take me into the family business. It will seem heaven after this.'

'What's the family business, Baker?' John asked.

'Butchers, sir.'

Baker didn't even smile.

Chapter Sixteen

The Convent of St Agnes and St Clare, India
August 1916

Maud brushed the flies from the table in her cell and re-read what she had written.

Letter I

Dear John,

I am sending this care of the Red Cross. I have heard that they don't always succeed in passing letters on to the Red Crescent, but I hope this will get through. I will date and number all my letters and copy this paragraph at the beginning of each one. As I intend to write to you three times a week until you reply, you can check how many of my letters have reached you, which may be useful in gauging how much of your other mail gets through.

I hope you won't tear this or any letter up that I send you before you read it. I want you to know that I am abjectly ashamed of my unforgiveable behaviour. I didn't realise how precious your love was until the last time I saw you, when told me you wanted a divorce.

I am full of regret, remorse – and hope. Hope that when this beastly war is over we can meet again, put the past behind us, and make a new life for ourselves together in that West Country village you used to talk about. Where you would be the village doctor and I would be just a housewife who cares for our children and our home.

I think of you constantly and can't bear the thought of you locked up in a Turkish prison. I hope and pray that you are in stronger and better health than the survivors of the siege of Kut who were returned to the hospitals in Basra. Angela Smythe told me most of the men were so weak and thin they couldn't even rise from their beds.

My father returned from Kut in remarkably good health compared to the other officers who were sent downstream. He asked me to move in with him but changed his mind when heard the gossip about me and ordered me to leave his bungalow. Given what people were saying about me I couldn't return to the Butlers. Michael Downe offered to help me, but rather than impose on the few real friends I have, like Angela and Michael, I thought it best to leave Basra and make a new life for myself elsewhere.

As you see from the return address, I am in India, living and working in the convent where I was educated. Mother Superior was kind to me when I was a pupil. The nuns run an infirmary alongside the school that cares for local people. I nursed in the Lansing for a short while and once Mother Superior realised that I'd received some training she agreed that I could work there in return for my keep.

Given the gossip about me in military circles both in Basra and here in India I am using the name Maud Smith, but I never leave the convent nor venture into the convent school that has officers' daughters among the pupils. I see and speak only to the nuns and the locals who seek treatment in the infirmary.

I gave birth to a boy last December. I asked Mrs Butler to place him in an American orphanage. I hope she will do so and that he will find adoptive parents who can give him a better life than I am able to. I am writing this so you realise that if you could bring yourself to consider taking me back, I would come unencumbered by further responsibilities.

As long as I remain in the convent I will be financially self-sufficient, and have no need to draw on my wife's allowance.

As I haven't heard anything from you, I have no idea whether you have divorced me or not, or intend to divorce me in the future.

If you are, I beg you with all my heart to reconsider, John ...

Maud stopped writing and considered how best to fill the space that still remained on the official Red Cross POW form. After gauging the number of lines she could squeeze in, she dipped her pen into the ink and continued.

So, as you see, I am supporting myself and hope to redeem myself in your eyes. I know what I am asking for when I plead with you to forgive me. All I can say is I am not the woman I was when you last saw me. It was hard to live in Basra in full knowledge of what was being said about me. I have suffered, but I know my suffering is nothing compared to yours. I will understand if I do not hear from you, but please, John, try and write even if it's only a few sentences to tell me that you don't want to see me again.

I send all my love, your own very sorrowful Maud who's only hope is that you allow her a second chance to be the wife she should have been.

Maud folded the letter, sealed it, and went to her washstand. She washed and dressed in the uniform she'd been given and covered her hair with a nurse's veil. When she looked at herself in the mirror she appeared more novice nun than nurse.

She resolved to have her photograph taken in the uniform. It was an image she wanted to project and imprint on John's consciousness. She wanted – no, she needed – to believe that she could make amends. That if she kept writing to John and sending him Red Cross parcels like the one she'd used Michael's money to buy, he would forgive her and take her back.

He simply had to. Because when she considered her life up until that point, she realised that John was the only person who'd loved her unselfishly and with all his heart.

Smythes' Bungalow, Basra
August 1916

'Thank you,' Angela took the tea tray from the maid and set it in a low table in the drawing room. 'And thank the cook for us. That was a lovely dinner.'

'Yes, ma'am Smythe.'

'It was a very good dinner,' Georgiana complimented. She rearranged the cushions at her back, and lifted Robin from his crib. 'You've no idea how welcome this blissful domesticity is after the day I've had in the hospital.'

'I heard a fight broke out among the Arabs in one of the streets down by the wharf.'

'It did. We admitted fourteen men with various broken bones

and degrees of concussion. On the plus side, no women and children were involved. They obviously had the sense to stay out of the way of the flying fists.'

'What was it all about?' Angela asked.

'Search me. We talked to them through interpreters but are none the wiser. It's possible the interpreters wanted to keep us in the dark but the injuries made a nice change from fevers and dysentery.' She looked down at the baby who was smiling up at her and playing with her rope of coral beads. 'Every time I see this child he appears to have doubled in size. The rate he's growing he'll be talking and running around in no time.'

'He will.'

Something in Angela's voice alerted Georgiana. 'You don't want him to grow up.'

'Of course. It's just that ...'

'You've become close to him and you're afraid Maud will return to reclaim him?'

'No,' Angela was emphatic. 'He's Maud's son and he'll always be Maud's son no matter how long I look after him. She gave birth to him, and that gives her the sole right to raise him. I only wished I knew where she was and what kind of a life she's living.'

'You're concerned in case it's not conducive to bringing up a child?'

'I'm concerned she might be in trouble and too proud to ask for help.'

'I've met her, of course, and saw her in the mission, but I can't say I really know her. I've also heard the rumours about her. My first impression was she didn't seem the type to attract John. Too shallow, pretty, and fluffy. I always thought he'd marry a sensible woman, his intellectual equal who'd be able to play chess and discuss literature and art with him. Not a woman whose conversation only extended as far as fashion, balls, and parties.'

'You didn't like her?'

'It's not a question of liking or disliking Maud. I just thought that she was wrong for John. After meeting her, I couldn't help wondering if John had married her simply because she was the most suitable woman around. There is a shortage of unmarried women in India, isn't there?'

'So I've heard.'

Angela poured the tea and set a cup on the side table beside Georgiana. 'I've always thought of Captain Mason as an exceptionally kind, considerate, and gentle man. Not an intellectual, though.'

'John's the most widely and best-read person I know. I was closer to him than Harry when we were growing up. Probably because Harry was always in trouble and I liked the quiet life too much to join my twin in his escapades.'

'John never mentioned books to me.'

'Did you ever talk to him when you were alone?'

Angela thought. 'Not often.'

'You were right when you said he was considerate. He always allows others to choose the topic of conversation rather than have them think he's talking down to them. Are you concerned that if Maud does reclaim Robin you might not be able to see him?' Georgiana ventured.

'I admit I would hate being separated from Robin, especially if I felt that Maud was taking him to a worse place than this one. I'm enjoying looking after him especially now that Peter's left. Between teaching in the Lansing, running the house, and setting aside some time each day for Robin, I've barely time to worry about Peter or consider where he is and what he's doing, except just after I wake in the morning and in the few minutes before I go to sleep.'

'It's better to be busy than sit and worry about what's happening upriver,' Georgiana agreed.

'I'm sorry, that was selfish of me. You must be worried about Michael and David.'

'Michael is a civilian and he has a battery of well-paid Arabs looking after him. David and I are friends. I like him, and he's fun to be with. But most people who are one-person parties are. Frankly,' she smiled, 'David is the sort of man my mother used to warn me about. Charming, good-looking, good company, an incorrigible flirt, and a wonderful friend provided you never rely on them. They make dreadful husbands.'

'Isn't that harsh on David?' Angela asked.

Georgiana's smile broadened. 'David would be the first to admit it's an accurate description of him. My husband, Gwilym, was the complete antithesis to David.'

177

'Charles told me he was killed on the Western Front.'

'Gwilym was a pacifist. Like many pacifists he volunteered as a stretcher-bearer. It never occurred to either of us that he would get killed or that we would never see one another again.' She fell silent and a faraway look stole into her eyes.

'You obviously loved him very much.'

'I adored him, but we were from different worlds. A bit like you and Peter. It wasn't easy for Gwilym to adapt to my world of doctors and family. Especially when my father flatly refused to allow him into his house.' Georgiana switched the conversation from her to Angela. 'But you couldn't have found it easy to marry into British military society.'

'It was strange at first, especially when some of the officers went out of their way to belittle me simply because I was American. But most of Peter's friends were welcoming. Especially your brother Harry. Peter and I would never been able to marry when we did, or have such a marvellous honeymoon if Harry hadn't arranged leave for Peter and given us his lieutenant-colonel's bungalow. I miss him so much. He used to call into the mission without ceremony every time he was in Basra. No matter how bad the war news he always managed to cheer everyone up and reassure me that Peter was safe and would remain safe. I can't bear the thought of him lying dead in an unmarked grave, with no one to mourn him or hold a proper service.'

Georgiana was finding it increasingly difficult to keep the secret of Harry's 'death'. 'Harry will always live on in the hearts of those who knew him,' she said ambiguously.

'He made friends with everyone. In that respect he was very like David.'

'But unlike David he fell in love with one woman and managed to remain faithful to her after they married, according to what Charles and Peter have told me.'

'I never met Furja but Harry's eyes positively glowed every time he spoke about her. She must be a very special woman. After news came of Harry's death I asked if anyone knew where she lived so I could visit her, but if she was still in Basra no one could give me her address.'

Georgiana looked down at Robin on her lap. He'd fallen asleep without her even noticing. Her coral necklace was entwined in his fingers, his feet tucked into the folds of her skirt.

'Here, I'll take him from you and settle him down.' Angela lifted him from Georgiana's lap and laid him in the cot before tucking him in. When she'd finished she looked at the tea tray. 'Shall I send for more tea or would you like a brandy?'

'A brandy, please.' Georgiana stretched out in the chair and lifted her feet on to a footstool. 'This really is pleasant. I'm never out of sight or earshot of the wards in the hospital, and on the rare occasions I make it as far as my room in the Lansing Mission I'm always on edge waiting for the telephone to ring to inform me of an emergency.'

'You could move in here,' Angela suggested shyly.

'No I couldn't. What if Peter returned suddenly?'

'You could move out if his presence would make you feel uncomfortable.'

'I don't know about uncomfortable. I'd certainly feel like a gooseberry.'

'Peter and I are well past the honeymoon stage.'

'Didn't look like it to me the last time I saw you together in the Basra Club.'

'We won't be taking Baghdad in a hurry, and Peter, Charles, and Michael are sure that's the objective. We have three bedrooms, I'm in one, the nanny and Robin occupy the other, and we have one free.'

'The thought of spending another leisurely evening like this is very tempting, especially if I could sleep over at the end of it,' Georgiana conceded.

'Then move in. We can cheer one another up. You must be feeling as forlorn and wretched as me now most of the men have gone up-country. I'd really welcome your company.'

'I wouldn't be here that much. I work long hours in the hospital and rarely make it back to the mission more than one or two nights a week.'

'You might make an effort to organise more free evenings for yourself if you knew you were more or less out of reach of the hospital.'

'I might at that.' Georgiana sipped the brandy Angela had given her.

'I've another reason for asking. I'm fairly sure I'm pregnant

179

and – you don't have to say yes to this – but I'd like you to take care of me, not an army doctor.'

Georgiana smiled. 'That's wonderful news, and I'd be delighted to take care of both of you.'

'Both of you …' Angela smiled as she repeated the words.

'Realisation has just dawned?'

'It has.'

'Does Peter know he's about to become a father?'

'No, I suspected I might be pregnant when he left but I couldn't be sure and I didn't want to give him any extra worries. I wish …'

Georgiana waited but when Angela didn't finish her sentence she did it for her. 'He wasn't in the army and didn't have to fight a war?'

'So many of our friends have been killed. I can't help wondering how many more will have to give their lives before it ends.'

'It can't go on much longer.'

'Do you really believe that?'

'I have to, every time I think of all the friends of Harry, Michael, John, and Tom who have died here or on the Western Front. If we lose the few who are left, an entire generation will be wiped out.'

'Reverend Butler says that America will be forced into the war sooner rather than later and they will come in on the side of the Allies.'

'Do you think he's right?' Georgiana asked.

'It's so long since I left America I have no idea what Americans believe. Theo seems to think that the German, Irish, and Scandinavian Americans will do all they can to keep America neutral, as does Dr Picard.'

'No matter what happens we can't do anything to change it. Harry used to tell me to ignore anything that can't be influenced. So how about we discuss the practicalities of me moving in here with you and your new baby. Do you want a boy or a girl?'

Angela smiled. 'A boy with red hair who looks exactly like Peter. That would be wonderful.'

'It would be.'

Georgiana couldn't supress the thought that it would be even more wonderful if there were no more wars left for him to fight when he reached his father's age.

Sheikh Saad
September 1916

Peter, Charles, and David walked down the gangplank of the ship that had taken them upriver from Ali Gharbi to Sheikh Saad.

'I would give whole worlds for an iced bath, a glass of good whisky, and a crack sniper to rid us of these bloody Arabs.' Charles instinctively ducked as a bullet whistled overhead.

'It's not the bullets you have to worry about, Major Reid, but your disappearing kit. The Arabs are lousy shots, but expert thieves. They creep about at night stealing blankets, rifles, and even tents and mosquito nets from under and over officers as well as men.'

'Captain Boris Bell,' Charles held out his hand and shook Boris's hand enthusiastically. 'I haven't seen you since you were hospitalised after that final failed push to relieve Kut. How are you?'

'As you see fit, active, and,' Boris fingered his insignia, 'captain no longer.'

'Then we're all majors. David Knight, medical corps, Peter Smythe, Dorsets, meet Boris Bell, 6th Indian Cavalry.'

Boris shook their hands. 'I take it you gentlemen are ready to have another go at Johnny Turk?'

'We owe them one for forcing Townshend to surrender at Kut,' Peter said bitterly.

'What's the organisation like here?' Charles asked.

'Better than it was when the Relief Force was trying to fight through to Kut.' Boris ducked as yet another bullet whistled overhead, hit a tent pole, and fell harmlessly to the ground. 'Maude has everything under control. The fittest men are being pushed straight on up to the front at Sannaiyat. The cavalry and mounted troops are being held back here because the animals require a greater quantity of supplies. You know what the grazing is like upstream.'

'What grazing?' Charles asked.

'Precisely. Ammunition, including the new Stokes trench mortars, is being stockpiled. Morale is good among officers and men ...'

'Really?' Peter was sceptical.

'Maude knows what he's doing and he's determined to march into Baghdad. Once we take the city Johnny Turk will have to retreat from this part of the world.'

'And all we'll have left to do is chase him back into Turkey,' David laughed. 'A month or two and we should have it cleared and ready for the civil servants. They can import the surplus from India. They'll love pushing forms around beneath the minarets.'

'But before that happens we have to advance.'

'Is there a hospital here?' David asked.

'Here and at Sannaiyat.'

'Shouldn't you report for duty?' Charles asked.

David shook his head. 'Command's managed without me until now. I'll wait until they track me down. So,' he turned to Boris, 'where does a man go for fine dining and wine here?'

It was Boris's turn to laugh. 'I see you brought the jokers with you, Charles.'

'More than one by the look of it.' He spotted Michael walking towards him in Arab robes.

'I've been in the desert interviewing the natives,' Michael explained, 'And say what you like about skirts, this outfit is more comfortable than khaki or civvies.'

'We'll take your word for it.' Peter was shaken by the sight of Michael in Arab dress. It reminded him of all the times Harry had sneaked into the Basra base after the nights he'd spent gambling in Abdul's.

'What's the story among the Arabs?' Charles asked. 'Are they on our side?'

'You've been in this country longer than me, Charles, you should know.'

'Know what?' Charles challenged Michael.

'I'm surprised that you haven't yet learned that the only side the Bedawi are on is their own.'

'Will they support us in the push upriver?' Charles pressed.

'For what's it's worth – and it is just an opinion, they'll support us as long as we're pushing out the Turks. Once the Turks have gone they'll probably start pushing us out.'

'It's rumoured the sepoys are making bully beef curry for

tonight, but it won't be served for another hour, how about all you gentlemen retire to my tent ...' Boris ducked as bullets started flying again.

'Where the hell are they shooting from?' Peter demanded irritably.

'Boats, camels, but they've yet to hit anything that bleeds. Brigadier sent out snipers earlier to see if they could cut them down. To continue, I have some Chianti and whisky in my tent, possibly enough for all of us. Anyone care for a pre-dinner snifter?'

'Sounds good.' Charles looked around. His bearer, Chatta Ram, was already erecting his tent. 'I'll just check on my gear and finish a letter that can go back downstream with the boat and I'll be with you.'

'To hell with my gear,' David said to Boris, 'I'll join you now.'

Chatta Ram had erected his own small tent and had started on Charles's.

'Have you seen my travelling desk?' Charles asked.

'Yes, sahib.' As always when they were in company Chatta Ram answered him formally. He unfolded a travelling chair, and handed Charles his desk.

Charles opened it and looked at the letter he'd started writing on the boat the night before.

My dear Kitty,

I know it must seem strange that I have to write what I couldn't say to you in words, but I wanted you to know how much and how totally and completely I love you and most of all how unworthy I am of receiving your love ...

Charles unscrewed the ink bottle, dipped the pen into it, and continued to write.

I have a son, Kitty. His name is Robin, his mother is Maud Perry. The wife of my closest friend. I cannot tell you how ashamed I am at having to confess that to you. I will understand if you never want to see me again. Believe me, you cannot possibly despise me any more than I despise myself. I have not only betrayed the moral code of decency all Englishmen try to live by but my best friend ...

'These damned snipers are getting to be a bloody nuisance, sahib,' Chatta Ram grumbled. 'I'm afraid to stand upright in this camp.'

'What do you mean getting to be, Chatta Ram?' David appeared and handed Charles a glass of whisky. 'They are a bloody nuisance. Come and join us, Charles, there are loads of fellows here we know.' He glanced at the writing desk. 'Your lady love can wait. You know what the post is like. That will be dumped in a mail bag in a warehouse at one of the boat changeover points like Qurna for a month or two.'

'I suppose you're right.' Charles capitulated. He blotted what he'd written, returned it to his desk, and took the glass from David.

They walked away from Charles's tent towards Boris's.

'Careful you don't catch the sun's rays with that,' David warned. 'It'll give Sniper Abdul a target and you'll lose your fingers.'

Even as David spoke another shot pinged, and Charles fell.

'Come on, old man.' David stooped down and turned Charles over. He stared in disbelief at the bullet hole in the centre of Charles's forehead.

Chatta Ram ran at speed towards them. Boris, Michael, and Peter charged from the tables and chairs in front of Boris's tent.

'Charles?'

No one noticed Chatta Ram had used Charles' first name.

'Is he?'

David looked up at Michael. 'Dead? Yes.' He stared down at Charles. 'I should never have taken him that whisky. I should have left him writing where he was. I should never ...'

Peter recognised the signs of clinical shock and laid his hands on David's shoulders. He shouted at the top of his voice.

'Stretcher-bearers!'

Chapter Seventeen

Internal Ottoman Empire border between Mesopotamia and Turkey
September 1916

'You, Private Evans, have the constitution of an ox.'

John took the corners of the blanket beneath Evans's head and shoulders, Baker the corners below his feet, and they lifted him and his blanket out of the hospital tent and carried him to the cart.

'I'm not going to die, am I, sir?' Evans asked when Mitkhal tucked a saddlebag beneath his head.

'You have my permission to live, Evans, but I can't answer for the feelings of our colleagues if you continue to makes the kind of jokes you have been inflicting on us of late.' John had to force a smile. Only ten minutes before he'd read the burial service over five men. One who'd died in their hospital tent and four sun-dried corpses Greening had found in a ditch, recognisable as British troops only by the ID tags that identified them as privates of the Norfolks. The collection of tags he'd accumulated was now so large, he'd emptied a dead man's kit bag to store them in.

'Comfortable, Evans?' Baker asked.

'No. The bottom of this cart is hard.'

'Then get out and bloody walk.'

'Give me your legs, corporal, and I will.'

John ignored the banter and watched the Turkish captain and his men walk out of their makeshift camp to greet a border patrol that was approaching on horseback.

'Leave the hospital tent until last, and let me know when the Turks return,' he ordered Jones and Williams who'd harnessed the mules to the second cart and brought it up ready to load the tents.

He ducked inside the hospital tent, Mitkhal followed.

'You'll be crossing into Turkey in less than an hour. This is where I and my men leave you.' Mitkhal lifted John in a bear hug.

'I'd hug you back if I had any breath left. You'll remember me to Hasan and Furja. Tell them I'd like to meet them again.'

'I will tell them. Perhaps when this war is over we'll all sit in the garden of Ibn Shalan's house in Basra and drink iced sherbet.'

'That garden was beautiful. I've never forgotten the time I spent there with Maud, Harry, and Furja. Will you go there from here?'

'No, as all your men want to stay with you I will return to Baghdad. It will be good to see my wife and son and Hasan again. Don't let the Turks lift the bag from under Private Evans's head. It's stuffed with sovereigns. Knowing the Turks you'll need to buy food and possibly even water.'

'Thank you, Mitkhal.' John returned Mitkhal's embrace.

Jones's voice echoed in from outside the tent. 'Captain coming, sir.'

'Thank you, Jones.' John picked up his medical bag. Mitkhal gathered together the spare mosquito nets and carried them out. He dropped them into the back of the cart they used to ferry their equipment.

'Your men will have to work harder from this point on, Major Mason. We are losing our Arab auxiliaries,' the captain warned.

'Do we have far to go?' John asked.

'A week, maybe two, of hard travelling.'

'We have transport?' John asked.

'You have your carts.'

'I was hoping we would complete our journey by train or failing that be supplied with fresh mules and horses.'

'The Ottoman government has more pressing and important concerns to consider than the fate of a few prisoners of war, Major Mason.'

'Can you at least tell me where we'll be taken in Turkey?'

'You are asking too many questions, Major Mason. Besides, if I gave you the name of the place it would mean nothing to you.'

'I have a fair knowledge of Turkish geography.'

'You will be east of Istanbul. Is that knowledge enough for you?'

'How far east?'

'Does it matter when you won't be allowed to leave the confines of the POW camp?'

186

'I need to know if there will be proper facilities for our sick.'
John reined in his exasperation.

'There will be facilities, Major Mason. You will be in charge of
them.' The captain walked away and John joined the privates, the
women, and the child, who'd already lined up behind the carts.

The last tent was loaded. Greening urged the mules forward.
Baker lifted the child on to his cart and followed. John turned to
take a last look at Mesopotamia before they entered Turkey.

Mitkhal was riding his camel behind those of his men. He saw
John and raised his arm in salute. John risked returning the wave.

Sheikh Saad
September 1916

Peter woke to a shaft of blinding light when his tent flap was flung
back. Keeping his eyes screwed tightly shut, he groped into
consciousness. A tide of nausea was creeping up his throat and
blasts of deafening snores resounded from the floor beside his cot.

He moved his head to the side of his pillow and looked down.
Boris Bell and David Knight were lying on a blanket that had been
flung over the groundsheet. Both were flat on their backs, their
mouths open to the flies that were swarming outside of the
mosquito tent that hung above his bed.

He tried to lift his head and a blinding pain shot through his
skull. He slumped back on to his pillow and remembered – Charles
was dead. The knowledge cut through his consciousness like a
knife.

'The funeral will be in half an hour, sahib.'

Charles's bearer was standing at the foot of his cot watching
him.

'Thank you. Chatta Ram, isn't it?'

'Yes, sahib.'

'Send my bearer in and Major Knight's and Bell's to their
tents.'

'Major Bell and Knight's bearers are already in their tents,
sahib.'

'Thank you. I'll wake them.'

'Yes, sahib.'

'We need to talk about Major Reid's effects and your future,

187

Chatta Ram. After the funeral?'

'Yes, sahib.'

Peter rolled from his cot and knelt on the floor. He reached out and shook first Boris, then David.

David opened an eye and glared at him.

'Funeral will be held in half an hour. Your bearer is in your tent.'

David struggled to his feet and left without a word.

Boris looked at him. 'I hoped it was a bad dream.'

'Don't we all,' Peter said feelingly.

A shadow loomed in Boris's wake and Michael ducked inside.

'You look rough.'

Peter squinted at him. 'I feel rough and you look healthier than any man should after what we drank last night.'

'Sobered up hours ago. I couldn't sleep.' Michael perched on the only stool in the tent. 'I can't believe Charles has gone. Yesterday he was walking around, talking, living then – nothing!'

'We old Gulf hands are used to death but ...' Peter took a moment to compose himself. 'When it happens to someone you're close to ... Harry ... Amey ... now Charles ... I'm sorry, I'm being selfish, you knew him before all this. You grew up with him, didn't you?'

'Yes.'

'I counted Charles amongst my closest friends, simply because he was friends with Harry and John, but outside of what we shared here I don't know the first thing about him.'

'There's not much to know,' Michael took a flask from his pocket and offered it to Peter. 'Hair of the dog?'

'Thanks.' Peter took the flask and opened it.

'Charles's father was – is again since the war started – a general. He works in the War Office in London. Charles's mother died when he was young so Charles's father sent him from India to my parents to be brought up alongside Harry, Georgie, and me, but because he was more Harry's and Georgie's age, he was closer to them and John than Tom and me. He went to school with Harry and John and spent every holiday with us but I only really got to know Charles after I came here.'

'Charles has no brothers and sisters?'

'None, although he, Harry, and John were closer than most

brothers. I can't even remember Charles having a girlfriend until he met Kitty. Not one he brought back to my parents' house. There must have been girls, but straight after school he went to Sandhurst and then he was posted to India. He wrote, of course. To my parents and Georgie and even on occasions me, but they were the usual sort of letters from siblings, accounts of parties, rides, sorties, and training with his command.'

'Kitty was so fond of Charles I think she'll take his death as hard as any wife.' Peter clambered awkwardly to his feet and held his head. 'There are ten little drummers inside my brain, thumping with sticks trying to get out.'

Peter's bearer entered and set jugs of hot and cold water on the travelling washstand. He handed Peter a mug.

Peter stared down at it. 'Hangover remedy?'

'With raw egg beaten into it, sir.'

'Not sure I'm up to it.' Peter tore off his clothes and washed while his bearer laid out his clothes. When he'd finished washing, he pulled on his underclothes and trousers. After lathering his face with shaving soap he reached for his cut-throat razor. 'Someone will have to go through Charles's kit, and arrange to auction off his uniform and anything else his family will have no use for. After that's done, his papers and documents will have to be sorted, his will read, and his personal stuff packed and sent down to Basra so it can be shipped home.'

'As I'm the civilian with time to spare, I'll do it,' Michael volunteered.

'Thank you, that's good of you. I've had to do it for so many good men in Kut I've come to hate the job, and I would find it doubly difficult to go through Charles's things. He was such a private man. I'd feel I was prying.' Peter finished shaving and splashed water on his face.

'Ready?' Boris's voice echoed outside the tent. Peter reached for his tunic, buttoned it on and picked up his belt and sword. When he'd finished dressing Michael handed him his hat.

They walked out into a silent and subdued camp. Men had lined up behind the officers. Peter stepped behind the padre. David, Boris, and Michael followed to the edge of the camp where the sepoys had dug a grave.

They stood at the side of the mass grave that held a row of

blanket-wrapped corpses and waited for the padre to begin.

Peter glanced at David and saw him watching him. He knew what David was thinking. How many more funerals would they have to attend before the war was over, and would their bodies be witnessing their last one from the bottom of the pit?

Sheikh Saad
September 1916

'You know we're averaging half a dozen deaths here a day from fever and dysentery,' David grumbled as they walked back to camp.

'Have you been posted to the hospital here or are they sending you upstream?' Boris asked. Like David he felt the need to break the suffocating silence that had fallen over the group after seeing earth shovelled over the shrouded corpses in the grave.

'I haven't a clue.'

'You still haven't reported for duty?' Peter questioned.

'There's time enough for that. Do you know what was so bloody awful? I didn't even know which one of those bodies was Charles.'

'None of us did,' Michael pointed out.

'Does it matter?' Peter questioned. 'Charles is not in that pit.'

'Please don't give us the "He lives on in our memory" lecture.' David snapped.

Peter stopped outside his tent. 'I frequently dream that the war hasn't broken out and I'm throwing a punch at Stephen Amey in the Basra mess because he's insulted Angela for being American. At that moment, I could swear that Stephen Amey is alive.'

'But you'd be asleep and you can't swear to anything if you're asleep,' David argued.

'Major Smythe, Major Bell,' A sub lieutenant ran up to them, stood to attention and saluted. 'Brigadier's called a conference, Major Smythe, Major Bell. He requests your presence.'

'Not mine,' David questioned.

'No, sir,' the lieutenant answered.

'Don't suppose you like to help me pack up Charles's personal effects?' Michael asked.

'Why not?' David shrugged. 'Anything to delay reporting to the senior medic. And, if I didn't help you, I'd only drink myself into another stupor. Lead the way, scribe.'

'I've packed Major Reid's uniform into his trunk, Mr Downe.' Chatta Ram lifted the lid and showed Michael. 'I've spoken to the brigadier. He suggested sending the chest downstream so the contents could be auctioned among the new recruits coming in. No one who's already here will want kit.'

'That sounds sensible, Chatta Ram,' Michael agreed.

'That only leaves Major Reid's desk and papers, sir.'

'Did Major Reid leave much in Basra, Chatta Ram?' David asked.

'A trunk, sir. Larger than this one.'

'Did he leave a will?' Michael asked.

'I believe there are copies of his personal papers in this desk and the trunk in Basra as well as personal possession like photographs. I put his watch, wallet, whistle, pencil, revolver, and notebook in the desk. I locked it. This is the key.' Chatta Ram placed the desk on the table, the key on the top and pulled up two camp chairs. 'Can I get either of you gentlemen anything?'

Michael glanced at David who shook his head. 'No, thank you. Chatta Ram, if you're prepared to stay on with the Force, I could offer you a position as my bearer,' Michael offered.

'You have a syce and Daoud, sir as well as a cook.'

'I think everyone knows Kalla is not my cook. But Daoud has enough to do without acting as my bearer. I will pay you whatever Major Reid and the army were paying. I know it won't be the same as serving an officer but it might be safer.'

'Thank you, Mr Downe, it is a generous offer, but I must decline. It was a pleasure and a privilege to serve Major Reid. Now he is dead I will return home. My mother is a widow. I have younger brothers and sisters. It is my duty to care for them.'

'I'll have a word with the quartermaster and get you a berth on the next boat going downstream. I'll ask him to ensure that you get a swift passage to India.'

'Thank you, Major Knight. I will take Major Reid's effects downstream with me. Please excuse me. I have my own kit to attend to.'

David sat opposite Michael. He eyed him across the desk. 'Are

191

you going to open it?'

'I feel as though I'm snooping. Perhaps we should ask Chatta Ram to take as it is, locked downstream.'

'And give it to ...?' David reached for his cigarettes.

'You're right. There really isn't anyone other than Angela and Kitty and it wouldn't be fair to ask them to do this.' Michael turned the key in the lock and lifted the lid on the desk. He took out Charles's gold pocket watch. He'd seen Charles use it many times. He pressed the button and the back flew open to reveal the inscription.

A gift to my son Lieutenant Charles Reid to mark the occasion of his twenty-first birthday. General G. Reid.

Michael reflected that if ever anyone needed reminding of the Reids' military background all they had to do was look at the watch. No mention of 'affection'.

He set it aside and removed Charles's wallet. A buttoned compartment was heavy with sovereigns. He counted out ten, a couple of half-crowns and two shilling pieces. The pocket at the back held four five-pound notes and two cigarette card-sized photographs. One was of Kitty in her nurse's uniform, the other of a beautiful woman in an evening gown who looked older than Charles. Although sepia it was obvious the women was fair.

David picked up the photograph of Kitty and stared at it. 'At this moment she believes Charles is alive. It seems unbelievably cruel to tell her otherwise.' He glanced at the second photograph. 'Another of Charles's loves?'

'I've no idea. She seems older than Charles. I've never seen a photograph of his mother, so I suppose it could be her, but as she died when Charles was a baby her dress seems too modern. What do you think?' Michael handed it to David.

David looked at it for a moment. 'I know her, or rather I did. This is a photograph of Emily Perry, Perry's wife. I met her in India when she and her daughter Maud spent the summer with the CO.'

'Odd photograph for Charles to keep in his wallet,' Michael commented.

'Not when you consider it alongside the gossip that they were having an affair. There was some sort of scandal about her death. It happened here in Basra and I was in India at the time but I heard she died on your brother Harry's veranda after being stung by a scorpion.'

'So there were other women in Charles's life.'

'If he were here now, I rather think he'd want us to set that photograph aside where it couldn't be seen by anyone else.'

Michael took the photograph and placed it in his own wallet. He looked down at the contents of the desk. 'I wish my travelling desk was as organised as this.' He flicked through the envelopes and extracted one marked *Last Will and Testament.* 'This seems the logical place to start.'

The envelope wasn't sealed. Michael removed the papers it contained. 'This is interesting,' he mused. 'Georgie witnessed this but she never said anything to me.'

'She wouldn't have if she considered it Charles's personal business.'

Michael started reading. 'Charles has left thirty thousand pounds to his bearer Chatta Ram.'

'Charles is rich?' David raised his eyebrows.

'I've never thought about it, but I suppose he would be. He comes from a long line of military people, and most seemed to be generals. Several served in India and investments made there generally paid well.' Michael continued to read.

'Did he leave any bequests besides the one to his bearer?'

'Twenty thousand pounds to Kitty.'

'Dear Lord, if a bullet hits me tomorrow I'd be lucky to leave sixpence.'

Michael looked sceptical.

'Possibly a little more than sixpence. I admit I haven't checked out my trust fund lately but my pay goes nowhere. In fact, do you have a fiver you can lend me?'

'Is that a joke?'

'Deadly serious, old boy.'

Michael pulled five sovereigns from his pocket and handed them over.

'Much appreciated.'

'He left twenty thousand pounds to Peter Smythe.'

'Any reason in particular?'

'He says in return for the kindness Angela Smythe showed to him when he was laid up for months in hospital.'

'Anything to me?'

'No.' Michael carried on reading.

'How much did he leave in total?'

'Even he wasn't sure, but by his calculations somewhere around two hundred thousand pounds.'

'So one hundred and thirty thousand pounds is going begging.'

'No, because he's left the bulk of his estate to Robin Perry.'

'Maud's son? Why on earth would he do that?'

'Because he's acknowledged him as his child.'

David fumbled for a cigarette. 'But John Mason was his close friend. Maud is John's wife …'

'And it would appear that Robin is Charles's son.'

Chapter Eighteen

Smythes' Bungalow, Basra
September 1916

Major Cleck-Heaton and Captain Reginald Brooke knocked the Smythe's door. The maid opened it.

'We're here to see Mrs Smythe.' Without waiting for an invitation, Cleck-Heaton pushed the maid aside and strode into the living room where Angela was sitting, feeding Robin a bottle of milk.

Angela saw the men and paled. The nursemaid took the child from her and she barely noticed.

'Peter ...' she whispered.

'Was well last time we received a communication from upstream, Mrs Smythe.' Reggie sat next to Angela and reached for her hand. She pulled it away before he could touch her.

Cleck-Heaton coughed. 'We have, however, received a wireless message informing us that Major Charles Reid was killed by a sniper at Sheikh Saad yesterday evening.'

'We know, Major ...?' Georgiana entered and looked from Brooke to Cleck-Heaton.

Reggie indicated his companion. 'Major Cleck-Heaton, I'm Major Brooke. May I enquire how you heard about Major Reid's death? The message has only just come down official lines, Miss ...'

'*Dr* Downe,' Georgiana corrected sharply. 'We heard last night. My brother, Michael Downe, is a war correspondent attached to General Maude's force upstream. He has access to the wireless.'

'The message we received in HQ suggested that you, Mrs Smythe, might be the best person to inform Major Reid's fiancée of his demise. I believe she's a nursing sister who works in the Basra Hospital.'

195

'Sister Jones is here and resting under my care, Major Cleck-Heaton. I trust it won't be necessary for you to see her?' Georgiana glared at Reggie.

'Not if you have everything under control, Dr Downe.'

'I do.' She continued to stare at him until he rose from the chair. 'Thank you for calling, Major Cleck-Heaton, Major Brooke. I regret that you had a wasted journey. The maid will see you out.'

Both officers were clearly unused to being dismissed in a perfunctory manner, especially by a civilian.

'As a fiancée Sister Jones is not entitled to a pension, but I may be able to arrange a hardship payment …'

Georgiana cut him short. 'That will not be necessary, Major Brooke. Major Reid left his fiancée well provided for.'

'If she requires passage home …'

'Matron has already arranged for Kitty to travel back to Britain with the next transport of sick and convalescent soldiers.' Georgiana nodded to the maid who opened the door. 'Good evening, gentlemen.'

Angela went to the window and watched them walk down the path. 'Horrible men. Peter can't stand either of them and every time I see Major Brooke I feel as though insects are crawling over my skin.'

'He's also younger and fitter than many of the senior officers with General Maude. Makes you wonder what strings he's pulled to stay here when so many men who are less fit and have already been wounded, as Charles was, are either already upstream or being posted to Maude's command.'

'After the way you turfed them out, they're not likely to be back. How is Kitty?'

'Sleeping off the effects of the draught I gave her. After the shock you've just had perhaps I should mix you one.'

'I should have realised they were here to tell us about Charles, not Peter. It's just that …'

Tears started in Angela's eyes and Georgiana gave her a hug.

'They had no business calling this late in the evening.'

'Unless Charles put Peter and I down as his next of kin. I didn't think to ask them. Charles, Peter, and I have become close over the last year, I think because Peter was Charles's last link to Harry and John.'

196

The nursemaid stood shyly before Angela.

'Yes, please, take Master Robin to his room and you can go to bed as well.'

'Thank you, ma'am.'

Angela went to the sideboard poured two brandies and handed one to Georgiana. 'I can't believe Charles has gone and I won't until Peter and the others return without him. That's if ...' her voice broke.

'Don't even think it, Angela,' Georgiana countered. 'Peter and the others will return. They *have* to.'

Angela thought of Peter, of the damage that had already been done that prevented them from ever sleeping another night in the same bed together. 'But after so much death and destruction,' she murmured. 'At what cost.'

Sheikh Saad
September 1916

Michael poured two glasses of Chianti and set them on the table. He pulled up a second chair and offered it to Chatta Ram.

'It wouldn't be proper for me to sit in your presence, sahib,' said Chatta Ram.

'It wouldn't if I was an officer, but I'm not, and you are no longer employed by an officer or entitled to draw rations and uniform from the British Army, so that makes us both civilians. Indulge me, sit down and have a drink with me.'

Chatta Ram took the chair.

'Have you read Charles's will?'

'No, but he told me he'd left some money to me.'

'On condition you look after your mother – and his.'

'He acknowledged me as his brother?'

'You seem surprised.'

'He said he would, but I didn't believe him. But then I didn't think he would get killed.'

'None of us believe ourselves mortal,' Michael agreed. 'My sister and I are executors of Charles's will. He left you thirty thousand pounds.'

'Thirty thousand pounds.' Chatta Ram repeated.

'Yes.'

'I didn't know there was so much money in the world.'

'Not just in the world but shortly in your bank account, Chatta Ram,' Michael assured him.

'I don't have a bank account, sahib. Only a strongbox.'

'Then we'll have to open one for you in a bank that has a branch in India. Once that's done we can arrange to have the money transferred there. If you need money for the journey, we can pay your expenses.'

'No, Charles was generous. He paid me well. I can meet my own expenses.'

'Charles wrote that you saved his life. That you ignored the demands of senior officers that he be left to die after Nasiriyeh.'

'Charles was kind. A good brother. When I found him I didn't know what to expect. Now … Our mother will shed many tears.'

'Will you take Charles's papers and personal belongings to my sister in Basra for safekeeping?'

'It will be an honour.'

'If there is anything you would like. His wallet – his watch'

'They should go to his son.'

'You know about his son?' It was Michael's turn to be surprised.

'I too was wounded at Nasiriyeh. When my wounds healed I returned from India and resumed my duties. Charles was still convalescing and had difficulty sleeping so sometimes we talked late into the night. We had no secrets from one another. I think he talked to me because he missed your brother and Major Mason.'

'Visit my sister as soon as you return to Basra. I will write to her so she will be expecting you. She will arrange the payment of the bequest and execute the rest of Charles's will. Are you sure you won't take anything of his to remember him by?'

'I don't need anything to help me remember my brother, sir.'

'Perhaps my sister will persuade you to rethink.' Michael rose and held out his hand. 'It's been a privilege to meet you, Chatta Ram.' He rose from his chair walked out of the tent with Chatta Ram and watched him salute David, who returned the Indian's acknowledgement before wandering into the tent and helping himself to wine.

'That's ten bottles you owe me,' Michael joked.

'You're counting?'

'Absolutely.'

'Send you a case after the war.'

'Do you say that to all the officers you sponge off?'

'Of course, you all have money, I don't. Comes of being the last in a long line of second sons. We never get to inherit or – I warn you now – pay our debts. But we're amusing company as well as great promisers. Rumour has it you're moving out tonight?'

'Upstream to write more articles about Maude,' Michael confirmed.

'Then you should be grateful I'm relieving you of some of your stock. Wine's too heavy to drag around the desert.'

'Thank you so much for your consideration.' Michael emptied the last of the bottle between their glasses.

'You'll be taking a detour to some of the tribal camps?' David fished.

'I'll talk to the Arabs,' Michael acknowledged.

'You, like your brother Harry before you, are a political officer.'

Michael debated whether to deny David's suggestion. Instead he reached for a fresh bottle and the corkscrew. 'Who else knows?'

'Anyone who's been watching your movements.'

'You've seen someone?'

'Perry has two subalterns monitoring you. Blake and Harries. Blake wandered up to my tent a couple of hours ago and offered me a glass of brandy.'

'You accepted.'

'I drank a good deal more than a glass.'

'Blake?'

'My bearer carried him back to his tent ten minutes ago.'

'He tried to get into a drinking competition with you?' Michael smiled.

'He asked a lot of questions about you, Harry, and John. At the risk of you snubbing me as John did when I asked him about Perry when we were in Kut, why is the colonel watching you?'

'I have no idea.'

'You do know that he tried to have John shot in Kut.'

'I heard.'

'John said he hated him and Harry. You've no idea why?'

'None other than the man seems to be the worst kind of

unbending stuffed shirt.'

'Watch your back, or,' David emptied his glass. 'Even better get Daoud to do it. Or ...'

'Or?' Michael prompted.

'Or you and I could conspire to get Perry into the front line.'

'One, I don't know anyone in command with the power to post Perry anywhere. Two, what little I know of the man suggests he's an expert lead swinger, if he wasn't he'd be in a POW camp in Turkey, not lording it here. Three, now he's a brigadier we'd have more luck trying to get the Prince of Wales into the front line in this forsaken place.'

'Leave it with me. I'll think of a strategy while I watch you pack.'

'Are you never on duty?' Michael stretched over David to pick up his saddlebags.

'Twelve hours last night.'

'Shouldn't you be sleeping?'

'And waste good drinking time?' David chuckled. 'Not likely. You have another four bottles there.'

'Pity help anyone who needs surgery tonight.'

'Doctors always operate better when drunk.' David glanced around the tent. 'Don't suppose you have anything good to eat in here?'

'Like what?'

'Your sister always has these little salt crackers ...'

'I don't know why she puts up with you.'

'My charm,' David rummaged in Michael's boxes.

'You'll find nothing edible in those. I have dried dates, or dried figs.' Michael tossed two paper bags at him.

'I'll take the figs, thank you. Have you written to John?' David asked.

'What would be the point when no one has the faintest idea where he is?'

'Sooner or later he'll reach a prisoner of war camp and when he does a letter sent through the Red Cross should reach him.'

Michael sat back on his camp chair still clutching his open saddlebags. 'You think someone should write to him about Charles's will?'

'If you were John, wouldn't you want a friend to tell you about

Maud's son as soon as possible rather than find out from a stranger after everyone had been gossiping about it?'

'I'll write to him after I've packed.'

'Pass me a clean sheet of paper, ink, pen, and your travelling desk and I'll write to him now. That way should one of our letters go astray he'll have the other.'

'Anything else I can pass you?' Michael asked in amusement as David propped his feet on his cot.

'An envelope. If you know John's number can you address it for me, please? It will save me having to look it up.'

Prisoner of War Camp, Turkey
September 1916

John saw the town long before they reached there. Nestling at the foot of gently sloping hills, from a distance it appeared almost like a fairy-tale illustration of what a small oriental country town should be. Neat and clean with red-roofed, whitewashed buildings.

Their guards escorted them and their exhausted mules through a network of narrow streets to the outskirts, where three fairly large buildings stood side by side enclosed in a garden fenced off from the street and surrounding woodland by high wire.

Orderlies dressed in the ragged remnants of British uniforms were hanging washing on rope lines stretched between trees. A knot of officers were walking the perimeter of the fence inspecting the plants. One turned in their direction, recognised John, and rushed to the gate. He would have run out into the street if the guards hadn't stopped him.

'I was hoping you'd make it here, sir.' Alf Grace shouted enthusiastically. 'Do you have all your original crew with you? You didn't lose any on the way?'

'Gathered a few.' John pointed to Evans as Corporal Baker helped the private down from the cart.

'You're alive, Evans,' Grace shouted.

'So Major Mason tells me, sir.' Evans waved.

Corporal Baker lifted Hasmik from the back of the cart and offered Mrs Gulbenkian his hand.

There was a rapid exchange of dialogue between their Turkish captain and the guards at the gate. A Turkish major appeared and started shouting at the captain. John approached, doffed his cap, and began speaking in Turkish.

'Since when has Major Mason spoken the local lingo?' Grace asked Greening when the sergeant moved within earshot of the gate.

'Since he started learning on the journey, Lieutenant Grace, sir. Good to see you.'

'Good to see you too, Greening.'

'What's this place like, sir?' Greening asked.

'I've been in worse, but it's no place for women.'

Crabbe looked at the two women who were standing either side of Hasmik.

'Armenians?'

'How did you know?'

'These houses belonged to Armenians before they were driven out of the town. Poor beggars have been treated even worse than us by the Turks. Bastards have wiped out the community here.'

John turned to Rebeka, Hasmik, and Mrs Gulbenkian and waved them forward. He slipped his arm around Hasmik's shoulders and carried on speaking to the Turkish major.

The Turkish major nodded, spoke to his men, and left with the captain.

'The commandant told us we can stay in rooms in the small house.' John pointed to the third house set back away from the others.'

'That's the hospital,' Grace said.

'It's kitted out as a hospital?' John asked hopefully.

'It's where the Turks put the sick men but it has more sick than beds to accommodate them. The two orderlies with us have done what they can but we've no medical supplies and we haven't had a doctor until now.'

'I told the major the women were nurses and the child belongs to one of them.'

'The major believed you?'

'He believes I've trained the two women as nurses.'

'I hope for your sake, they can give a good imitation of being competent.'

John lifted his bag from the back of the cart. 'We'll soon find out.'

Crabbe took the canvas bucket of broken rocks from Private
Crocker and emptied it on top of the debris the German engineers
had loosened with their blasting. The truck was three quarters full
and he was deliberately taking his time to fill it, in the hope of
making it the last truck of the day. He had no way of knowing the
time but dusk was falling and all he could think of was stretching
out on the dirt floor that served as his bed and closing his eyes.

'Almost full, sir.' Private Barnabas, universally known as
'Barney' tipped his bucket on top. 'Shall we start hauling it, sir?'

Crabbe eyed the Turkish corporal who was guarding the British
POWs working on their section of rock face.

'This truck will take another two buckets, lad,' he answered
loudly. Under his breath he muttered, 'Slow down, I know you've
just had a rest in sick bay but we can wait until the knocking off
whistle to push this one out. The light's fading, we'll be sent back
to our cells soon.' He took a bucket of stones from a third private
who barely had the strength to remain upright and emptied it into
the truck.

'Yallah ...'

'Enough!' Crabbe whirled round and yelled back at the Turk.
He knew the man couldn't understand a word he said but he hoped
the guard would pick up his meaning from the tone of his voice.

'Yallah!' the guard repeated, shaking his fist at Crabbe.

Crabbe faced him square on and mimed spooning food into his
mouth. 'Enough for today. Time to finish and eat.'

A second guard pushed his way towards them. He pulled a
whip from his belt and lifted it high in the air before bringing it
down full force across Crabbe's shoulders.

Crabbe screamed.

'No work. No money. No money. No food. No food you don't
eat,' the guard shouted in pidgin English.

Crabbe staggered and fell back. Barney and Crocker caught him
and propped him upright.

The guard with a whip stepped closer to Crabbe and repeated.
'No work! No food!'

Crocker released his hold on Crabbe, took another canvas

bucket of stones from a prisoner and emptied it into the truck. 'Look, work,' he addressed the guard.

A whistle blew, loud and piercing.

'Finish,' Crocker tried smiling at the guard who didn't smile back.

'Truck!' The guard raised his whip above Barney's head. Crabbe grabbed the end and pulled it from the guard's grasp. He grasped the handle and slammed it across the guard's cheek.

Half a dozen guards charged towards the melee. Barney and Crocker were pushed aside as the newcomers joined their Turkish comrades. The guard who'd lost his whip cracked Crabbe soundly on the jaw. The major crumpled to the ground. The guards closed in around him. He curled on the floor and attempted to protect his head with his hands and arms as the guards booted him from all sides.

Blood spurted from Crabbe's nose, ears, and mouth, sinking into and staining the dust on the track.

'Bastards! Leave him alone!' Without sparing a thought for the consequences Crocker grabbed one of the guards' whistles and blew it, hard. More guards came running and so did the prisoners, although they trailed and limped at a slower pace.

Shouts and screams filled the air as the more robust among the prisoners tried to pull the guards away from Crabbe. A shot was fired. Both guards and prisoners turned to the commandant who was standing on a block holding his revolver high in the air. The commandant shouted in Turkish and the guards began herding the prisoners back towards their accommodation.

Crocker and Barney fought to stay with Crabbe. Crocker bent over him and refused to move even when the guards tried dragging him away. Crocker pointed at Crabbe and shouted as loud as he could, 'Major,' while holding the insignia on the collar of the remains of Crabbe's tunic.

The commandant stepped down from the block and loomed over them. Crocker stared up at him. The commandant barked at the guards and four of them physically lifted Crocker and dragged him away, still shouting and screaming. Two more guards pushed Barney behind the truck.

'Push! Push!'

Barney put his shoulder against the truck and pushed with all the strength left to him. It didn't budge an inch.

The guards started laughing.

'Push! Push!'

Barney looked down at Crabbe's bloody broken body on the track and tried pushing again.

The guards' laughter escalated, ominous, terrifying.

A gun butt was rammed into Barney's back, another his stomach. The last thing he saw as he fell headlong alongside his major was his blood drying in the dust alongside Major Crabbe's.

Chapter Nineteen

Turkish Prisoner of War Camp
October 1916

'If there's a louse left in this house, it's a dead lonely louse, sir,' Greening said proudly to John as they walked through the rooms, Baker, Williams, Roberts, Jones and all the other orderlies had scoured with boiling water and evil smelling powders. John had bought the powders from one of the merchants who were allowed to 'sell' goods to the British POWs in exchange for promissory notes, exchangeable for gold at the end of the war.

John had been amazed at the trust placed in the British POWs by the merchants, the high value of credit extended to them and the quantity and quality of the goods on offer that included food and much-needed clothes.

'There's no way of knowing if the boiling water or the powders killed off the blighters. But they certainly appear to have gone.' John bent down and examined cracks in the floorboards. He spotted a mouse hole in a skirting board but when he looked at it closely he saw that it had been blocked up with clay.

'It's an old one, sir,' Greening reassured him.

'So I see. You've done a great job here, Greening.'

'I only supervised, sir.'

'Like an officer,' John joked.

'Exactly, sir.'

'When I first saw this place a month ago, I doubted that it would ever be fit for habitation let alone a hospital, now it's probably cleaner than the hospital in Kut was, even in the early days of the siege.'

'So can I tell the orderlies to move the quilts in, sir? The cold weather's coming and the sick are freezing in the tents in the garden.'

'Yes, Greening. As discussed keep the surgical cases on the

ground and first floor. The medical cases on the second. Mrs Gulbenkian, Rebeka, and Hasmik can move into two of the attic rooms on the top floor. I'll take the third. You take the small room at the foot of the attic stairs to the right. Dira can take the one on the left. Baker, Roberts, Williams, and Jones can share the one at the back as it's the largest. If they all agree, Evans can join them. He seems to have become a volunteer orderly since he recovered.'

'More like our resident joker and jester, sir, but the men seem to like him. I'll ask our orderlies what they think of the idea of him moving in here with us. I'll get things going now, and we'll have this hospital organised and operational by the end of the day.'

'Greening,' John stopped the sergeant as he was about to leave.

'Sir.'

'Let the men know how much I appreciate what they and you have done here.'

'I will, but we enjoyed having something to do. It was a pleasure, sir.'

'Pleasure?' John repeated. 'Killing lice and scrubbing out a filthy building is a pleasure?'

'The men will do anything for you, sir. They even set up a sweepstake on who would kill the most bedbugs.'

'Who won?'

'Need you ask, sir?'

'Evans?'

'He found a filthy old mattress in one of the attic rooms he christened "Bedbug Heaven" then proceeded to turn it into "Bedbug Hell". None of the guards here seemed to know who lived in this building before we took it over and moved in, but judging by the amount of blood Evans squashed out of the little beggars the poor souls must have been anaemic, sir.'

'Bedbugs are known to be inveterate survivors, even during long droughts and famines when they've had no humans to feed on. There haven't been any problems with the Armenians, have there?' John asked.

'Not since you asked me the same question yesterday, sir. Every POW is looking out for them, and with one or two exceptions, on the whole our guards ignore them.'

'What kind of exceptions?' John asked, instantly on the alert.

'It's the little girl, sir. I've seen one or two of the guards trying to give her cake and sweets, nothing wrong with that, they're probably fathers who are missing their own children, but for all of that she never takes anything off them, which isn't surprising after hearing what they've been through from Miss Rebeka. Can I give you a hand to move your things out of your tent and into the building, sir?'

'My things are my doctor's bag and kitbag,' John answered in amusement. 'I think I can manage those on my own. What on earth is going on out there?'

The sounds of shouting and excitement echoed in from the garden. John and Greening left the building. Bowditch and Grace were standing behind a rough wooden table set beneath the veranda of the officer's accommodation emptying out sacks of letters.

'Is that what I think it is?' John shouted.

'Mail, sir.' Grace ran his hands through the letters, lifted them high in the air, and allowed them to fall through his fingers.

'There's Red Cross parcels too, sir,' Bowditch added. 'Some have names on and some are for general use. The colonel's ordered the general ones put into storage for the common good. He asked if you could find a secure cupboard in the hospital to lock them into.'

'If there isn't one, I'll find someone who can make one, Bowditch.'

'Here's a parcel for you, sir.' Bowditch looked through the pile of Red Cross boxes that had been heaped on a wooden bench behind him, extracted one, and handed it to John. 'You probably have letters too, sir, but as you see, we haven't had time to sort them yet.'

John took the parcel and looked around at the men. Even with the food procured though the merchants most looked as though they were starving, but they were undoubtedly healthier than they'd been when he'd arrived a month ago. And certainly a lot fitter than they were when they'd left Kut.

'Baker,' he spotted the corporal and called him over. 'You've had letters?'

'Three, sir, from my wife, my mum, and my sister.'

'Do you have the key I gave you to the store cupboard where we decided to keep drugs and medical supplies?'

'Safe, sir.' Baker took it from his tunic pocket.

'Put this in there for me please,' John handed him the Red Cross parcel. 'And if you want to read your letters in peace you can shut yourself inside. No one will think of looking for you in there.'

'I may just do that, sir.' He took the parcel. 'But this food parcel is yours, sir. Shouldn't you keep it in your quarters?'

'I'll open it later and check the contents. We're not badly off for food at the moment, but things can change and it won't hurt to have extra supplies we can draw on if we have a sudden influx of sick.'

'I'll lock it in the cupboard, sir.'

Baker left and Greening joined John. 'Six letters for you, sir.'

'Thank you.'

'It's good to know that the outside world hasn't entirely forgotten us, isn't it, sir.'

'It is. You heard from your wife, Greening?'

'Yes, sir,' Greening beamed. 'I have a son, sir. John Mason Alfred Greening.'

'You named him after me!' John was shocked.

'The Alfred's for me, sir. After Kut ... well you know what we all went through there, sir – I wrote to Harriet and told her that if we had a son I wanted him named after the finest man I knew. I know it's an imposition, sir, and I shouldn't do it, but if we were in Basra I'd have asked if you'd minded standing godfather, sir.'

'It would be an honour, Greening, and I'm touched that you invited me, much less named your son after me.' There was a sudden unaccountable lump in John's throat that made his voice oddly tremulous. 'But how did you get your letter to Harriet?'

'I gave it to Major Knight to take downstream, sir. When General Townshend surrendered, Major Knight passed the word around that he'd take anything we wanted sent out with him when he escorted the sick, sir.'

'Well congratulations, Greening. We'll toast young John's health tonight.'

'In what, sir?'

'We'll find something.' John winked. He took his letters, went into his tent, moved the kitbag and doctor's bag he'd packed earlier, sat in his camp chair, and looked at the return addresses.

One was from Michael Downe, another from David Knight,

both sent a month ago from Sheikh Saad. One from Georgiana had only taken three weeks to travel up from Basra but a letter from his brother Tom, also posted in Basra, had taken over six weeks. There was one from his parents with a six-month-old postmark. The sixth, with an Indian return address, was from Maud.

He opened Georgiana's letter first. As he read he imagined her frown as she pushed her spectacles back up her nose as she wrote, squinting down at the paper in between dipping the pen into the ink well.

Dear John,

It's extremely odd to be writing this when I know perfectly well the odds of you ever getting it are almost negligible. However, here goes. I do hope that you are well and totally out of character caring for yourself better than you are looking after your patients. What's that phrase Helen was so fond of using in the London Hospital? 'Physician heal thyself because if you don't you won't be a blind bit of use to your patients'. Well, this is the point at which I stop rambling and say what I have to before I run out of paper.

Charles is dead, John, killed by a sniper at some awful place on the Tigris between Basra and Baghdad. David, Peter, and Michael were with him when it happened and they have all written the same thing. That there wasn't a single thing any one of them could do. One minute Charles was with them, talking and walking from one tent to another across the camp, the next he was dead with an Arab bullet in his skull. I know what reading this is doing to you. I loved the stiff upper-lipped idiot too, and I can't imagine carrying on living without him but living without him we must. I am too devastated to resort to platitudes about King and Country and a better place. The better place was here on earth with us. How dare Charles go and get himself killed! He left an absolute fortune which wasn't surprising when I thought about it. He and his father lived fairly frugally and there were an awful lot of generals in his family trees on both his mother and father's sides. Aren't they the ones who get the pick of the loot after battles?

Anyway, Charles appointed me and Michael executors of his will. Which brings me to the second awful bit of news, apart from bequests to Chatta Ram – Charles's half-brother as well as his

211

bearer – I'll save that story – and Kitty, Charles's nurse girlfriend, Charles left the bulk of his estate to Maud's son, Robin, and acknowledged the baby his son. How the hell that happened I have no idea. If you want me to do anything for you about Maud – like start divorce proceedings – I will. Unfortunately I can't whiplash her, which is what I'd like to do as she disappeared after leaving the child at the Lansing and asking Mrs Butler to put him into an orphanage. At the risk of you thinking I'm being the over-protective cousin, she was never the right one for you, John. Too silly and flighty by half.

Robin is with Angela at present – how long for, neither I nor Angela have any idea. Now the baby is wealthy I suppose guardians need to be appointed and to that end I have written to Charles's father to ask him what he'd like to do with the child. As Robin is undoubtedly a bastard I can guess his reply. Damn, I'm running out of paper so my writing is getting smaller. Hope you can read this. Tom was invalided out and sent back to Blighty, he and Clary married in Basra just before they left. David feels terribly guilty at leaving you to go into captivity while he is living in the lap of luxury with the Relief Force – now rechristened the Baghdad Force I suppose.

John, I really am sorry that it didn't work out for you and Maud, but you don't need my sympathy. This bloody awful war is messing up everyone's lives. I love you and will always be here for you, and I'm staying in Mesopotamia until the bitter end – or Michael leaves, whichever comes first.

Your loving cousin, who kisses your photograph (on the cheek) and says a prayer for you every night,
Georgie

John sat back and considered what Georgiana had written. He explored his feelings and was disconcerted to realise that he didn't feel anything much at all. He tried to recall his reaction when he found the cache of letters Maud had exchanged with one of her lovers among the effects of a man killed in battle. All he remembered about that night was getting drunk and remaining drunk for months afterwards – in fact, right up until the moment he'd been court-martialled and sentenced to death in Kut.

But then that had been a somewhat sobering experience.

How did he feel about his wife's child? But not just Maud's child, Charles's too, poor boy, abandoned by Maud to live out his life in an orphanage, or if he was fortunate, an adoptive home.

He thought about the boy for a moment. He was Charles's son and Charles was dead, so the boy was in need of a guardian. Peter and Angela would be ideal, especially as they were already caring for the child, but what if they had their own child. And then there was General Reid. No one could deny he was the boy's closest living relative, apart from Maud, who'd abandoned him, but General Reid had at best been an absent and remote father to Charles even when they'd lived under the same roof.

The obvious course would be to take the boy back to Clyneswood and Stouthall where he, his brother, sister, cousins, and Charles had grown up. Tom would probably already be back there with Clary. At the end of the war Georgie would possibly return to Clyneswood and him –

He had a sudden vision of a Sunday afternoon in the garden on a sunny day, playing cricket with Tom, Michael, Harry, Charles, Georgie, and his sister Lucy, while their respective parents drank tea on the terrace with the vicar.

Tom and Clary would hopefully have children. Charles's son – he scanned Georgie's letter to check his name – Robin should have at least one or two cousins to play with, if not, there were always the village children.

He had a sudden longing to be sitting on the terrace where his parents had sat, watching the next generation play cricket, tennis, and rounders.

His dreams had never moved far from Stouthall, or the old Georgian manor in a West Country village that he had planned to buy and live in with Maud and a houseful of children. The one and only thing that had changed in his dream was the identity of his wife.

Bagtsche Turkish Prisoner of War Camp
October 1916

Captain Gerald Vincent walked down the long dark stone corridor in company with a Turkish guard and German sergeant. The stench was foul and overpowering. Raw sewage mingled with cold sweat, vomit, and the feral odour of rats. He looked through the metal gratings into cells floored with filthy damp quilts and blankets so louse-ridden he could see the creatures moving from six feet away.

'The conditions in this camp are execrable,' he railed at the German sergeant. 'None of the men moving rocks outside were fit to work. These living conditions are not even fit for wild beasts. By your own admission you have no hospital or even a sick bay so men suffering from contagious diseases can be quarantined away from their healthy comrades.'

'We keep the sickest men in here, and this is where you'll find the officer you have been sent to replace, Captain Vincent.' The German nodded to the guard who stepped forward and unlocked the metal cell door.

The cell was about fifteen feet square, stone walled and floored. The only light came from a small grating close to the ceiling. It took Vincent a few minutes for his eyes to become accustomed to the gloom. The smell was even more intense, foul, and overpowering than it had been in the corridor. He blinked and focused on three emaciated men slumped on the floor with their backs against the wall opposite the door. All three were dressed only in shorts without boots or shirts, and all were perspiring.

He stepped towards them. The quilts and blankets squelched beneath his boots, lice scurrying deeper into the folds of the bedding.

'Captain Vincent, sir.'

He peered at the man who'd spoken. 'Do I know you?'

'Pearce, sir. You treated me when I was shot by a Turk in Kut.'

Vincent advanced towards the man. 'How are you, Pearce?'

'As you see, sir. I've been better.' He held up his arms which were skinned and bloody.

'What happened?'

'Slipped down the rock face, sir, when I was gathering blasting debris. Caused a landslide that caught Radcliff and Purcell.' He pointed to the men either side of him and Vincent saw that their hands, faces, and arms were as raw as Pearce's.

'I'll see if I've anything that might help ease the pain.' Vincent opened his doctor's bag.

'It's not us you should be looking out for, Captain Vincent, it's Major Crabbe, sir. He hasn't moved or opened his eyes in two days.' Pearce pointed to the corner.

Vincent went over too what he'd assumed was a bundle of rags. He used the tips of his fingers to move the quilt that covered Crabbe's face and body.

Vincent checked Crabbe's breathing and temperature before turning to the German sergeant. 'This man's face and body are badly bruised. What happened to him?'

The sergeant didn't answer but Pearce did. 'Major Crabbe took a terrible beating from the guards a month or so back and hasn't been right since, sir, but the Turks drove him out to work just the same. He was complaining about pains in his chest before he collapsed.'

Vincent folded back the filthy blanket and ran his hands over Crabbe's bare chest. He looked up at the German sergeant. 'The state of this man is bloody disgraceful. He's obviously been viciously attacked. He has two broken ribs and severe concussion. You have a moral duty to take care of these men, yet you have worked them ...'

'They are POWs and we have every right to work them,' the German reminded him harshly. 'They are paid for their work and we need that money to buy their food and pay for their lodging.'

'Food and lodging. You call this lodging?' Vincent demanded indignantly. 'How much do these men get paid?'

'Seven piastres a day, and every piastre is spent on them, but you cannot expect the Ottoman command to provide enemy soldiers with all the ridiculous luxuries they demand. We have our own troops to feed and care for. As for yours, we have complied with the conditions of the Hague Convention.' The sergeant kicked a corner of Crabbe's blanket. 'We have given all of your British soldiers bedding, clothes, and food and we also allow them to rest when they are too lazy to work, as these men are.'

'I see no care, and there is nothing in the Hague agreement about working men to death, and this man ...'

'Major Crabbe was beaten because he refused to obey orders.' The Turkish commandant stood in the open doorway of the cell.

'The conditions here are unacceptable and barbaric. The men are filthy, undernourished, and ...'

'They are prisoners, Captain Vincent, who refuse to wash or eat the food provided for them. If anyone is barbaric it is them. As they have thwarted all our efforts to clean themselves up we have assumed that they like living this way.'

'Major Crabbe needs urgent medical attention, now.'

'You are a doctor as well as an officer, are you not, Captain Vincent? You can treat him.'

'I need medicine and bandages, not just for Major Crabbe, but these men, disinfectant, drugs, men to help me clean this cell and wash the bedding ...'

'You have money to pay for medicine, bandages, disinfectant, and replacement bedding while this is washed?'

'I will sign a promissory note. The money will be paid by the British government at the end of the war.'

'Not good enough, captain. If we provide these things and pay for them out of our own pocket we will never be reimbursed. Disinfectant, medicines, and bandages are expensive.'

'I have two sovereigns.'

'Three and I may be able to bring you some of what you ask for.'

'Don't give him anything, sir,' Pearce warned. 'He'll take your money and give you nothing.'

The commandant nodded to the guard who held out his hand.

'Three sovereigns, but only after I've seen what they will buy,' Vincent warned.

The cell door banged shut. The men walked away. Vincent went to the door and shouted through the grille but the men kept on walking.

'Welcome to the cemetery, sir.'

Vincent turned to Pearce. 'Sorry, Pearce, what did you say?'

'Welcome to the cemetery, sir. That's what they call this place. Only one hundred and forty of us Dorsets reached here out of the three hundred and fifty who left Kut. Last headcount Major Crabbe took we were down to less than a hundred and that was a month ago.'

216

Chapter Twenty

Turkish Prisoner of War Camp
November 1916

John had slung a blanket around his shoulders but he was still shivering when he sat on the wooden bench on the veranda of the hospital. A cold wind blew dead dry leaves around the enclosed space, piling them high beneath the corners protected by the overhanging balconies. Rebeka left the building wrapped in an army greatcoat. She carried a tray that held a brass pot and three glasses. She set it on the table in front of John and took a small book from her pocket.

'Are you sure you want to progress to written Turkish?' she asked.

'There's no point in speaking a language if you can't read it. The merchants could be adding half a dozen camels on to the bills they ask me to sign and I wouldn't know.'

'You would because I always check the papers before you sign them.'

'You're not always around, Rebeka, besides, I need something to take my mind off this place and your lessons are the highlight of my day.'

Rebeka laughed. He reflected it was a delightful sound before realising he'd never heard her laugh before, and rarely seen her smile.

'Your days are very sad, Major Mason, if these lessons of ours are the highlight, and it's cold out here. We would be warmer and more comfortable in the kitchen.'

'But we wouldn't get fresh air. All prisoners' days are sad. None of us can go where we want, or do as we wish, but as prisons go this one is not as bad as some.'

'You have been in other prisons?' she asked in surprise.

'Not as a prisoner, but as a visiting medic when I worked as an army doctor in India. I visited a military prison there once a week.'

Sergeant Greening walked across the garden with the colonel who was the longest-serving and highest-ranking British officer in the camp, and as such had been unanimously elected commander of the British POWs. John rose to his feet and saluted.

'At ease, Mason. Mind if I join you?'

'Not at all, sir. You're welcome to join us for our Turkish lesson. Sergeant Greening and I would welcome a new fellow pupil.'

'I'm grateful you've seen fit to learn the lingo, Mason. But it's beyond my capability. Language sounds like monkey gibberish to me.' The colonel lowered himself carefully on to the end of the bench. He knew and John knew he had yet to recover from the ill effects of the fever he'd picked up on the march from Kut.

'The commandant just came to see me. He asked if I'd have any objection to the Turks sending prisoners here from other camps for medical treatment.'

'British prisoners, sir?'

'He did say there might be a few French and Russians as well, but mostly British.'

'What was your answer, sir?'

'No objections whatsoever provided they give us the accommodation, equipment, medics, and orderlies we needed to treat them.' He nodded to the nearest house outside the wire. 'He said he'd look into requisitioning that place.'

'Provided we have the rooms, drugs, and equipment, sir, I'd welcome the work.'

'Thought you'd say that which is why I told him yes. Although he did warn that finding more POW medics to assist you might be a problem.'

'Townshend allowed too many of our doctors to go downstream with the wounded when he surrendered Kut.' John nodded when Rebeka offered him and the colonel tea.

'Townshend made a great number of mistakes when he surrendered Kut. That was one of many and not the worst.' The colonel took the glass Rebeka handed him.

'The fact that he wants us to treat prisoners suggests that there are other POW camps within easy travelling distance of this place, sir,' John commented.

'It does. He also said that given the isolated nature of the countryside around here, the distance from the sea, and how far we are from any densely populated areas or railway lines, there's talk among the higher echelons of the Turkish command of giving all British POWs greater freedom.'

'In exchange for what, sir?'

The colonel hesitated then looked John in the eye. 'Signed guarantees from every officer and orderly that we won't try to escape.'

John fell silent.

'So, my suspicions are correct, there are plans afoot in the camp?'

'I've already said I won't leave Turkey while any of our men remain in captivity and need medical care, sir.'

'So I can rely on you to sign the guarantee and stay put, Mason. I wouldn't expect any the less of you. But you've avoided answering my question.'

'I know nothing about any escape plans, sir.'

'And you've probably taken care to know nothing about the subject.'

'I'm busy in the hospital, sir. I spend practically every waking hour here. I have no time left for gossip.'

'I understand you. Be so kind as to pass down a warning from me. If anyone does manage to get out of this place, they've a long trek in front of them. The chances of any one of us, even the fittest – and heaven only knows there are few in here who can be described as even moderately healthy – walking to Russia, or reaching the coast, stealing a boat, and sailing to Cyprus are not good. Just ask anyone with thoughts running in either if those directions one question. Are they prepared to risk every man they leave behind being punished for what will undoubtedly turn into a foolhardy and failed attempt to gain their freedom?'

'I'll see that your message is passed on to all the officers and orderlies, sir.'

'I suppose I can't ask any more of you.'

'Before you go, sir, is there any more news on the situation of the Armenians?' John glanced at Rebeka. 'I would hate to lose either of my nurses.'

'The last time I spoke to the commandant about them was shortly after your arrival. I told him what you told me, that you found their nursing services invaluable. He hasn't mentioned their presence here since, neither have I. Least said, least thought of, but I have noticed that the little girl, Hasmik, isn't it?'

'It is, sir.' John confirmed.

'Has become something of a favourite both with our men and the Turks. She adds a touch of humanity and home to this foul situation of ours.' The colonel rose awkwardly to his feet and leaned heavily on his cane.

'You should rest, sir,' John advised.

'If I rested any more I'd be dead, Mason. See you at the chess club this evening?'

'If I'm not needed here, sir.'

'Hope you're not. You're the only decent player we have.'

'One day I may even beat you, sir.'

John looked at Greening after the colonel had left to walk back to the officers' quarters. 'You have some people you need to talk to urgently, Greening?'

'I do, sir.'

'Pass on the colonel's message in it's entirely.'

'I will, sir.'

'Do you think Mrs Gulbenkian, Hasmik, and I will be able to stay here with you until the end of the war, Major Mason?' Rebeka asked after Greening had followed the colonel.

'I hope so. We had mail again yesterday. I've been meaning to ask, has Mrs Gulbenkian heard from her cousin in America yet?'

'No, sir, but she's sure she will, and when she does he'll send her money for passage to America for her and Hasmik.'

Rebeka felt the side of the small brass teapot. It was still warm so she refilled John's glass and poured a tea for herself.

'We've never really talked about your family, or Mrs Gulbenkian's. You don't have to now, but this war can't last forever and we all need to make plans for when it's over.'

'Where will you go, sir?'

'Back to my country I hope.'

'To work as a doctor?'

'With my father if he'll have me.' He began to tell her about Stouthall, the house he'd grown up in, and of his family, the clinic

220

his father ran, how he'd like to turn his father's hospital into a facility that catered for the men who'd become sick as a result of the wounds and injuries they'd sustained in the war. Then he realised, yet again she'd turned the subject away from herself.

'What about your home and your family?' he asked. 'Will you return to your home town at the end of the war?'

She shook her head. 'Mrs Gulbenkian and I have talked about it, but all our people are dead. Not just our families but our neighbours. Everyone we knew.'

'Are you sure?'

'All except Mariam, the sister I told you about.'

'But you have Mrs Gulbenkian and Hasmik.' John shivered. 'I'm cold.'

'So am I, but I warned you it was freezing outside, sir.'

'So you did.' He finished his tea, loaded the tray and led the way into the kitchen that served the hospital. Most of their food was cooked in the building that housed the junior officers and carried over to them but they used their small kitchen to make tea and toast bread.

She took the tray from him. He sat on the bench next to the stove, and held his hands out to the warmth.

'Don't tell anyone this,' she looked over her shoulder before shutting the door, 'but Hasmik is not Mrs Gulbenkian's daughter.'

'Then why would Mrs Gulbenkian say she is?'

'She didn't, really. I think you men just assumed Hasmik was Mrs Gulbenkian's daughter."

John thought about what Rebeka had said. 'You're probably right, but that doesn't explain why Mrs Gulbenkian would want us to believe that she's Hasmik's mother.'

Because all they have left from the old life is each other.'

'And you?'

She sat opposite him. 'Mrs Gulbenkian was our neighbour. Her husband was murdered along with my father, my brother-in-law, and all the other men in the town. She had no children and because she had only herself to worry about, she stood up to the gendarmes who force marched us into the desert. Hasmik's mother was the butcher's wife. When they killed her and Hasmik's sisters Mrs Gulbenkian held out her arms to Hasmik. None of the rest of us dared. Hasmik ran to her and Mrs Gulbenkian has taken care of her ever since.'

'The only one of your family you've spoken about is your sister Mariam who was taken by the tribesmen. What happened to the others?'

She looked down at the floor and began to talk, and once she started she couldn't stop. John sat beside the stove and listened as she recounted the horrors. How Mehmet, a common criminal that the Turks had made a gendarme and placed in a position of power over the Armenians, had tried to drag Veronika away from her mother, Mariam, Anusha, and her in the church, and how Mehmet had shot and killed Veronika and her mother when her mother had protested.

'After Mehmet killed my mother he pointed his rifle at Mariam and me. Anusha went with him to save us. Only Anusha returned to us in the morning. The gendarmes took Veronika and my mother's bodies in the night. I saw them lying next to those of my aunts when we were marched out the next morning. They were all naked and covered in blood. After the gendarmes finished using them, they killed all the women and girls who'd tried to fight them. Like my aunts had fought.'

'What happened to your sister Anusha?'

'She threw herself in the river when she could no longer bear to be used by Mehmet. She was shot before she drowned.' Rebeka raised her eyes to John's. 'The guards used all the women, except the very old. Some of the children like Hasmik escaped sometimes because the older women hid them in the dark. They covered them with their skirts. But they didn't always escape, and before the Arabs found us they used Hasmik. You know the guards used me too … they … they …'

She broke down, sank beside him on the bench and sobbed. Harsh, rasping sounds that tore from her throat and lungs. John slipped his arm around her.

'What they did to you was disgusting and unforgiveable, Rebeka.' He pulled a clean bandage from his pocket and handed it to her.

She took it wiped her eyes and straightened her thin shoulders. 'I should have found the strength to kill myself as Anusha did. Or at least fight back like Veronika …'

'You would have been killed, Rebeka, and life is precious.'

'Not my life, not after what the gendarmes did to me. They shamed me in the eyes of the world.'

'They shamed themselves, not you. You are better than them. You found the strength to survive. You have your whole life ahead of you.'

'A life without family, or work …'

'You have all the work you can do here and more. As for family. You have good friends. Mrs Gulbenkian, Hasmik, me and every man you have nursed here.'

'They don't know what I am.'

'Yes they do. They know you are a good, kind woman.'

'They don't know what the Turks did to me.'

'What the Turks did to you is not who you are, Rebeka,' he said emphatically. 'When the war is over you can leave here and go anywhere in the world. You'll make a new and wonderful life for yourself. You're bright, intelligent, speak three languages, Turkish, Armenian, and English …'

'I speak French as well. My father insisted we all learn.' The memory brought a smile to her face.

He took the damp scrap of bandage from her. 'Whatever brought that smile to your face keep thinking about it, you're beautiful when you smile.'

'It was one of my memories from my memory table. My father sitting in his chair next to the fire on a winter's evening trying to make my sisters and I converse in French when we only wanted to speak Armenian.'

'Your memory table?' He asked quizzically.

'It was something my grandmother gave all us girls. She told us that we should imagine our dining table set out with memories. Only the best and the happiest ones, and whenever we were unhappy we should take a memory, hold it close, and remember it until we were sad again. Then we should exchange it for another.'

He pulled her close. 'That is a lovely idea. Can I borrow it? Not your memories, but the idea for the table. I have some wonderful ones to set out on mine.'

'What kind of memories?' she asked.

'My home, growing up with my brother, sister, and cousins. Of drunken nights spent celebrating being a medical student in London.'

'Of a girl.'

He smiled. 'There were many girls.'

'No one special.'

'One, but she left me a long time ago.'

'I can't believe any woman would leave you. You're so kind.'

'It's not easy being married to a doctor or a soldier, especially in wartime, and I'm both.'

'You have no children?'

He shook his head. 'Were there young children in your family?'

'Mariam was the youngest and she was five. There was no time for Anusha and Ruben, they had only been married a few months but already my mother and his were nagging them to produce grandchildren.'

There was a knock at the door. John moved his arm from around Rebeka's shoulders. 'This is a kitchen, no need to knock.'

'Yes, sir,' Dira looked around the door.

'Is there a problem?'

'Lieutenant Bowditch's abscess just burst.'

'Thank you, Dira. Nothing like a burst abscess to stop a man thinking of home.' John turned to Rebeka. 'Want to help?'

'It's time I made tea for the patients.'

'Wish I could do that instead of cleaning and draining an abscess.' He reluctantly left the warmth of the stove and moved to the door. 'Thank you, Rebeka.'

'For what, sir?'

'My memory table. I will furnish it as soon as I have time.'

Turkish Prisoner of War Camp
October 1916

John rarely went to bed before midnight. That night it was two o'clock in the morning by the pocket watch he'd managed to hang on to despite Turkish 'searches' for what they termed contraband, which covered any valuables they considered worth stealing.

He closed the door of his bedroom, sank down on his cot, and mulled over the treatment he'd given Bowditch. He'd intended to lance the abscess on his spine before it burst but the abscess had decided otherwise. And now Bowditch was running a high fever which suggested the infection had already entered his bloodstream.

Bowditch's condition would have been regarded as serious in a London hospital, here, given the primitive conditions and instruments he was forced to operate with, it was life threatening, but he'd done all he could for the present. Jones and Baker were in charge of the night shift and he'd left them strict instructions to fetch him if there was any change in Bowditch's condition. He could do no more.

He sat on his bed, unlaced his boots, and in an effort to divert himself recalled his conversation with Rebeka about setting out a memory table.

He spent a few enjoyable moments recalling his childhood and student days, and a pleasant affair he'd had with an older and more sexually experienced fellow doctor, Helen, that had ended amicably leaving the deep friendship between them intact. His early military days in India, the balls, parties, mess dinners, flirtations with senior officers' daughters, rides in the countryside. Then – then – came Maud.

It would be churlish of him to say there were no good memories of Maud. Their courtship had been wonderful, marred only by Charles's clandestine affair with Maud's mother Emily. He'd suspected from the outset it would end badly for Charles, although he'd never thought it would end with Emily's untimely death. His wedding to Maud on the day of Emily's funeral had been sombre and not an occasion he wanted to remember. Their honeymoon in Harry's Arab father-in-law's house in Basra could have been wonderful but it had been spoiled by Maud's antagonism towards Harry's Bedouin wife and all things Arab.

From that moment on, he suddenly realised, there were no memories he wanted to cherish or put on his memory table. Only events he'd rather forget, like conducting make-shift surgery on trestles in trenches, extracting bullets and amputating the limbs of smashed young bodies. Drunken days and night when he'd sought oblivion and solace from the knowledge of Maud's adultery in any alcohol he could lay his hands on.

An endless parade of faces of the dead and wounded that he hadn't been able to help out of pain or save from death flashed through his mind's eye. Skeletal men dying of malnutrition and disease in Kut. The blanket-wrapped bodies of the men he'd read the burial service over in the desert, who'd died from wounds,

225

disease, and the Turks insistence on force-marching them in temperatures of a hundred and thirty degrees at the height of summer.

He re-read Maud's first letter and tried to imagine her living and working in a convent and simply couldn't.

Maud belonged in a party, surrounded by attentive men, and liveried servants with trays of capes and chilled champagne, smiling, talking, laughing …

He looked at the paragraph that had annoyed him most in the first letter he'd received from her.

I gave birth to a boy last December. I've asked Mrs Butler to place him in an American orphanage. I hope she will do so and that he will find adoptive parents who can give him a better life than I am able to. I am writing this so you realise that if you could bring yourself to consider taking me back, I would come unencumbered by further responsibilities.

So like Maud: she'd given birth to a child but instead of taking responsibility for him, she'd abandoned him to an orphanage and the care of mythical adoptive parents who, she believed, would be better placed to look after him than his own mother. That the child was unlikely ever to see the inside of an institution was down to Charles's generosity in acknowledging him as his son and leaving him an inheritance, and Angela Smythe's kindness in taking the child in.

He preferred not to dwell on Maud's infidelity, especially with Charles, but to his surprise he realised the idea of Maud sleeping with Charles didn't hurt him as much as the knowledge of her affairs had when he first discovered she'd been unfaithful to him.

He re-read the final paragraph.

I have suffered, but I know my suffering is nothing compared to yours. I will understand if I do not hear from you, but please, John, try and write, even if it's only a few sentences to tell me that you don't want to see me again.

I send all my love, your own very sorrowful Maud who's only hope is that you allow her a second chance to be the wife she should have been.

'Sorrowful' in truth or 'sorrowful' that she had been caught out? If he did reply, what could he say? It was easier to leave Maud's letters unanswered.

He picked out Georgie's last letter.

There's a sister in the Lansing, a real martinet called Sister Margaret. I spend most of my time fighting with her because she disapproves of female doctors. She's unbent slightly since she discovered I was married, but only slightly, and still tries to insist that I should examine men only when they're fully clothed as a naked man 'is a sight unfit for a woman's eyes'.

When I get free time I spend it with Angela, she absolutely dotes on the baby and I don't mean to hurt you, John, but he looks exactly like Charles. That's how I guessed who his father was.

I can't understand Maud leaving the child but I try not to judge others. Even if you've forgiven her I can't. She should never have treated you the way she did.

You are my cousin, and you always were a better big brother to me than Harry, but then as I was apparently born first, strictly speaking he was never my big brother.

I love you fiercely and protectively, John, look after yourself until we meet again and I can look after you. Whenever I write to you I imagine you sitting in front of me, listening intently, you head slightly to one side, never condescending or impatient ...

He picked up his pen, unscrewed his inkwell, and took a clean sheet of paper.

Dear Georgie,

You have no idea how much your letters mean to me. You say they are full of nothing, that's what so marvellous about them. They enable me to picture a sane, normal world (apart from the Turkish POWs) and there are times here when I'm ashamed to say I begin to doubt I'll ever live in the normal world among normal people again.

It's horrid being cooped up with men who long to be active. None of want to be here and there are days when some of us can't even summon up energy for a game of chess.

I'm more fortunate than most because I have the hospital and the sick to keep me occupied. I also have two marvellous nurses who've lost their homes and all their family to the Turks, yet they show so much kindness to all of us every day.

Today one of them gave me a memory table. I'd like to share it with you ...

Chapter Twenty-one

Bagtsche Prisoner of War Camp
December 1916

Captain Vincent ducked his head under the doorway of the small cell he used to isolate the camp's fever patients in the hope that separation might contain some of the diseases that were sweeping through the camp. Eight men were lying comatose on the floor. Warren Crabbe was the only one of his patients who'd moved since he'd last checked them. The major was leaning back against the wall, gasping.

'Still breathless and still have that pain in your right lung?' Vincent asked.

'I'd be worried if I didn't,' Crabbe joked. 'It would mean my broken ribs are dissolving.'

'A cart has arrived. We're loading it now. The Turks have agreed that six sick POWs can be moved to a hospital in another camp.'

Crabbe checked the men nearest him were really unconscious before whispering, 'Do you think there really is another camp close by with a hospital?'

'Macefield was hauled out of his cell last night by the guard with a limp. He was returned two hours later, unconscious. The men who shared his cell created a fuss until the guards woke me. There was nothing I could do. He died two hours ago. If they wanted to kill you and the others, Crabbe, they'd have no compunction about doing it right here and now in front of me and anyone else who was around.'

'They're allowing you to send six men, you say?'

'Yes.'

'Give my place to one of the younger men the guards are using every night.'

'The other five are all younger men who are being raped on a regular basis by the guards. You're going because if someone doesn't operate on those ribs of yours and set them properly, your lungs won't heal and you won't last out the winter.'

'I'm tougher than I look, and I've done most of my living.'

'You're an experienced officer who wields considerable authority. I need to send someone who has clout with the men, someone the guards won't try to bully. You know how impressed these dunderheads are by rank. I also told the commandant that your family are Scottish nobility.'

Crabbe made a face. 'Don't! Please don't make me laugh.' He clutched his chest. 'The idiots believed you?'

'They believe everything I say because I take care to keep a straight face when I say it. Over here,' Vincent shouted to two men who carried in a makeshift stretcher improvised from a pair of saplings and two greatcoats.

'I can walk.' Crabbe pressed the palms of his hands against the wall in an effort to lever himself upright.

'No you can't. Move him carefully and don't put any pressure on his chest,' Vincent warned.

'I can walk,' Crabbe repeated stubbornly.

'Out of this cell, down the full length of the corridor, and out into the courtyard?' Vincent checked.

'I may need an arm to lean on.'

'Assemble the stretcher and lift the major on to it,' Vincent ordered.

'Don't you dare,' Crabbe warned the men.

'Medic's orders take precedence over senior rank in all matters pertaining to health. Lift him on to the stretcher.'

Vincent escorted the stretcher-bearers and Crabbe into the courtyard. Five men were already in the back of the cart. The stretcher-bearers lifted Crabbe from the greatcoat 'sling' and laid him in the cart before fastening the tailgate.

The commandant left his office and looked into the open cart.

'These are the six you have chosen?'

'They are the most seriously ill. How long will they be travelling?' Vincent had asked the commandant several times as to the exact location of the camp with the hospital, and how long it would take the patients to travel there, but he had yet to receive an acceptable answer.

The commandant waved his hands in the air. 'One day, maybe two.'

'It gets cold at night. Put the greatcoats in the cart,' Vincent ordered the stretcher-bearers.

'But, sir, they're ours ...'

'Do it.' Vincent went to the commandant. 'There are many more sick POWs who should not be working.'

'Your men are lazy. The Germans do ten times more work than you and there are not so many of them.'

'The Germans are housed in clean dry rooms with clean dry bedding and they are given good food. Our men are being kept in appalling, filthy, damp conditions without adequate clothes or bedding, fed scraps that are not fit for animals, and beaten, raped, and mistreated by your guards.'

'I refuse to believe that a single one of your men has been mistreated by one of my Turkish guards. Every penny your men earn working on the railway line is spent on them as well as some Turkish money my government can ill afford. They have a roof over their heads, don't they?'

'An inadequate one.'

'If they work harder they may earn some more money which will buy better food, clothes, and blankets. The solution to your problems is in the hands of your men, Captain Vincent.'

'And the beatings,' Vincent steeled himself, 'and the rapes.'

'If your men obeyed orders there would be no need for my guards to chastise them.' The commandant watched the cart move across the courtyard. He barked the order to open the gates. As soon as the cart was driven through them the sentries closed and locked the massive doors.

'They will be all right, won't they, sir,' one of the stretcher-bearers asked Vincent. 'I mean, Major Crabbe and the others will be looked after?'

Vincent wasn't convinced that Crabbe and the others would be cared for, but the last thing he could afford to do was spread alarm or lower morale which was already at rock bottom among the remaining men so he repeated the same words he'd said to Crabbe.

'If Johnny Turk had wanted to kill Major Crabbe and the others, I think they would have saved themselves a lot of trouble and done it here. All we can hope for is that there really is a hospital staffed by qualified doctors. British would be marvellous.'

'You think we'll see them again, sir?'

'I certainly hope so.' He headed back to the isolation cell. 'I certainly hope so, Pearce, and wouldn't it be bloody marvellous if we were all on a boat heading to Blighty out of Constantinople harbour.'

Abdul's, Basra
November 1916

'So, you are back, my friend.' Abdul embraced Michael as he entered the coffee shop with Kalla and Daoud.

'Only for two days, Abdul. Then I will have to go upstream again.'

Abdul fell serious. 'I am very sorry about Major Reid. It is a grievous loss for you.'

'Thank you, Abdul. It is a heavy loss to us all.'

'A fine man and a fine English gentleman.'

Kalla touched Michael's sleeve. 'I will go up and check the rooms.'

'They have been cleaned regularly, Kalla. If anything is amiss come and find me.'

'So you can beat the maids? No, Abdul,' she shook her head. 'There's no need for me to trouble you, I will beat them myself.'

'I will lend you my stick,' he shouted after her.

'I have my own,' came back.

'She is getting cheeky, that one,' Abdul said as Daoud disappeared into the back room and Kalla ran up the stairs. He pulled a chair out from 'his' table for Michael, then clicked his fingers and a waiter appeared with fresh coffee, glasses, and brandy.

Michael looked through the window at the wharf. 'There are more boats than usual berthed on the quayside.'

'With General Maude demanding more and more supplies be sent upstream the river traffic's never been so heavy, except perhaps when the wounded are sent downstream after a battle.'

Michael lowered his voice. 'You sent a message?'

'Mitkhal is back in Basra. He called in last week and said he wanted to see you. Urgently.'

'What did you tell him?'

'That I could get a message to you, as I did. If I hadn't you wouldn't be here.'

'Is Mitkhal staying here?'

'No, at his brother-in-law Ibn Shalan's house.'

'I don't know where that is.'

'I do.'

'You will take me there?' Michael knew just how careful most Arabs were to keep the whereabouts of their family secret from all but a few trusted people.

'No. but I can get a message to him as I did you.'

'Tell him I will wait for him here all day tomorrow.'

'Not tonight?'

'I need to visit Mrs Smythe and my sister. I have letters for them.' Michael opened his pocket watch and checked the time.

'Do you want me to order you a carriage?'

'Please. To be at the door in ten minutes.' He finished his brandy and went upstairs, knowing ten minutes in Abdul time equated half an hour to an hour of normal time. The door to his rooms was open and Kalla was laying fresh linen on the bed.

She turned as he came in and shut the door. 'Do you want me to order a meal for later?'

'Just for yourself. I'll probably eat with Angela and Georgie. They're bound to have a hundred and one questions about Peter and David.' He stripped off his shirt, tipped water into a bowl, and washed his hands and face. 'I wish you would come with me. Angela and Georgie are dying to meet you.'

'A native girl visiting military ladies, don't be silly. Even if the guards manning the compound gate allowed me through, Angela's servants would think it bizarre.'

'Why? You're as good as my wife in all but name.'

'Really?' she smiled.

He soaked a sponge in water, rubbed soap on to it, and started washing. 'More of a wife than my British wife ever was.' He leaned over and kissed her. She pushed him playfully away.

'You're wet.'

'I should have taken more notice of the letters my brother Harry sent me after he married his Arab wife. As a race you're far more

233

loving, understanding, and easy-going than English women.'

She handed him a towel. 'I'll wait up for you.'

'You don't have to.'

'I want to.'

He finished drying and took the linen shirt she handed him. He looked around. 'Where did I put those letters?'

'If you mean the ones Major Smythe and Major Knight gave you, they're in here.' She opened his briefcase, took them out and handed them to him.

He glanced out of the window. 'For once Abdul was as good as his word. The carriage is already here. See you later.'

She walked him to the door.

'Lock it behind me.'

'I will, but if there are any problems all I have to do is shout for Abdul or Daoud.'

'See you soon.' He kissed her on the lips, a long lingering kiss he was reluctant to end. 'I suppose I could visit Angela tomorrow ...'

'You promised Peter you'd see her tonight.'

'Heartless woman.' He left.

Kalla locked the door behind him and leaned against it. There was knock at the door that connected with Daoud's room.

'It's open, Daoud,' she picked up the sheets and carried on making the bed.

'The cook is making lamb stew. Do you want me to bring some up for you?'

'Please, and some bread flaps, and just enough for me. Michael has gone out.'

'He has more energy than me, after three days of sailing downstream in rough water.'

'You know Michael.'

'Has he said anything to you about leaving me here when he goes back upstream?' she asked.

Daoud looked at her in surprise. 'No.'

'You're telling me the truth?'

'I am, but if you have any doubts you should talk to him.'

'You do know that the fighting will start again very soon?'

'Everyone knows that the British army is almost ready to advance, and as I can't see the Turks up and decamping to allow them through to Baghdad I think there'll be fighting.'

'Michael says he doesn't want me near any battles. You would tell me if he said anything to you about leaving me here?'

'No, I wouldn't, but Michael would.' Daoud adjusted his kafieh. 'Michael's only really happy when you're with him, Kalla.'

'You mean that?'

He smiled. 'You'd be a fool not to believe it.'

Turkish Prisoner of War Camp
December 1916

John left the building that housed the senior officers, crossed the garden and entered the hospital. The kitchen door was open and Mrs Gulbenkian, Hasmik, and Rebeka were in there, washing the patients' evening tea glasses and dishes.

Hasmik ran to him and offered him a basket.

'What have we here?' he asked lifting her in his arms.

'Turkish Delight,' she giggled, 'look, it's very good.' She took a piece and stuffed it into his mouth.

John didn't like the sickly cloying sweet but he smiled as he ate. 'Did you make it, Hasmik?'

'No the guard with a limp gave it to me. His wife made it.'

'And you have eaten quite enough of it, little one. Any more and you will be sick. Time you were in bed,' Mrs Gulbenkian ushered the child towards Rebeka. 'Say good night to Rebeka and Major Mason.'

Hasmik dutifully offered both of them kisses.

Mrs Gulbenkian picked up Hasmik. 'I'll come down and finish the dishes after I've settled her.'

'No, there's hardly anything left. I'll finish, it,' Rebeka volunteered. 'Get a good night's rest. You look tired.'

'Thank you, I am. Good night, Major Mason. See in the morning.'

'Good night,' John called after them as he sat down.

'Did you have a good game of chess?' Rebeka carried on washing and drying the tea glasses.

'No, I lost three games to the colonel.'

'You must give me a game sometime.'

'You play? Why didn't you tell me?'

235

'My father taught all of us to play. I was never as good as him although I could beat all my sisters.'

'I'll check on Bowditch; if he's stable I'll get my set and board and we'll have a game now.'

'You haven't had enough for one night?' she asked.

'I'd enjoy playing someone I could beat.'

She laughed. 'I meant to tell you when you came in but Hasmik couldn't wait to give you her Turkish Delight. When I took the orderlies tea earlier Private Williams told me that Lieutenant Bowditch's temperature had dropped to normal.'

'That is good news. I hope it would. It was almost normal when I left. I won't be long.' John left the kitchen and toured the wards. Everything was clean, all the men were sleeping and Williams was sitting next to Bowditch's bed.

John examined Bowditch. 'I thought Dira was on duty tonight.

'Dira's been sitting here night and day, sir. Now Bowditch is finally showing signs of recovering I persuaded him to go to bed.'

'Thank you, Williams. If Dira has fault, it's tendency to work himself too hard.'

'Like you, sir?'

'Like all the orderlies,' John corrected.

'It's impossible to take it easy when the men need help, sir. Do you think Lieutenant Bowditch will recover now, sir?'

'I hope so. The signs are good but it could be a long haul. Blood poisoning is the devil to get over. Is anyone relieving you?'

'Corporal Baker at two, sir.'

'I'll be round again before then, but if Lieutenant Bowditch wakes or there's any change in his condition come and get me. I'll be in the kitchen.'

'Yes, sir.'

John went to his room, picked up the chess set and board a patient had made him, and returned to the kitchen. Rebeka had finished washing the dishes and set out two glasses of water and a plate of crackers. He put the cloth board and pieces on the table.

'You and Mrs Gulbenkian have turned this room into a warm and welcoming domestic oasis.'

'The orderlies like to come here, sir. It's somewhere for them to sit and talk when they have a few spare minutes.'

She opened the box that contained the chess pieces and looked at them.

'Not your conventional set. One of my patients made it from two walking sticks so all the pieces are the same shape if not the same size. It's as well he drew pictures of what each piece is on the top or we wouldn't recognise them.'

'But the set is perfectly playable,' she said seriously.

'Perfectly,' he concurred, watching as she set out the board. 'You can take white which in this case is red as he had no white paint.'

She set up the pieces and made the first move.

'You must have been close to your father if he taught you languages and chess. Did he teach you anything else?'

'Sketching, painting, literature, and music. He was passionately fond of music. We had a gramophone at home and he always spent more than we could afford, or so my mother said, on recordings.'

'What did he like?'

'Mozart, Beethoven, and the later composers like Chopin and Tchaikovsky.'

'I can imagine your evenings at home, with literature and music, you sitting at the table making jewellery.'

'I never worked at home, only in the workshop. We kept all the jewels and precious metal there.'

He moved a piece, and they played in silence for a few minutes.

'Like my brother you're a careful player who places pawns meticulously. I, on the other hand am reckless.' He moved his queen out into the middle of the board.

'How did you spend your evenings in England?'

'Much the same as you, reading, talking, listening to music. Playing chess and other games. We had a billiards room and a room with a gramophone so the girls were always nagging the boys in the family to dance.'

'Girls?'

'My sister and my cousin.'

'Sounds fun.'

'It was. Our upbringings couldn't have been that different.'

'Check.'

He looked down at the board. 'I haven't been paying attention. No matter what move I make, you'll checkmate in three moves.'

'My father was a good teacher, and you've had a long day and you're tired,' she said diplomatically. 'Would you like a cup of tea?'

'Not at this hour, but thank you for the offer.' He thought of the letters from Maud that were still waiting to be answered. 'I have a few things to do in my room before I make my next round.' He watched her pack away the chess set. 'You seem restless.'

'I can't stop thinking about the future.'

'Who knows what it holds for any of us.'

'I can't imagine any kind of a future without my family. Yet I have to.'

'Do you want to carry on making jewellery?'

She thought for a moment. 'I was good at it.'

'That's not the same thing as wanting to do it.'

'It's a way of earning a living, but since Mrs Gulbenkian and I have been working with you and the orderlies and I've seen the difference we can make I've realised there are more useful things to do with my life than make jewellery.'

'You've certainly made a great deal of difference to the men who've had to come in here.' He rose to his feet and without thinking held his arms out to her. She went to him and he hugged her.

Then she did something totally unexpected. She stood on tiptoe and kissed him. He looked down at her. Her eyes stared back into his. Dark, enigmatic pools that gave away none of her thoughts. She stood on tiptoe again, and that time he bent his head to hers and kissed her. She tensed in his arms and he suddenly realised what he was doing.

'I am so sorry.' Overcome with remorse for taking advantage of the girl, John stepped back from Rebeka. 'I have no excuse. I simply wasn't thinking. If I had I would never have kissed you.'

'I shouldn't have kissed you, sir.'

'After what you've been through you have every right to come to me for comfort. I took advantage of you, which is unforgivable.'

'I ...' tears started in her eyes.

'Sir,' Private Williams opened the door. He stepped back surprised to see Rebeka there. 'Didn't mean to interrupt, sir.'

'You're not, Williams,' John hadn't meant to snap.

'Lieutenant Bowditch is awake, sir.'

'I'll be there now, Private.'

'Yes, sir.'

Williams left and John looked at Rebeka who was standing at the sink, drying a clean tea glass. He reflected it wasn't the time to talk to her, not with Bowditch needing attention. He picked up his bag and left for the ward.

Chapter Twenty-two

Smythes' Bungalow, Basra
December 1916

'That was the best roast lamb I've eaten in years, Angela. Thank you.' Michael turned from Angela to his sister. 'It's good to be here with both of you.' He reached for Georgie's hand and squeezed it.

'Things must be bad upstream if you're looking for reassurance from your big sister.' Georgie returned the pressure.

'They're not bad – at the moment,' Michael qualified.

'When will the assault begin?' Angela signalled to the maid to clear the dishes.

'Command doesn't confide in war correspondents.' Michael picked up his wine glass.

'Come on, Michael, we've seen the supplies being shipped upstream,' Georgiana finished eating and set her knife and fork on her plate. 'This is us you're talking to and we need to know. Peter's there, you're there …'

'And David's there.'

'He survived the Expeditionary Force foray from India in 1914 and the siege of Kut. I'm not worried about him.'

'You should be. He never stops talking about you. Every time I see him he asks if I've heard from you.'

'Really,' Georgiana retorted sceptically. 'If he does, it's only because you haven't any women with you. He likes to have a new girl on his arm every night.'

'There aren't any women upstream,' Michael protested.

'Not even camp followers?'

'Camp followers are always attached to someone and that someone will be loath to allow their womenfolk out of their sight,' he replied, thinking of Kalla. 'That doesn't detract from the fact

241

that David will be in the forefront of the advance.'

'Doctors are never in the front line.'

'Oh, yes, they are. John and David have both worked in the forward trenches and operated under fire.'

'David's made of India rubber, he'll bounce back,' Georgiana declared. 'To repeat Angela's question, when is the assault likely to start?'

'So you can tell everyone?'

'Who will we tell? Men in HQ who already know? Americans in the Lansing who are playing guess the date? We need to know so we can start praying for your and Peter's safety.'

'I suppose I won't be telling you anything that the sepoys and auxiliaries haven't already guessed and spread far and wide among the natives. Everyone is expecting orders to start the offensive around the middle of the month.'

'In a week?' Angela paled.

'Week to ten days. But don't worry, Peter will be fine,' Michael assured her.

'You haven't known him that long. You've no idea how reckless he can be.' Angela bit her lip.

'I've heard the late night camp fire stories about Townshend's Regatta. How Peter sailed single-handedly into nests of Turks and fought and overcame them all when he was outnumbered ten to one,' Michael joked, 'but that was Peter the subaltern. Peter is now a cautious, responsible major.'

'Being promoted didn't make him any more sensible.'

The maid came in and curtsied.

'You can bring the coffee, fruit, and cheese when you've finished clearing the dishes.' Angela handed her the gravy boat.

The maid filled a tray with dirty dishes and disappeared back into the kitchen.

'Peter's responsible for the lives of the junior officers and ranks under his command, Angela,' Michael reminded her. 'And majors almost always remain in relative safety in the trenches to oversee operations.'

'You expect me to believe that Peter will stay behind the lines after sending his men out to face the Turks?'

'That's exactly what he'll do – most of the time.'

Georgiana decided that a change of subject was called for. 'You didn't return to Basra just to give us letters from Peter and David, did you?'

'No, Harry's old orderly sent a message that he wants to see me.' He met Georgiana's eye and shook his head slightly to warn her off mentioning Harry.

'You think he has information about the Arab auxiliaries fighting with the Turks?' Georgiana moved their coffee cups to the centre of the table so the maid could fill them.

'I have absolutely no idea why he wants a meeting.'

'Did you catch the man who shot Charles?' Angela questioned.

'No one even saw him.'

'Do you have any idea what tribe he belonged to?'

'None. Charles was incredibly unlucky. Arab snipers fire at us day and night and rarely hit anything.'

'So Charles wasn't a target?' Georgiana pressed.

'No more than any man in an officer's uniform.' He saw tears start in Angela's eyes. 'Peter really will be all right ...'

'Please, excuse me.' Angela left the table and ran from the room.

'Shouldn't you go after her?' Michael asked his sister.

'She'll be fine after she's had a few minutes to compose herself. It's the strain of worrying about Peter while working in the Lansing and looking after Robin. Have you heard from John?'

'A postcard to say he's arrived in a Turkish POW camp, and was fine but would welcome Red Cross parcels. You?'

'The same, but I've been writing to him a couple of times a week. To be honest it was either that or start keeping a diary. John's always been a brilliant listener. I thought reading my letters might give him something to do. Apart from the news about Charles and the paternity of Maud's baby I've tried to keep them fairly light. From what we've heard in the Lansing and seen of the Turks, the British POWs taken at Kut have had a foul time.'

'I've heard that too,' Michael murmured.

'From the Arabs?' When Michael didn't confirm her suspicions she said, 'Don't look so surprised. I know exactly how you spend your days. I've read the articles you've written in the paper – granted often weeks after you've penned them – but it's obvious, even without what you've said tonight, that you spend a great deal of time with the locals. I've also heard rumours that you're a political officer.'

'Like Harry I sympathise with the natives. We may be fighting their hated overlords, the Ottomans, but nothing can alter the fact that we're doing it by invading their country. Like the average Tommy I have absolutely no bloody idea why we're here. Apart from trying to steal the oil the Arabs have chosen not to exploit.'

'Have you talked to any Arabs who've seen the Kut POWs?' she asked.

'A few. Apparently the Turks and their Arab auxiliaries marched the captives into the desert at the height of summer without food, water, or sufficient protective clothing. Tribesmen stole everything they had of any value including their boots. Hundreds if not thousands have died en route to Turkey.'

'Do you think John is safe now?'

'You can't get much information from a postcard. He's alive at the moment but I doubt the Turks will keep the POWs in one place for long. They'll move them around to prevent them from building a network of contacts to help them escape. I only hope John doesn't end up in the hands of a group of sadists. Every army has a few and the ones that are wounded and invalided into prison guard duty can be among the worst, or so I've been told.'

'Do you know why Mitkhal sent for you?'

'I've no idea.'

'But you'll see him?'

'Hopefully.'

'Will you ask him if I can see Harry?' she pleaded.

'I'll ask, Georgie, but you saw Harry as well as me. He obviously wants to live as an Arab with his Bedouin wife and children. And, from the state of him I wouldn't blame him for turning his back on the army or England.'

'And us?'

'We haven't been part of his life for a very long time, Georgie.'

'I know he's made his choice but I'd still like to see him one more time and meet his wife and children. We were so close …'

'When he wasn't teasing you and driving you to distraction,' Michael smiled.

The maid brought in fruit and cheese and Angela reappeared. 'I'm sorry, Michael, I don't know what's the matter with me these days. I just can't seem to stop crying.'

'Given what's happening in the world, it's a wonder we haven't all drowned in tears,' Georgiana commented. 'How are you coping upstream, Michael?'

'You know what men are like, especially soldiers.'

'You're pretending it's a Boy Scout camping trip.'

'The supply of alcohol helps.'

'Georgie told me that you've written to Charles's father about Robin. I take it you haven't had a reply from him?' Angela asked.

'It's too soon for letters to have gone both ways, but even if General Reid wanted the boy to live with him, there's no way we could get Robin to England at the moment. No military ship heading for Blighty would take a baby, and there are precious few civilian vessels prepared to risk sailing with German U-boats patrolling the Med.'

'Have you discussed Robin's inheritance with Peter?'

'He knows Charles recognised the boy as his son and left him a legacy.'

'Did Peter say anything about my looking after him?'

'Only that he hoped you won't get too fond of the boy because General Reid might claim him.'

'Do you think Charles's father will want him?' Angela's hand shook as she poured the coffee.

'Difficult to say. What do you think, Georgie?' Michael turned to his sister.

'As I've already said to Angela, it's impossible to predict how Uncle Reid will react. Especially after losing Charles. But I can't see a seventy-year-old man wanting a small child running around his house. And by the time this war is over, Robin will be at the handful stage.'

'The situation is a mess. It must be dreadful for John to know that one of his closest friends fathered his wife's child but a part of me can't help feeling glad that Charles has left a son.' Michael rose from the table.

'Thinking of having a family, Michael?' Georgie asked, surprised by his attitude.

'Not until after the war.'

'Everyone says that about everything these days,' Angela left her chair.

'Please don't get up, Angela. I'm beat and I have no doubt you want to read your letters.' He indicated the letters he'd placed on Angela's desk.

'You'll call again before you go back upstream?'

'I'll try, Georgie, but I make no promises. If you want to send replies to your letters ...'

'We will,' Angela assured him.

'I'll send Daoud to pick them up tomorrow evening if I can't come myself.' He left the table and Angela and Georgie followed him to the door. He kissed Angela's cheek then Georgie's.

'You'll give Peter my love?' Angela begged.

'I will. Goodnight to both of you.'

It was only when he went outside that Michael realised Angela had sat through the entire evening with her shawl pulled around her shoulders although the stove was lit and the bungalow warm. He hoped she wasn't sickening for something.

Turkish Prisoner of War Camp
December 1916

Mrs Gulbenkian was woken by the sound of someone sobbing as though their heart was breaking. She left her bed and checked Hasmik in her low cot. The child was sleeping soundly. She opened the door and tiptoed into the small adjoining room where Rebeka lay face down on her bed.

She sat beside her and stroked her hair. 'Whatever's the matter, Rebeka?'

Rebeka reached into her pocket for the scrap of bandage she'd put there. She turned and dried her eyes but kept them averted from Mrs Gulbenkian.'

'Are you crying for your parents and sisters?'

'I cry inside me every day for them.'

'As I do for Mr Gulbenkian.' Mrs Gulbenkian made the sign of the cross and lowered her eyes for a few minutes. 'If you're concerned for the future,' she said, 'don't be. My cousin will send money enough for passage for all of us to go to America. And wherever I go I will take you and Hasmik. I promise you. After what we have suffered together we are closer than a family.'

'Thank you, Mrs Gulbenkian ...' Rebeka shook her head and more tears fell from her eyes.

'You're crying because of Major Mason, aren't you?'

Rebeka finally looked at her.

'You've fallen in love with him?'

'I don't know,' Rebeka whispered.

'You don't know? Whenever he comes into the room you are in, you can't stop looking at him. And now you tell me don't know whether you love him or not. Well, I don't believe you.'

'It's hopeless for me to love any man. I was never pretty and no man would want or love me, not after what the Turkish gendarmes did to me.'

Mrs Gulbenkian wrapped her arms around her. 'You're no different from any Armenian girl the Turks laid their hands on. They dishonoured thousands of us.'

'Knowing that I have company doesn't make it any easier to bear.'

'No, it doesn't, but you must learn to accept that when the Turks dishonoured us they made less in the eyes of the world, and to any man who is aware that we have been dishonoured. Major Mason knows what the Turks did to you and although he is kind no man wants a wife without honour. And have you spared a thought for Major Mason? A man like him would have a wife and children.'

'If he has, he's never spoken about them.'

'Probably he finds it too painful because he misses them so much.' She stroked Rebeka's hair. 'The best thing you can do is forget about Major Mason, Rebeka, concentrate on your work here as a nurse. If we don't make trouble and work hard perhaps the Turks will allow us to stay here until the end of the war. Then, when the ships start sailing again, we can go to America. Once we are there we won't tell anyone what happened to us and we can start our lives afresh.'

'By lying?'

'By not telling anyone what the Turks did to us.'

'I must look for Mariam before we leave Turkey. I am all she has left. If it wasn't for her I would want to be with Veronika and Anusha and our parents ...'

'Of course.'

Rebeka could tell from Mrs Gulbenkian's tone of voice that she didn't really expect her to find Mariam.

247

'But you have to remember, Rebeka, that when we start our new life in America, you are not to tell anyone, not a soul, what the Turks did to us and the others.'

'They will have heard about it from others.'

'What others, Rebeka? Everyone except us is dead.'

'There were other groups from other towns,' Rebeka pointed out.

'Which is nothing to do with us.'

'A man will know whether or not his bride has been dishonoured.'

'Once married, a decent man won't ask his bride any awkward questions.'

'I was happy living without a husband. I don't want a husband ...'

'Just Major Mason?'

Rebeka nodded wretchedly.

'A man like Major Mason can have any girl he wants. He is an Englishman, a gentleman. We are Armenians, simple farmers. We have not been taught to understand the English or their ways. They are complicated people with their kings and queens, lords and ladies. You only have to see them here. This is a prison, every man who is a prisoner should be equal to every other, yet the colonels do not speak to the captains or the captains to the lieutenants.'

'That is the same in every army, even the Turkish.'

'Rebeka, Major Mason is a nice, kind man. You have lost your family, you trust him, and that is why you have fallen in love with him. You are mistaking his kindness towards you for love.'

'Kindness – that's all you think it is?'

'After what's happened to you, Rebeka, I don't think you can expect any more from any man. But my cousin will welcome us and we will go to America together.'

'But first I must look for Mariam.'

'We will go after you have found Mariam.' Mrs Gulbenkian didn't sound convincing but she embraced her and held her close. Rebeka didn't enjoy the sensation. Mrs Gulbenkian smelled of onions, goose grease, and oatmeal, the ingredients they mixed to make poultices for patients' ulcers that were proving difficult to heal.

All she wanted was to be left alone to try and imagine what her future would be like in a country where the only familiar faces she would see from her past life were Mrs Gulbenkian and Hasmik – and no one else.

Basra
December 1916

After spending the best part of three days travelling downstream cooped on an overcrowded boat, Michael decided to walk back to Abdul's from the Smythes' bungalow. The air was cold but the night crisp and clear and he stepped up his pace to keep warm.

When he left the narrow street that connected the British compound to the wharf, a figure emerged from the shadows and blocked his path.

'The boat you ordered is up ahead on the left, sir.' The man's English was heavily accented but there was no trace of any dialect that Michael recognised. He wasn't tall but he was broad and well-built and had a vicious-looking dagger tucked into his brown cloth belt. His face and head were swathed in a kafieh he'd pulled over his nose and mouth to conceal his features. His gumbaz and abba were clean, well made, and a nondescript beige that was worn by half the working men in Basra.

Michael had a gun in his pocket but he knew it would take him longer to retrieve it than it would for his companion to pull a dagger and slice into him.

'Thank you.' Michael headed towards the vessel.

The man grabbed the mooring rope, pulled the boat against the quayside, and held it steady. Michael glanced at him before boarding.

The man followed. 'The river air is cold tonight. You will be warmer beneath the awning.'

Michael picked his way carefully over the planking of the low-slung native barge towards the curtain that separated a makeshift cabin from the rest of the boat. An unseen hand moved the cloth aside.

'Thank you for joining me, Michael.' The language was Arabic, the voice, soft, low.

'Mitkhal, good to see you.' Like Mitkhal, Michael whispered. He ducked his head and entered the 'cabin'. An oil lamp hung from the rafters. It burned low, sending eerie shadows dancing over the camel hair cloth walls, throwing Mitkhal's features into sharp relief.

'I came downstream as quickly as I could after receiving your message, Mitkhal.'

'Thank you.' Mitkhal called out to the boatman.

There was a splash as the man untied the painter and dropped the rope into the water, swiftly followed by the thud of wood knocking on wood when he pushed the boat away from the wharf with an oar. The boat rocked and they moved out into mid-stream.

'Don't,' Mitkhal warned when Michael reached for the curtain.

'We're going to Shalan's house?'

'We're going where we won't be seen or overheard.'

Michael took a pack of cigarettes from his pocket and offered Mitkhal one.

Mitkhal shook his head. 'I saw John.'

'Where? When?'

'Keep your voice down.

'Sorry. I've just left Angela Smythe and my sister. We're all worried about him.'

'With good reason as he's in Turkish hands. He was coping when I last saw him. Many British troops died on the march from Kut into Turkey. There would have been far more fatalities if it wasn't for John Mason. I left him on the border between Turkey and Mesopotamia over a month ago.'

Voices drifted in from outside and Mitkhal held his finger to his lips. Knowing how every sound magnified on water Michael remained quiet. Mitkhal called to the boatman. Moments later the harsh grating of metal on metal filled the air. The boat stopped then moved forward and thudded against a bank.

'We're here.' Mitkhal moved back the curtain and stepped out on to a small dock. Michael followed and came face to face with the tall, hawk-nosed, commanding figure of Ibn Shalan.

British Relief Force Camp
December 1916

David cradled his glass of whisky, sat forward on his camp chair and watched the flames dance in the fire his bearer had lit in front of his tent. Deep in thought, he was barely aware of the camp noises beyond the fire. The sounds of men conversing in loud, alcohol-fuelled conversation. Camels, mules, and horses snorting in protest as the syces tethered them for the night. The cries of the sepoys manning the canteen offering last orders of food.

Peter and Boris walked up carrying their own chairs.

'Any whisky going spare?' Boris asked.

'Help yourself. I sent my bearer to bed. I've just finished a twenty-hour shift and he was with me every step of the way, fetching, carrying and keeping me awake when all I wanted to do was sleep. Now, when I can sleep, I'm past it.' David handed Boris the bottle.

'There've been more sniper victims?' Boris took a glass from his pocket, filled it, and handed the bottle on to Peter.

'Four sepoys, poor beggars, and five Arab auxiliaries, which made for a busy day on top of the dysentery and fever cases, and two of the Eton wet bob subalterns decided to crack open one another's skulls. I hope Maude's takes stock of our strength before we move on. He needs to cut the useless dead weight loose, especially the youngest idiots, and send them back downstream.'

'We came here to be cheered up,' Boris complained, 'not listen to you moaning. Whatever happened to diverting David?'

'Diverting David has been transformed into depressing David. Do you two realise we're now well into the third year of this damned war?'

'I don't need reminding.' Peter finished his drink and refilled his glass.

'The best years of our lives are slipping by.' David looked up from the fire. 'But not for you, Smythe. You've a pretty wife waiting for you in Basra.'

'What's this, Knight? The bachelor life palling on you all of sudden?' Boris teased.

'Some bachelor life here. Not an available woman in sight.'

'Just not one you fancy. What's brought on this fit of maudlin introspection?' Peter queried.

'Just wondering what life's all about.'

'Drink some more of this,' Peter topped up David's glass, 'and you won't need to wonder.'

David tried to focus on Peter. 'Is that what it's all about? A search for oblivion?'

Peter opened his watch, not to tell the time but to look at the photograph of Angela he tucked under the glass plate in the lid. 'I hate to say it, but until we march into Baghdad and get victory leave long enough to go home, it probably is.'

Chapter Twenty-three

Ibn Shalan's house, Basra
December 1916

The message Michael had received upstream implied that Mitkhal wanted to meet him urgently, but whatever the reason, it wasn't urgent enough for Ibn Shalan to dispense with the lengthy ceremony that marked every visit to a Bedouin household. Michael was shown into a small, exquisitely decorated room and offered coffee, sugar, and pastries while male servants laid out trays of sweetmeats, dates, and almond cakes.

The room was warm, heated by an iron stove and comfortably furnished with low divans and carved tables. Michael sat on a divan, his host sat opposite him and after receiving and making polite enquiries about their respective health, they were joined by Mitkhal.

Michael rose when the Arab entered the room and Mitkhal embraced him as any Arab would a close friend, kissing him on both cheeks.

'You look good, Michael, campaigning in the desert suits you.' Mitkhal sat opposite him next to Shalan.

'It's easier now the cold weather is upon us.'

'Your Arabic has improved.'

'Daoud is a good teacher.'

'Just in Arabic, or all things Arab?'

'All things Arab.' Michael was careful to observe Bedouin formality. He kept the soles of his feet firmly on the floor and touched nothing with his left hand. Tired after a long day and looking forward to returning to Kalla more than he would have admitted to Mitkhal or Ibn Shalan, he attempted to move the conversation on. 'The arms, ammunition, and livestock I arranged to be supplied to you before the fall of Kut were satisfactory?'

253

Ibn Shalan inclined his head and reached for his tobacco pouch. 'They were satisfactory,' he echoed, 'but the situation has changed since Kut surrendered. As demanded by British command, I sent many of my men to the North to assist the British troops who were being marched to Turkish prison camps, this, despite the increased number of hostile tribesmen who massed in the Karun Valley in preparation to attack the British Relief Force from the rear.'

'British Command knows that Ibn Shalan is safeguarding their flanks and they are grateful for his friendship and assistance.' Michael sat back and waited for the request he suspected was coming.

'The British surrender of the town of Kut al Amara has given some men in the tribes reason to believe that the British will lose this war,' Shalan observed.

'We won't,' Michael refuted.

Shalan finished rolling his cigarette and proceeded to light it. Mitkhal continued the conversation.

'The Bakhtairi Khans have been more active, not just in the Karun Valley and on the northern borders. We did not have sufficient men to control them, so I recruited men from some of the smaller tribes friendly to us and the British, but,' Mitkhal shrugged, 'although they were prepared to fight they had no horses, camels, or guns.'

'So these men you recruited were of no use to you?'

'I supplied a few of the strongest with weapons, ammunition, and camels from the last of our stock,' Shalan explained. 'I cannot deny the British have been generous in giving us what we need to fight the Turk, but we have lost many men between Kut and the Turkish border. And not just men: livestock, ammunition, and weapons.'

'You need more weapons?' Michael didn't know why he was asking when it was obvious what the sheikh wanted. The chief political officer, Percy Cox, had given him considerable leeway when it came to fulfilling the tribes' requests for stock and ammunition, provided the tribe in question could prove loyalty to the British. But his remit did not extend to guns. A tighter control was kept on weapons because Cox was all too aware that they could be used against the British if they fell into the wrong hands.

'We urgently need weapons, ammunition, horses, camels, and

goats. With the war raging in every corner of the desert the women cannot tend our livestock.'

'How much do you need?' Michael asked.

'A thousand rifles would be good, two thousand better. Ammunition sufficient for six months' use of the guns, plus mounts and goats,' Shalan said.

Michael decided the honest approach was the best one. 'The livestock and ammunition won't present a problem. Mitkhal and I can go to the supply department and the markets tomorrow. You'll have whatever you need in a day or two.'

'The guns?' Ibn Shalan asked.

'The British Command makes a note of every gun they distribute among the tribes. Your men have more British firepower than any other tribe in Mesopotamia.'

'We fight longer and harder for the British than any other tribe.'

'And we are grateful.'

'But not grateful enough to give us more guns?' Shalan pressed.

'It is not my decision. If it was, I would give you everything you ask for. But the men in power are concerned as to what will happen when the last Turk has been driven back over the border into Ottoman Turkey.'

'Until that moment we will fight resolutely by your side.'

'And afterwards?' Michael's question was met by a silence so dense, so absolute it prompted a buzzing in his ears.

'We all know what will happen then, Michael.' The curtain that covered the doorway moved.

'Harry!' Michael jumped up and stared at his brother before clasping him in his arms and hugging him.

'Hasan. Harry Downe is dead.' He returned Michael's embrace before pushing him back and studying him with his one eye. 'You look good, Michael, as handsome as I remember myself before I fell into the hands of the Turks.'

'You haven't lost your sense of humour.'

'I've needed it since I left England. Your Arabic is good.' He took a seat on the divan next to Michael.

'So is yours.'

'I've been speaking it longer and had more practice than you.'

Ibn Shalan and Mitkhal rose and went to the doorway.

'You don't have to leave,' Hasan protested.

'We will return shortly,' Mitkhal followed Shalan out.

Michael smiled at his brother. 'I've thought about you often since Georgie and I saw you walk onto that boat in Basra wharf. As has Georgie. You do know that we saw you?'

'I knew. I hoped that both of you would understand why I chose to remain an Arab.'

'Your injuries? The Turks did that to you?'

'They tortured me.'

There was a tone in Hasan's voice that warned Michael not to enquire further. 'Was that your wife and children on the boat with you?'

'Yes. And Mitkhal's wife and son.'

'The twin girls ...'

'Are mine and as beautiful as my wife, Furja. I will introduce you to them and my baby son later, but first ...'

'You want to explain to me why Ibn Shalan needs all the guns he can lay his hands on.'

'The reason is simple. A question of survival of the tribe.'

'Your tribe will fight anyone who threatens you.'

'Exactly.'

'Turk, Germans, Bakhtairi Khans, and ...' Michael hesitated, 'the Allies including the British.'

'You know what will happen when the Turks leave this land. Once the British take Baghdad – and they will, the Turks will return to Turkey to lick their wounds ...'

'And you and your fellow tribesmen will turn the guns on the British?'

'Only if the British refuse to leave and train their guns on us. It is our land, Michael. We have a God-given right to govern it as we chose without interference from any foreign power, no matter how well intentioned. And contrary to British patriotic belief, the British are not, and never have been, anything other than self-seeking and self-serving. They are here to fill English coffers, not to free the Arabs from their Ottoman yoke.'

Michael couldn't stop looking at his brother. The one-handed, one-eyed, battle-scarred Arab next to him was not Harry, but he was a shell of what Harry had once been. At that moment he suddenly realised that Harry was as dead to him as if he really had been buried out in the desert by the Turks.

'You don't agree, Michael?'

'I agree, but …'

'You have joined Cox's tribe of British officers and, for all your sympathy with the Arabs and our cause, if it comes to war between us you will fight for your British paymasters and kill Arabs.'

'I would never pull a gun on you or fight against you.'

'And my tribe?' When Michael didn't answer, Hasan said, 'There may come a time when you have to do just that, Michael.'

'War correspondents don't fight.'

'They fight with the most dangerous weapon the world has ever invented. The pen.' Hasan gave Michael a lopsided grin that was so familiar it tore at his heartstrings. 'Do you know what the British plans for Mesopotamia are when they oust the Turks?'

'I've heard rumours that the country will be handed over to the Indian Office.'

'That's not what we've heard.'

'It's too far from Westminster for the British government to rule,' Michael observed.

'On that we agree.'

'So what do you think will happen to Mesopotamia?' Michael pressed.

'There are many Arabs of many tribes fighting with the British, not just here in Iraq but elsewhere in the Middle East. Some of those Arabs have the ambition to rule, even over those who are not of their blood or their tribe.'

'You think the British will install an Arab puppet overlord?'

'I think they will listen to people who know nothing of our lands, like Lawrence. Possibly they will even name whoever they decide should reign over us "king". That notion hasn't occurred to you?'

'It has now.'

Ibn Shalan and Mitkhal returned and stood in the doorway.

'You will try to get us the things we asked for?' Hasan questioned Michael.

'I will try. Meet me early tomorrow, Mitkhal, in Abdul's. We'll visit HQ together.'

'I will be there.'

'And now, come, meet my wife.' Hasan rose. 'If you return

with Georgie tomorrow evening you must bring Kalla.'

'You know about Kalla?' Michael asked.

'You would be surprised by how much Hasan knows about you, Michael. You and his British family are often his thoughts,' Mitkhal revealed.

Turkish Prisoner of War Camp
December 1916

John was tired but restless and beset by remorse. He couldn't stop thinking about the incident with Rebeka. He made a round of all his patients – twice – although most of them were sleeping and he could do nothing for them. Then he checked all the supply cupboards and made an inventory of the stocks of drugs and dressings. When he'd finished those he looked over the patient charts that he'd taught Mrs Gulbenkian and Rebeka to update.

The guilt he felt at kissing Rebeka burned painful overwhelming, and all the more bitter because he could recall in graphic detail the injuries she'd suffered after being raped by the Turks.

He was standing in the kitchen debating what to do next when he heard a knock on the front door. Greening, who was on night duty reached it before he did.

Grace was outside with two Indian sepoy orderlies. Behind them, parked on the garden with absolutely no consideration for the plants several of the officers had spent hours tending, was a mule cart.

'Apologies, Major Mason, for disturbing you at this late hour. The colonel's compliments, sir. A cart of six sick men has just arrived, sent on from another POW camp. The men inside it are in bad shape.'

'Do you and your orderlies need help to get them in here, Grace?'

'More muscle wouldn't go amiss, sir. The men cannot walk unaided.'

'I'll wake Baker and Jones.' Greening stepped back into the hall.

'Tell them to clear the six-bedded ward we keep for quarantine cases. The two fever patients in there have almost recovered and

258

can be moved into the main ward. We need to keep these men separate until we can be sure they're not incubating anything.'

'Yes, sir.'

John lifted an oil lamp from a niche in the hall, held it high and walked out to the back of the cart with Grace. The drivers had climbed down and were standing smoking and talking to a guard who'd accompanied them from the gate.

'One of the sick is Major Crabbe, sir,' Grace warned John. 'He looks in particularly bad shape.'

John lowered the tailgate and stepped up into the cart. All the men were painfully thin, half naked, and all had open sores on their bodies. But only Crabbe was unconscious. If Grace hadn't told him that Crabbe was in the cart he would never have recognised his friend. As it was, he did so purely by process of elimination. The other five men were years younger than Crabbe, and they all had haunted expressions in their eyes that belied those years.

John ran his hands over Crabbe's forehead and face. His skin was cold, clammy; his breathing shallow and laboured.

John looked up and saw Williams and Jones running from the building. 'Get a stretcher and take Major Crabbe into the examination room.' Williams ran back inside.

'Sergeant Greening and I have prepared the quarantine ward. It's ready, sir.'

'Thank you, Dira, I knew I could rely on you to turn up even when you're off duty. See these five men settled in ward and make them comfortable. No food other than tea and thin gruel until I say otherwise. Too much nourishment too soon could rupture their stomachs. I'll be in to examine them as soon as I've seen to Major Crabbe.'

One of the men screamed in agony as Jones helped him from the back of the cart.

'Sorry, sir,' he apologised, his eyes bright with tears. 'It's my back, sir.' He stepped into the pool of light in the doorway and John saw the unmistakeable marks of a whiplash on his naked back. It had stripped the skin down to the muscle in several places.

'Who did this to you?' John demanded furiously.

'Turks, sir. They beat everyone in the camp, beat the Major to a pulp, more than once. Captain Vincent tried to stop them, sir, but it was sport to them. Will we be beaten here?'

'Not if I or the other officers can help it, Private.' John fingered the deep wide cuts on the man's back. They were raw, infected, and running with pus. He shouted in Turkish at the driver and the guard who'd accompanied him.

Both men turned to him and shrugged. 'The guards in the camp at Bagtsche did it. Nothing to do with us,' the driver retorted.

John didn't trust himself to reply to them. 'Grace, get an escort and insist these men are kept locked up here until morning. I want them taken to the commandant.'

The guard who'd been on duty at the gate approached John. 'As they said to you, these guards are from another camp, Major Mason. They are not under our jurisdiction. We have no control over them and cannot keep them here against their will.'

'It's not in any Turkish guard's jurisdiction, or remit, to whip prisoners to the point of death,' John remonstrated.

'Prisoners will be punished if they refuse to obey orders or cooperate with their guards.'

'Punished by being whipped to death?'

'You don't know what that man did to be whipped.'

'I will take a deposition from him, attesting to his crime – if he committed one. I will also make a full and comprehensive account of his injuries.'

'You won't be able to send it anywhere,' the guard taunted.

'Not immediately, perhaps,' John met the guard's steady gaze. 'But the war won't last forever and when it ends I will make sure that you and your ilk will face justice.'

The man stepped forward. So did John. They stood facing another in silence until Williams interrupted.

'We're about to move Major Crabbe, sir.'

John turned on his heel and followed Greening and Williams who'd lifted Crabbe on to the stretcher inside the building.

'Rebeka, what are you doing here?' John asked when he entered the room they used as an operating theatre, to find her gowned and masked and scrubbing down the table.

'Mrs Gulbenkian and I were woken by the noise of people walking up and down the stairs,' she lied, as neither of them had fallen asleep. 'Sergeant Greening told us that more patients had arrived from another camp and you needed to operate on one so we offered to help. Mrs Gulbenkian is cleaning and dressing the injuries of the men in the quarantine ward. Sergeant Greening is washing the patient who needs surgery, so I thought I'd prepare this room.'

'Thank you. It's good of you both to give up your sleep.' He reached for an apron and mask.

Rebeka took the chloroform apparatus from the box it was stored in. Greening and Dira carried Crabbe in on a stretcher and placed him on the table.

John studied Crabbe as Dira prepared to administer chloroform. It hadn't been easy to control his temper when he'd seen the damage the Turks had inflicted on his friend and it was harder still to keep his temper when he had to start operating.

'Major Crabbe is ready, sir.'

'Thank you, Dira.' John reached for a scalpel, opened Crabbe's chest, spread his ribs, and set to work. Slowly, painstakingly, he began to remove bone splinters from Crabbe's punctured lungs. He worked carefully and in silence, acutely aware of Dira administering chloroform, Rebeka monitoring and sterilising the instruments as he used them, but most of all of Crabbe, lying wounded and helpless on the table.

After an hour's steady work, he made one final check before removing the clamps he'd used to spread Crabbe's ribs and stitching up his chest. He placed the last stitch, and monitored his pulse.

'Major Crabbe is strong, sir, he will survive,' Dira reassured.

'I hope you're right, Dira. I've done all I can.'

'It is in God's hands now, sir. Where would you like us to take him?'

'The examination room please, Dira, in case I need my instruments.'

'I'll get help to carry him there.'

Rebeka untied her apron and veil, removed her mask, and dropped them into the linen bin.

'Would you like tea, sir?'

'If it's not too much trouble, Rebeka.'

'No trouble, sir. I'll see if the orderlies, patients, or Mrs Gulbenkian want any as well.'

John stripped off his surgical clothes and left for the bathroom.

He washed his hands and face in cold water and checked his watch. Four thirty. Another hour and half and he would have been up for twenty-four hours.

He went into the quarantine ward. Mrs Gulbenkian was sitting next to the bed of one young man, holding his hand.

'They just want to sleep, sir.'

'You gave them the painkillers I prescribed?'

'And fed and cleaned them, sir.' Greening came in with two cups of tea and handed Mrs Gulbenkian one. 'Rebeka's just made tea, sir. Yours is in the kitchen. If you don't mind me saying so, sir, after you drink it you should get some rest.'

'I will, but not until after Major Crabbe's regained consciousness.'

'I'll come and get you when he does, sir.' Greening hesitated. 'The major will make it, sir.'

'He might, provided infection doesn't set in. But if wishes can make things happen, he'll be dancing around here tomorrow.'

John looked in on Dira and Crabbe before going to the kitchen. Rebeka had made tea and toast. She handed him a plate and mug.

'Dira says Major Crabbe's breathing is getting stronger.'

'It's still too early to give a prognosis.' John sank down on a chair. 'We have a full hospital again and from what the colonel said a few days ago we may soon have even more patients.' He looked up at her. 'Rebeka, about what happened …'

'I'm sorry, sir. It was my fault. I shouldn't have …'

'Shouldn't have what?' he broke in sharply.

'Touched you, sir.'

'Why not?'

'Mrs Gulbenkian explained everything, sir. I can't expect any decent man to forget what the Turks did to me. I am dishonoured.'

'Dishonoured!' he exclaimed. 'You're not dishonoured. You saw the men who've just come in. You can see what the Turks have done them. Are they dishonoured because the Turks whipped, beat, and raped them?'

'They are men. They were overpowered.'

'And you are a woman. A brave survivor, who fought for your life when so many others would have given up.'

He cupped her face and kissed her gently on the lips. This time neither of them pulled away.

Chapter Twenty-four

The Convent of St Agnes and St Clare, India
December 1916

Maud knocked and waited outside the Mother Superior's office. A novice opened the door and showed her in. The senior nun was sitting behind her desk, a prayer book open in front of her.

Maud curtsied. 'You sent for me, Mother Superior.'

'I did, Maud. Please sit down.' Mother Superior closed the book, sat very upright, and looked Maud in the eye. 'When you came here six months ago you told me that you were troubled and felt as though you'd reached a crossroads in your life with no obvious path before you.'

'That is correct, Mother Superior.' Maud thought rapidly. Had she done anything recently to incur the Mother Superior's or any nun's displeasure? She'd hoped to remain in the convent until the end of the war when she was absolutely certain that John would come for her. How could he do otherwise after reading her letters?

She'd pictured the scene in her imagination many times. He would walk into the infirmary. A nun would point him in the direction of a ward. She'd be dressed in her nurse's uniform, ministering to a sick child. John would take one look at her and realise not only that she was a kind, experienced, and sympathetic nurse who'd lived out the war in the sanctified respectable atmosphere of the convent, but how much he loved her and had missed her in his life …

'Is your mind any clearer now, Maud?'

'Pardon, mother?' Lost in her daydream Maud hadn't heard Mother Superior's question.

'Has God given you a sign as to the path you should take?'

'No, mother.'

'You have prayed for guidance?'

'Yes, mother.'

Mother Superior clasped her hands in front of her on the desk, but she kept her gaze fixed on Maud. 'A convent is a place for reflection, on life and on spirituality. It is primarily an institution where women who have chosen to dedicate their lives to God can live and work in harmony while seeking out ways on how best to serve Him. Some convents,' she inclined her head, 'including this, also offer temporary refuge, hospitality, and respite from daily care to those who seek spiritual guidance. But no convent can provide a haven for those attempting to hide from themselves or the world, Maud.'

Maud was afraid of the reply but she had to ask the question. 'You are unhappy with my work in the hospital?'

'On the contrary, every nursing sister who has worked with you agrees that you are a dedicated and competent nurse.'

'Then what is the problem, mother?'

'The problem is your lack of spirituality. I have watched you during mass, Maud. Your thoughts clearly do not dwell on God but upon worldly matters.'

'I told you when I came here, Mother Superior, that I do not wish to take a nun's vows. You know I am a confirmed Anglican.'

'I never sought to convert you to the Catholic faith, Maud. But I expected – no, rather, hoped – that you would become closer to God. This has not happened because you have not sought his blessing.'

Maud's blood ran cold and she suspected that she hadn't escaped the gossips, even here. 'You have heard rumours about me?'

'Surely, Maud, you are aware that rumours can even permeate the walls of a convent. As I've already said, no convent can offer sanctuary to those attempting to hide from themselves or the result of their sins.'

'I can explain …'

'It is not for me to judge you. Only God can do that, and I have asked for his guidance in considering your situation. He has sent what may prove to be a solution to the lack of direction in your life. I was approached this morning by a man whose wife is close to death. I suggested he conveyed her to our infirmary but he refused because he wishes to spend as much time as possible with her before God takes her from this world. He asked if I could recommend day and night nurses to care for her. I thought of you. It would mean you moving out of the convent, into his home. Perhaps when you are once again surrounded by worldly objects your mind will turn to worldly things. Or possibly you will reject them and welcome God into your life. Either way, you won't be able to continue to hide from whatever demons drove you here. I will send Sister Luke with you. Should you have any problems of a religious or spiritual nature you may discuss them with her. One thing is certain, you won't be as protected outside this convent as you have been inside these walls. Your patient may even teach you to think of and calmly accept the inevitable end we all face. Every one of us, no matter who we are, needs to spend some time in our lives preparing to meet our maker. It is my hope that in caring for this terminally ill lady you will find time to reflect on your own life and future commitment.'

Maud realised there was no point in trying to argue her case for remaining in the convent. 'I am expecting a letter ...'

'Should one arrive for you I will ask the gardener to deliver it to you.'

'Does the patient have a contagious disease or a condition that requires special treatment aside from usual nursing?'

'I wondered when you would ask about the countess.'

'A countess?'

'A Portuguese countess.' The inflection suggested a Portuguese countess was somewhat lower than any other nationality of aristocrat, but Mother Superior was a Catholic of English origin. 'The countess was perfectly healthy until six months ago when she was diagnosed as suffering from cancer of the brain. I have spoken to the doctor who is monitoring her. It was he who suggested the count engage professional nurses to care for his wife. The countess has not woken for twenty-four hours and the doctor does not expect her to regain consciousness. There is no hope of recovery. It is merely a question of time. One week, perhaps two, or possibly even as long as a month. Do you envisage any problems in caring for a patient who cannot communicate their needs?'

'No, Mother Superior.'

'Should you find yourself unable to cope with the patient, send a message to me and I will relieve and replace you. Father Ignatius will call every day, but Sister Luke will be the senior nurse and I expect you to discuss any matters that concern you, including personal ones, with her first. Do you have any questions?'

Realising that the decision had already been made and was irreversible, Maud resisted the temptation to argue. 'No, Mother Superior.'

'You may go and pack. A carriage will be here in half an hour to convey you and Sister Luke to the count's residence. There is no need to change from your nurse's uniform. You will wear your nurse's cape and bonnet for the journey. Your patient is Countess D'Souza, her husband, Count D'Souza, is the Portuguese consul. I will expect you to conduct yourself not only as a nurse but as a representative of this convent at all times even when you are outside these walls.'

'Yes, Mother Superior.'

'I hope you find the peace that you are searching for, Maud. There is no need to return to your ward before leaving.'

Maud still sought reassurance. 'You will send any letters on to me, Mother Superior?'

'As I've already told you, any communication that arrives for you will be sent on to you the day we receive it.'

'Thank you, Mother Superior.' Maud wondered why she was thanking the woman when she was so intent on sending her from the convent against her will.

She went to her room, took her Gladstone bag from the bottom of her wardrobe, and started packing. Not that she had much to pack. Her jewellery case, writing materials, and the few clothes and essentials she'd brought with her. She looked at the Bible the Mother Superior had given her and packed it, lest leaving it give the nuns yet another excuse to berate her for her lack of spirituality and religion.

She looked at the silver-framed photograph of John she'd picked up in the bungalow in Basra almost as an afterthought, and slipped it into her bag. The cell, with its neatly made bed and crucifix hanging above it, was suddenly as bare and impersonal as when she'd arrived.

Would she ever return to this room? Even if she had the opportunity, would she want to? She slipped on the nurse's cape and hat. As mirrors weren't allowed even in the convent guest bedrooms she had no way of knowing if it was on straight.

266

There was a tap at her door. She opened it.

Sister Luke was outside. 'The carriage has arrived.'

'I'm ready.' Maud took one last look around, picked up her bag and left.

Ibn Shalan's house, Basra
December 1916

Kalla and Michael sat next to Furja and Gutne, Mitkhal's wife, on a divan in the corner of Ibn Shalan's large reception room, watching Georgiana and Hasan. It was difficult to know which twin was most affected by the reunion. They'd been together for over two hours and Georgiana still couldn't stop looking at or talking to Hasan, who answered her questions slowly and with difficulty in his rusty English.

Michael sensed movement, glanced up, and saw Mitkhal beckoning to him from the doorway. He reached into his pocket, pulled out two Fry's Five Boys chocolate bars, gave them to his nieces Hari and Aza who'd been climbing over his lap, then walked outside to the open veranda with Mitkhal.

The overhanging balcony sheltered them from the worst of the rainstorm that was blowing in from the west but it did nothing to raise the temperature. Michael shivered and drew back close to the wall of the house.

'I'm sorry I couldn't persuade HQ to give you all the guns you wanted this morning, Mitkhal.'

'Five hundred is more than I hoped for, the first time of asking. This morning Ibn Shalan received an estimate of the number of Arab auxiliaries massing with the Turks below Kut al Amara. When your command also receives reports of their strength, they'll give us everything we asked for today – and more when we need it.'

Ibn Shalan walked out of the room and joined them. Michael salaamed.

'You're going upstream tomorrow, Michael?'

'Before dawn,' Michael confirmed.

'More of my men will be following you shortly.'

'Do you think we will take Baghdad this time?' Michael ventured.

Ibn Shalan smiled. 'If your forces don't, it won't be for the want of trying. Or the result of a shortage of supplies, weapons, and men as it was before your forces were cornered at Kut. General Maude appears to have asked for and acquired everything he needs for success.'

'You will be fighting with us, sir?' Michael enquired.

'On one front or another,' Shalan replied ambiguously. 'It's cold out here. Shall we go inside, gentlemen? There is still that small matter you were going to broach with Michael, Mitkhal.'

Michael was curious, but when it came to dealing with the Bedouin he had learned to be patient. They returned to the living room and Michael smiled at Georgiana who was making friends with their nieces while cuddling their baby nephew.

'The small matter.' Mitkhal pointed to a young girl clinging to Gutne's skirts. Michael hadn't noticed her before, which was hardly surprising as she was sandwiched between the wall and Gutne. She was tiny, painfully thin, extremely nervous, and appeared to be no more than four or five years old, yet her eyes looked dark and older. As though they had witnessed horrors no child of her age should have seen.

Mitkhal saw Michael studying her. 'She's an orphan, Michael. I hoped that you or Georgiana could help her.'

Georgiana heard her name mentioned, turned and saw the child. 'Is she well?' she asked Mitkhal diplomatically while privately thinking the child appeared cowed and beaten.

Frightened by the attention she was attracting, the child moved even closer to Gutne. Mitkhal picked up a large cushion, set it between Michael and Georgiana, and sat close to them.

'I was hoping one of you could help us by caring for the child until the end of the war when it may be possible to reunite her with the one remaining member of her family. However I should warn you, such a reunion is by no means certain.'

'I'm going upstream in the morning,' Michael pointed out. 'An army camp is no place for a child, especially just before an action.'

'Are you taking Kalla?'

Michael frowned at Mitkhal.

Mitkhal laughed. 'The walls are thin in Abdul's, everyone who frequents the building has heard you two arguing.'

'The British will advance soon and I will be going with them.

Kalla doesn't want me to leave her behind, but Kut and Nasiriyeh has taught us that anything can happen when a military engagement doesn't go to plan. Even camp followers can end up as casualties.'

'What about you, Dr Downe?' Mitkhal asked. 'Could you care for an orphan?'

'I work full time in the Lansing Memorial hospital so I am in no position to look after a child.'

'But you are living with Mrs Smythe who is already fostering Mrs Mason's baby.'

'You are well informed, Mitkhal.'

'I have also heard that Mrs Smythe is unwell and keeps to the house but she has servants and a nursemaid to see to her and the baby. This child can do many things around the house. She is quiet, tries very hard to please, and is in desperate need of a home and the love that should be given to every child.'

'She is obviously fond of your wife. Why can't you keep her?' Georgiana asked.

'Because we also leave tomorrow for the desert, Dr Downe, and like the British Army our future and that of our tribe is uncertain.'

'But the girl is settled here. She's an Arab,' Georgiana was loath to heap any more responsibilities on Angela who was suffering a difficult pregnancy plagued by sickness that lasted all day and more often than not, late into the night.

'She is wearing Arab clothes because we had no other clothes to give her. She is a Christian.'

Georgiana gave the girl another smile, but the gesture only drove her closer to Gutne.

'She looks like a cornered fox at a hunt,' Michael commented.

'Hardly surprising, she's Armenian,' Mitkhal revealed. 'And that's exactly what the Turks did to her and her family. Hunted them down and killed them in front of her as if they were vermin.'

'Are the rumours about the Turkish genocide of the Christian Armenians true?' Georgiana asked.

'All too true,' Michael confirmed. 'I've seen the bodies in the desert myself and heard first-hand accounts from tribesmen who tried to save some of the women and children. They were marched out into the desert by Turkish gendarmes who allowed them neither food nor water with the deliberate intention of killing them.'

'Some put the number who've been murdered at a million some put it even higher,' Mitkhal added.

'This girl really saw members of her family killed by the Turks?' Georgiana asked.

'Turkish gendarmes – policemen – yes. Only most of them weren't really policemen. The Turks emptied their prisons of their worst criminals and put them in charge of what they called the "Armenian resettlement".' Mitkhal confirmed.

'You saved this girl?'

'Not by being heroic, Dr Downe. I bought her from a man who rescued her only to enslave her. His family used her to tend their flocks of goats and gather animal dung for fuel. Her name is Mariam. Her father was shot along with all the men in her town. Her mother was also shot. Afterwards the Turks killed two of her sisters. I picked up her one remaining sister, Rebeka ...'

Georgiana saw the child look at them when she heard her sister's name. A light suddenly kindled in her eyes and Georgiana felt as though the sun had touched the child's face.

'Rebeka,' Mitkhal repeated when he saw the child's reaction, 'was one of only three survivors of a Turkish death march in the northern desert. She told me about her sister Mariam who had been taken at night along with other children from the column by bandit tribesmen. She begged me to look for Mariam. I did and I found her.'

'Where are Rebeka and the other two survivors now?' Georgiana asked.

'I took them to John and left them with him.'

'Michael told me you'd seen John in the desert. He was able to keep the Armenians?'

'He told the Turks that Rebeka and the woman she was with were trained nurses and he needed them to work in his makeshift field hospital. They had another child with them, an orphan. John told the Turks she couldn't be separated from the women. As John treats the Turks and natives as well the British, the Turkish guards allowed him to keep the women.'

'Do you think the Turks will allow John to keep the Armenian women with him once he reaches a prison camp?'

'You know John, Georgie.' Hasan's daughters climbed back on

to Michael's lap and he delved into his pockets for more of the chocolate bars he'd bought in the British canteen at HQ earlier that day. 'He can persuade anyone to do exactly what he wants, while convincing them it was their idea in the first place.'

'We were hoping that one of you could care for Mariam until she can be reunited with her sister after the war.'

'Much as I'd like to, I can't, Mitkhal,' Michael demurred.

'I can certainly pay for her keep. I'll talk to Mrs Smythe. If she can't look after her perhaps she can stay in the mission house and I'll visit her there.'

'Thank you, Dr Downe.'

'As you're my twin's foster brother you must call me Georgie, Mitkhal.' She watched Michael take their twin nieces across the room and helped them share out the chocolate between them and Mariam. 'War is so hard on everyone, men, women, and children,' she murmured.

'If we can survive, Georgie, it will be something.' Hasan leaned over her and lifted his son from her arms. 'Thank you for agreeing to take Mariam. I know she will be safe with you.'

Turkish Prison Camp
December 1916

John was deep in sleep, lost in his recurring dream of standing on board a ship that was heading out to sea. He felt the breeze blowing across his face. Then suddenly he jerked, lost his balance, and opened his eyes to see Rebeka standing next to his bed holding a tray.

He sat up rubbing his eyes. 'What time is it?'

'Seven in the evening, sir. You said you wanted to be woken …'

'At four in the afternoon.'

'I came in at four, sir, and couldn't wake you. Dira said all the patients were fine and none needed attention so I should leave you sleep.'

'Major Crabbe?'

'Woke briefly at three o'clock. He drank water and went straight back to sleep. Dira is sitting with him.'

John momentarily forgot that he was naked and sat up in the

bed. When he saw Rebeka staring at his chest he pulled the sheet to his chin.

'Thank you for the tea.'

'Take your time drinking it, sir. All the patients are comfortable.'

'Rebeka?'

'Sir?'

'Is anyone out there?' He pointed to the open door.

'No, sir, Mrs Gulbenkian and Hasmik are in the kitchen. Can I get you anything else, sir?'

'No, thank you. Stay, just a minute, please,' he said when she went to the door.

'Sir?' She looked back at him in confusion.

'This isn't a good time for us to talk, not with me in bed and you in my bedroom, it's against what my mother would call "all propriety", but we never seem to be alone for a minute ... You do know I'm married, don't you?'

She hesitated before answering him, confirming his suspicions that the growing affection he felt for her wasn't entirely one-sided.

'No, sir, I didn't.'

'My wife and I ... she left me and had another man's child. If there wasn't a war, I – we – would probably have been divorced by now.'

'Why are you telling me this, sir?'

'Because ...' He threw all caution to the wind. 'I would find it very easy to fall in love with you.'

She turned aside so he couldn't see her face. 'Are you making fun of me, sir?' she whispered.

'No, Rebeka, I would never do that,' he said seriously. 'It's just that I don't want you to have any illusions about me.'

She looked up at him and her eyes widened in wonder. 'You really think you could love me, sir?'

'Could ... to be truthful, Rebeka, I already do.'

Uncertain how to reply or what to make of his declaration, Rebeka froze, speechless.

'If you're horrified ...'

'No, sir. I don't know anything about the love between a man and a woman. All I've known is what the Turks did to me. And – what I feel for you now, sir.'

'I love you, Rebeka,' John smiled, 'and I'm delighted to hear that you feel something for me. There's no need to say more at present, other than there has to be honesty between us, which is why I told you about my wife.'

'Yes, sir.'

'Do you think you could bring yourself call me John when we're alone together?'

She nodded.

'Thank you for the tea. I'll be downstairs as soon as I've finished it.'

'The kitchen sent over bully beef stew tonight. There's some left. I could cook you rice to go with it.'

'That sounds good, Rebeka. I'll eat after I've done the rounds. Have you eaten?'

'Not yet, sir. I've been too busy helping the orderlies with the new patients.'

'Perhaps we can eat together,' he suggested.

She smiled. 'I'd like that – John.'

Chapter Twenty-five

Count D'Souza's Residence and Portuguese Consulate, India
December 1916

An Indian butler dressed in dark blue, gold-braided livery ushered Maud and Sister Luke into a magnificent marbled hall. A footman, attired in similar livery with a marked absence of gold braid, took their bags and spirited them away. Maud felt most peculiar. She had lived in the Spartan surroundings of the convent for only six months, yet it had been long enough for her to accept unadorned whitewashed walls and stone floors as normal. In contrast, she found the luxury of her present surroundings overwhelming.

The gilding on the mirrors and furniture glowed, a deep dark tarnished gold. Her feet sank into the thick pile of the crimson and blue Persian rug centred on the marbled floor. The paintings on the wall, some portraits, some landscapes, shimmered in opulent shades of crimson, cerulean blue and jade, fostering an overall effect of glittering, glamorous splendour.

'I'd forgotten people could live like this,' Sister Luke whispered.

'Sisters?' the butler indicated the stairs. 'If you would please follow me?'

They walked up the massive curved marbled staircase and on to a marbled gallery.

The butler led them down a corridor to a door at the far end. He opened it and showed them in. 'This is the suite of rooms the count ordered prepared for you, sisters.' He walked across the room and opened three doors. 'Two bedrooms, a bathroom, and this, as you can see is your sitting room. Your keys.' He set them on a table. 'Should you require anything, at any time of the day or night, please ring the bell.' He pointed to a bell pull next to the fireplace. 'There is always a servant on duty in the hall and in the kitchens. The count is with your patient the countess, at present. I will wait outside to escort you to them.'

'Thank you.' The butler left and closed the door softly behind him. Maud looked into the bedrooms. The servant had placed her bag on a luggage trestle in one of the rooms. She went in, removed her hat and cape, and stowed both in the wardrobe. She poured water into the basin on the washstand, washed her hands and face, tipped the water into the slop pail, and looked at herself in the mirror.

It was the first opportunity she'd had since entering the convent to study her image in a larger reflective surface than the back of a spoon.

Her skin had always been pale but now, probably because of lack of exposure to the sun, it was deathly white. Her hair needed washing and curling. She hid most of it beneath her nursing sisters' veil.

'Maud?' Sister Luke knocked her door. 'Are you ready? We shouldn't keep the count waiting.'

'Coming.' On impulse Maud opened her bag, dug into her toilet bag, and found her bottle of perfume, which she'd kept closed since she'd left Basra. She dabbed a few drops on her neck and behind her ears. The scent kindled memories, of starlit Indian evenings spent on verandas, balls, parties, dinner parties – and John.

'Maud, the butler is waiting.'

Maud opened the door. 'Sorry, I couldn't find my veil.'

Sister Luke sniffed long and hard to show Maud that she smelled and disapproved of the perfume.

The sounds and atmosphere of the house closed around them as they walked down the corridor. The heavy scent of hothouse roses emanated from vases set in niches in the corridors overpowering a mixture of strong cigar smoke and incense. Maud could distinguish the subdued murmurs of distant conversations, hints of music – a radio or gramophone? The clink of glassware and silverware vied with the echo of unseen footsteps somewhere ahead. The butler finally stopped outside the door nearest to the staircase. He knocked quietly, waited for a command, and opened it.

A tall, distinguished, grey-haired man walked across an exquisitely decorated and furnished morning room to greet them.

'Sisters, how kind of you to answer our call for help.' His

276

English was excellent, carefully enunciated and barely accented. 'I am Count D'Souza.'

'Sister Luke.' The nun gave a small curtsy.

'Maud Smith.' Maud offered him her hand. He took it and lifted it to his lips.

'You are not a nun, Sister Smith?'

'No, Count D'Souza. I am a nursing sister but not a nun.' Maud returned his cool appraising stare. There was a glint in his eye and an expression on his face she had seen many times before in other men.

'Please, allow me to introduce you to my wife. Her maid is with her at the moment but she requires more nursing care than the servants can give her.'

He crossed the room and opened a door at the far end. The bedroom was even more splendid, extravagant, and feminine than the morning room with white and grey silk hangings and pearl marbled walls and floor.

The count introduced them to his wife as if the countess were conscious. 'Countess, may I present Sister Luke and Sister Smith. Sisters, my wife, Countess D'Souza.'

Maud looked down at the figure in the bed. The countess was beautiful, with regular features and full generous lips. Her hair had been recently brushed and shone, long and black. Maud imagined her eyes as dark as hair.

'You have been acquainted with my wife's condition, sisters?'

'We have, sir.' Sister Luke pushed herself forward, standing in front of Maud to assume the mantle of senior nurse.

'The doctors can do nothing for her. My only concern is to ensure that the countess remain as comfortable as possible. I am a busy man and cannot afford to neglect my duties, which is why I now work as much as is reasonably feasible in the morning room next door. Unfortunately it is not always practical. We have been married for fifteen wonderful years. It would be of great comfort to me to know that she is being looked after while I have to leave this room and occasionally the house.'

'We will do everything we can to nurse Countess D'Souza with dignity, kindness, and respect, count.' Sister Luke went to the bed and picked up the countess's hand.

'If you remain with the countess, Sister Luke, I will show Sister

Smith over the house so she will know where everything is to be found.'

'There is no need ...'

'A tour with Sister Smith now may save precious minutes later, Sister Luke.' He went to the door and held it open. 'Sister Smith?'

Maud meekly followed him out of the room, down the stairs, and through a bewildering number of extravagantly and opulently furnished rooms.

'You and Sister Luke are of course, free to go wherever you choose in the house when you are not actually caring for my wife.'

'You have a beautiful home, Count D'Souza.'

'Thank you for the compliment, but everything you see, the décor, the furniture, the ornaments, were all chosen by my wife. This is the main drawing room, and this is the library.'

They left the drawing room and entered a room lined with teak bookshelves each one laden with leather bound volumes. A painting of a woman Maud recognised as the countess hung over the fireplace. As in the hall, a deep pile Persian rug covered most the floor. The sofas and armchairs were upholstered in crimson leather.

The count went to the drinks tray on a side table and poured two cognacs. He handed Maud one.

'This, as you see, is the library. It is my favourite room in the house. I like to relax here at midnight with a nightcap. You would be very welcome to join me if my wife is peaceful. Do not be concerned about leaving her. I have instructed the maids to ensure that two of them are in my wife's suite at all times to see to her needs – and her nurses'.'

'Thank you for the invitation.' Maud watched him over the rim of her glass.

'So,' he smiled. 'I'll expect you here at midnight?'

'Yes, sir.'

Turkish Prison Camp
December 1916

John drank the tea Rebeka had brought him before reluctantly climbing out of the hard, narrow bed, which had never looked so warm or appealing. He went to the washstand, and washed shaved, and dressed. When he picked up his hair brush he looked at the tin box next to it. It was where he kept all the letters he'd received during his captivity – including Maud's.

He'd received six letters from her since he'd been in the camp, less than a third of the number she'd sent him judging from the notation she'd put at the top of each one. He'd meant to but hadn't got around to answering any of them. He opened the tin and picked them out. Maud's were easy to find because he'd stowed them at the bottom of the pile.

He read the final paragraphs of the last letter he'd received from her, which was identical in in sentiment to her first and subsequent ones. But then, if what she said about never leaving the convent or the infirmary was true, what else could she possibly write about?

I gave birth to a boy last December. I asked Mrs Butler to place him in an American orphanage. I hope he will find adoptive parents who can give him a better life than I am able to ...

He had thought long and hard about that sentence, especially after discovering Charles was the father of Maud's son. She had obviously told Charles he was the father, because he had recognised the boy in his will. Had Maud told Charles he was the father of her son before she'd abandoned the child? Had Charles doubted her? If so, it would explain his delay in acknowledging the child. But if Charles had been prepared to claim the child, why had Maud left the baby in the Lansing? Was it to hurt Charles, or had she hoped that she and the world, including Charles, would simply forget the boy's existence?

I am writing this so you realise that if you could bring yourself to consider taking me back, I would come unencumbered by further responsibilities.

Unencumbered by further responsibilities ... as if the child was a stray dog or cat she'd picked up in the street and could walk away from without a second thought.

I have no idea whether you have divorced me or not, or intend to divorce me in the future. If you do, I beg you with all my heart to reconsider, John ... I send all my love, your own very sorrowful Maud whose only hope is that you allow her a second chance to be the wife she should have been.

He set the letter aside. He should have replied to Maud, months ago when he'd received her first letter. Whether it was the kiss he'd exchanged with Rebeka, her diffidence and ridiculous assertion that she'd been 'dishonoured' by what the Turks had done to her, or not, he was beset by a sudden urge to put an end to the pitiful remnants of his marriage to Maud as swiftly as he could.

He took Maud's last letter, refolded it so her return address was on the outside, and scribbled a note below her signature.

Dear Maud, our marriage is over. I will instigate divorce proceedings as soon as I can. John

He fastened the letter as best he could, slipped it into the pocket of his white coat, and dropped it into the mailbox when he reached the bottom of the stairs. As he headed for the kitchen he amused himself by picturing the Georgian house he'd so often dreamed of. Set in a quiet West Country village of old stone houses with pretty cottage gardens filled with harebells, bluebells, apple and cherry blossom – why did he always imagine his dream house in May time?

He pictured the door opening, his wife and children running down the lawns to greet him. That was the moment he realised he wanted a wife with the same simple tastes as his, a wife who wouldn't flirt with every man in sight. A wife who would love him, no matter what he did or what happened to him, until the end of his days ...

Hasmik ran out of the kitchen, giggled, and held out her small arms to be picked up. He couldn't help smiling as he swung her on to his shoulders.

A wife – who would perhaps in time, even give him the children he wanted?

He walked to the end of the passage. 'Back into the kitchen, young lady.' He lifted Hasmik down and pointed to the kitchen door. She ran off still giggling. He waited until she was in the kitchen before entering the examination room.

Crabbe was awake and talking to Dira.

'You look better than you did when you arrived last night, Crabbe. I'm sorry if you're sore. I had to poke about inside you for quite some time. It wasn't very pretty in there.'

'The way I feel I'm not sure I should be thanking you, but I will,' Crabbe's voice was weak, his skin pale and clammy. 'Dira told me that unlike all the king's men, you put this poor Humpty Dumpty back together again.'

John checked Crabbe's temperature. 'This Humpty Dumpty had better stop fighting Turks now they've taken his rifle away. We can't win, you know. Not now we're prisoners. Our war is over.'

'I'm beginning to realise that.'

'I'll get fresh drinking water for Major Crabbe, sir.'

'Thank you, Dira.' John sat beside Crabbe.

'This hospital ...'

'The Turks allow me to run it because I treat them and the locals as well as our men.'

'It's in a camp?'

'An officers' camp.'

'You're lucky. The one I've come from for the ranks ...' Crabbe stopped talking and breathed deeply in an attempt to control his pain. That in turn initiated a coughing fit. 'They have it rough,' he whispered when he could speak again.

'We know how rough. We heard about it last night from the men who came in with you.'

'Some of the men we left behind are in an even worse state than us.'

'So I gathered.'

'We need to make an official protest.'

'I delivered medical reports on you and the others to our colonel and the Turkish commandant after I operated on you. The colonel was framing a demand for an official enquiry into the Turkish treatment of our POWs by both the Allied and Ottoman commands when I left.'

'It will be too late for most of the poor beggars in the camp I was in. I have to get back there ...' Crabbe struggled to sit up as if he were getting ready to leave.

'No you don't.' John pushed him back down. 'Lie still and quiet and give your lungs a chance to heal. I dug around in them

281

quite a bit.'

'The ranks back in the camp ...'

'Have Captain Vincent looking after them. He's a good man and hopefully once our colonel's complaints reach the Turkish command that camp will be closed.'

'How are the boys who came in with me?'

'Exhausted, starved, sick with beriberi and dysentery. Three have syphilis.'

'Bloody raping Turkish guards. The boys are too weak to fight back.' Crabbe looked at him. 'What's this camp really like? Don't bother sugar-coating it. I intend to recover so I can go back and strangle the bastards who put me in this bed.'

'Before I saw you I would have complained about this place. The food's monotonous, my fellow officers are bored witless, and we lack essentials, especially medical supplies. But since I've been here no one's been beaten, and although the food isn't great we get Red Cross parcels and even the occasional letter from home.'

'So,' Crabbe managed a grin, 'although you've nothing to really complain about you still gripe.'

'You know me so well.'

The door opened and Mrs Gulbenkian bustled in carrying in a tray. 'Dira said the patient might try some clear chicken broth.'

John rose and smiled. 'As I'm only the doctor I wouldn't dream of arguing with Dira. Your English is improving, Mrs Gulbenkian.'

'Rebeka's father taught me languages in school so all I had to do was – how does Dira say it – "brush up".'

'You've brushed up very well. Major Crabbe, meet Mrs Gulbenkian, she and her friend Rebeka are our Armenian nurses, so I'll leave you in her capable hands.'

'We'll talk later?' Crabbe asked.

'Of course, and courtesy of the Turks we have all the time in the world for conversation.'

British Relief Force
December 1916

'That's Kut, sir?' Peter's adjutant Lieutenant Sweeney was taken aback. 'That miserable dilapidated little village is Kut al Amara?'

282

'That's it, the place we called home sweet home.' David ducked, although given that he was lying on the ground, and the country was a flat as a pancake, he couldn't go much lower.

Fortunately for him, and Peter's command, since the order for them to halt had been passed down, the Turkish shells were falling a hundred yards or more short of their intended targets and the bullets were even more off course than the shells.

'You ever get tired of this.' David took advantage of the temporary respite in the advance, rolled on his back and pulled out his cigarettes.

'The rain or the fighting?' Peter asked.

'Both, but of the two the fighting irritates me more.'

'I grew tired of it after my first battle in 1914. You?'

'I was never enamoured with the thought of active service even before I saw it. The reality was worse than I expected, and that's saying a great deal.'

Peter took the cigarette David offered, lit it, and passed the match on to David. 'What the hell are you doing in the army?'

'Told you, second son of a second son.'

'You studied medicine.'

'Only because my uncle, who incidentally was the first son of a first son, told me that doctors didn't have to go to Sandhurst to get a commission. What he didn't tell me was that we still had to do a certain amount of boring military square-bashing.'

'You're the laziest sod and worst soldier in this man's army,' Peter laughed.

'Not when it comes to the hospitals.'

'I'll grant you, when you finally do decide to go on duty you look after your patients.'

'Cheeky blighter! That's like me saying when you do finally decide to lead your men into battle you pick up your gun.' David shivered. 'I'm colder than a polar bear's arse. Not to mention wet through.'

'At least you're wearing serge. Spare a thought for the men who are still in their summer khaki. Supplies can never get anything right.' Peter spotted a lieutenant slithering through the mud towards them. 'Orders?' he asked.

'Dig in and hold fast until morning, sir.'

'Oh, thank you, high command, for the joys you bring.' David rolled his eyes.

'Take no notice, Lieutenant, water has got into Major Knight's brain.'

'And rusted it,' David said mournfully. 'Is there no one who can tell me what we're doing here?'

Peter passed him his flask.

'We're here just to get drunk.'

'The drink is to silence you.' Peter called down to his second in command. 'Dig in until morning, every man roll out his blanket.' He raised his voice. 'Bearers, officers need their blankets.'

'Dry blankets, if possible,' David added.

'No point,' Peter took the sodden blanket his bearer handed him and rolled himself into it. 'It'll be damp in no time once the rain gets to it.'

Chapter Twenty-six

Basra
December 1916

Georgiana waited until their driver had stopped the carriage, dismounted from the box, and was holding the horses steady before opening the door and helping Angela down on to the unpaved street.

'I could have come here with Mariam and bought whatever you needed for the baby,' Georgiana admonished as Angela reached ground level.

'I want to see the quality of the fabric they have for myself, both for baby gowns and Mariam's winter wardrobe.'

Mariam held out Angela's handbag, which she'd given to the child for safekeeping.

'You are a darling, Mariam. I don't know what we'd do without you. Perhaps we can find a ready-made dress for you to wear to the church service on Christmas morning. If not we'll have to buy some material and get one made. But you have to choose the fabric yourself.'

'Red?' the child asked hopefully.

'Most certainly, if they have a shade you like.' Georgiana pushed the door open. The assistant took one look at Angela and rushed from behind the counter to bring her a chair. Within minutes the counter was covered with a bewildering array of bolts of cloth and ready-made girls' dresses. Georgiana smiled when Mariam made a beeline for a red velvet smock and stroked it as if it were a kitten, while Angela debated the relative merits of cream winceyette against white brushed cotton. Georgiana told the assistant to set the dress aside in Mariam's size and asked to see silk stockings. She heard a footstep on the internal stairs and turned. The door opened and Reggie Brooke and Major Cleck-

Heaton strode in. They saw her and Angela and doffed their caps.

'Merry Christmas, Dr Downe, Mrs Smythe, and who is this?' Reggie bent down and tickled Mariam under her chin. The child shrank back behind Angela's chair.

'Mariam,' Angela introduced the girl, who curtsied behind the chair.

'Charming,' Cleck-Heaton gushed insincerely. 'A relative?'

'My foster child, Major Cleck-Heaton.'

'Christmas shopping, I see,' Reggie commented.

Bored by the exchange of pleasantries, Georgiana nodded.

'Have you heard from Major Smythe, Mrs Smythe?'

'I had a card this morning, Major Cleck-Heaton. Thank you for enquiring.'

'I've heard it's rough up there.'

'As have we,' Georgiana said shortly.

'Major Cleck-Heaton and I have been posted upstream and will be leaving first thing in the morning. If you have messages for friends or relatives who are with General Maude it would be an honour to take them.'

'Thank you, Major Brooke, but Lieutenant Grace called this morning. We gave him our letters and parcels,' Angela replied politely.

'Then it appears we can't assist you ladies in any way.' Reggie Brooke looked coolly at Georgiana.

'I'm afraid you can't. Major. Major Cleck-Heaton. I wish both of you a good journey.'

'Thank you, Dr Downe.' Reggie turned his attention to Angela. 'Your very good health, Mrs Smythe.'

Georgiana watched the men leave the shop before joining Angela. She dropped her voice to a whisper. 'Have you written to tell Peter about the baby?'

'I know I said I would, but once I heard that hostilities had broken out I couldn't bring myself to do it. You know how Peter worries about me. If he knew I was having a baby he'd only worry all the more.' She looked through the shop window at the two officers who were climbing into a carriage. 'You don't think either of those odious men would tell him, do you?'

'I think they'd have no compunction about telling him, and adding that you looked ill. I have no idea why they dislike Peter

286

and John so much, or why they disliked Charles and Harry. I only know that every time I see them they go out of their way to be obnoxious. When it comes to Peter finding out about your baby, it would be far better if he heard the news from you.'

'We've already given Lieutenant Grace our letters and parcels.'

'Write another letter when we get home and I'll send a boy to deliver it to Lieutenant Grace's quarters. He's not embarking until the morning.'

'I really wanted the baby to be a surprise.'

'After it's born?' Georgiana questioned in amusement.

'I thought it would be better because then I could write and tell Peter we're both well and healthy. But you're right. I've kept it secret long enough. I'll write to Peter today.'

'Excuse me, ma'am, I couldn't help overhearing. If you'd like to write a letter, we have comfortable rooms upstairs. We could supply you with writing materials and bring you tea while we pack up your purchases.'

'And we can drop the letter off on our way home. Wonderful idea. You'd enjoy having tea here, wouldn't you, Mariam? They have the most wonderful cakes and sandwiches and scones and jam.' Georgiana set the stockings she'd chosen aside.

The door opened and two ladies entered, both carrying babies.

Angela rose unsteadily from the chair and held out her hand. 'Mrs Greening?'

'Mrs Smythe, how kind of you to recognise me!'

'Not at all, I remember you from your days before the war with Mrs Perry and Maud.' Angela embraced the sergeant's wife. 'We were just about to go upstairs and have tea. Please, join us.'

Harriet Greening turned to Georgiana. 'We wouldn't want to intrude.'

'You wouldn't be,' Georgiana assured both women. She held out her hand. 'If you knew the late Mrs Perry and Maud, you must have known my brother Harry Downe and my cousin John Mason.'

'Harry Downe was such a kind, wonderful man.' Tears started into Harriet's eyes when she mentioned his name. 'And Captain Mason – Major Mason now of course – was very good to me when I worked for Mrs Mason.' She shook Georgiana's hand and introduced her companion. 'Mrs Ida Jones, her husband was at Kut with my husband, Major Smythe, and Major Mason.'

'Then your husbands are …'

'Prisoners, in Turkey.

'It appears we have a great deal to talk about, ladies. Those are both adorable babies. Is yours a boy or girl, Mrs Greening?'

'A boy. I wanted to name him Alfred Greening for my husband but when I sent a wireless message to Kut when he was born, Alfred sent a message back, insisting I name him John Mason Greening after the finest man he knows. That should tell you what my husband thinks of Major Mason.'

'So this is John Mason Greening.' Georgiana looked down at the baby.

'John Mason Alfred Greening,' Harriet corrected. 'I don't think it's good for husbands to have it all their own way.'

Georgiana held the door open for Angela, Mariam, Mrs Jones, and Harriet. 'No, Mrs Greening, it certainly does not. I can't wait to make young Master John's acquaintance.'

Turkish Prison Camp
New Year's Eve 1916

'Here's to the New Year and whatever 1917 will bring to us.' John lifted the tin mug Greening had handed him high in the air.

'The end of the war I hope.' Crabbe took one of the mugs of raki Greening was distributing among the patients in the ward and waved it at John.

'That would be the bonus we're all hoping for,' John agreed.

'If our boys take Baghdad, it will be over, won't it, sir?' asked Lieutenant Johnson, who was recovering from an appendicitis operation.

Crabbe drank his raki and made a face as the liquor percolated down his throat. 'Despite any miracles General Maude performs in Baghdad, there won't be an armistice until the Germans surrender on the Western Front and that could take months,' he warned.

'Years,' Jones echoed gloomily from the other side of the ward where he was filling water jugs. 'My daughter will probably be married with children by the time we're released from here.'

'We'll be home before then.' Reverend Spooner slapped Jones gently on the back and he took one of the mugs from Greening's tray.

'No gloomy predictions allowed on New Year's Eve. This is the one time of the year optimism is compulsory,' John insisted. 'And we've a lot to be optimistic about. Everyone here is recovering. The only disease that's rampant in the camp is boredom ...'

'Thank to the measures you insisted the Turks take,' Reverend Spooner interrupted.

'Most importantly of all, we have all the raki we can drink,' Crabbe held out his mug to Greening for a refill.

'Make that a small one for, Major Crabbe,' John warned Greening.

'Spoilsport.' Crabbe winked as he spoke to show John there were no hard feelings.

John opened his watch and watched the second hand move towards midnight in line with the other two hands. 'It's here, gentlemen,' he raised his tin mug again. 'May 1917 take every one of us back to our families and loved ones.'

'And may God watch over them until we return,' the Reverend echoed.

'As I am first and foremost your medical advisor, gentlemen, finish your raki ...'

'That a medical command?' Crabbe joked.

'It is, because Greening will put out the lights in five minutes. I say five minutes because I know that Sergeant Greening will give you five minutes' grace. I wish you all a healthy New Year because I know for all of us the beginning will not be a happy one. Goodnight to you all, gentlemen.'

'And to you, sir,' the patients echoed.

John took a candle from the hall, lit it in the flame from an oil lamp, and climbed the four flights of stairs to his room. He lit his oil lamp and blew out the candle before sitting at the battered desk he'd scrounged from the Turkish commandant.

There were six unopened letters on his desk, all of which he'd kept for that evening, Tom, Georgiana, Maud, and his sister Lucy had all written to him, and to his surprise so had Angela Smythe. The last letter was from his parents, but he knew his mother had penned it as his father had never written to him, even before he'd been taken prisoner.

He checked the date on the missive from Maud. As there hadn't been time for her to reply to his letter telling her he intended to divorce her, he tucked it unopened at the bottom of the tin.

He opened Tom's letter first. It was fairly cheerful when he considered that it had been written in the middle of a war. Tom had taken over their father's London practice and he and Clary were living in their father's London house. Most of Tom's patients were injured soldiers and he was doing a fair amount of surgery in a London hospital that had been requisitioned by the military.

Tom mentioned that he and Clary had recently visited their parents and his father had persuaded two of his ex-colleagues out of retirement to help him with the clinic on the estate, which now almost exclusively catered for wounded officers. Their mother and Lucy had turned over half of the house to convalescent soldiers. He finished by telling him he was much loved and missed and could expect to become an uncle in the summer of 1917 and he and Clary hoped that he would be home in time to stand godfather to their child.

Georgie's letter was much in the same vein, and he imagined his cousin sitting back in a chair conjuring entertaining and positive thoughts for the poor prisoner. He was surprised to hear that Georgie had moved in with Angela Smythe. Not on Angela's account, because Angela was one of the kindest, sweetest women he knew, but because Georgie was so driven and dedicated to her profession he'd expected her to move into the Lansing Hospital for the duration.

Lucy's missive was an elegant Christmas and Happy New Year greeting, with the addition of, 'It's odd to be sending you this in May. I hope it reaches you and 1917 is the year we see you.'

Angela wished him a Happy Christmas and New Year and said she often thought of him, that he was missed by his Basra friends.

His mother's letter, the one he'd most looked forward to opening, was devastating. It reminded him so strongly of her presence he could almost hear her reading the words.

Dear Darling John,

The last thing I want to do is upset you or make you unhappy, especially now when you are a prisoner and incarcerated so far from everyone who loves you. I don't want to alarm you, and I want to reassure you that everything that can be done is being done for your father, who is dying. Tom and Lucy know and Lucy especially is taking it very hard. Your father diagnosed himself as suffering from inoperable cancer some months ago, although he only recently told me.

John checked the date on the letter. His mother had posted it in September. Knowing his father and how he hated any kind of fuss, he suspected that he'd only told his mother he was dying when he couldn't hide his condition any longer, which probably meant he was dead and buried by now. He was finding it difficult to envisage a world without the man who had steered him through boyhood into manhood.

Your father says he has only one regret, and that is that he cannot have a long face-to-face talk with you. He misses you a great deal, John. He has put his affairs in order and hopes that you will be able to move into this house with your wife when the war is over and you finally come home. He also hopes that you will continue to run the clinic which is now exclusively for ex-servicemen. So many broken young men are returning from the war, it is heartbreaking to see them.

The mention of his wife struck a chord and John felt guilty for not informing his parents of the situation between him and Maud in any of his letters. He realised that Tom couldn't have told his parents about the situation either. If he had, his mother wouldn't have suggested he install her as mistress of the family home.

Lucy has helped me to set up convalescent wards in the house for soldiers. We are kept busy doing what we can for them, but it is easy to see that Lucy is deeply hurt by what she sees as Michael's desertion. She never hears from him but your father insists I have no right to interfere in their lives.

It seems so unfair, my darling, to think of you locked up in a prison camp when all you have done is fight for your country. I hope and pray that you will return home before your father dies although I doubt that is now possible.

I pray for you, Georgiana, and Michael, and Harry's soul every

291

night. I don't know how your aunt copes knowing that Harry will never come home to her, but then, there are so many other mothers in the same position.

I trust that I will be able to hold you in my arms, if only once more, and I know your father feels the same way.

We love you so much, John, and are very proud of you and everything you have accomplished.

Good night, John, God Bless.

Your loving mother and father who has just walked into the bedroom and sends his love along with mine.

Look after yourself, my darling. You must come home to us again. You must.

John set the letters aside. He didn't have the heart to answer any of them that night. There was tap at his door. He called out, 'Come in,' hoping it wasn't a medical emergency.

Rebeka crept inside and closed the door quietly after her.

'I thought you'd be fast asleep by now.'

'I couldn't sleep and I wanted to be with you.' She walked over to him. He left the chair, folded his arms around her, and kissed her.

'Can I sleep here, with you?' she asked when he released her.

'You could, but I doubt I'd be able to keep my hands off you so that isn't a very good idea. And Mrs Gulbenkian …'

'Mrs Gulbenkian knows how much time I spend with you, so it won't be a surprise for her to know that I've spent all night here.' She hesitated, before continuing and he realised she was summoning up courage to say something important. 'My grandmother used to say that love between a man and a woman can be the most beautiful thing in the world. I've never seen the beauty. Only the ugliness. Can you show me the beauty, John?'

'Rebeka, you know I love you …'

'And you keep telling me that you will wait for me until I ask you to make love to me.'

'I told you when it happened it would have to come from you.'

She left him and folded back the bedclothes.

'Are you sure?'

'Quite sure.' She dropped her robe and the breath caught in his throat. She stood before him naked before slipping between the sheets. He blew out the candle, undressed, and lay beside her.

He reached out to her. It was comforting to be with someone, to know that he wasn't alone, and he blessed the impulse that had led her to seek him tonight of all nights.

He lifted her on top of him. She felt light, fragile, reminding him of a fledging bird. Slowly, infinitely slowly, he explored her body with his fingertips and then his lips. When he finally entered her, it was gently, unhurriedly. But then they had all the time in the world. And after the war – an entire future they could spend living and loving together and neither of them need ever be alone again.

British Relief Force, Shumrun
February 1917

Peter stepped down from the trench's firing step, where he'd been monitoring the advance of his troops, and squelched ankle deep in rainwater. He beckoned to Sweeney.

'Bring that lantern over here,' he ordered.

The subaltern did as Peter asked. Peter fished his note book from his pocket opened it, held it to the light, and tried to make sense of the scribbles he'd made at the last briefing. At the time his orders had sounded simple enough.

'Supervise one of the three ferry crossings on the river to the opposite bank held by the Turks. Ensure sufficient men sail over in ten pontoons to seize a firm foothold on the enemy-held bank, while covering two identical operations further upstream in case supporting fire is required.

As soon as a foothold is established, order the pontoons brought back to the bank on the British side of the river bank, fill the pontoons with the second wave of troops, and cross again. Repeat the operation until the entire battalion is on Turkish ground.

Then order the battalion to rush Turkish trenches and dugouts, scupper the Turkish riflemen and machine-gun teams, and hold our ground on the opposite bank to give our engineers time to build a permanent bridge that can be used to ferry more of our troops and artillery across to Turkish ground.'

It had sounded simple. But the heavens hadn't been open at the briefing, they hadn't been ankle deep in water or soaked to the skin, or on duty for sixteen straight hours.

'Sir,' a lieutenant ran up to him. 'Orders have come through. Ferries 2 and 3 are being abandoned because of because of unsustainable casualties. They're running at fifty per cent.'

Peter stepped back up on the firing step and lifted his field glasses again.

'We're holding but we won't be for long unless we get cover from the artillery. As soon as all the men manning Ferries 2 and 3 are back on this side ask command to give the order to our guns to open fire in the area where Ferries 2 and 3 were operating.'

'Shall I tell command you'll hold, sir?'

'You can tell them we're doing our damnedest.'

The runner raced past Perry, Cleck-Heaton, and Brooke who were striding towards him.

'Smythe,' Perry barked.

'Sir,' Peter stepped up back on the firing step and renewed his monitoring of the river crossing, partly because he was anxious to do so and partly to remind Perry he was no longer under his command.

'What the hell is delaying the river crossings?' Perry demanded. 'My men are chafing at the bit. Can't wait to get across and start clearing Johnny Turks out of their trenches.'

'The delay is down to heavy casualties, over fifty per cent in the other two crossings ... sir.' Smythe was careful to leave a noticeable pause before the 'sir' a trick he'd learned from Harry.

'There are a solid line of Hampshires close to the bank who could supply supporting fire to all three ferry crossings. They haven't moved in an hour. I've kept the idle bastards in sight of my field glasses,' Cleck-Heaton raged. 'Why haven't you sent them orders, Smythe?'

'Because they're all dead ... Major.'

'Don't be ridiculous ...'

'Please, feel free to go down there and check for yourself. But if you do keep low because you'll be within the sights of the Turkish guns.'

A runner came up. 'Major Iles compliments, Major Smythe. Ferries 2 and 3 have retreated and retrenched, sir ...'

'Bloody cowards,' Perry railed. 'I suppose you're set to continue sitting your arse here, Smythe, so you can get back to your wife. The baby must be born by now ...'

'Baby ...'

Before Peter could say another word a shell burst in the trench. Afterwards there was only a blanketing silence and a vague consciousness of sinking down, deep down, into an all-enveloping sticky wetness that closed, warm and comforting around and over him.

Chapter Twenty-seven

British Field Aid Station, Shumrun
January 1917

'Bring the lamp down lower. Hold it steady.' David felt as though he'd been operating for eternity, not days. His legs were leaden. He was having problems focusing and was too weary to expend an ounce more energy than he absolutely had to.

Every time he raised his head, it was only to see more wounded men piling in at the mouth of the trench. Those unable to sit or stand had been dropped onto tarpaulins to free the stretchers for yet more wounded. And because of the unrelenting rain every tarpaulin was under at least an inch of standing water, which made for soaking wet patients who, when it came to their turn to be operated on, drenched his trestle table. The 'walking wounded' sat or crouched alongside the tarpaulins, the majority uncomplainingly in the face of those with more serious injuries.

David brushed the water from his eyes with his sleeve and continued to saw through a corporal's thigh bone. He loathed carrying out amputations in the field because of the increased risk of infection but the man's leg was shattered into so many shards of bone and flesh he'd had no choice but to cut into the healthy leg above the injury to stop the haemorrhaging.

'Make way there. Make way! Wounded senior officers coming through.' A shadow loomed across the trestle table. 'Remove that man immediately, medic. There's an injured colonel here.'

'Get out of my light,' David snapped.

'Didn't you hear me, major? I said there's an injured colonel ...'

'I don't care if you have an injured general. Move out of my light and take him to the orderlies.' David kept his head down and his attention fixed on his patient's leg.

'You don't understand …'

'Get out of my light before I give the order to shoot you and your bloody colonel. You're putting this man's life at risk.'

'You ridiculous medic, you're not even a real military man …'

'Singh!' David shouted to his orderly. 'Remove this officer from the surgical area.'

Cleck-Heaton drew himself up to his full height and puffed out his chest. 'Do you know who I am?'

'You're a bloody pain in the arse.' David sawed through the last inch of bone, set the saw aside, and reached for a scalpel.

'I'll have you for insubordination!'

Without thinking, David handed Cleck-Heaton the remains of the leg he'd severed.

Cleck-Heaton dropped in alarm and shrank back in disgust. 'What the hell do you think you're doing, man?'

'Tying off this man's blood vessels. Singh!'

'Here, sir.' Singh appeared with four Gurkhas.

'Escort Major Cleck-Heaton and his companions from here while I get out of this man's leg.'

One of the Gurkhas gripped Cleck-Heaton's arm. The major pushed the Gurkha aside. 'That man on the table is a corporal …'

'And I'm a surgeon,' David snapped. 'Move!'

'I'm Colonel Perry's adjutant …'

Colonel Allan finished operating on the next table, and walked over to join them. 'What the hell's the ruckus here, Knight? Cleck-Heaton, I can hear you above the noise of the guns.'

'Colonel Perry and Major Brooke are injured, sir. This medic point blank refuses to give their treatment precedence over that of the ranks.'

'Amputation,' David explained succinctly when Colonel Allan glanced at his table.

Colonel Allan looked over Cleck-Heaton's shoulder at Brooke and Perry, who were leaning against the side of the trench. Perry's shoulder was blood-stained and he was breathing heavily. The lower sleeve of Brooke's greatcoat was bloody but he appeared otherwise unharmed.

'Arm wound?' he shouted to Brooke.

Brooke nodded.

'Shoulder?' Allan shouted to Perry.

'Yes.'

'As you can both walk, the wounds can't be that serious. Go to the walking wounded section. An orderly will take out the bullets if they haven't passed through.'

'These officers need treatment from a doctor ...'

'Treatment is administered according to need, not rank, Cleck-Heaton. Knight and I could have ministered to a dozen men in the time we've spent arguing with you. Take Perry and Brooke to the area set aside for the walking wounded, Cleck-Heaton, and return to your post. That's an order.' Colonel Allan turned his back on Cleck-Heaton. 'Need help with that, Knight?'

'Nearly done, sir. Just the blood vessels to tie off. Singh, clear the leg from the floor and pass me catgut and needle.'

'Badly wounded coming through.' Two stretcher-bearers charged up with a mound of muddy, blood-soaked body.

'On my table,' Allan shouted. The man was plastered in so much detritus it was difficult to make out his rank, features, or figure.

'Bastard! You'd see to this man ...'

Allan motioned to the Gurkhas. Before they reached Cleck-Heaton a burly sepoy orderly stepped from the side of the trench and hit Cleck-Heaton on the jaw. He went down instantly, splashing into the standing water in the bottom of the trench.

Allan gazed at the mess on his operating table. 'I can't make head or tail of this. Give us a hand, Knight.'

David joined him. 'Kill or cure. Singh, bring up buckets of water.'

The orderly brought two over. David tipped one over the stretcher. The mud and blood washed away to reveal an arm and two severed legs lying on top of a body.

'I've seen some sights ... but this ...' Allan picked up the legs and handed them to Singh who threw them into the medical waste container.

'I think they're dead, sir, as is this arm.' David passed the limb to Singh before tipping the second bucket of water over the stretcher to reveal Peter Smythe's face. Peter opened his eyes and glared up at him.

'This, however, is alive, sir,' David grinned.

Peter struggled to sit up.

299

Allan shouted for more water.

'Anything hurt, Smythe?' David asked.

'I can see your lips moving but I can't hear you.'

'Anything hurt?' David shouted.

Peter swung his legs over the side of the table, and ran his hands down his arms and legs.

'Only his hearing by the look of it,' Allan shouted when Peter didn't reply.

David smiled. 'Clean the blood off him, Singh. See if you can find his bearer and a clean uniform. A couple of hours' rest and Major Smythe can go back and get all muddied and bloodied up again.'

Smythes' Bungalow
February 1917

'Why didn't anyone tell me how painful labour is?' Angela muffled her moans in her pillow lest she disturb Hasmik or Robin.

'Because if women knew what childbirth was really like beforehand there'd be no more babies – ever – and the supply of people would dry up.'

'That might make the world a better place. There'd be no men to wage war and the animals could take over ...' The rest of Angela's sentence dissolved in a tight-lipped, restrained cry.

Georgiana took a towel she'd soaked in lavender water and wiped Angela's forehead. 'You're doing fine. Not long to go.' She called to the maid, 'bring more clean towels please, and prepare the baby's cot.'

'Yes, Dr Downe.'

Georgiana glanced at the clock on the dressing table. It was four in the morning. Angela's labour had begun at midday. She'd sent a message to Theo, who sent a note back by return informing her that he and Dr Picard were dealing with an unexpected influx of Turkish wounded, but if she needed help to she should send again. She'd managed to resist the impulse to write back to him asking if he could assist by enlarging his sister's hips.

'This is taking so long. The baby will be all right, won't it?' Angela panted in between pains.

'The baby will be fine,' Georgiana reassured. 'It's you I'm

concerned about. You must be exhausted. The problem is I rather suspect this child is built like his father and you're the size of a gnome.'

Angela didn't smile at the poor joke.

Georgiana checked Angela's pulse. 'Tell me if the pain become unbearable.'

'How much longer?' Angela gasped.

'When the next pain comes give one almighty push with every particle of strength you can summon.'

Angela did just that and as she pushed, Georgiana heard a knock at the door.

'That will be Dr Wallace. Show him into the living room,' she ordered the maid without looking away from Angela. 'I can see the baby's head, Angela. One more push when the next pain comes.'

Five minutes later Georgiana was holding a red, squirming baby in her arms.

'Has it red hair?' Angela fell back on to her pillows.

'That's a strange question for a new mother to ask.'

'It's a boy, isn't it?'

'A beautiful boy with fair hair. He's all in one piece and absolutely gorgeous.' Georgiana wrapped the baby in a towel and gave him to Angela. 'I'll cut the cord, wash you and the baby, then get your brother.'

By the time she had made Angela and the baby comfortable and gone into the living room, Theo had fallen asleep, although he was sitting bolt upright in a chair.

Georgiana poured two small brandies, woke him, and handed him one. 'You look as though you haven't slept in days.'

'Just two.'

'What's happening?'

'Heavy fighting upstream. Turks have been flooding into the Lansing again.'

'What about British wounded?' Georgiana's blood ran cold when she thought of Michael, Peter … and David.

'I spoke to a British medic on the wharf. He said they've been warned to expect an enormous influx. Initial reports suggest a fifty per cent casualty rate.'

'Any news on lists of names?'

'It's too early. Angela?'

'Come and meet your nephew.'

Theo prised himself out of the chair and followed Georgiana into Angela's bedroom. Angela was lying in bed staring at and cuddling her son. She didn't even look at Theo, just held out her hand to him. He squeezed it.

'He's beautiful, isn't he?'

'A handsome fellow.' Theo stroked the baby's cheek with his forefinger.

If Georgiana didn't know Theo better, she'd have said he'd sounded emotional.

Angela finally looked away from her son long enough to see how tired her brother was. 'You're sleeping on your feet.'

'Just finished a long shift.'

'There's fighting upstream?'

'Not for officers above the rank of captains. The majors will be standing at the back pushing the ranks forward,' Theo reassured her clumsily. 'I have to get back. You did write and tell Peter that he was going to be a father, didn't you?'

'Yes, but he hasn't replied. The mail is so uncertain.'

'I could call into the wireless room at HQ on the way and ask them to send him a wire.'

'Would you?'

'I would,' he smiled. 'Have you picked out a name for young Smythe?'

She gazed down at the child. 'Peter Charles Theodore Smythe.'

'Charles for our father?'

'And another Charles I knew and loved and valued as a friend.'

Georgiana turned away from Angela and Theo and folded back the sheets and blankets on the baby's cot. Theo stroked the baby's cheek again, dropped a kiss on Angela's head, and went to the door.

'Would you like tea, coffee, something to eat, Theo?' Georgiana asked.

'No, thank you. I have to go.' He walked past her. Georgiana saw that she wasn't the only one struggling to hold her emotions in check.

British Relief Force, Shumrun
February 1917

302

The sky grew gradually paler, but the grey was unrelenting. Simply a lighter shade than that of the night. Rain teemed down in sheets, cold, penetrating, and interminable.

'This trench is a right bloody sodden mess, isn't it, sir?' A private in the Cheshires addressed Michael who was crouched beneath a flimsy shelter he'd patched together from his mackintosh and two ammunition boxes.

Michael carried on scribbling in his notebook. 'No more than any other sodden mess of a trench in this area, private. You know the saying, "if God meant for soldiers to be content with their lot in life he would have staffed the army with angels".'

'You're a war correspondent, sir?'

'*Daily Mirror.*'

'My missus likes reading that. I'm not much of a reader myself.'

Michael had learned long ago that the man who admitted that he 'wasn't much of a reader' generally couldn't read much beyond his own name.

A runner came down the line, 'Anyone seen Major Smythe?'

Michael held his hand out from under his waterproof to attract the runner's attention. 'Who's asking?'

'Message just come down the wire for him, sir.'

'I'll look for him if you're busy.'

'I am, sir. Thank you. Much obliged, sir.' The runner handed Michael a piece of sodden folded paper. There was no envelope, Michael opened it carefully.

Peter Charles Theodore Smythe born 4.15 a.m. Mother, son, well. Congratulations, Theo

Michael checked the date – 3 hours ago. 'This is one piece of news I can't wait to pass on to Major Smythe.' He pushed his notebook and pencil into his pocket, shook out his mackintosh, and slipped it on.

'Do you know where Major Smythe is, sir?' The runner asked.

'I'll find him.' Michael fought his way through the trenches until he reached the river. He found Peter in the front line trench on the British side, standing on a rifle step watching through his field glasses as the Turkish guns blasted the British foothold on the opposite bank. Michael tapped Peter's shoulder. He stepped down.

'The Gurkhas are advancing. We're getting there. You here to write copy, Michael?'

'Why are you shouting?'

Peter pointed to his ears. 'Shell blast.'

Michael handed Peter the scrap of paper. 'You play your cards close to your chest,' he yelled in Peter's ear. 'Not a word.'

Peter read and re read the note. 'It makes sense.'

'What?' Michael yelled.

'Perry said I was a coward who wanted to get back to my wife and child. I thought he was talking about Maud's baby ...'

Michael laughed at the bewildered expression on Peter's face. He dug out his flask and handed it to him. 'You're a father, Smythe, Congratulations.'

'Congratulations, sir ... congratulations ...'

Within seconds Peter was surrounded by a sea of junior officers slapping his back and wishing him well.

'I need to send a return wire.'

Michael pulled out his pencil and notebook. 'I'll do it for you,' he mouthed above the noise of the shelling and congratulations of officers. 'What do you want me to say?'

'If wishes could carry me, I'd be home tonight. Love to both of you, Peter.'

Michael walked back and looked for the command post. General Maude insisted on hourly wireless updates, which infuriated most of his staff officers. It took twenty minutes to set up the wireless and fifteen minutes to take it down. Thirty-five minutes during which Maude and his staff were forced to remained static. Minutes the majority of his senior officers believed could have been put to better use.

He walked past the staff tent to the wireless operator's shelter, which also held a tea station manned by sepoys. He was in luck. The lieutenant was just about to disconnect the wireless. He persuaded him to keep it open a few more minutes, handed over Peter's message, and watched him send it.

'Two sugars isn't it, sir?' A sepoy who remembered Michael from previous visits, asked from behind the tea urn.

'It is,' he took the tin mug the man handed him and warmed his hands on it. 'Thank you, just what I needed.' As he'd stocked up in the stores before the battle, he offered the sepoy a full pack of cigarettes. The man beamed.

'Thank you, sir. You just come up from the river, sir?' the sepoy asked.

'I have.'

'Do you know if we've crossed to the Turkish side?'

'We most certainly have.' Michael tried to forget just how precarious the British foothold was.

'Do you think we'll win, sir?'

'It would be unthinkable to put in all this effort and get nowhere.'

'That's probably what the Expeditionary Force thought before they surrendered at Kut, sir.' A wounded private with bandages around his head, arm, and leg limped towards them on crutches.

'Pessimism's a court martial offence, private,' Michael joked.

'If the cell's dry, I wouldn't mind, sir.'

David's orderly, Singh, ran up. 'Mr Downe, sir, you on your way somewhere?'

'Not particularly, why?'

'We're desperate for help in the field hospital, sir. The doctors are overwhelmed by the numbers of wounded. Men are still flooding in and half the stretcher-bearers have been hit.'

Michael turned back to the wireless operator who was busy disconnecting wires.

'Any plan to advance?'

'Not for the next twenty-five minutes, sir.'

Michael turned up the collar of his mackintosh, headed towards the river and the booming artillery, and hit a crowd of walking wounded. He glanced over to the trenches that held the aid stations and field hospitals. They were so packed with injured and bleeding bodies he couldn't see the surgeons.

Behind the mounds of wounded waiting for attention was a hillock of bodies. He paled. Lying on top was the corpse of Boris Bell; beneath him, a stretcher and two dead stretcher-bearers, their skulls riddled with bullets. He lifted Boris's corpse and placed him gently on a line of sandbags before extricating the stretcher. He looked around. A sepoy was standing, staring, mesmerized by the mass of walking wounded. Michael hailed him and held up the stretcher. The sepoy joined him. Without exchanging a word they headed towards the river.

Chapter Twenty-eight

David swam slowly out of confused dreams into consciousness. Disorientated, he opened his eyes. The oil lamp in his tent was flickering low, shedding amber light that sent shadows dancing on his cot and the walls of his tent. He reached for his pocket watch and opened it. Four o'clock. It was dark so it had to be early morning. But which day?

He had a vague memory of going to bed in daylight but he had no idea of the month let alone the day. He also recalled a letter from home. Had he dreamed it?

He found it on his campaign chest, opened it, and read it. He hadn't dreamed its contents. The impact of the life-changing news it contained hit him anew with full force. All his life he'd managed to avoid taking responsibility for any and everything, especially his mistakes, and the debts he incurred, but fate had conspired against him – or so it would appear.

He returned the letter to its envelope and stowed it in the top drawer of his chest. He'd placed a framed photograph of himself with Georgiana on top. It had been taken by a Jewish photographer in the Basra Club shortly after he'd travelled downstream with the wounded from Kut. He'd paid the man for a copy and if Georgiana remembered it being taken she'd never mentioned it again, so the print had remained his secret.

He looked at it for a long time. Georgiana certainly couldn't be described as beautiful, not in the conventional sense, but neither was she as plain as she tried to make out. One thing was certain, he adored her more than any woman he'd ever known simply because she treated him as her intellectual inferior, which in his most honest moments he admitted he probably was.

She'd lent an element of surprise to his life which had jerked him out of cynicism and complacency. He never knew what she was going to say or do next and the only thing he was absolutely certain of was he didn't want to imagine a life without her.

He took out his writing case, opened it flat to give himself a surface to press on, unscrewed the top of his ink bottle, and picked up his pen.

Dear Georgie,

This isn't going to be a letter about what we're doing upriver because frankly you don't want to know, I don't want to write about it, and even if I did, the censor would have to paint thick black lines all over my nice clean letter to you and that would spoil it. Especially in view of what I want to say and the importance history will bequeath on this epistle.

I've had news from home. Frankly I don't want to talk about that either because I don't want to think about it.

The only thing I do want to write about is us.

Marry me, Georgie.

I'll list all the reasons why you should.

First, you're absolutely the only woman other than my mother who's willingly put up with my company for more than a few hours.

We'd look really good together I'll be the handsome one and you can be the intelligent one.

I need you to be my mentor and give me good medical advice which will benefit my patients and hopefully prevent me from making any more fatal mistakes than I've already made. Not that I know of any that I've made as yet. (I put in that last sentence for legal purposes in case someone sees this and remembers that I doctored a friend or relative of theirs who has subsequently died.)

I miss you more than anyone would believe it possible for a devastatingly handsome man like me to miss a girl. It's very cold at night wrapped in a damp soggy blanket with no warm body to cuddle.

I expect to receive your acceptance by return of post – given it's wartime I'll allow six months for it to reach me,

Your loving fiancé, David.

P.S. Peter is over the moon at the news that he's a father. He's handed out cigarettes to everyone in between firing salvos at the Turks. We have no cigars upstream and that should tell just how uncivilised the conditions are here.

David read what he'd written and added another postscript.

If I wrote what I really feel about you I'd probably frighten you off but I want you know that my heartfelt feelings aren't entirely the result of being terrified of being blown into oblivion at any moment.

He pushed it into an envelope, sealed it, and wrote Georgiana's name and address on the back. He cleared away his writing case, pen, and ink and lay back on the bed.

If by some miracle Georgiana did agree to marry him, would she be as appalled and devastated as he was by the life-changing news he'd received?

Turkish Prison Camp
March 1917

John went into the kitchen after he finished patients' rounds to find Mrs Gulbenkian in tears and Hasmik and Rebeka trying to comfort her.

'What on earth is the matter?'

Mrs Gulbenkian's English had improved to the point where she understood him. She looked up, saw the sympathetic expression on his face, and sobbed all the louder.

Rebeka wrapped her arm around Mrs Gulbenkian's shoulders and shook her head at John.

He retreated to the room that had been claimed as a day room by the fittest among the convalescent patients. They'd enlisted the help of the POW officers and orderlies, and moved the beds to clear an area for chairs and makeshift tables. John found Crabbe playing bridge with Bowditch and two other officers, and in direct contradiction of all medical advice, smoking.

'Missed us so much you had to come back, or did you forget to discharge one of us to the officers' accommodation?' Crabbe asked.

'I'm hiding from the nurses in the kitchen. Something's upset Mrs Gulbenkian.'

'She's heard from her cousin in America.' Crabbe took the hand on the table, shuffled the cards together with the others on his pile, and led with another trump.

'And?' John pressed.

'The cousin pleaded poverty and said he could neither send her the money for passage to America nor sponsor her to go there even if she found the money herself. Nor could he offer her a room to stay should she somehow make her own way to the land of milk and honey.'

John sat on the end of Crabbe's bed which was close to the table. 'That leaves Mrs Gulbenkian with nowhere to go at the end of the war.'

'Exactly.'

'She was so sure her cousin would come to her aid. She was going to take Hasmik with her. She even offered to take Rebeka.'

'I thought Rebeka might be making other post-war plans.'

Crabbe's wink suggested to John that he and Rebeka hadn't been as successful at concealing their relationship as they'd believed.

'Don't worry, we can always take them back to England with us when the peace treaties are signed.' Crabbe took another hand and threw away a low club. 'Mrs Gulbenkian and Rebeka have cared selflessly and without payment for British troops, therefore we can hope the powers that be will regard them as British nurses.'

'We can hope.' John echoed. He waited until Crabbe finished the hand. 'Fancy a walk outside? It's dry.'

'But freezing cold.'

'It will disinfect your lungs.'

Crabbe picked up his greatcoat, which he used as an extra blanket on his bed, and followed John outside.

'I'll make an appointment to see the colonel,' John wrapped the muffler that Mrs Gulbenkian had knitted him from wool sent in a Red Cross parcel around his neck. 'If enough officers sign a letter asking the War Office to accept Mrs Gulbenkian, Rebeka, and Hasmik into Britain, someone in authority might take notice.'

'They might. They might take even more notice if I marry Mrs Gulbenkian.'

'Marry?' John thrust his hands deeper into his greatcoat's pockets to warm them. 'You're seriously thinking of asking Mrs Gulbenkian to marry you?'

'Why not? She's a fine-looking woman.'

John thought for a moment. 'You're right. It's just that I've never thought of her that way.'

'Hardly surprising; you're what, twenty-eight, twenty-nine?'

'I feel a hundred and ten most days,' John murmured.

'Mrs Gulbenkian – Yana – is forty.'

'Yana? I had no idea you were so close.'

'We have a few things in common. I'm closer to fifty than forty. Even before I was wounded I knew I'd be put out to grass after this show. I've a major's pension to look forward to, which is not insignificant, and I've a bit put by as well, so I can afford to lead a comfortable life in retirement. I think I'd enjoy sharing it with a woman.'

'The way you play cards I'm guessing you've more than a bit put by.'

'Enough to buy a small house in the country with a garden big enough for a few chickens, and a goat. Yana's fond of goat's milk and fresh eggs.'

'There are several cottages on my father – my family's estate,' John corrected. He still found it difficult to believe that his father wouldn't be there to greet him when he returned home.

'You're going back there after the war?'

'If I survive until the peace treaties are signed.'

'You'd sell me a cottage?'

'Or rent, whichever you prefer. You'd make an excellent neighbour, one I could bore with war reminiscences any time I chose. Does Mrs Gulbenkian – Yana – know you're making plans?'

'She will before the day is out.'

'And Hasmik?'

'I've always wanted a daughter.' Crabbe turned when they reached the fence. He gazed back at the winter shrivelled, uninviting garden. 'I could adopt Rebeka as well.'

'No, you couldn't, she'd object. She's too old to be adopted by you or any man.'

'You're married.'

311

'You don't need to remind me. I've written to Maud telling her I want a divorce. I've also written to my brother Tom asking him to begin divorce proceedings.'

'A divorce can take years.'

'I know, but I have other means of persuading the authorities that Rebeka is my indispensable nursing assistant.'

'Such as?'

'A godfather who's a general and a father who's the King's surgeon.'

'That should help your case. I'm bloody frozen. Are my lungs disinfected enough for you now?'

'You have my permission to go back inside. Just one thing: when and where do you intend to propose?' '

'Why?'

'So I can hide and watch.'

'That is exactly why I won't tell you.'

Count D'Souza's Residence and Portuguese Consulate, India March 1917

Maud was last to finish breakfast. Sister Luke had excused herself almost as soon as Maud had entered the dining room and left for upstairs. Maud presumed to pack, although she couldn't imagine quite what the sister was packing as she, like Maud, had brought very little beyond a change of clothes and a Bible with her. To Maud's disappointment if the count had breakfasted he'd eaten early, because there was no place set for him at the table.

She finished her coffee, blotted her lips on a napkin, and went into the hall. Before she reached the stairs a footmen handed her a letter on a silver tray. She turned it over twice before realising that John had written her address on the outside of one of her own letters. She tore it open in the hope he'd written a reply to her in the margins. It couldn't be a long message but everyone knew prisoners of war were kept in appalling conditions where necessities were in short supply and presumably luxuries like notepaper unobtainable.

She saw that John had written something in the corner on the page, but his writing was cramped and she had to move closer the window to read it.

Dear Maud, our marriage is over. I will instigate divorce proceedings as soon as I can. John

'Good morning, Mrs Smith.'

'Good morning, Count D'Souza.' She forced a smile and pushed the letter into the pocket of her dress.

'You are pale, not bad news I hope.'

'A letter from my cousin. He is a being held a prisoner of war in a Turkish camp. I have been sending him food parcels. It appears not all of them are getting through to him.'

'Hardly surprising. It is common knowledge the Turkish army is full of cut-throats and thieves. Sister Luke, good morning. Please, would you both care to accompany me into my study?'

Maud and Sister Luke followed the count. He closed the door and offered them chairs before walking around behind his desk. He opened a drawer and removed an envelope.

'I wish to thank both of you for remaining with my wife until the end, which took a great deal longer than the doctors initially envisaged. This,' he handed Sister Luke the envelope, 'is a donation to the convent over and above what I agreed to pay Mother Superior for both your services. Thank you for remaining for the funeral and thank you for the spiritual comfort you have given me and everyone in this house throughout this difficult time. Also for the comfort you offered the mourners yesterday.'

Sister Luke took the envelope. 'God bless and keep you, Count D'Souza, and God bless and keep the Countess D'Souza's soul.'

'Thank you, Sister Luke. You are packed and ready to leave?'

'I am, sir.'

'You must be anxious to return to the convent.'

'We are needed in the infirmary, sir. I received a message from Mother Superior yesterday. Smallpox has broken out in the streets in the north of the town and the isolation wards in the convent are overflowing with the sick.'

'I have summoned a carriage to convey you to the convent. A footman will accompany you and carry your bags.'

'Sister Smith?' Sister Luke looked at Maud as she rose from her chair.

'I won't be returning to the convent with you, Sister Luke.' Maud looked down at her hands to avoid meeting Sister Luke's gaze which given the strain between them she suspected would be full of contempt.

'I've offered Mrs Smith the position of housekeeper on my staff, which I am delighted to say she has accepted. She will remain here,' the count explained. 'Thank you again for your assistance, Sister Luke.'

Maud rose from her chair and offered Sister Luke her hand. The nun bowed but did not take it. She swept out of the room without another word. A footman reached in from the hall and closed the door the sister had left open behind her.

The count smiled at Maud. 'I would like you to pack my wife's personal possessions. Secure all her jewellery in a strongbox and her clothes in mothproof trunks. Her personal maid will help you. Do you get on with her?'

'Very well.' Maud knew that the mixed-race girl was terrified of losing her place.

'In which case you can tell her that she will be kept on to serve as your lady's maid. When you've cleared my wife's room, please begin on the rest of the house. Start with the cut glass, crystal, and silverware in the dining room. I received official confirmation this morning. I have been recalled to Lisbon. I leave at the end of the week.'

Maud's heart beat a tattoo. 'And me, sir?'

'I will need a housekeeper wherever I am posted, Mrs Smith, and I was hoping you would accompany me. I will continue to pay you the salary we negotiated yesterday as well as all your living and travel expenses. I trust that will be satisfactory?'

'It will, sir.'

'I have an appointment with the mayor but I will return for lunch. Will you join me?'

'I will be happy to. Thank you, sir.'

'I'll see you then.'

'May I borrow some notepaper so I can write to my relatives in England to inform them that I am leaving the convent and that I will forward a new address to them as soon as I have one?'

'Of course.' He rose from his desk, squeezed her breasts, and kissed her. 'See at lunch – and siesta,' he added suggestively. 'And summon the dressmaker. I would like you to see you in something more colourful and becoming than that drab nurses' uniform.'

As soon as he left the room, Maud opened the stationary cabinet. She ignored the house stationary and removed a dozen sheets of official Portuguese Consulate notepaper and envelopes. She placed them in a file and carried them up to her room. The door to the bedroom Sister Luke had occupied was open and the maids had already stripped the bed.

Maud took the file into her own bedroom, placed it on the desk, and closed and locked the door. She used the pen, ink, and paper she found in a drawer, and began practising handwriting. Her own, which slanted to the right, was too distinctive so she tried to write in a clear, upright hand.

Only when she was happy that her writing wasn't recognisable as hers did she take the consulate paper and envelopes. She addressed one envelope to her father, another to John, and a third and fourth to Angela and Mrs Butler.

Apart from the name, she penned the same message on all of them.

Regret to inform you Mrs Maud Mason died of smallpox yesterday afternoon. Mrs Mason's remains were immediately interred with those of other victims in a mass grave in the public cemetery as a necessary precautionary measure to contain the spread of the disease.

Mrs Mason left her personal effects and all her worldly goods to the convent of St Agnes and St Clare.

Yours sincerely,
pp Count D'Souza
Portuguese Consul
on behalf of the sisters of the convent of St Agnes and St Clare.

When she finished writing five letters she placed four in the envelopes and sealed them. She took them and half a sovereign from her purse and went downstairs in search of a footman. She handed the envelopes to the man and gave him the coin.

'These letters are urgent. Please take them to the Post Office at once and ensure that the correct postage is placed on them.'

'Yes, ma'am.'

'You may keep the change.'

'Yes, ma'am.'

'On your return journey call on the countess's dressmaker and ask him to visit me here at his earliest opportunity.'

She returned upstairs, entered the countess's suite, and looked around. How long would it be before she succeeded in cajoling the count to house her in similar quarters? Recalling his instructions, she went to the cupboard and found the strongbox. The key was in the lock, she lifted the lid in preparation to take the countess's jewellery.

While stowing away the pieces in their original boxes, she amused herself by imagining her future. Should her father, John, Mrs Butler, or Angela write to the consulate, Count D'Souza would have long gone and all the new consul would be able to do was confirm the outbreak of smallpox. She doubted that the count's replacement would contact the convent, but if he should consider it, the fifth letter she'd penned, a copy of the one she'd sent to her father, left in the consulate's file on the convent, should deter anyone from making further enquiries.

As for Maud Smith, she might be a housekeeper now – albeit one with her own lady's maid – but her future beckoned as bright and glittering as the jewels she was packing. There'd have to be period of mourning of course. But the count enjoyed the private moments they shared.

She knew, because she'd had extensive experience of similar private moments with many other men. The count was taking her to Lisbon. No one knew her there, so there'd be no risk of encountering any gossip about her past. A few more months and then, what could be more natural than that the bereaved count should turn to his beautiful young widowed housekeeper for consolation.

Six months, a year at the outside, and wedding bells would be ringing for Maud Smith and Count D'Souza. Maud Mason née Perry was dead and buried in a common unmarked grave. She'd make sure her ghost never rose to trouble her again.

Not while Maud Smith, soon to become Countess D'Souza, remained very much alive.

Chapter Twenty-nine

British Relief Force, Baghdad
13th April 1917

'Take cover!' Peter yelled as a grenade was thrown from a heavily shrouded harem window on the top floor of a private house. It landed a few feet away from the gallows his men were constructing to hang fifteen looters Perry had arrested on his march into the town.

Most of the sappers clamped their hands over their heads and dropped to the ground but Private Hawkins dived forward, snatched the grenade, and lobbed it back into the building. Seconds later the front of the house blasted outwards and both men and street were covered inches deep in dust and debris.

'Anyone hurt?' Peter rose to his feet and dusted himself off, trying not to think about what he'd been lying in.

'I think something hit me, sir.'

Hawkins emerged from a ragged pile of splintered wood. Blood streamed through his hair and dripped down on to his face, neck, and uniform.

'I saw medics enter that building half an hour ago.' Peter pointed across the street. 'Let's get you seen to. Sergeant, carry on. You're in charge.'

'Sir.' The sergeant snapped to attention then started shouting at the men. 'Get a move on, you lazy beggars. Do you expect these looters to hang themselves ...'

Peter helped Hawkins across the street and into the building. The noise was ear-shattering. Michael and David were standing in the hall, shooting at a tide of rats that raced squealing towards them, pouring out of a narrow corridor.

David waved at Peter. 'Be with you in a moment,' he shouted. 'The orderlies are herding these beggars towards us. The entire bloody building is filthy, unsanitary, and infested.'

When David finished emptying his gun, he reloaded and holstered it. An Arab ran through the front door shouting in German. To Peter's surprise, David answered him in the same language after telling Michael to stop shooting.

'I don't care if every stupid rat we've killed is your most beloved and cherished pet. I'm the senior officer here and I've given the order to shoot as many rats as we can get in our gun sights. And for your information,' David pulled at the insignia on his collar. 'This is a British uniform. The Turks and Germans left last night. We're in charge now and,' David switched to English. 'I've passed a death sentence on all rats in the city. No appeal, no reprieve. Singh?'

David's orderly emerged from a second corridor.

'Is there a clean room in this place?' David asked.

'No, sir.'

'Bring me a chair and a medical kit, and take them outside. These stupid bloody rats haven't yet realised that this is an execution chamber.' David shot at and killed another rat before walking out.

Peter helped Hawkins who was having trouble standing, onto a marble bench in the courtyard. 'Joined the medics?' he asked when Michael sat beside them.

'I carry a gun and don't often get chance to use it. That rat hunt was fun.'

Peter looked back through the door at the tiled walls and floors of the hall. 'What was this building?'

'Haven't a clue,' David shrugged. 'Arabs were burning papers in the garden when we got here but they ran off when they saw us. I think they must have disturbed a few rats' nests and the creatures ran inside to join their chums who'd already taken up residence.'

Singh arrived with the chair. David helped Hawkins on to it and examined his head. 'The good news is nothing's broken. The bad you'll need a few stitches. Singh, I need my bag. Make sure there's catgut and disinfectant in it.'

'That'll teach you to play ball with grenades, Hawkins.' Peter reached for his cigarettes.

'I didn't think, sir.'

Peter lit three cigarettes and passed one to Michael and another to Hawkins. He held up the packet to David who shook his head. 'Your "not thinking", Hawkins, probably saved at least a dozen of our men from injury if not death.' Peter took his notebook from his pocket and scribbled a reminder to put Hawkins up for a medal.

Michael read the note over Peter's shoulder. 'Can I have the full story?'

'In return for what?' Peter raised his eyebrows.

'Jug of raki.'

'You're on.'

'Excuse me, Major Knight, sir,' a runner arrived and addressed David, 'we've found a hospital.'

'A nice big clean one, I hope.'

'A large one, sir.'

Something in the runner's voice made David look up from his stitching. 'It's filthy?'

'It's full of patients, sir. Mainly cholera and typhoid cases. Looks like most of the staff have succumbed.'

'Singh, muster the medics and orderlies from wherever they're hiding, we're on the move again.'

David fastened the last stitch in Hawkins's head and eyed Peter. 'Tell me again, why did we fight to take this forsaken, verminous, insanitary city?'

'Because a politician overdosed on the *Arabian Nights* when he was a child and wanted to see "the golden minarets shine and glitter in the setting sun"?' Michael suggested.

'I see no golden minarets.'

'You obviously haven't looked in the right place – yet,' Michael rose from the bench.

'Can't wait for my first night off to look for them.' David returned his instruments to his bag.

'If you find any *Arabian Nights* splendours, let me know, Michael.' Peter helped Hawkins to his feet.

'You'll be the first I'll tell,' Michael volunteered.

'As you're the one with the least work to do, you can look for them,' David shot two more rats before picking up his doctors' bag and leaving.

Turkish Prison Camp
May 1917

319

'It feels as though summer's brought a taste of heaven with it. Just wandering around the garden breathing in the scents of apple and cherry blossom and feeling the warmth of the sun on my face is absolute bliss.' John checked for protruding nails before sitting alongside Rebeka and Hasmik on a wooden bench Grace had inexpertly patched together from the branches of a tree that had blown over in a winter storm.

'None of your patients need you?' Rebeka asked.

'Not for five minutes. If I'm fortunate maybe even ten.'

'Or half an hour.'

'That's probably too much to hope for.' He reached for her hand. Crabbe and Yana Gulbenkian were walking around the perimeter, arm in arm, heads bent, immersed in deep and earnest conversation.

'They are planning their future together,' Rebeka explained. 'Reverend Spooner agreed to marry them as soon as the relevant permissions come through from your army.'

'You do know I'll marry you the minute my divorce comes through.' John meshed his fingers into hers.

'I know.' She watched Hasmik run over to Bowditch and Grace. Grace had brought out the doll he was whittling for her. He'd made a reasonable job of the head and torso, but the dolls' arms and legs were somewhat mismatched, with the left side limbs twice the size of the ones on the right.

'If it doesn't come soon enough for this little one to be born with married parents, I'll insist on Mason being on the birth certificate.' He laid his hand on her abdomen.

'Don't,' she moved his hand away. 'Not here, where everyone can see you.'

'They're going to find out soon enough. You're nicely plump.'

'Fat, you mean.' She leaned against him. 'I really don't care about us not being married. I love you.'

'You couldn't possibly love me as much as I love you and we'll both love this little one when he or she arrives.'

'It's not a "one", it's a boy.'

'Or girl. We have to think of names. I'll be happy with anything you chose.'

'Really?' She was surprised.

'You'll be the one doing the work so you should pick the name.

We could call him or her after your father or mother. They must have been incredible parents to make you the woman you are.'

'My father's name was Erik.'

John repeated it. 'Erik Mason, that's an excellent solid name. Your mother?'

'Elen.'

'That's beautiful.'

'So we've settled on names.'

'Only for our first two children.'

'You want more?'

'Dozens more.' He faltered when he recalled saying the exact same words to Maud. He dismissed the memory from his mind, then slipped his arm around Rebeka's shoulders and sat back, closing his eyes and turning his face to the sun. The sound of marching feet echoed from the gate. He opened his eyes. 'What's happening?' he asked Crabbe when he walked up with Yana.

'New influx of guards. I talked to one of the younger ones.'

'And?'

'And?' Crabbe teased.

'Something must have happened to make you grin like the Cheshire cat in *Alice in Wonderland*.'

Whoops echoed across the garden from the officer's quarters.

'The war's over?' John sat up.

'One thing at a time, Mason. We've taken Baghdad.'

'As of when?'

'Last week apparently. That's why we have new guards. The Turks have pulled back half their army. With luck this is the beginning of the end in Mesopotamia. Now the War Office can concentrate on taking the Western Front.'

'Hopefully sometime soon.' John drew Rebeka even closer to him. 'And then we can all go home.'

Baghdad
May 1917

'Baghdad nightlife, here we come,' David finished shaving and splashed cologne on to his chin and cheeks.

'Hoping to attract the mosquitoes?' Peter asked.

'You never know, there might be a stunning belly dancer

prepared to throw herself at me.'

'I'll tell Georgie.'

'Do and I'll tell Angela you went out on the town to look for loose women. Did you know that John worked here?'

'Here? You mean Baghdad here?'

'I mean hospital here. Apparently he arrived heading a medical escort of sick British POWs. One of the orderlies who was working here at the time told me. The German doctors fled with the Turks, so when we took over this place, cholera and typhoid cases included, there were only nurses and orderlies managing the facility. But to be fair they didn't try to wreck the place or destroy any of the medical supplies or instruments.'

'Did the orderly say how John looked?'

'Apparently he'd been driven into the ground. Once he'd been reassured that his patients would be attended to, he slept for days. But that's John.'

They left David's room and walked out into the courtyard which was packed with scores of locals sitting patiently waiting for medical attention.

'I feel guilty walking away from them,' David confessed.

'You've been on duty for months without a break.'

'That's war for you. No matter how hard we work or how many of us are on duty the queues of patients never get any shorter. As for the locals, they don't need medical attention, only a good scouring and clean-up of their living conditions. I've seen more infected flea, bedbug, rat, sand fly and mosquito bites, and impetigo than any doctor should in several lifetimes.'

'Forget them for the next couple of hours.' They walked out of the gates of the hospital and turned into the street.

'And all the sores, abscesses …'

'Enough disgusting medical talk,' Peter pleaded.

'You want to go down here?' David halted at the entrance to a narrow alleyway.

'Do you?'

'It looks interesting. Just look at those second-floor balconies, they're touching to form a roof over the street. Do you think the houses have moved since they were built?'

'Perhaps they wanted to kiss.'

'You're a romantic idiot, Peter Smythe.'

322

'You would be if you had a wife like mine – and a son.'

David sniffed Peter's breath. 'Have you been drinking?'

'Only the medicinal brandy my doctor recommends to keep germs at bay.' Peter continued walking on the main thoroughfare which was only marginally wider than the narrow lane they'd looked down.

'Have you ever seen such a stinking slum?' David questioned.

'I'll concede it's worse than Basra, Amara, and Qurna.'

'Worse – this place is a cesspit.'

'We cleaned up the towns in the south, give us time we'll do the same to this one,' Peter said.

David stopped outside a café and looked through the window. 'Michael, Bowditch, Grace, Brooke, and practically every convalescent officer I've signed off duty are in there. Want to go in and find out what the attraction is?'

Peter pushed the door open. Half the café was filled with Arabs lounging on wooden benches cradling glasses of mint tea. The other half was occupied by British officers, jugs of water and raki in front of them.

A naked girl was dancing on top of a large table in the centre of the room. Musical accompaniment was provided by a trio: two men were playing peculiar stringed instruments that resembled lyres while a third thumped an out-of-tune piano. The resulting noise was weird and deafening.

David raised his eyebrows at the expression on Peter's face. 'I presume this is what they call "Eastern Promise".'

Peter grabbed a chair and squeezed it in next to Michael's at his crowded table. 'Researching a political article or still searching for golden minarets?'

'Absorbing background,' Michael winked at David who joined them. 'British majors at play. How do you spell "Knight" and "Smythe"?'

Turkish Prison Camp
June 1917

Rebeka had set the table in the small kitchen in the hospital for her and John's evening meal. She'd grated tinned cheese from a Red Cross parcel and beat it together with a few slices of leftover potato into an egg, milk, and tinned butter mix. She'd laid out tin plates, knives, and forks, and arranged a few flowers she'd picked in the garden in a bully beef tin she'd cleaned and polished. She looked at the clock on the wall. Another ten minutes and John should have finished his last patient round for the day.

She was looking forward to spending some time alone with him. Mrs Gulbenkian and Hasmik were helping Major Crabbe move into a room in the officers' quarters. John had discharged him from the hospital that morning to make room for four new fever cases and everyone was worried that the fever would spread throughout the other inmates in the camp.

The door opened. She turned and smiled, expecting to see John. She backed into the wall when Mehmet advanced towards her. 'You ...'

Mehmet tugged at the insignia on his sleeve. 'I was promoted and sent to the regular army for killing people like you. What are you doing still alive?'

'I work here – for the British soldiers,' she added, in the hope he'd leave her alone.

'An Armenian has no right to draw breath.' He reached behind him, closed the door and turned the key. Locking them in together.

Rebeka screamed.

'Shhh.' He pulled a long-bladed knife from a sheath on his belt. She opened her mouth to scream again.

He silenced her by clamping his hand over her mouth. She felt his hand pulling at her dress, the bite of the tip of the blade at her throat. The sensations were horrifyingly familiar.

Unlike in the desert, though, they galvanised her to fight back. She tried to wrench her head away from him but he forced his hand into her mouth. She bit down hard. He slapped her, sending her reeling into the wall.

'Not again,' she shouted, 'not ever again.'

Someone tried the door. When the lock held they banged on it. 'Rebeka?'

'John!' Something sharp, agonisingly so, jabbed into her neck. She staggered. Dark shadows crowded in on her, rising from the ground, drifting down from the ceiling, closing in from the corners of the room.

Warm, wet liquid ran down her neck, soaking her. The door

crashed open.

Someone hauled Mehmet from her. She saw Major Crabbe standing behind the Turk, heard the crack of bones snapping. Mehmet disappeared from her view.

John wrapped his arms around her, and lowered her gently on to his knees. She looked up at him and clutched her stomach in an attempt to protect the child within her. She saw John's soft brown eyes cloud in sorrow, felt his hand, warm, gentle on hers.

She smiled up at him.

'Don't leave me … Rebeka …'

She tried to say 'never' but she couldn't speak. She could still see John, still hear him, but he was moving away from her. He grew smaller and smaller while the shadows continued to grow, swallowing him until there was only darkness and his voice, faint, fading into a single pulse that kept time with her heartbeat …

John never knew how long he remained on the floor of the kitchen cradling Rebeka. But when Crabbe gently took her from him, he realised she'd died in his arms.

Chapter Thirty

'Did you hear me, Knight?' Colonel Allan looked him over with a professional eye. 'I said General Maude's dead.'

'I heard you, sir. He'll be sorely missed.' It was the standard phrase David resorted to whenever anyone mentioned the dead or the dying.

The entire force was immersed in death and had been for months. He was tired of administering morphine to ease men out of life and sitting beside death beds waiting for the last breath to be drawn so he could give the order to remove the corpse and bring in the next sick man.

He continued to stand in the centre of the ward. He couldn't see the floor for men laid head to toe in every available inch of space and in every direction. Cholera had broken out eight weeks ago closely followed by typhoid fever. They'd run out of beds in the first two days.

The only saving grace was the lack of wounded. The battle for Mesopotamia was, in theory at least, still be being waged against the Turkish troops retreating North back to their own country, but according to dispatches all fight had left the Ottoman Empire. Meanwhile his battles were continuing here.

'Where do you want me to put him, sir?'

David stared uncomprehendingly at the two orderlies carrying a stretcher.

'This man, where do you want me to put him, sir?'

'Anywhere where there's an inch of space, orderly.' He looked around for Allan but there were simply too many people crowded into the ward, upright and horizontal.

'Corridor's full, sir. The ward's full …'

David glanced at the stretcher. 'No! Please, no. Not Smythe.'

'Colonel Allan says it's Typhoid Fever, sir.'

David opened Peter's shirt and saw the rash. 'The office. Push the desk and chair against the wall.'

He tried to follow the orderlies but his legs refused to obey the commands his brains sent. The room swirled around him, gathering speed it moved faster – and faster – than any childhood roundabout. He grabbed a kidney dish from the stretcher and retched.

'Sir ... sir ...'

Singh caught him. David heard his orderly say, 'Make up two beds in the office.' He closed his eyes. He would leave everything to Singh. Just for a little while.

Turkish Prison Camp
November 1917

Crabbe watched John walk into the kitchen and sit at the table. Yana took a plate of food she'd put in the stove to keep warm and set it in front of him.

'Thank you.' John looked at it but made no attempt to eat it.

Yana pushed Hasmik towards him. The girl offered him a piece of paper that had been torn from a notebook. 'I made a drawing for you, Major Mason.'

John took it from her and Hasmik climbed on to his lap.

She laid the drawing on the table. 'That's me.' She pointed to a small round-faced figure with stick arms and legs. 'That's you.' She indicated a similar larger figure standing behind her. 'And that's Rebeka looking down at us from heaven.'

John sensed Crabbe and Yana holding their breath. He smiled in an attempt to put them at their ease. 'That's beautiful, Hasmik.'

'Mrs Gulbenkian says Rebeka's watching over all of us all of the time. And the man who hurt her has gone and will never hurt anyone again.'

'That's right, Hasmik. He won't hurt anyone ever again. '

'Come on, young lady. Bed for you.' Yana scooped the child from John's lap.'

'Must I?'

'If you're good I'll tell you a story.'

'*Hagop and the Hairy Giant*?'

'If you give Major Mason and Major Crabbe goodnight kisses.' Yana held the child fast while she swooped down and kissed first John then Crabbe.

'Clean plate by the time I get back, Major Mason. We haven't an ounce of food to waste.'

'I know, Yana, thank you.' He picked up his fork.

'Hasmik didn't mean anything,' Crabbe explained by way of an apology after Yana left with the child.

'I know.'

'We had to tell her something.'

'I know, Crabbe,' John reiterated.

'Foul thing to happen. If I'd been in the kitchen when that bastard came in …'

'If any of us had been in here it wouldn't have happened. You killed him with your bare hands. That's more than most men would have done.'

'Too late.'

'There's no point in going over it or talking about it, Crabbe. What's done is done.' There was no anger, only immense sadness in John's voice.

Crabbe indicated John's plate. 'If you don't eat that Yana will have your guts for garters.'

'It's been a long time since I heard that expression.'

'I warned you I climbed out of a Glaswegian gutter.'

'You've been a good friend, Crabbe. I wouldn't have survived without you.'

'Nonsense.'

'I'm serious.' John countered. 'The war will end soon. If we're fortunate we'll be allowed to go home, and I meant what I said about you, Yana, and Hasmik coming to Stouthall with me.'

'If you're absolutely sure there'll be real work that I can do there and you'll rent or sell us a house, we'll come.'

'There's just one thing. I want to sail home from Basra.'

'Why on earth would you want to go back to that God-forsaken hole? It will only remind you of Harry and Charles …'

'It will, but that's why I want to return. There's someone there I need to say goodbye to.'

'Mitkhal and Harry's wife?'

John dropped his fork. 'Please, eat this for me, so I won't offend Yana.'

'You have to eat.'

'I will tomorrow. I promise. It's just that now, right now, I need to be alone, Crabbe. Thank you.'

'What are you thanking me for?' Crabbe pulled the plate of bully beef stew towards him.

'Killing Mehmet. If you hadn't I would have tried and I would have made a right mess of it because I've no experience of killing – intentionally that is. And that's the last I want to say about him.'

'But not Rebeka,' Crabbe murmured. 'We all have to remember Rebeka.'

'As if we could ever forget her.' John rose and left the room.

Baghdad
December 1917

David was only vaguely aware of his surroundings. Whenever he opened his eyes it was to see orderlies cleaning the blood, secretions, and pus that flowed from every orifice of his and his Peter's bodies. The entire ward, including the office he and Peter were laid out in, was soaked in bodily fluids and hazy, almost as though they were all under water. Sometimes he managed to focus. When he could, he looked across at Peter, who always seemed to be tossing and turning in delirium. His friend had aged decades, not years, since they'd been struck down. His skin had thickened until it resembled old yellowed parchment, and there was an underlying ominous bluish tinge which he'd come to dread seeing as a doctor, because it invariably heralded death.

His mind constantly wavered and he found it difficult to retain a grasp on reality or determine whether it was his or Peter's breathing that sounded so loud. When he screamed in the agony of muscle cramps, he often turned to see it was Peter, not him making the noise.

He retained enough medical acumen even in delirium to know that he and Peter were both dying and it was only a matter of time before the burial party would pick up their shrouded corpses. Having lost all control over his body he lay on the thin pallet

330

drifting in and out of consciousness, amazed every time it registered that he was still breathing – until the moment he realised Peter was no longer lying next to him.

He reached out to the empty mattress. Singh stayed his hand. He looked into his orderly's eyes.

Singh nodded.

He moved his hand. It felt ridiculously heavy. He laid it on Singh's arm. 'I'll be with him soon. Get ...get ...' David knew what he wanted to say but he lacked the strength to say it. 'Dressings ...Plug me.'

'Sir?'

He could see Singh thought he wasn't rational. 'Plug my ears, nose ...every orifice, I'm leaking, dying ... make no difference ... save you work ... you shouldn't clean my mess ... Tell Georgie I love her.'

He was vaguely aware of Singh bringing a sheet and dressings, of lifting him on to the sheet ...wrapping him ... then nothing.

Smythes' Bungalow
December 31st 1917

'Happy New Year.' Georgiana touched her glass to Angela's. 'Christmas wasn't like Christmas at all and this New Year doesn't feel very celebratory.'

'It might tomorrow when we lunch at the Lansing. That was a knock at the door.' Angela rose, glanced in the mirror, and patted her hair into place. Georgiana knew Angela had hoped, just as she had, that Peter and David might wangle leave for Christmas. When they hadn't arrived for the holiday the hope had been postponed to the New Year.

The maid knocked and opened the door. 'Dr Wallace, ma'am.'

Theo walked in. Angela took one look at him, stepped back, and sank down on a chair. Her hand flew to her mouth.

'Angela ...'

'*No!*' Her scream was agonising, bestial in its intensity. 'The fighting's over ...'

Theo kneeled before his sister and wrapped his arms around her. 'It was typhoid, Angela. They did all they could ...'

'No!'

Georgiana stood back, helpless, as Angela buried her head in Theo's shoulder and wept.

Theo pushed his hand into his pocket, pulled out a telegram wireless message and handed it to Georgiana.

From Michael Downe war correspondent to Dr Theodore Wallace, Lansing Memorial Hospital. Majors Peter Smythe, David Knight, dead. Typhoid Fever. Tell Angela and Georgie. Send love and sorrow.

Chapter Thirty-one

Baghdad Hospital
January 1918

'You're not in trouble, any of you.' Allan looked from Singh to the corporal in charge of the burial party. 'I just want you to tell me what happened.'

When all the men remained obdurately silent, he turned to Singh. 'Let's start with you, Singh. What did you do?'

'It wasn't me, sir, it was Major Knight. He ordered me to plug him.'

'I don't understand. What do you mean, "plug him?"'

'Plug his mouth, ears, and nose with dressings, sir.'

'Was Major Knight delirious?' Allan asked.

'I think so.'

'But you went ahead and did it?'

'Yes, sir. Major Knight insisted. He said I had to do it so I wouldn't have to clean up his mess because he was leaking.'

'And when you finished plugging him?'

'He stopped breathing, sir. I wrapped him in a sheet and told the orderlies to take him to the corpse room ready for the burial party as they'd done with Major Smythe an hour before.'

Allan looked to two of the orderlies. 'You took Major Knight's body to the corpse room?'

'Yes, sir.'

'He was dead?'

'He wasn't breathing or moving sir.'

'His face was uncovered?' Allan asked.

'Sergeant did that when he removed Major Knight's name tags, sir. The sergeant collects them after we've shifted and stacked the bodies in the corpse room, sir. Then he hands the tags to the clerk who makes a note of the deaths for the regimental musters and paymasters, sir.'

Allan turned to the burial party. 'What happened then?'

'We went to the corpse room to pick up, sir.'

'How often do you go there?'

'About every two to three hours in daylight, sir. We don't do night pickups, sir. Orders are not to leave bodies unattended in darkness, sir. The Arabs dig our boys up to steal the sheets they're wrapped in and any clothes they're still wearing, sir.'

'I'm aware of the rampant thieving by the natives.'

'We don't just work in this hospital, sir ...'

'Understood, corporal,' Allan said impatiently. 'You went to the corpse room and picked up the bodies?'

'I told the men to leave Major Knight for the next pickup, sir.'

'Why?'

'He didn't look quite right, sir. Dead people look grey, sir. Grey and waxy. Major Knight had too much colour for my liking.'

'Did you leave any other corpses?'

'No, sir.'

'Did you return to the corpse room again that day?'

'Twice more, sir.'

'And you left Major Knight both times?'

'He still didn't look right to me, sir.'

'And yesterday? How many times did you come here to pick up bodies?'

'Four times, sir.'

'Let me guess: each time you left Major Knight because he didn't look quite right?'

'Yes, sir.'

'What happened this morning?'

'We were ordered to clear all the bodies, sir, because the corpse room was jammed packed after all the deaths that had occurred in the night. When we lifted Major Knight he opened his eyes.'

'Has that ever happened before?' Allan demanded.

'Never to my knowledge, sir. And I've been an orderly for over ten years,' Singh said proudly.

'Major Knight?'

'Is sitting up in bed, sir, drinking tea, but the clerks are not pleased.' Singh failed to suppress a smile. 'They say they've notified everyone in his family of his death and written out the death certificate. They say he is no longer entitled to pay, sir, and they've auctioned off his uniform.'

'Make enquiries, Singh. Try and find out who bought Major Knight's effects, and buy them back. Should you need money, see my bearer and ask him to supply you with what you need from petty cash.'

'Yes, sir. Thank you, sir.'

'Corporal?'

'Sir.'

'Should you decide that a corpse doesn't look "quite right" again, please fetch me. If I'm busy leave a message with my bearer and also ensure that all "not quite right" corpses are left in a separate area – a room might be better – than the corpses who do appear "quite right".'

'Yes, sir.'

'Off the record. Well done every one of you. You've saved the life of a doctor the force could ill afford to lose.'

'Thank you, sir.' The corporal in charge of the burial party replied.

'However, all of you are guilty of breaking military rules and regulations in respect of leaving a corpse unburied for three days. I regret I don't have sufficient voice left to berate you. All of you please consider yourself admonished for treating military procedure in cavalier fashion. Dismissed.'

Smiling, the men marched out.

'Singh?'

'Colonel Allan.' The orderly stood to attention.

'Tell the mess orderly to give every man in the burial and corpse disposal party free drinks for the evening on my tab.'

'Yes, sir.'

'I'll arrange for a bonus to be added to your pay.'

'Thank you, sir.'

'Resume your duties, but return to this office at the end of your shift. In the meantime think hard about what you did so you can tell me exactly what steps you took when you "plugged" Major Knight.'

'Yes, sir.'

Allan left his office and walked down to the convalescent ward. David Knight was sitting up, lighting a cigarette.

'Knight.'

'Sir, you won't mind if I don't get up?'

'Not this once.' Allan pulled up a chair and sat down. 'For Lazarus you're looking pretty good. Want me to telegraph someone for you?'

'No, sir. Thanks to the efficiency of the army, everyone who knows me will have heard that I'm dead by now. I'll enjoy surprising them.'

'You'll be going downstream to Basra as soon as you're fit enough to travel. I've recommended six months' convalescence.'

'That's good of you, sir.'

'You'll continue to receive full pay. By the time you're fit for duty it's anyone's guess what will be happening here. Aside from a little mopping up the war is practically over in Mesopotamia. We've pushed the Turks back into Turkey and hopefully put an end to their Ottoman Empire once and for all. But although the soldiers' war has ended, it's still going on for us medics. We're losing more men now from disease than wounds. As for the rest of the world, it's up to those fighting on the Western Front, but I'd like to believe there are more years of war behind us than ahead.' There was a wistful note in Colonel Allan's voice.

'It will be good to back in England, sir.'

'Away from this cursed climate. I agree with you, Knight. By the way, the paymaster told me about your change of name. You've inherited a country pile and title. Earl isn't it?'

'I was hoping to keep it quiet, sir. Not sure what to make of it. This war has really messed up my family.'

'You won't be the first second son of a second son to inherit by the time the peace treaties are signed, Knight. Or should I call you the Right Honourable …'

'Knight is fine, sir,' David cut in.

'Good luck to you. You're the first officially dead man I've had a conversation with. Hope to see you downstream soon, if not back in England at a reunion when we're all well out of this.'

Lansing Memorial Hospital
February 1918

Georgie had just finished cutting the last of the necrotised tissue from a Turk's amputation stump when Theo appeared in the operating theatre.

'Stop whatever it is you're doing. I'll take over.'

'Why.'

'Your brother's here.'

She pulled off her gloves.

'Take time to clean up. He looks remarkably healthy considering he's come down from upstream and it would be good if he could stay that way. You don't want to pass any infections on to the poor man.'

She untied her coat and apron, and scrubbed her hands in the basin kept for the purpose at the door.

Michael was waiting for her in the small hallway at the end of the corridor. She ran down to meet him and hugged him. 'How wonderful to see you.'

'You have to come with me.'

'To where?'

'I have a carriage waiting …come on, I'm paying the driver by the minute.'

'Now?'

'Right now.'

'I can't go anywhere. Just look at me …'

'You look fine,' he said irritably.

'My hair's a bird's nest. I'm wearing my oldest skirt, blouse, and sweater. My stockings are darned. I'm not fit for the Basra Club.'

'We're not going to the Basra Club.' He pulled her coat and shawl from a peg in the corridor, gave them to her, grabbed her hand before she had a chance to put them on and pulled her after him.

She finally managed to put her coat and throw her shawl around her shoulders when she climbed into the carriage.

'We're going to Abdul's?' she guessed when the carriage turned down towards the wharf.

'We are.'

'Why all the mystery, Michael?'

'Wait and see.' He helped her down to the street when the driver stopped the carriage. 'You know the way to my room?'

'Of course. I've been there, remember,' she added.

'Kalla's ordered lunch. We're eating in the small dining room at the back.'

'I'm not hungry, but thank you for the invitation.' She gave him a backward glance as she went into the coffee shop. She nodded to Abdul walked up the stairs and knocked on Michael's door.

It opened.

She froze.

'I'm not a ghost, Georgie. I'm real.'

Tears poured down her face.

David opened his arms. 'Georgie …'

Michael heard Georgiana cry as he joined Kalla.

'They may be some time. I think we should go ahead and order – just for ourselves.'

June 1918

Dear John,

Thank you for your letter of condolence. I was deeply moved when I read your heartfelt words about Peter. It is comforting to know that others who knew him also held him in high esteem. I am so sorry for your devastating loss, John. After your letters and speaking to Mariam I feel as though Rebeka was a close friend. Life can be unbelievably cruel to take Rebeka and your unborn child away from you, and Peter from me and his son.

Georgie and I have moved back into the Lansing Mission House. After Peter died I had a week's notice to vacate our bungalow and although Georgie and I searched Basra, we couldn't find anywhere large enough to take us, the three children, and the boys' nurse, so Mrs Butler kindly agreed to take us in.

Theo has given notice to the Lansing and intends to leave for America as soon as hostilities cease which he believes will be before Christmas. His decision has left me several problems. Thanks to the money Charles left Peter and me and the inheritance he bequeathed to Robin, the children and I are financially secure. Theo has asked me to return to America with him and I have agreed to lend him what he needs to buy into a medical practice in New York which is being managed by an old friend of his who was at school with him.

I know that it makes sense for me to accompany Theo back to the States when passenger shipping can once more sail without risk of being sunk by U-boats. The problem is Robin. I cannot bear the thought of leaving him. I love him as dearly as I love my own darling Peter, and then there is Mariam. She was, as you can imagine, heartbroken when I told her that Rebeka had died. Theo has assured me that he will find a home large enough to take all of us, so accommodation is not a problem, but Robin and Mariam sadly are. I have no legal rights over either child. General Reid replied to my letters about Robin and says he wants to meet the boy. I respect him as Robin's grandfather but Georgie tells me he is over seventy and I can't help wondering what will happen to Robin if the General dies when Robin is still a child. Georgie has said she and David will look after him, but that would mean Robin growing up in England while I am in America.

I'm sorry, John, please accept my apologies, I should not be burdening you with my concerns when you are hundreds of miles away and have more than enough to cope with in surviving prison life.

You mentioned that you too received a letter from the Portuguese embassy informing you that Maud had died. I am sorry, John. I feel guilty for not trying to help her when she most needed a friend. She was a troubled woman but the one thing I do know from my conversations with her is that she loved you very much and regretted the weakness that prevented her from showing it as she would have wished to.

I so wish I could sit and talk to you, especially about Peter and Rebeka, because I know that you, like me, are bereft. It is so hard to know that the one person you loved most in the world has gone forever. I am sure that you, like me, can't stop listening for their footstep at the door, and their voice in another room.

Now I have almost run out of paper.

Thank you for being you, John, for being a true and good friend, for understanding exactly how I feel, and corresponding with me, I do so hope that you return to Basra before I go to the States so that I can see you and hug you one last time before I leave Mesopotamia forever.

Georgiana and David are waiting until you to return so you can all sail home together. Georgiana is trying to persuade Michael to sail with you but at the moment he is most insistent that he wants to remain in Basra.

I send you my special love and also Mariam's love and gratitude because you cared for her sister.

Your friend,
Angela

August 1918

Dear Angela,

Your letters have kept me sane, simply because you recognised my pain as mirroring yours. You know all too well the impotent feeling of emptiness that is perhaps the worse aspect of bereavement. How life loses all meaning and there seems little point in struggling to live another day. I'm not ashamed to admit that I dread the future. I am not a man who ever wanted to live alone. When I married Maud this war was only a rumour of 'what might happen', and I dreamed of a large house with an even larger garden in the English countryside where I could live with my wife, children, and animals surrounded by love, warmth, and a peace that bordered on boredom.

You say you don't want to leave Robin and Mariam. Don't, Angela. Marry me, we'll sail to England with David and Georgie, and move into the family home I've inherited. I'll work in the clinic my father founded and come home every night to you.

The one thing I envied Peter was not you, that would have been mean and petty of me, but his close and loving relationship with you. You're a special woman, Angela. Good, kind, charming, and beautiful, and I promise I'll bring up young Peter, Robin, and Mariam as if they were my own children. Major Crabbe is going to buy a house close by and I'm sure Georgie and David will visit often, so we won't lack for friends.

What do you say, Angela? I know I'll never replace Peter in your affections, but I am confident that in time we could – like the Bedouin who marry 'unseen' as Harry did with Furja – learn to love one another – after a fashion.

If it seems too convenient a proposal to you, then perhaps it is, but I'm tired. Tired of war, tired of fighting, tired of doctoring dying young men who should have died in their own beds of old age.

What do you say? Could you marry a man, damaged but not entirely broken by war? A man who yearns for peace and a family life who promises to cherish you and our children all the days of our lives? I accept that our relationship will never have the passion of first love, but what I can promise you, Angela, is that I will care for you and respect you as long as I live.

If you are no longer in Basra when I arrive, I'll take it your answer is no. Or if you haven't been able to leave because of a shortage of ships, just say 'no' when I see you.

You mentioned money; I have enough for both of us and the children I hope to be able to call my own.

John Mason, who has always admired you, and begs to be given the opportunity to learn to love you as you deserved to be loved.

September 1918

Dear John,

The war must be as close to an end as everyone here in Basra insists, as letters are not taking as long to travel between here and Turkey. I even allowed myself the luxury of thinking about your proposal for three days before writing this in answer your letter.

Aside from Peter I cannot think of a man I admire or respect more than you, John. You say you are damaged but not entirely broken by war. Before I received your letter I felt broken. So much so I never wanted to leave my bed. If I hadn't had the children to care for I believe I would have curled into a corner and wished for death.

You letter has given me hope. For the first time since Theo brought the telegram to tell me that Peter had died I can envisage a future, not only for myself but my three children. Thank you, John. It would be an honour to become your wife.

I send you love from all of us, and if it is not yet the love of a wife for her husband I trust in God that when we are together I will be able to make it so. I will not tell anyone of our plans, not even Georgie or Theo. I will leave that task to you when you return to Basra. If possible I would like to marry as soon as you arrive so we can sail to England as man and wife and make the journey a new beginning for us both.

Angela

October 1918

Dear Angela,

We all know the Armistice is imminent so our Turkish captors, admitting defeat, have released us early. Major Crabbe, Crabbe's wife Yana, their adopted daughter Hasmik, and I will be travelling to Basra tomorrow morning. In fact we may reach the town before this letter.

I received the letter you sent me accepting my proposal. I thank you sincerely for the trust you have placed in me. As soon as I arrive in Basra I will speak to the padre and arrange a swift and quiet wedding ceremony. Just us and a few friends. One person who will be especially pleased to welcome you to England is my aunt, Harry, Michael, and Georgie's mother. She has been the only American in our quiet corner of England for many years.

I send you and our children love,
Your fiancé, John

Abdul's
November 1918

The last goodbyes had been said the previous day in Ibn Shalan's house. Neither John nor Georgie had expected to see Michael, Hasan, or Mitkhal again before they sailed, but the three of them had turned up unexpectedly in Abdul's where they were waiting for the boat to carry them downstream to the Gulf and the ocean-going liners.

As soon as the boat arrived, David, Angela, and Major and Mrs Crabbe took the children on board to give John and Georgiana a few last private moments with Hasan and Michael, but while Hasan and Georgiana embraced for the last time, Michael took the opportunity to explain – yet again – to John just why he was staying in Mesopotamia.

'If the Arabs don't get a mandate to rule themselves after helping us to win the war against the Turks, there will be a revolt ...'

'And you want to be here to see it?' John interrupted.

342

'I do,' Michael conceded.

'It's hard losing both of you to the Bedouin.'

'You haven't lost us, John. You can write to us care of Abdul. He always knows where to find us.' Hasan turned away from Georgiana and hugged him.

'My Arab cousin. Or is that now cousins?' John turned from Hasan and Michael to Mitkhal.

Abdul knocked and opened the door. 'The boat's ready, sir.'

'Thank you, Abdul. Georgie? Time we left.' John offered her his arm.

They walked downstairs and on to the boat. David and Crabbe were leaning on the rail.

'After all the sacrifice, all the killing, all the death, this is this how it ends?' David asked. 'With a boat trip down the Shatt al-Arab?'

'We're the lucky ones. For us, it ends with a journey home.' John watched Georgie take Robin from David. Mariam and Hasmik were running up and down the deck, under the eagle eyes of Yana Crabbe, who was watching every move they made.

John walked over to where Angela was sitting with Peter. He knew that they were all thinking of the ones who wouldn't be going home. Peter, Charles, Stephen Amey, Boris Bell – faces swirled in his mind's eye. Men he'd loved, men he'd cared for, even men he'd disliked, but above all, men he'd never forget.

John wrapped his arm around Angela. He looked up at the three robed Bedouin who stood side by side at an upstairs window in Abdul's and tipped his hat to them.

'Shall we walk to the prow, Mrs Mason?'

'To take a last look at Basra? Yes, please.'

He slipped his arm around her waist. Angela smiled up at him, then turned to look ahead towards the horizon, a shawl covering her head and that of her child. John watched and felt an overwhelming love for both of them.

He remembered the recurring dream that had begun in Kut.

The sky was blue, the breeze fresh. He was surrounded by light. It danced and shimmered, clear, beautiful and blinding above and around him. Below him the river glistened with reflected sunbeams that tipped the surface of the waves with winking gold and silver flashes. The wind carried the taste of fresh salt air blowing up from

343

the Gulf. The vessel moved out from the river banks and glided, slow and stately, past the anchored boats into mid-stream.

HISTORICAL NOTES

Most scholars outside of Turkey now accept the genocide of the Armenians in 1915-16 by the Turks as fact. Possibly two of the best accounts are Henry H. Riggs' *Days of Tragedy in Armenia* and Tacy Atkinson's *The German, the Turk and the Devil made a Triple Alliance*. Both authors were American missionaries and both had first-hand knowledge of the atrocities. British POWs marched into Turkey after the surrender of Kut al Amara mentioned seeing abandoned Armenian villages and the bones of massacred Armenian men, women, and children in the desert. The report of the US Ambassador to the Ottoman Empire, Henry Morgenthau, Sr., is recognized as one of the main eyewitness accounts of the genocide. Morgenthau published his memoirs in a 1918 book, *Ambassador Morgenthau's Story*.

The Mesopotamian campaign in the First World War has been called 'The Sideshow War' and 'The Forgotten War.' It's certain that the surrender of Kut al Amara by General Townshend was an embarrassment the British would rather forget. The British Relief Force suffered heavy casualties both inside and outside Kut: in the effort to relieve the town between January and April 1916. 14,814 were killed or died of wounds, 12,807 died from disease, and 13,494 ended up in captivity or were posted missing. The treatment British POWs received at the hands of the Turks was savage and brutal, and classified as torture. Thousands died on forced marches or in captivity. There was talk of reprisals, some of the guilty Turks were arrested, but freed after the Treaty of Lausanne was signed in 1923.

Scorpion Sunset is the end of a journey I began in 1985 when I met Christopher Marley, a Welsh volunteer and survivor of the Mesopotamian Campaign, who at the age of eighty-nine showed me his death certificate. It stated that he'd died of typhoid fever in Baghdad in 1918. His corpse didn't look 'quite right' to the burial party, who put it aside. Four days later he woke up in the temporary mortuary. By then the army had declared him officially dead, notified his family, and refused him rations or a replacement uniform on the grounds that he was deceased. It took six months of arguing while begging for food and clothes from his companions before he was eventually restored to the strength of his battalion.

To my shame I hadn't heard of the First World War fought by the British against the Ottoman Empire's Turks in Mesopotamia (modern Iraq) until Christopher told me about it. His tales inspired me to write *Long Road to Baghdad*, *Winds of Eden*, and *Scorpion Sunset*. It's been a long road! *Long Road to Baghdad* lay unpublished in a drawer for over 25 years. Editors who read it offered me contracts to write other books while insisting no one wanted to know about the First World War in Iraq. Fortunately Accent Press invited me to complete the trilogy in 2013, and readers have since proved otherwise! I am indebted to everyone at Accent for their continued faith in me, especially my editor Greg Rees.

Hasan Mahmoud/Harry Downe is based on Lt Col Gerard Leachman, Officer Commanding the Desert, who remained in Iraq at the end of the war in 1918. He, like so many, both Arab and British, had hoped that the Arabs would be given the opportunity to rule themselves. It was denied them at Versailles when the peace treaties were signed and the Allies carved up the Middle East. In 1920 the Arabs made a bid for freedom when they orchestrated the Arab Revolt. But that's another story …

In 1928 William Seabrook published his *Adventures in Arabia*. In it, he mentions seeing European men living in the black tents of the Bedouin in both the Arabian and Mesopotamian Deserts. They had invoked the hospitality of the desert and as such no questions were asked of them regarding their origins or motives for seeking a life among the Arabs. Were some surviving British POWs?

Finally, there is a plaque in the crypt of St Paul's Cathedral in London:

KUT EL-AMARA
5TH DECEMBER 1915 TO 29TH APRIL 1916
TO THE MEMORY OF
5746 OF THE GARRISON WHO DIED IN THE SIEGE
OR AFTERWARDS IN CAPTIVITY.
ERECTED BY THEIR SURVIVING COMRADES.

Catrin Collier, 2015

The *Long Road to Baghdad* series

by

Catrin Collier

For more information on **Catrin Collier**

and other **Accent Press** titles, please visit

www.accentpress.co.uk

Lightning Source UK Ltd.
Milton Keynes UK
UKOW04n0826100915

258362UK00001B/3/P

9 781783 753772